Bantam Books by Kay Hooper

STEALING SHADOWS
HAUNTING RACHEL
FINDING LAURA
AFTER CAROLINE
AMANDA
ON WINGS OF MAGIC
THE WIZARD OF SEATTLE
MY GUARDIAN ANGEL

BEWARE OF WHAT YOU SEE

It's dawn when the police arrive at the murder scene.
The victim is propped against a tree,
her eyes still open, her head tilted, her lips parted in a silent cry.
Just as Cassie Neill predicted.
Just as she saw while she was inside the killer's mind.
The killer knew she was there.
And next time he won't let her get away.

"Peopled with interesting characters and intricately plotted, the novel is both a compelling mystery and a satisfying romance."

—*Milwaukee Journal Sentinel*

"Kay Hooper has crafted another solid story to keep readers enthralled until the last page is turned."

—*Booklist*

"Joanna Flynn is appealing, plucky and true to her mission as she probes the mystery that was Caroline."

—*Variety*

AMANDA

"*Amanda* seethes and sizzles. A fast-paced, atmospheric tale that vibrates with tension, passion, and mystery. Readers will devour it."

—Jayne Ann Krentz

"Kay Hooper's dialogue rings true; her characters are more three-dimensional than those usually found in this genre. You may think you've guessed the outcome, unraveled all the lies. Then again, you could be as mistaken as I was."

—*The Atlanta Journal-Constitution*

"Will delight fans of Phyllis Whitney and Victoria Holt."

—*Alfred Hitchcock Mystery Magazine*

"Kay Hooper knows how to serve up a latter-day gothic that will hold readers in its brooding grip."

—*Publishers Weekly*

"I lapped it right up. There aren't enough good books in this genre, so this stands out!"

—*Booknews* from The Poisoned Pen

"Kay Hooper has given you a darn good ride, and there are far too few of those these days."

—*Dayton Daily News*

STEALING

SHADOWS

Kay Hooper

BANTAM BOOKS
New York Toronto London Sydney Auckland

STEALING SHADOWS

A Bantam Book / September 2000

ISBN 0-553-57553-8

Published simultaneously in the United States and Canada

Bantam Books are published by Bantam Books, a division of
Random House, Inc. Its trademark, consisting of the words "Bantam
Books" and the portrayal of a rooster, is Registered in U.S. Patent
and Trademark Office and in other countries. Marca Registrada.
Bantam Books, 1540 Broadway, New York, New York 10036.

PRINTED IN THE UNITED STATES OF AMERICA

OPM   10   9   8   7   6   5   4   3   2   1

There aren't enough good teachers in the world.

*This book is dedicated to
Mary Anne Head
Jane Biggerstaff
and Betty Hough,
with appreciation and thanks
for helping to make school an interesting place
for my niece, Beth.*

PROLOGUE

"Talk to me, Cassie."

She was all but motionless in the straight-backed chair, head bowed so that her hair hid her face. Only her hands stirred, thin fingers lightly tracing and shaping the red tissue petals of the exquisitely handmade paper rose in her lap.

"I think . . . he's moving," she whispered.

"Where is he moving? What can you see, Cassie?" Detective Logan's voice was even and infinitely patient, betraying none of the anxiety and urgency that beaded his face with sweat and haunted his eyes.

"I . . . I'm not sure."

From his position a few feet away, Logan's partner spoke in a low voice. "Why's she so tentative with this one?"

"Because he scares the shit out of her," Logan

responded, equally quietly. "Hell, he scares the shit out of me." He raised his voice. "Cassie? Concentrate, honey. What does he see?"

"Dark. It's just . . . it's dark."

"All right. What is he thinking?"

She drew a shaky little breath, and those thin fingers trembled as they held and traced the paper rose. "I— I don't want to . . . It's so cold in his mind. And there are so many . . . shadows. So many twisted shadows. Please don't make me go any deeper. Don't make me touch them."

Logan's already grim face grew bleaker at the fear and revulsion in her voice, and it was his turn to draw a steadying breath. When he spoke, his voice was cool and certain. "Cassie, listen to me. You have to go deeper. For the sake of that little girl, you have to. Do you understand?"

"Yes," she replied forlornly, "I understand." There was a moment of silence so absolute, they could hear the soft crackle of the tissue paper she touched.

"Where is he, Cassie? What is he thinking?"

"He's safe. He knows he's safe." Her head tilted to one side, as though she were listening to a distant voice. "The cops will never find him now. Bastards. Stupid bastards. He left them all those clues and they never saw them."

Logan didn't allow himself to be distracted by the disturbing information. "Stop listening to him, Cassie. Look at what he's doing, where he's going."

"He's going . . . to get the girl. To take her to his secret place. He's ready for her now. He's ready to—"

"Where is it? What's around him, Cassie?"

"It's . . . dark. She's . . . he's got her tied up. He's got her tied up . . . in the backseat of a car. It's in a garage. He's getting into the car, starting the engine. Backing out of the garage. Oh! I can hear her crying. . . ."

"Don't listen," Logan insisted. "Stay with him, Cassie. Tell me where he's going."

"I don't know." Her voice was desolate. "It's so dark. I can't see beyond the headlights."

"Watch, Cassie. Look for landmarks. What kind of road is he on?"

"It's . . . a blacktop. Two lanes. There are mailboxes, we're driving past mailboxes."

"Good, Cassie, that's good." He glanced aside at his partner, who grimaced helplessly, then returned his attention to that dark, bent head. "Keep looking. Keep watching. You have to tell us where he's going."

For a few moments there was nothing but the sound of her breathing, quick and shallow. And then, abruptly she said, "He's turning. The street sign says . . . Andover."

Logan's partner moved a few steps away and began talking softly into a cell phone.

"Keep watching, Cassie. What do you see? Talk to me."

"It's so dark."

"I know. But keep watching."

"He's thinking . . . horrible things."

"Don't listen. Don't go too deep, Cassie."

She lifted her head for the first time since they had begun, and Logan flinched. Her eyes were closed. He'd never seen such pallor in a human face before. Not a living face. And that pale, pale skin was stretched tautly over her bones.

"Cassie? Cassie, where are you?"

"Deep." Her voice sounded different, distant and almost hollow, as though it came from a bottomless well.

"Cassie, listen to me. You have to back off. Just see what he sees."

"It's like worms," she whispered, "feeding on rotting flesh. On a rotting soul . . ."

"Cassie, back off. Back off *now*. Do you hear me?"

After several moments she said, "Yes. All right." She was trembling visibly now, and he knew if he touched her, he would find her skin cold.

"What do you see? What does he see?"

"The road. No mailboxes now. Just winding road. He's getting tense. He's almost at his secret place."

"Watch, Cassie. Keep watching."

Several minutes passed, and then a frown tugged at her brows.

"Cassie?"

She shook her head.

Logan stepped aside quickly and spoke in a low voice to his partner. "Any luck with Andover, Paul?"

"There are five variations on the street name Andover within two hundred miles. Bob, we can't even get to them all, much less cover them effectively. She has to give us something else."

"I don't know if she can."

"She has to try."

Logan returned to Cassie. "What do you see, Cassie? Talk to me."

In a tone that was almost dreamy now, she said, "There's a lake. I've seen the lights shining on the water. He's . . . his secret place is near the lake. He thinks he'll dump her body there when he's done. Maybe."

Logan looked swiftly at his partner, but Paul was already on the cell phone.

"What else, Cassie? What else can you tell me?"

"It's getting harder." Her voice became uncertain, shaky once more. "Harder to stay inside him. I'm so tired."

"I know, Cassie. But you have to keep trying. You have to keep us with him."

As always, she responded to his voice and his insistence, drawing on her pitifully meager reserves of strength to maintain a contact that revolted and terrified her. "I hear her. The little girl. She's crying. She's so afraid."

"Don't listen to her, Cassie. Just him."

"All right." She paused. "He's turning. It's a winding road now. A dirt road. I can see the lake sometimes through the trees."

"Do you see a house?"

"We're passing . . . driveways, I think. There are houses all around. Houses on the lake."

Logan stepped aside as Paul gestured. "What?"

"There's only one Andover Street close to a lake. It's Lake Temple. Bob, it's only fifteen miles away."

"No wonder she's picking him up so well," Logan muttered. "She's never been this deep before, not inside this bastard. The teams moving?"

"I've got everybody en route. And we're chasing down a list of all the property owners on the lake. I'm told this is one of those places where the people name their houses, give them signs and everything. If we get really lucky . . ."

"Keep me advised," Logan said, and returned to Cassie.

"Lake Temple," she said, dreamy again. "He likes that name. He thinks it's appropriate."

"Don't listen to what he thinks, Cassie. Just watch. Tell me what he's doing, where he's going."

Five minutes of silence lasted seemingly forever, and then she spoke suddenly.

"We're turning. Into a driveway, I think."

"Do you see any mailboxes?"

"No. No. I'm sorry."

"Keep watching."

"It's a steep driveway. Long. Winding down toward the lake. I see . . . I think there's a house ahead. Sometimes the headlights touch it. . . ."

"Keep watching, Cassie. When you see the house, look for a sign. The house has a name."

"There—there's the house." Her voice quickened. "It has a sign near the door. The sign says . . . 'retirement fund.' "

Logan blinked, then glanced at Paul, who mouthed, "Typical."

Logan turned back to Cassie. "Talk to me, Cassie. Is he stopping the car? Is this house where he's going?"

Cassie said, "Wait . . . we're going past it. Oh. Oh, I see. There's . . . a boathouse. I think it's a boathouse. I see . . ."

"What, Cassie? What do you see?"

"It's . . . a weathervane on top. On the roof. I can see it moving in the breeze. I can . . . hear it creaking."

"Hear it? Cassie, has he stopped the car?"

She seemed startled. "Oh. Oh, yes, he has. The lights are out. I can see the shape of the boathouse, the darkness of it. But . . . he knows his way. He's . . . he's getting her out of the back. Carrying her into the boathouse. She's so little. She hardly weighs anything at all. Ohhhh. . . ."

"Cassie—"

"She's so afraid. . . ."

"Cassie, listen to me. You can only help her by paying attention to what he's doing. Where he's going." He looked at his partner. "Where the hell are they?"

"Almost there. Five minutes."

"Goddammit, she doesn't have five minutes!"

"They're moving as fast as they can, Bob."

Cassie was breathing quickly. "Something's wrong."

Logan stared at her. "What?"

"I don't know. He feels . . . different about this one. Sly, somehow, and almost . . . amused. He means to give the cops something new. He—oh. Oh, God. He has a knife. He wants to just cut her open—" Her voice was thready with grief and horror. "He wants to . . . he wants to . . . taste . . ."

"Cassie, listen to me. Get out. Get out, *now*."

Logan's partner started forward. "Bob, if she stays with him, she might be able to help us."

Logan shook his head, never taking his eyes off Cassie. "If she stays with him, and he kills the girl, it could pull her in too deep, into his frenzy. We'd lose them both. Cassie? Cassie, get out. *Now*. Do it." He reached over and plucked the tissue-paper rose from her fingers.

Cassie drew a shuddering breath, then slowly opened her eyes. They were so pale a gray, they were like faint shadows on ice, strikingly surrounded by inky black lashes. Dark smudges of exhaustion lay under those eyes, and her voice shook with strain when she said, "Bob? Why did you—"

Logan poured hot coffee from a thermos and handed her the cup. "Drink this."

"But—"

"You helped us all you could, Cassie. The rest is up to my people."

She sipped the hot coffee, her eyes on the rose he still held. "Tell them to hurry," she whispered.

But it was nearly ten long, long minutes later before the report came in, and Paul scowled at Cassie.

"The boathouse was empty. You missed the fork in the driveway. One branch led to the boathouse, and the other led to a cove less than fifty yards away, where a cabin cruiser was tied up. He was gone by the time we found it. The little girl was still warm."

Logan quickly caught the cup that fell from Cassie's fingers and said, "Paul, shut up. She did her best—"

"Her best? She fucking missed it, Bob! There was no weathervane on top of the boathouse—there was a flag flying above the boat. That's what she saw moving in the wind. And the creaking she heard was the boat in the water. She couldn't tell the difference?"

"It was dark," Cassie whispered. Tears filled her eyes but didn't fall. Her shaking hands twisted together in her lap, and she breathed as though struggling against an oppressive weight crushing her lungs.

Paul said, "Five minutes. We wasted five minutes going the wrong way, and that little girl's dead because of it. What am I supposed to tell her parents? That our famous psychic blew it?"

"Paul, shut your goddamned mouth!" Logan looked back at Cassie. "It wasn't your fault, Cassie." His voice was certain.

But his eyes told her something else.

Her own gaze fell, and she stared at the tissue rose he held, its delicate perfection emphasized by the blunt strength of his cop's hand.

Such beauty to have been created by a monster.

Sick fear coiled in the pit of her stomach and crawled on its belly through her mind, and she was barely aware of speaking aloud when she said huskily, "I can't do it. I can't do this anymore. I can't."

"Cassie—"

"I can't. I can't. I can't." It was like a mantra to ward off the unbearable, and she whispered it over and over as she closed her eyes and shut out the mocking sight of the paper flower that now lived in her nightmares.

ONE

As towns went, it didn't have much to boast of. It was about as broad as it was long, with more acreage than buildings. There was a scattering of churches and car lots and small stores that didn't call themselves boutiques but charged enough for their plain little dresses to be considered just that. There was a Main Street with a grassy town square, enough banks to make a body wonder where all the riches were, and a drugstore so old, it still had a soda fountain.

Of course, there was also a computer store on Main Street, as well as two video stores and a satellite dish dealership, and just two miles away from the center of town was the very latest thing in movie multiplexes.

So Ryan's Bluff was staring the coming millennium right in the eye.

It was also, on most levels, a small Southern town, so the politics were largely conservative, church on Sunday was the norm, you couldn't buy liquor by the drink, and until the previous year the same sheriff had been voted in at every election since 1970.

In 1998 his son got the job.

It was, therefore, a predictable town by and large. Change came as reluctantly as heaven admitted sinners.

There were few surprises, and even fewer shocks.

That's what Ben Ryan would have said. What he believed, after a lifetime of knowing this place and with generations of family history at his back. This town and its inhabitants could never surprise him.

That's what he believed.

"Judge? Someone to see you."

Ben frowned at the intercom. "Who is it, Janice?"

"Says her name is Cassie Neill. She doesn't have an appointment, but asks if you can spare a few minutes. She says it's important."

Ben's very efficient secretary was not easily persuaded by people without appointments, so he was surprised to hear a note almost of appeal in Janice's voice. Curious, he said, "Send her in."

He was still jotting down notes and didn't look up immediately when the door opened. But even before Janice announced "Miss Neill, Judge," he felt the change in the room. It was as if an electrical current had been set loose, making his skin tingle and the fine hair on his body stir. He looked up and rose to his feet in the same instant, noting Janice's disconcerted expression as she gazed warily at the visitor.

They were all three disconcerted.

The visitor was functioning under an enormous level of stress. That was his first realization. He was accustomed to weighing people, and this young woman weighed in as someone carrying a burden too heavy for her.

She was of average height but too thin by a good twenty pounds, a fact obvious even under the bulky sweater she wore. She might have been pretty if her face hadn't been so thin. Her head was bowed a bit, as if her attention were focused entirely on the floor, and her shoulder-length, straight black hair swept forward as if to shelter her face, the long bangs all but hiding her eyes.

Then she looked at him through those bangs, a quick, surprised glance darting warily upward, and he caught his breath. Her eyes were amazing—large, dark-lashed, and a shade of gray so pale and clear, they were hypnotic. And haunted.

Ben had seen suffering before, but what he saw in this woman's eyes was something new in his experience.

He found himself coming around his desk toward her. "Miss Neill. I'm Ben Ryan." His normal speaking voice had softened, so much so that the uncharacteristic gentleness startled him.

Something else startled him. Ben was a Southern lawyer, a one-time judge, and had been for years involved in politics at the local and state levels; shaking hands with strangers was as natural to him as breathing, and sticking out his hand during an introduction was automatic. Yet somehow this woman not only managed to elude shaking hands with him, she did it so smoothly and with such perfect, practiced timing that there was nothing obvious in the avoidance of physical contact, and nothing at all awkward. He was not left with his hand hanging in the air, and was conscious of no slight.

She simply circumvented the gesture by moving promptly toward his visitor's chair and glancing casually around at his office. "Judge Ryan." Her voice was low and beautifully modulated, the accent not Carolina. "Thank you for seeing me."

When she looked at him doubtfully with another of

those guarded, darting glances, he realized that she had probably expected him to be older. More . . . judgelike.

"My pleasure." He gestured to the chair, inviting her to sit, then looked toward the doorway with a lifted brow. "Thank you, Janice."

Janice took her gaze off the visitor finally and, still frowning slightly, backed out of the office and closed the door.

Ben returned to his chair and sat down. "We're pretty informal around here," he told her. "I'm Ben." His voice, he noted in some surprise, was still gentle.

A faint smile touched her lips. "I'm Cassie." Another quick glance at his face, and then she stared down at the hands clasped in her lap. Whatever she had come there to say, it was obviously not easy for her.

"What can I do for you, Cassie?"

She drew a breath and kept her gaze fixed on her hands. "As I told your secretary, I'm new in Ryan's Bluff. I've lived here a little less than six months. Even so, that's long enough to get a sense of who's respected in this town. Who is apt to be . . . listened to, even if what he says is unbelievable."

"I'm flattered," he said, very curious but willing to let her get to it in her own time.

She shook her head. "I've done my homework. You're descended from the Ryans who founded this town. You left only to go to college and law school, returning here to practice. You became a much admired and highly respected district court judge—obviously at a young age— but chose to retire after only a few years because you felt your true vocation was as a prosecutor. You were elected district attorney for Salem County, and you are very involved in community affairs as well as local and state politics. Your . . . support would count for a lot."

"My support in what?"

She answered his question with a matter-of-fact one of her own. "Do you believe in the paranormal?"

That was unexpected, and threw him for a moment. "The paranormal? You mean ghosts? UFOs? ESP?"

"Specifically extrasensory perception. Telepathy. Precognition." Her voice remained calm, but she was sitting just a bit too stiffly and her clasped fingers moved nervously. She darted another glance at him, so fleeting that all he caught was a flash of those pale eyes.

Ben shrugged. "In theory I always thought it was garbage. In fact, I've never encountered anything to make me change my mind." It was the fairly cynical mind common to many law enforcement officials, but he didn't add that.

She didn't look discouraged. "Are you willing to admit the possibility? To keep your mind open?"

"I hope I'm always willing to do that." Ben could have told her that he himself was given to hunches, to intuitions he found difficult to explain rationally, but he said nothing since it was a characteristic he hardly trusted. By training and inclination he was a man of reason.

Still utterly matter-of-fact, Cassie said, "There's going to be a murder."

She had surprised him again, unpleasantly this time. "I see. And you know that because you're psychic?"

She grimaced, registering the disbelief—and the suspicion of a prosecutor—in his voice. "Yes."

"You can see the future?"

"No. But I . . . tapped into the mind of the man who intends to commit a murder."

"Even assuming I believe that, intentions don't always translate into actions."

"This time they will. He will kill."

Ben rubbed the back of his neck as he stared at her. Maybe she was a kook. Or maybe not. "Okay. Who's going to be murdered?"

"I don't know. I saw her face when he watched her, but I don't know who she is."

Ben frowned. "When he watched her?"

She hesitated, her thin face tightening. Then she said, "I was . . . in his mind for only a few seconds. Seeing with his eyes, listening to his thoughts. He's been watching her, and he's decided to kill her. Soon."

"Who is he?"

"I don't know."

"Wait a minute. You claim you were inside the guy's head, but you don't know who he is?"

"No." She answered patiently, as though to an oft-repeated question. "Identity isn't a conscious thought most of the time. He knows who he is, so it wasn't something he was thinking about. And I didn't see any part of him, not his hands, or his clothing—or his reflection in a mirror. I don't know who he is. I don't know what he looks like."

"But you know he's going to kill someone. A woman."

"Yes."

Ben drew a breath. "Why didn't you go to the sheriff?"

"I did, last week. He didn't believe me."

"Which is why you came to me."

"Yes."

Ben picked up a pen and turned it in his fingers. "What do you expect me to do about it?"

"Believe me," she answered simply. For the first time, she looked squarely at him.

Ben felt as if she had reached across the desk and placed her hand on him. It was a warm hand.

He drew a breath, holding her gaze with his own.

"And assuming I can bring myself to do that? Is there anything you can tell me that might stop this murder from taking place?"

"No. Not . . . yet." She shook her head, unblinking. "I may see more. I may not. The fact that I connected to him without holding something he had touched, without knowing him, is unusual. It must have been the . . . intensity of his thoughts and plans, his eagerness, that reached out to me. Maybe I did touch something he had touched without knowing it. Or maybe he was physically nearby, and that's why I was able to steal the shadows—" She broke off abruptly and looked down once more.

He missed that warm hand. It was another surprise.

"Steal the shadows?"

Reluctantly Cassie said, "It's what I call it when I'm able to slip into a killer's mind and pick up bits and pieces of what he's thinking, planning. Their minds tend to be dark . . . filled with shadows." Her fingers were really working now, their nervous energy in stark contrast to her calm face and voice.

"You've done this before?"

She nodded.

"Have you worked with the police?"

"In Los Angeles. Some of the police out there are quite open-minded about seeking the help of psychics—especially when those psychics never seek publicity."

Ben leaned back in his chair and studied her. Weighed her. "Los Angeles. So what brought you all the way across the country to our little town?"

Her upward glance, he thought, was just a little wary once more. It put him on guard.

"An inheritance," she answered readily enough. "My aunt died last year and left me a house in Ryan's Bluff."

Ben frowned. "Who was your aunt?"

"Alexandra Melton."

He was startled, and knew it showed. "Miss Melton was a fairly well-known . . . character in Ryan's Bluff."

"She was quite a character in our family as well."

"Word around here was that she broke with her family."

"She was my mother's elder sister. They quarreled years ago, when I was just a child. No one ever told me what it was about. I never saw Aunt Alex again. Being notified last year that she'd left me a house and some acreage in North Carolina was quite a shock."

"So you decided to move three thousand miles."

She hesitated. "I don't know if it's permanent. I was tired of the city and wanted to spend some time in a place with an actual winter season."

"The Melton place is pretty isolated."

"Yes, but I don't mind that. It's been very peaceful."

"Until now."

"Until now."

After a moment Ben said, "Give me the name and number of somebody I can talk to in L.A. Somebody you've worked with."

She gave him the name of Detective Robert Logan, and his number, and Ben wrote down the information.

"Does that mean you're willing to believe me?" she asked.

"It means . . . I'm interested. It means I'll do my best to keep an open mind." He shook his head. "I'm not going to lie to you, Cassie. Your claim to be able to get inside the heads of killers is something I'm having a hard time with."

"I understand that. It's alien to most people."

Ben circled the name and number he'd written on the legal pad before him. "In the meantime, is there anything else you can tell me about this would-be murderer?"

She gave him another of those direct looks that was a warm touch. "I can tell you he's never killed before—at least, not a human being."

"He might have killed something else?"

"Maybe. Have there been any unexplained animal deaths or disappearances around here?"

"You mean recently? Not that I know of."

"It could have been recent. It's more likely, though, that he did that sort of thing as a child."

"If he did, he got away with it."

"Probably. It's the kind of thing that often gets dismissed when young boys do it. Unless it's extremely frequent or especially vicious. Not many people realize it's one of the earliest signs of homicidal tendencies."

"Particularly among serial killers. Along with, if I remember correctly, unnaturally prolonged bed-wetting and starting fires."

Cassie nodded. "Did you take one of the FBI courses for law enforcement officials?"

"Yes, shortly after I got this job. How about you?"

She smiled slightly. "No. I've just . . . picked up information along the way. I think it helped me, at least a little, to understand the clinical terms and explanations."

"For monsters?"

She nodded again.

"I'm sorry," Ben said.

Her eyes widened slightly, and then her gaze fell. "Never mind. I've taken up enough of your time today. Thanks again for seeing me. And for keeping an open mind."

They both rose, but a faint gesture from Cassie kept Ben on his side of the desk. Still, he wasn't quite ready to let her go. "Wait." He looked at her intently. "Your name. Is it short for Cassandra?"

"Yes."

Softly he said, "She tried to warn them—and nobody believed her."

"My mother was psychic. She'd knew I'd be. Sometimes I think she gave me that name just to make certain I'd go through life prepared for doubt and scorn. A reminder I'd always carry with me."

"I'm sorry," he said again.

"Don't be. We all have our crosses." She shrugged and began to turn away, then paused when he spoke again.

"That other Cassandra knew she couldn't change what would happen. She knew she wouldn't be believed. It destroyed her. Don't let it destroy you, Cassie."

Without looking at him she said, "Something else that other Cassandra knew. She knew her own fate. And she couldn't escape it."

"Do you?"

"Know my own fate? Yes."

"I thought you couldn't predict the future."

"Just mine. Just my fate."

He felt a little chill. "It's something you want to escape?"

Cassie went to the door and paused once again, this time with her hand on the doorknob. She glanced back at him. "Yes. But I can't. I ran almost three thousand miles, and it wasn't far enough."

"Cassie—"

But she was gone, slipping through the door and closing it quietly behind her.

Alone again, Ben sat down in his chair and for a moment gazed down absently at the name and number he'd written on his legal pad. Then he buzzed his secretary. "Janice, there's some research I need you to do ASAP. But first, there's a cop in L.A. I need to talk to."

· · ·

She walks like a whore.

Those short skirts make it worse, the way she twitches her ass when she walks.

Disgusting.

And just look at her—flirting with him. Tossing her hair and batting her eyes.

Whore.

You whore, I thought you were different!

Just another twenty-dollar whore. And not even worth that.

Not even that.

Matt Dunbar came from a long line of lawmen that stretched all the way back to a Texas Ranger who'd roamed the West in 1840, and it was a heritage he was proud of. He was also proud of the way he looked in his crisp sheriff's uniform. He worked out religiously in his basement exercise room six days a week to make damned sure no excess flab hung out over his belt.

No way was he going to become the familiar carica-ture of a fat, indolent Southern sheriff. He'd even gone to some effort to lose his accent, though the results were, he had to admit, less than what he'd been aim-ing for.

A lover had once told him he had a drawl that stretched out lazy like a cat in the sun.

It was a simile he liked.

So maybe he drawled a bit when he told Becky Smith that next time she ought not to park right smack in front of the fire hydrant even if she *did* plan to just run in and out of the drugstore.

As a stern official warning, it lacked something.

"Oh, I'm sorry, Sheriff." She smiled widely at him and pushed glossy brown hair back over her shoulder in a gesture that was a little flirtatious. "But I was only gone a couple of minutes, I promise. I'll move it right now."

He started to tell her she didn't have to move all that fast, but then he saw Ben Ryan's Jeep pull in behind his cruiser, so he touched his hat courteously to Becky and walked back to meet his boyhood friend, occasional poker buddy, and sometimes pain in the ass.

Today Ben looked like the last.

"Matt, when did you talk to Cassie Neill?" Ben asked as he got out of the Jeep.

The sheriff leaned back against the Jeep's front fender and crossed his arms over his chest. "She came into the office the end of last week. Thursday, I think. You mean she went running to you with that wild story?"

"Are you so sure it's wild?"

"Oh, for Christ's sake, Ben—"

"Look, I was doubtful too. But did you bother to check her out? Because I did."

"And?"

"And the LAPD detective I talked to says there are half a dozen multiple killers behind bars today because of Cassie Neill. And that's just in his jurisdiction."

Matt narrowed his eyes. "Then how come I never heard of her?"

Ben shook his head. "There's been very little press, and nothing national. The way she wanted it, apparently— which I count as a point in her favor. The cop told me his superiors were delighted that she insisted the department take the credit and keep her out of it. Naturally they weren't too eager to admit that they'd used the human version of a crystal ball to track down bad guys."

Matt grunted, and gazed absently at the peaceful scene of downtown Ryan's Bluff on a mild Tuesday afternoon. "I just don't buy that psychic bullshit, Ben. Last time I checked, neither did you."

"I'm still not sure. But I think we'd better pay attention to what the lady says."

"Just in case?"

"Just in case."

After a moment Matt shrugged. "Okay. You tell me what I'm supposed to do about the lady's so-called warning. She says somebody's going to die. That somebody is a woman—only she doesn't know who. All she knows is that the woman is possibly dark-haired, possibly between twenty and thirty-five, medium height and build—possibly. Which narrows down the *possible* victim to, oh, a quarter of the area's female population, give or take a few hundred. And our helpful psychic knows even less about the aspiring murderer. Don't even have a possible on him except that he's male. Eliminating you and me, and every man over sixty just on logical grounds, that leaves me with—what?— a few hundred conceivable suspects inside the town limits? What the hell do I do with that, Ben?"

"I don't know. But there must be something we can do."

"What? Panic a town by announcing one of our ladies is being stalked and doesn't know it?"

"No, of course not."

Matt sighed. "My gut says to have somebody watch Cassie Neill, and watch her close. Maybe there's a good reason she's so sure there's going to be a murder."

Ben stared at him in disbelief. "You can't be serious. If she weighs a hundred pounds, I'd be surprised."

"What, killers have to have muscles? You know better, Ben."

"I just meant she's too . . . fragile to have that in her."

The sheriff cocked an eyebrow. "Fragile?"

"Don't even start with me." Ben could feel heat rise in his face, as aware of his uncharacteristic credulity as his friend was but unwilling to examine it at the moment.

Matt hid a grin. "Okay, okay. It's just I've never heard you use that word before."

"Never mind my words. What are we going to do about this, Matt?"

"Wait. Nothing else we can do. If your *fragile* psychic comes up with something useful, great. If not—I guess we twiddle our thumbs and wait for a body to turn up."

TWO

"He's done it."

Ben pushed himself up onto an elbow and turned on the lamp beside his bed. The clock told him it was five-thirty. In the morning.

Christ, it was still dark.

He wedged the phone between ear and shoulder. "Who's done what? And do you know what time it is?"

"He's killed her," Cassie Neill said softly. Starkly.

Ben woke up.

He shoved the covers aside and sat up on the edge of the bed. "Are you sure?"

"Yes." She drew a breath. "It happened hours ago. There was nothing anyone could do, so—so I waited to call you. As long as I could."

Ben wondered what it was like to be awake and alone through the long, dark hours of the night—and aware of horrors. The professional part of him pushed that aside to say, "You should have called me right away. Evidence—"

"Won't be changed by the passing of a few hours. Not what little he left behind." Cassie sounded impossibly weary. "But you're right, I should have called immediately. I'm sorry."

Ben drew a breath. "Do you know where?"

"Yes, I think so. There's an old abandoned barn on the north end of town, about five miles out."

"I know it. Used to be a stockyard there."

"She's . . . he left her in the woods behind that barn. He didn't kill her there, but it's where he left her. I think . . . I think she'll be easy to find. He didn't bury the body or try to hide it in any way. In fact . . . he posed her somehow."

"Posed her?"

"Sat her up with her back against a tree. He was very careful to get the look just right. It must mean something." Cassie's voice faded on the last words, and she sighed. "I don't know what. I'm sorry. I'm tired."

Ben hesitated, then said, "I'll go take a look."

"Before you call the sheriff?" There was wry understanding in her tone.

Ben was unwilling to admit that he didn't want to look like an even more gullible fool if this turned out to be a false alarm. So he merely said, "I'll probably want to talk to you later."

"I'll be here." Cassie hung up quietly.

Dawn was just lightening the sky when Ben parked his Jeep at the old Pittman stockyard. He turned on the flashlight he'd brought along in order to pick his way around the barn and through a ragged gap in what was left of the fence to the woods in back of the place.

It was quiet. Too quiet.

He didn't go very far into the woods before halting

and directing the flashlight in a slow arc ahead. These were hardwood trees, bare of leaves in February, the undergrowth scant, so he could see quite well.

He hadn't really believed she would be there.

When the light fell on her, Ben heard his own sharply indrawn breath.

Just as Cassie had described, the victim sat with her back against a tree, facing the barn, easily visible. Her eyes were open, her head tilted a bit to one side and her lips slightly parted as though she had paused in saying something to listen politely to a companion. Her hands lay folded in her lap, palms up. She was fully dressed.

Ben knew her. Becky Smith, a girl barely twenty who worked—had worked—at the drugstore in town while she attended the local community college. She had wanted to be a teacher.

Her throat was cut from ear to ear.

"Goddammit, Ben, you know better!" The sheriff was furious, and it showed.

"Like you wouldn't have done the exact same thing?" Ben shook his head. "As convincing as she sounded, Matt, I didn't really believe I was going to find anything. So, yes, I walked within twelve feet of the body. I didn't realize it was a crime scene until it was too late. But I didn't touch her or disturb anything."

"Why the hell didn't you call me before coming out here?"

Ben glanced past the sheriff, toward the rear of the barn, where most of the dozen or so deputies Matt had brought were carefully combing the ground. The sun was well up now, and Becky's body had been taken away.

Her body being zipped into the black bag was a sight he would not soon forget.

"Ben?"

"We've been through this, Matt. I didn't want to look like a jackass if I dragged you out here and there was nothing to find."

"So you came out on your own. Unarmed. What if the bastard hadn't finished his work, Ben? Jesus, she was hardly cold."

"I wish I *had* found him here. I'm not a twenty-year-old girl."

"And he might have had a gun. Did you think of that? Did you think at all?"

Normally Ben wouldn't have allowed his friend to censure him—loudly—in a fairly public arena, but he knew Matt well enough to recognize that the sheriff was badly shaken.

Before today, the last murder in Salem County had occurred ten years back, when Thomas Byrd had come home early from work to find another man keeping his bed warm. To say nothing of Mrs. Byrd. It had been an entirely understandable crime of passion.

This crime was everything but understandable.

"Matt, can we please get past my reckless actions and move on?"

Matt's mouth tightened, but he nodded.

"Okay. Now, since you were elected by the good citizens of Salem County to catch criminals, and I was elected to prosecute them, I'd say we have work to do."

"Yeah." Matt turned his head to look toward the activity behind the barn and scowled. "And the first thing I want to do is talk to Cassie Neill."

Ben hesitated, then said, "You and your people have to finish up here. Why don't I go get Miss Neill and bring her to the station? I'm very interested in what she has to say."

Matt turned his scowl to his friend. "It isn't your place

to investigate crimes, Ben. Your job starts when I catch the bastard."

"My job is made a lot easier if I'm involved early on, and you know it."

"Maybe. And maybe in this case your involvement would be a bad idea. You aren't exactly impartial, are you?"

"What the hell do you mean by that?"

"What I mean is that you obviously have a soft spot for your fragile so-called psychic. I won't let you get in my way, Ben."

It took a moment, but then Ben got it. "Ah, I see. You think Cassie Neill killed Becky Smith."

"And you obviously don't."

"I know she didn't." Ben heard the words come out of his mouth and was more than a little surprised by them.

Matt didn't seem to be. "Uh-huh. And you know that because—"

"I told you. She doesn't have it in her to kill someone. Especially not like that. Come on, Matt. It takes a particular brand of brutality to cut a woman's throat from ear to ear. Don't tell me you saw that in Cassie."

"The first thing you learn as a cop is that the most likely explanation is probably the right one. Cassie Neill did a hell of a good job describing a crime scene. I say it's because she'd seen it."

"I agree. But I don't think she was here."

"The psychic bullshit. Yeah, right."

"Matt, try to keep an open mind." Once more Ben glanced past the sheriff at the uniformed people searching for clues, then added quietly, "You know those hunches I used to get when we were kids?"

"Yeah."

"Well, I've got one now. I've got a hunch that this is just the beginning." He returned his gaze to Matt's face.

"And the psychic bullshit may be the only thing we've got going for us."

The old Melton place consisted of a Victorian-style house and various outbuildings that sat on twenty acres more than ten miles from town. Alexandra Melton had bought the place back in 1976, arriving in Ryan's Bluff from the West Coast with, apparently, plenty of money and nobody but herself to spend it on.

She had been quite a character. Her outfit of choice had been jeans and T-shirts, often paired with unusual hats or flowing silk scarves. Still beautiful right up until her death from pneumonia at sixty-plus the previous year, she had black hair that had been touched by silver only in a narrow streak above her left temple, and her figure had remained striking enough to attract admiring eyes whenever she came into town. Which was rarely. Once a month for supplies, no more often.

The odd thing was that Alex Melton had struck most as a warm and outgoing woman with a brisk, no-nonsense manner and a big heart. Yet she had made it plain from the outset that she did not want or need visitors and that she had no intention of becoming involved in community affairs.

Or affairs of the heart, apparently. Ben had heard the stories. Because she had been so beautiful, more than one man had made an attempt over the years, only to be firmly, if kindly, rebuffed. Word had it that a woman or two had also tried, and received the same decisive refusal.

It apparently wasn't a question of which way Alex Melton swung, but the fact that she didn't swing at all.

Ben thought of all that as his Jeep wound its way up

the long dirt drive to the house that now belonged to Alex's niece. She didn't mind the isolation, she'd said. It was peaceful. Or had been.

She'd also said that she had "run" three thousand miles to escape the fate she saw for herself, only to fail.

Ben didn't know if he believed Cassie Neill saw her own fate, but he was certain she was running away from something. And another one of his hunches told him that understanding what that was would be important to him.

He parked the Jeep in the circular drive in front of the house and got out. For a moment he just studied the house, noting that it was being slowly redone on the outside. New shutters, new paint on the railing of the wraparound porch, and he thought the front door, with its oval leaded glass inset, had also been refinished. The house hadn't been in bad shape before, but the new work definitely improved it.

Ben knocked on the door, and Cassie opened it holding a paintbrush in one hand.

"Hi," he said. "I would say good morning, but it isn't."

"No, it isn't. Come in." She stepped back and opened the door wider.

Just as in his office, she looked at him directly only in flickering glances. But this time, with her hair tied back away from her face and with her dressed in jeans and a close-fitting thermal shirt, he got a much better look at her.

She wasn't just fragile. She was almost ethereal.

"The coffee's hot. Would you like some?" If she was even conscious of his scrutiny, Cassie didn't seem bothered by it.

"Please." He followed her through an open living area

with little furniture—where she'd been painting a small table on newspapers spread out in the center of the room—and into the kitchen.

Cassie took a moment to rinse her paintbrush and leave it in the sink, then washed her hands and poured coffee for them both. "Black, right?"

"Right. More ESP?"

"No. Just a guess." She handed him the cup without touching his fingers, then took her own to the scarred old wooden table in the center of the room. "Do you mind if we sit in here? I need to let the paint fumes in the other room dissipate."

"No problem." He joined her, sitting in the chair on the other side of the table. "I always liked this room." It was warm and cheery, sunny with numerous windows and brightly painted in yellow.

"You knew my aunt, then?"

"Slightly. I came out here a few times." He smiled. "I wanted her vote. Besides, she was an interesting lady."

Cassie sipped her coffee, her gaze on the cup. "So I've been told. There's lots of her stuff packed away; sooner or later I'll have to go through it. Looks like she kept a journal, as well as all her correspondence. Maybe I'll finally get to know her myself. I'm not in a hurry about that though. There's so much else to do."

Ben had a hunch that she had put off going through her aunt's things not because of being busy elsewhere but simply because she was not yet ready to open herself up, even to the personality and memories of a dead woman. From what the L.A. detective had told him, Cassie had been worse than walking wounded when she had retreated here nearly six months before. Detective Logan believed she had been about a breath away from a complete physical, emotional, and mental breakdown, the result of living through one nightmare too many.

But Ben accepted her explanation, at least for the moment, and said only, "You're renovating the house?"

"No, just updating a bit." Her glance flickered toward his face, then fell again. "I like working with my hands. Working with wood."

"Touching beautiful things because you can't touch people?"

That brought her gaze to his face, and this time it stayed. There were smudges of exhaustion underneath her pale eyes and he could read nothing in them, yet he still felt the warmth as clearly as though she had reached out and laid her hand upon him. It was an unnerving sensation, yet one he knew he had wanted to feel again.

"That's too simple," she said.

"Is it? You avoid physical contact with people. Or is it just me?"

Cassie shook her head. "It's . . . uncomfortable for me. I'm a touch telepath. It's very difficult for me to block out someone else's thoughts and emotions when I'm in physical contact with them." Her shoulders lifted and fell.

"So you just avoid touch."

She looked back at her cup. "There are things in the human mind that are not meant to be seen or touched, things seldom even acknowledged by our conscious selves. Fantasies, impulses, rages, hatreds, primitive instincts. They're buried deep, usually, and that's where they belong. In the darkest parts of our minds."

"The parts you can see."

Again she shrugged. "I've seen enough. Too much. I try not to look."

"Except when murderers blast their way in?"

"I tried to shut him out, believe me. I didn't want to know what he was going to do. What he did."

"But if there was even a chance you might stop him—"

"I didn't, did I? Stop him. I went to the sheriff. I went to you. I even opened myself up and crawled into his . . . darkest places. But it didn't stop him. It never stops them."

"That's not what Detective Logan told me."

Cassie shook her head. "They're caught eventually. Maybe I can help with that, maybe not. But people still die. And there's not a single goddamned thing I can do to change that." Her voice was soft.

"So you ran here, is that it? Here, in this isolated house near a small town where you could hope for peace."

"Don't I have a right to peace? Doesn't everyone?"

"Yes. But, Cassie, you can't ignore what you see any more than I could ignore it if I saw someone stabbed on a street corner. I would have to do what I could to help. So do you."

She drew a breath. "I've spent ten years doing what I could to help. I'm tired. I just want to be left alone."

"Do you think he'll leave you alone?"

She was silent.

"Cassie?"

"No," she whispered.

Ben wished she would look at him again, but her gaze seemed welded to her coffee cup. "Then help us. Becky Smith was just twenty, Cassie. A college student who loved kids and wanted to be a teacher. She deserved her life. She deserved her chance. Help us catch the bastard who took that away from her."

"You don't know what you're asking."

"I have some idea. I know it'll take a lot out of you. But we need your help. We have to do whatever it takes to get this guy before he gets away. Or before he kills again."

Finally her gaze lifted to meet his, and there was something lurking in the depths of her eyes that made him flinch. Something small and hurting.

"All right," Cassie said quietly. "I'll get my jacket."

"So?" The sheriff wasn't openly hostile, but close. "Let's have it."

They were in Matt's office, seated side by side in the visitors' chairs in front of the old slate-top desk that had been his father's, and the sheriff was already in a nasty mood because his people had found absolutely nothing useful at the crime scene.

And he didn't believe in psychic bullshit, he just *didn't*.

"I can't tell you much more than I already have," Cassie said. "The killer is male—"

"How can you be so sure of that?" Ben asked. "You said identity isn't a conscious thing. Is gender?"

"Sometimes. But in this case . . ." She avoided his gaze, fixing hers on the hands clasped in her lap. "When he was watching her . . . planning what he would do to her . . . he was . . . aware of his erection."

It was the sheriff who reddened slightly and shifted in his chair, but his voice was sharp when he said, "This wasn't a sexual attack."

"They're always sexual attacks."

"This woman was not touched sexually," he insisted. "Preliminary reports say no semen was found anywhere on or near the body. For Christ's sake, she still had her panties on."

"That doesn't matter. He was in a state of sexual excitement when he stalked her, and he achieved release when he killed her."

"My God, you were in his mind during all that?" Ben said, startled.

"Yes. When he first went after her and then again, after he'd tied her up and was . . . was ready to hurt her. That time I was with him for a few minutes. It didn't take long, and just as he killed her I . . . managed to break away."

Ben wondered what it must be like to observe—maybe even experience intimately—the orgasm of an insane killer, and thought it was undoubtedly one memory Cassie would happily part with. For the first time, he began to truly understand what lay behind her haunted eyes.

Monsters indeed.

The sheriff had something else on his mind. "So he tied her up, did he?"

"Not with ropes," Cassie said. "A belt, I think. For her wrists. He didn't tie her ankles. He—he made her sit with her legs apart."

"Why?" Ben asked.

"It was . . . part of the pose somehow. Part of what he needed to see. He was taunting her. He kept . . . he kept putting the knife between her legs and threatening to put it inside her. He wanted her to be afraid. She was. She was terrified."

"You know this because you saw it," Matt said.

"Yes."

"Through his eyes."

"Yes, Sheriff."

The sheriff was looking at her squarely, his gaze narrowed in suspicion. "I'm having a hard time understanding this, Miss Neill. You claim not to know the murderer. So how is it you're able to see what he does? Know what he was feeling? Do you always *pick up* the thoughts and plans of strangers? Like a bad filling picks up stray radio signals?"

She shook her head and explained what she had explained many times before. "Maybe I touched something he touched. That's most likely."

"Touched something like what?"

"Like . . . a door he'd just passed through. Something on the shelf of a store. A theater seat he'd been in the night before. Or I might have bumped against him in the grocery store. Our eyes might have met for a moment on the streets. But—"

Ben interrupted. "Eyes meeting? Something so . . . impersonal?"

Cassie's head turned slightly toward him, but her gaze remained on her hands. "It's . . . a question of connecting. I've never been able to—to read anyone without some kind of connection. It's almost always a physical touch, either of the person or something the person came into contact with recently. An object. A bit of clothing."

"But eyes meeting?" Ben repeated. "Two strangers on opposite street corners—it could be as brief and simple as that?"

"Ben, do you mind?" the sheriff said.

"It's an important point, Matt. If all she needed to make this connection was a glance—"

Sourly, the sheriff said, "I know goddamned well what it means, Ben. A town full of suspects. Assuming, of course, that I believe any of this bullshit. So far I haven't heard a good reason to."

"Cassie knew someone would be murdered," Ben said. "She told both of us a couple of days ago. She called me this morning to tell me it had happened—and where."

"Yeah, and you know what I think about that. Maybe she was able to do that because she'd been there. Maybe she knew the details because she killed Becky Smith."

Cassie lifted her gaze for the first time. "No. I didn't

kill her. I didn't even know her." Then a frown flitted across her brow. "But neither did he, really."

Ben leaned forward. "What? He didn't know her?"

Cassie turned her head and looked at him. "No. He'd been watching her. He knew who she was. He thought he knew . . . what she was."

"What do you mean—what she was?"

"Somehow . . . she wasn't what he thought. He was disappointed in her. Maybe because of something she'd said or done. He was angry at her. Enraged. Yet . . . I didn't get a sense of intimate knowledge. And I don't believe she had known him in any real sense before he grabbed her."

"She didn't know who he was?"

Cassie shook her head. "I can't be sure, but I don't think so. She might have recognized him as someone she'd seen around town, maybe even on a regular basis, but I didn't get the sense that she really knew him. He might have done something to disguise himself, of course, though that doesn't seem likely if he knew he was going to kill her. As for what she saw, she was pleading with him not to hurt her, but she never said his name. If she'd known his name, if she'd recognized him, she probably would have."

"You get sound too?" the sheriff said.

Ben swore impatiently, but Cassie's gaze returned to him and a faint smile without real amusement curved her mouth. "Sometimes it's just like turning on a television set."

"Turn it on now," he invited. "Let's see what the bastard's doing at the moment."

"I wish it were that easy."

His chair creaked angrily as he leaned back. "Yeah, I thought so. Not *quite* like turning on a TV, I guess."

It was obviously an attitude Cassie had encountered before. "I'm sorry, Sheriff. I wish I could just flip a switch or say a magic word and climb inside this monster's head to get the answers you need." She drew a breath. "If he kills again, I'll probably connect again. Murderers like this one tend to get progressively more wound up and excited when the lust to kill starts building in them. Those powerful emotions broadcast strongly. Now . . . now he's probably in a cooling-down period. Very calm, maybe tired. His mind is quiet, contained. It isn't reaching out. And without a physical connection, I can't reach out to him."

Ben glanced at Matt but said nothing.

There was a moment of silence, and then the sheriff said grimly, " 'Cooling-off period' is the phrase those behavioral sciences boys at Quantico use. Miss Neill, are you trying to tell us we've got a serial killer here? On the basis of one murder?"

Cassie hesitated visibly. "I can't say for sure. I only know there's . . . something abnormal about him. About the way his mind works. And she was a stranger to him, or as good as. People who kill are almost always driven—by rage, hate, jealousy, greed, even fear. People who kill the way he did, using a knife, getting the blood on him . . . that can only be done in an extreme emotional state. It's hard to feel so strongly toward a virtual stranger, for someone whose life never touched yours in any meaningful sense. But serial killers . . . they have their own mad reasons to kill. And they almost always kill strangers."

"You seem to know a lot about the subject," the sheriff said.

"I've spent a lot of time around some very good cops. I learned as much as I needed to in order to try to help them. Enough so that it's been a long time since I had a good night's sleep." Her voice was matter-of-fact and without self-pity.

"Monsters," Ben murmured.

She glanced at him. "When I was a child, my mother told me that if I turned on a light, I'd see there was no monster hiding in the closet or under my bed. She was always right about that. Then. I'm all grown-up now. And the monsters in my life aren't under my bed. They're inside my own mind, where I can't shine a light on them."

The sheriff was unaffected by her words. "Ever talk to a shrink, Miss Neill?"

"Lots of them." Her voice was as dry and unemotional as his had been. "Sheriff, I can give you plenty of references. Testimonials from lots of cops on the West Coast, all of them as hardheaded and rational as you are. They'll tell you that they were doubtful too, in the beginning. That they also suggested I talk to someone about these . . . voices and images in my head. And they'll tell you that time and experience convinced them that sometimes—not always, but sometimes—I could help them catch killers."

She drew a breath, her pale eyes fixed on his. "No matter what you believe or don't believe about what I can do, Sheriff Dunbar, there's one thing you can be very, very sure of. I hate this. I didn't ask for this, and I wouldn't wish it on my worst enemy. It is not a pleasant thing to be jolted awake in the middle of the night with the screams of a dying woman ringing in your ears and the smell of her blood so real, you expect to find yourself covered in it.

"It is not a pleasant thing to sit across a desk from hard and suspicious men like you and talk calmly about vicious crimes and monsters who can't be banished by the light of day or sanity. And it is more traumatic and debilitating than you will ever know for me to force myself to drop all the guards I've spent a lifetime building and climb inside the mind of something that is not human.

"So give me a break, *Sheriff*. I did not kill that poor woman, and since I did not, you will never find a shred of evidence against me. Now, I will give you the references I spoke of, and you can check them out or not. Believe them or not. If you want my help, I will do everything I can to help you. If not, I'll go back to my peaceful house and my peaceful life. And the next time I'm awakened by the screams of a dying murder victim, I'll pull my pillow over my ears and try my damnedest to ignore them."

Ben looked at Matt but said nothing. Cassie was obviously her own best champion, at least where her psychic ability was concerned, and if there was ever going to be any kind of understanding between her and the skeptical sheriff, it would have to be reached by the two of them.

It would not be easy.

"I don't believe in psychics, Miss Neill," Matt said. "And I don't trust you."

"That is your prerogative, Sheriff." She matched him stare for stare, and her voice was cool, her steel core suddenly evident. "Judge Ryan asked me to help, and I said I would. But I am not going to jump through hoops for you, especially when my help is not wanted. If you think I'm a killer, lock me up. When the next body turns up, I'll have a cast-iron alibi. Unless you *do* believe it's possible to walk through walls and bars."

He ignored that. "I don't suppose you have an alibi for last night?"

"The same one you have. I was home in bed. Of course, I was alone."

Matt stiffened. "Meaning?"

"Meaning you weren't."

Ben was surprised but kept his mouth shut.

"Nice guess, Miss Neill," Matt said.

"It wasn't a guess. I don't even have to try very hard to read you, Sheriff. You're an open book. The lady has red hair. I believe her name is . . . Abby. Abby Montgomery."

Ben said, "For God's sake, Matt—if Gary finds out, he'll come after you with a gun. She's still his wife."

"They're separated," Matt snapped.

"Not in his mind."

Matt stared at Cassie. "You probably saw us together."

"You've been very circumspect, both of you," she said. "Nothing in public. As Judge Ryan said, her husband hasn't accepted the separation. He has a bad temper. It's why their marriage broke up." She frowned suddenly. "Be careful, Sheriff. Be very careful."

"Or?"

"Or you'll never be able to take her to Paris next summer the way you want to."

THREE

"Shit," Matt said, obviously shaken. "You couldn't have known that. I haven't even told Abby. Nobody knows."

"*You* know."

There was a long, tense silence, and then Cassie shook her head. "I don't usually do that. Invade someone's privacy. I'm sorry. But you made it easy for me, Sheriff."

It was Ben who said "Because he was acting like an ass?"

Cassie smiled slightly but didn't look at him. "No. That just made it easy for me to try to read him. You're simple, Sheriff. You think loudly."

Ben had to laugh, and after a moment even Matt smiled.

"Well, stop listening, will you?"

"I didn't listen very closely," she promised him. "And I'll try not to do it again. You just made me mad."

Matt nodded slowly. "Okay, I admit that little parlor trick was fairly convincing. And if those references of yours pan out, it's another point in your favor. But I'm still not a believer, Miss Neill."

"All I ask is that you keep an open mind." She glanced at Ben, then added, "And give me a chance. Maybe I can help. Maybe I can't. But I will try if you want me to."

"Can you tap into this guy directly? You said it required a connection, which obviously already exists."

"If he were sitting right in front of me, I probably could. But for me to reach out over distance and try to tap into his mind when I don't know who he is or where he is . . . that's difficult. I'd need something of his, something he touched. Something I could touch physically."

"What about . . . something Becky was wearing? He touched her."

Ben thought Cassie's face tightened. But her voice remained calm.

"We found out . . . that's dangerous for me. To touch the belongings of a murder victim, especially the clothing worn during . . . during the crime. I connect with the strongest, most recent emotions permeating that clothing. The moment of greatest terror. Usually that's the moment of death."

"What happened when you tried it?" Ben asked.

Matter-of-factly she answered, "It was like falling into a deep black well. I didn't have the strength to pull myself out. If someone hadn't been there to break the physical connection, I don't think I would have made it. As it was, I was in a coma for a week. And afterward . . . it was like all the psychic pathways in my mind had been cut or burned out. It was six months before I got my abilities back." She paused, then added almost wistfully, "It was so quiet. It was the first time I could understand how normal people sense things."

After a moment of silence Matt said, "So you need something belonging to the killer. Something he touched that wouldn't have been . . . affected by her death."

She nodded. "The coin might work."

Matt stiffened and shot a look at Ben, who spoke immediately.

"I didn't tell her."

Cassie said, "I broke the connection before she died, but it came back faintly a little while later, when he put her in the woods. When he posed her like that. It's how I knew where you'd find her. And I saw him put the coin into her hand."

"What do you think it means?" Ben asked her. "The coin?"

"I think it has something to do with her worth in his eyes. It was a silver dollar, wasn't it?"

"It was," Matt said. "No prints."

"Yes, he was very careful about not leaving traceable evidence, so the coin itself probably won't lead you to him." Cassie frowned as she looked at Ben. "Her worth in his eyes. How he posed her, the coin, the way he taunted her before he killed her. He thought she was a whore."

"She wasn't," Matt objected immediately. "She was just a kid."

Cassie's eyes fixed on the sheriff, and she spoke gently. "What she actually was didn't matter to him. In his mind she was a whore. If you want to find him, you have to figure out how his mind works."

"Yeah, I know." Matt sighed heavily. "But I don't have to like it."

"Not much fun trying to think like a madman, is it?"

Matt looked at her. "You've made your point."

Cassie didn't push it. "Do you have the coin?"

"Maybe this isn't such a good idea," Ben said. "Today, I mean. Cassie, you said you were awake most of the night—you must be tired." He didn't add that she was visibly exhausted.

"I'd like to try, Judge."

"I wish you'd call me Ben."

She glanced at him and nodded but spoke to the sheriff. "I'd like to try. If you have the coin."

Matt opened the center drawer of his desk and brought out a small, clear plastic bag labeled EVIDENCE. He pushed it across the desk to Cassie.

She didn't touch it immediately, but instead sent Ben another quick glance. "I'll need a lifeline."

"A what?"

"A lifeline. Somebody to . . . talk me through. Keep me focused. Keep me from going too deep."

"What happens if you go too deep?"

Cassie smiled faintly. "I don't come back."

Ben looked at Matt, who lifted an eyebrow silently, then back at her. "Okay. What do I do?"

Cassie reached for the bag. "Just keep talking to me. If I make a connection, don't let go."

Her trust disturbed him, but Ben nodded.

Either seeing or sensing his uneasiness, she said reassuringly, "I'll make the connection as shallow as I can this time, just to find out if there's anything there. If this coin didn't belong to him or wasn't in his possession for a while, there may not be much I can get."

Ben watched as she opened the bag and slid the coin out onto her palm.

Her head bent and her eyes closed as she began turning the coin in her fingers. It was what someone would do when she was trying to identify something by touch alone, probing the shape and texture of a thing.

"Cassie?" Ben said when he thought the silence had lasted too long.

Her face turned a little toward him in a clear and instant response to his voice. She was even more pale than she had been before, so much so that it startled Ben.

But her voice was steady when she slowly said, "This

was his. It was part of a . . . collection. And he has more. Laid out in a row. There was a place for the dollar, but now that's empty. There was . . . a set. He still has a fifty-cent piece, a quarter, a dime, a nickel, and a penny."

"Does he mean to use them all?" Ben asked.

"I don't know." She winced. "It's difficult to touch his mind. He's tired, drained. He's looking at the coins, but I don't know what he's thinking or feeling."

Matt spoke then, his voice low and filled with the fascinated suspicion of a man unwillingly impressed by the show but still searching for the wizard behind the curtain. "Can she see what's around him?"

"Cassie? Can you see what's around him? Can you describe where he is?"

"Not really. It's dark. He likes the dark. His head doesn't hurt so much in the dark."

"Is it a room?"

"I think so. But . . . I don't see any furniture. Just the coins laid out in a row. Black velvet behind them. All his attention is focused on them. It's like he's . . . mesmerized. Almost in a trance."

Cassie shook her head suddenly and opened her eyes. "That's all. That's all I get." She slid the coin back into its bag and pushed it across the desk to Matt. "I should try again in a day or two. Right now he's . . . too distant. Too drained."

Matt glanced down at the notes he'd made on a legal pad. "Part of a collection. Do you think he collects coins?"

"Could be. The ones he had laid out before him are definitely important to him, I know that." She sounded tired.

"Are you all right?" Ben asked her.

"I'll be fine."

"But are you all right now?"

She looked at him, and he felt the difference. The warmth of that direct gaze was less than it had been, as though some furnace of energy inside her had used up too much fuel and now burned dangerously low.

"It's draining. But I'll be fine." To Matt she said, "I'm sorry I couldn't be more help. This time."

Matt looked up from the legal pad, his face grim. "Is there anything else you can tell me about him? Anything at all?"

"Just what I'd already told you and Judge—you and Ben. I don't believe he's killed before, but I think he will again. He has the taste of it now. And he likes it." She paused. "There's something young about his mind, about the way he thinks. Guessing, I'd say he's still in his twenties."

Cassie shrugged. "And then there's what a profiler would probably tell you. White male between twenty-four and thirty-two. Probably single and unlikely to be involved with a woman. Probably came from an abusive background and undoubtedly had at least one domineering parent—probably his mother. Sexual problems—possibly impotence. He's found a way to achieve sexual gratification, and that's important to him. The ritual worked. The way she was posed, the coin in her hand—those are things you'll find at the next scene. His M.O., in that way, is probably established."

"What about the weapon?" Matt asked. "We didn't find the knife. Will he use it again?"

"It's a guess . . . but I don't think how they die is as important to him as how they're found. He may not use the same means next time." She gestured wearily. "But I'm not sure."

"Come on," Ben said, rising. "I need to get you home." He had to fight the instinct to reach out and offer his hand.

Cassie got up. "I'll wait outside. The sheriff wants to talk to you."

"Stop doing that," Matt said as he also got to his feet.

"I'm sorry—you were thinking loudly again." She offered him a small smile, then left the office, closing the door quietly behind her.

"Well?" Ben said.

Matt shook his head. "I still don't know if I buy any of this."

"She's reading you like a book."

"Yeah, yeah. And a fake fortune teller can read a total stranger pretty well just with body language. It's a skill, Ben. And not a paranormal one."

"Did your body language tell her about Abby Montgomery? It sure as hell never told me. And be careful with that, will you?"

Matt ignored the warning. "I don't know how she knew about me and Abby. But I'm still not convinced. My investigation of this murder is going by the book. Most murder victims know their killers, so family and friends have to be checked out. Coworkers, classmates. The usual drill. We'll look for witnesses who might have seen Becky talking to somebody in the last day or two. We'll check out her background and recent history, look for connections, for motives. What we will not do is start thinking we've got a serial killer on the basis of one crime."

"I can't tell you how to do your job."

Matt grunted. "Why stop now?"

Ben smiled but said, "What have you told Eric?" Eric Stephens published the local daily newspaper.

"Bare facts. That Becky was murdered. With any luck at all, word won't get around about how she was found. Or about the coin. I sure as hell don't expect a copycat killer, not around here, but the less the public knows about the details, the less likely we are to have a panic on our hands."

"Maybe they should panic," Ben said soberly. "Matt, if we do have a serial killer—"

"If we do, I'll slap a curfew on this town and have all the girls escorted by family or traveling by twos at all times. I'm not afraid to scare the hell out of them, Ben. I just won't do it needlessly."

"Let's hope you won't have to," Ben said.

"Hi."

Cassie, who had been leaning back against a decorative lamppost on the sidewalk in front of the Sheriff's Department with her face turned up to the mild February sun, looked around at the greeting and blinked to focus. She found herself being studied by a smiling woman maybe a few years older than herself, a very attractive blue-eyed blonde.

"Hi."

"Excuse me—I didn't mean to bother you, but you remind me of someone. Alexandra Melton. Any relation?"

"She was my aunt. I'm Cassie Neill." Her voice was friendly, but she kept her hands on the post behind her.

"Ah, that explains the resemblance. I'm Jill Kirkwood. Nice to meet you. I knew your aunt—though not very well, I'm afraid. I own the craft store across the street there, and she came in occasionally."

"She must have liked you," Cassie commented.

"Because she came in the store?"

"No." Cassie smiled. "Because she didn't do crafts."

Jill Kirkwood blinked. "But—she bought things. Supplies. And all kinds of kits."

"I know. I found them in her house. In a trunk in a

spare room. As far as I can tell, she never even opened any of the kits."

After a moment Jill laughed. "I'll be damned. I figured she had a house full of the stuff by now, even though she never brought anything in to show me, the way most of my customers do."

"As I said, she must have liked you."

"I know I liked her. She was . . ."

"Odd?"

"Different." Jill smiled. "She told me once where I could find a ring I'd lost. Said she had a knack for things like that. And she was right. The ring was right where she'd said it would be."

Whatever Cassie might have responded to that was prevented by the arrival of Ben, who joined them on the sidewalk.

"Hi, Jill," he said.

"Ben. Have you met—"

"Yes, Cassie and I have met. As a matter of fact, I'm giving her a ride back to her house."

"Oh? Well, then, I won't keep you." She smiled at Cassie. "Nice meeting you. Come into the store sometime—if you're more interested in crafts than Miss Melton was."

"It was nice meeting you," Cassie said with a smile, not committing herself any further.

"Bye, Ben."

"Jill."

Cassie walked slightly ahead of him to his Jeep. She didn't say anything until they were inside and heading down Main Street. Then, mildly, she said, "If you'd come out of the Sheriff's Department a few minutes later, I might have had a new friend."

"What?"

"Jill Kirkwood. I liked her."

Ben shot her a glance. "Good. She's a nice lady."

"Um. But she doesn't like me. Not now."

"Why not?"

"Because of you. Some ex-lovers don't want to let go. She doesn't. Other women are a threat—even without reason."

Ben was silent for a moment. "Now I know how Matt felt. It's a little unnerving to be an open book."

"You aren't," Cassie said. "But Jill Kirkwood is. Her emotions were . . . strong. They were hard to ignore. Impossible to ignore."

Again Ben hesitated before speaking. "Can you read me?"

She shook her head, then looked at him rather curiously. "Not the way I can some, without even trying."

"Could you if you touched me?" Instantly he could feel her tense, almost draw in on herself.

"Probably. Usually. It's a rare person—a very rare nonpsychic—who is able to shield thoughts and emotions, especially well enough to withstand physical contact. For most people there was never a reason to learn, so they didn't."

Ben held a hand out palm up between them. "Care to put it to the test?"

She looked at his hand, then met his eyes. "If you don't mind, I'd rather not." Her voice was very steady.

He put his hand back on the wheel. "I'll try not to take it personally."

"Please don't. You noticed right away—I avoid touching people. All people. It's . . . simpler for me. Their mental voices don't slip through my walls so easily. Think of what it's like to be in the center of a huge room filled with people. All of them talking."

"The noise can be overwhelming," he agreed.

"Not just the noise of thought. The . . . jagged edges of

emotions. The dark flashes of fantasy. The secrets they don't even tell themselves." She shrugged. "It's just much less painful and distracting if I shield myself as much as possible. That means doing my best to keep my walls up—and avoiding touch."

"It's all right, Cassie. I really didn't take it personally."

"Good."

A silence fell, and neither of them broke it until Ben turned the Jeep into the long driveway at the Melton place. "I'll have to start thinking of this as your place rather than the Melton place," he said absently.

"It doesn't feel like my place yet."

"You said you'd been here only a few months?"

"Since the end of August."

He glanced at her. "We had a lot of snow in December. It must have been lonely out here."

"There's lonely . . . and then there's *lonely*. Believe me, the peace and quiet was wonderful. Being alone was just what I needed." As he stopped the Jeep near the walkway, she added, "You don't have to get out."

He did anyway, and then opened the passenger door for her. "I was raised right. Always walk a lady to her front door."

Cassie didn't protest again. On the front porch, she dug in her jacket pocket for keys. "I guess I didn't have to lock the door, but habit dies hard."

Ben frowned. "Keep the door locked. And if you don't have a security system or a big dog around, get both. Soon. A week ago I would have said it hardly mattered, but after what happened to Becky, and what you said about her killer, this town doesn't feel safe anymore."

"That really bothers you."

"Of course it does."

"No—I mean that's something you *do* take personally. Why? Because your family founded the town?"

"Maybe. And I'm an elected official, very much concerned with the safety of the people of Salem County." He knew he was being deliberately offhand, that he did, in fact, take this threat very personally, but since he didn't have a ready answer and in any case wasn't given to explaining his emotions to anyone, it wasn't something he was willing to talk about.

Cassie unlocked her front door. "Understandable. I'll try the coin again in a day or two. In the meantime, if I pick up anything else about the killer, I'll give you or Sheriff Dunbar a call."

"Do that."

She stepped into the house and turned back to face him. "Thanks for the ride."

"You're welcome. Cassie . . ."

"Yes?"

Ben heard himself say, "Jill and I, we broke up last summer. A long time ago."

"I see." Neither her face nor her voice revealed anything other than polite interest.

"I just wanted you to know. It's been over for months."

"All right," Cassie said.

Since there was no graceful way out of it, Ben just said, "See you later," and went back to his Jeep.

He wished he could have believed that Cassie watched him leave, but he was reasonably sure she had not.

Putting the Jeep into gear, he muttered, "Jackass."

FEBRUARY 19, 1999

Matt Dunbar wanted to throw something across his office but contented himself with glaring at Cain Munro, who had the misfortune of being Salem County's medical examiner.

"So, in other words," the sheriff said, "you can't tell me a fucking thing I didn't already know."

Dr. Munro wasn't about to take that attitude from somebody he'd delivered with his own hands. "Watch your language, Matthew. I did you the courtesy of coming down here to report instead of calling you to the hospital, and I'd appreciate a little respect in return."

Matt sighed and leaned back in his chair. "Right. Sorry, Doc. I'm just a little tense about this."

Somewhat mollified, the doctor said, "I can understand that. Murder is never pretty, but this one was especially bad. Especially cruel. He nicked the artery first, let her bleed for a while before he finished the job."

"Do you know what kind of knife he used?"

"A sharp one." Dr. Munro grimaced. "Fairly short blade. Could have been a pocket knife."

"Great. That's just great. I figure most of the male population over the age of twelve has at least one pocket knife."

"I figure you're right. Sorry, Matt, I wish I could be more help. If you want to get a forensics expert in from Charlotte, you won't put my nose out of joint. But the girl's family has already called twice asking when they can bury her."

The sheriff hesitated. "No ego here, Doc, I need the truth. Do you think a forensics expert could find something you might have missed?"

Munro pursed his lips for a moment in thought but finally shook his head. "I'd have to say no. We went over her body with a magnifying glass, Matt. Sent samples of her blood off for a toxicology report, but I'll be surprised if it comes back positive for anything. No alcohol, no drugs. Still, I'd say she never got a chance to struggle, or was too scared to. Sure as hell never fought him. No skin or tissue under her nails, no defensive wounds. She sat there with her hands bound behind her, probably with a belt, as I told you, and he cut her throat—and she died."

"But not in the woods."

"No, there wasn't enough blood there."

"Any idea where?"

"Nope. Have you checked her house?"

"Of course. Her parents never heard a sound, and the family dog, being old and deaf, never barked. We didn't find a sign of forced entry, but her folks say she usually slept with the window open even in winter."

"So you're thinking he just climbed in the window and persuaded her to get dressed and go with him?"

Matt scowled. "Maybe. But I don't really like that possibility. You say time of death was around two o'clock Thursday morning?"

"About that."

"Then, there's a chance he was waiting for her at her house when she came in late Wednesday night, and got her before she could unlock the front door. Her bed wasn't made, but her mother said she often didn't make it, so we have no way of knowing if she actually came in and went to bed."

"Who was she out with?"

"A group of friends. They all left that club out on the highway just after midnight and headed home in their individual cars. Becky was alone when she drove off in hers."

"I've kept her clothes as evidence, of course, in case you want her friends to take a look and say if it was what she was wearing when she was with them."

Matt grimaced. "Yeah, okay. But it wouldn't be conclusive, since she could have gotten up out of bed and put on the clothes she'd worn earlier."

Doc Munro got to his feet. "So what do I tell her folks?"

Matt pushed the warning of a psychic out of his mind. "Let them schedule the funeral."

"Okay. I'll send my report along tomorrow. Get one of your boys to come over and collect her clothes and the bits of grass and leaves we found on her."

Matt considered reminding the doctor that his deputy force was made up of roughly forty percent "girls," but in the end he just let it slide. "I'll send somebody over this afternoon."

"Good enough."

Matt was left alone in his office with his thoughts, and none of them were pleasant.

She shouldn't have done that.
  Bitch.
  Why did she have to do that?
  My head hurts.
  I'm still tired, and my head hurts.
  But I can't let her get away with it.
  She has to pay.
  They all have to pay.
  They'll never laugh at me again.

The knocking at her front door on Friday afternoon didn't surprise Cassie. She'd been expecting him. Sooner or later.

She went to the door and opened it. "Hi," she said to Ben.

He was carrying a manila folder, and his face was set in grim lines. "May I come in?"

"Sure." She idly wondered whom he'd gotten to research for him. Janice, probably. She'd looked quite efficient.

Three days. Not bad.

Most of the furniture was back in the living room, since she'd finished the painting and refinishing, so she led the way there. She left the entire sofa for him, sitting down in a wing chair at right angles to it. "Have a seat."

He didn't. Instead, he opened the folder, took out a sheet of paper, and handed it to her. "Care to explain this?"

It was a copy of a newspaper story taken from microfilm. There was a not very good photo of her much younger self, looking frightened. And headlines. Big headlines.

SERIAL KILLER TARGETS PSYCHIC

FOUR

"Did Janice find this for you?" Cassie asked.

"Yes."

"You don't pay her enough. That article was buried. The wire services never picked it up." Cassie put the sheet of paper on the coffee table and pushed it toward him, then made herself comfortable in the chair, sitting sideways with knees drawn up. He finally sat down on the sofa so that they were on eye level again.

He reached for the paper and held it. "According to this," he said, "a little more than ten years ago your mother was the one helping the police look for a killer. But before she could help them find him, he found her. And killed her."

Cassie drew a breath and said tonelessly, "He didn't just kill her. He butchered her. She was home alone, since I was away on a school trip. There was no one to . . . hear. He took his time killing her. They never let me go back into the house, but I understand there was blood everywhere." She held on to her detachment simply because there was no other way to remember or speak of such horrors.

Ben seemed to understand that. "You had to deal with that alone? Didn't you have any other family out there? The article says your father had been killed in a car wreck a couple of years before."

"My only other family was Aunt Alex, and she never replied to the telegram about Mother's death." Cassie shrugged. "I was eighteen, a legal adult. I handled what I had to. And I went on. There was insurance, enough to invest and provide a fair income while it put me through college. It took two more years, but the house eventually sold."

"And all your roots were gone."

"My roots were gone the night Mother was killed."

Ben drew a breath. "This article doesn't say anything about you also being psychic."

"No, the police were kind enough—and smart enough— to keep that to themselves. They wanted my help."

"You mean they asked you to help them find the man who had murdered your mother?"

"Yes."

"My God. Did you?"

"Yes."

"It must have been unimaginably painful for you."

Cassie hesitated. "Remember when I told you and the sheriff about what happened when I touched the clothing of a murder victim to try to connect to the killer?"

"It put you in a coma. Damn near killed you."

"It was Mother's clothing I touched."

"Jesus," Ben muttered. "Cassie—"

"They had guards around me at the hospital, and for months after I got out. Their fear was that the killer would be able to target me as he had my mother—through the psychic connection I had made very briefly when I touched

Mother's clothes. But either it hadn't been a very strong connection, or he just wasn't interested, because he never came after me in all those months. By the time I finally got my abilities back, he'd killed half a dozen more people, so I had to try again, had to risk . . . drawing his attention to me."

"What happened?"

"They got him." Her voice was matter-of-fact. "He was executed about three years ago."

"But before they got him, did you draw his attention?"

"I was much younger then," Cassie said. "Inexperienced. I didn't know how to keep the connection shallow, to get into another mind without revealing my own presence."

"Did you draw his attention?"

She grimaced slightly. "Yes."

"What happened?"

"Nothing happened, Ben. He came after me, and the police were waiting for him."

"They used you as bait."

Cassie shook her head. "It wasn't that calculated. I touched his mind too deeply, I realized it, and I told the police he'd probably come after me. They protected me—and caught him. End of story."

Ben leaned forward with his elbows on his knees and stared at her. "End of story, my ass. Why the hell didn't you tell Matt and me that in touching this maniac's mind you could be drawing his attention, making yourself a target? Don't you think that's something we needed to know?"

"Sheriff Dunbar doesn't believe I can touch the maniac's mind," she reminded him dryly. "Assuming there even is a maniac, and not just a garden-variety one-time impulse killer, which is what the sheriff believes. What he wants to believe. And you have your doubts, both about my abilities and whether there'll be another murder." Her shoulders rose and fell briefly. "Besides, I've learned a lot in ten years. It's been a long, long time since I was at risk in that way. I know what I'm doing now."

"But catching his attention is still a possibility."

"A very slight one."

"And you're living way the hell out here, alone, without even a dead bolt on the front door. Jesus, Cassie. If you'd told us, at least we could have taken steps to keep you safe. A security system, a dog. A gun."

"I don't know how to use a gun. I don't want to know. And you may have noticed that I'm fine."

"Now. But what happens if you tap into this guy again?"

"I'll make sure he doesn't know I'm there."

"And if you make a mistake? If he realizes you can watch everything he does when he's committing a murder?"

"He won't."

"But if he does?"

Cassie drew a breath. "Ben, I came to terms with that threat a long time ago. I had to. It's a risk I have to take. All I can do is be careful, and I've learned how to be."

"I don't like it, Cassie."

"You don't have to like it. It's my risk to take." She made sure her voice was calm and sure.

"I know that, dammit."

Fooled them again. Cassie wondered how much longer she could do that, could fool those around her into believing that taking the risk of inviting a psychopath into her mind—into her soul—didn't scare her half to death.

A little longer, maybe.

Trying to distract him, she glanced at the manila folder he'd laid on the coffee table. "What else is in there?"

"Not much. Sketchy background information, school records, that sort of thing. As far as the official record is concerned, you've led a quiet, unexceptional life."

It was amazing, Cassie thought, how little of someone's life could be revealed by official record. And how much lay hidden.

"I guess Sheriff Dunbar has checked out my references by now?"

"Yeah."

"And still doesn't believe I can do what I claim."

"He's hardheaded. It's his biggest fault."

"Most cops consider that a necessary character trait." She smiled, and saw that Ben was watching her steadily. It was unnerving. He should *look* like a judge, dammit, silver-haired and forbidding. Instead, if he had celebrated his fortieth birthday, Cassie would have been surprised; there wasn't a single silver thread among the dark ones, and there was youthful energy and strength in the way he moved and carried himself. Along with that, he possessed a warmth and empathy so strong, she felt it reaching out to her.

Rare. That was so rare, especially among men, that ability and willingness to feel the pain of another human being. But Ben could do it, even though she doubted it was a skill he enjoyed.

That was why this was going to tear him to pieces.

"Cassie?"

She blinked, then conjured another smile. "I was just thinking that I hope Sheriff Dunbar is right. I hope that poor girl's death was an isolated incident and that he finds her killer quickly."

"But you don't believe he will."

"No. I'm afraid not."

"Neither do I." Ben picked up the folder, returned the copy of the newspaper article to it, and got to his feet. "I have an appointment in an hour, so I'd better go."

Cassie walked with him to the front door. "I guess you'll tell the sheriff what you found out. About my mother."

"Not if you don't want me to. But I think he should know, Cassie."

She opened the front door. "Okay. Tell him what you like."

Ben hesitated. "You know, there's something I don't think you've considered."

"Oh? What's that?"

"You're not in L.A. now, protected by the sheer number of strangers all around you. This is a small town, Cassie. Not so small that absolutely everyone knows everyone else, but small enough. And people talk. Your trips to Matt's office, and to mine, have been and will be noted. Eventually word will get out about your abilities. So even if you do manage not to alert the killer when you're in his mind, chances are that sooner or later he's still going to know who you are. And you won't be a disembodied voice in his mind. You'll be a flesh and blood person with an address in the phone book—and no dead bolt on your front door."

After a moment Cassie said, "I'll keep that in mind."

"And nothing's changed."

"No. Nothing's changed." *I have to do this. I have to.*

His hand lifted slightly, as though he would touch her, but then it fell when she tensed visibly.

"I'll see you later, Cassie."

"Bye, Ben."

This time he had the sure knowledge that she stood in the open doorway and watched him drive away.

But it didn't make him feel good.

It didn't make him feel good at all.

"Maybe she really is psychic." Abby Montgomery banked the pillows behind her and sat up in bed, absently drawing the sheet up over her naked breasts.

Matt Dunbar sat on the edge of the bed to put his socks and shoes on. "I don't believe in that shit."

"Then how did she know about us?"

"A lucky guess. Hell, maybe she saw you slipping in here the other day. But she did not read my mind."

Abby was familiar with her lover's stubbornness. Usually it amused her, just as his occasional macho posturing amused her; she had good reason to know that despite both, he had a generous nature and a heart, as the saying went, like a marshmallow. But today the reminder of how bullheaded he could be made her uneasy.

"Matt, if she can help find Becky's killer—"

"I don't know that she can. The cops out in L.A. gave her a glowing recommendation, but when I pushed, the detective I talked to finally admitted that she'd sent them down a few blind alleys, and that those detours were costly."

"Most conventional investigations do the same thing, don't they? I mean, you always explore at least a few possibilities that don't pan out in the end."

"Yeah. But it's a hell of a lot easier to explain why you followed a lead if you've got something solid to point to. Anything a so-called psychic tells you is about as substantial as fog, and just as quick to vanish." He shook his head. "No, I just don't buy it, Abby. She must have seen us together, and that's how she knew."

"In public? We barely look at each other in public. And nobody saw me slipping in here to meet you, Matt. I'm always careful, and you know it."

He looked at her quickly, hearing the slight tremor. "Honey, has Gary been bothering you again? Because I can sure as hell get a restraining order against him, you know that."

She shook her head. "No, he hasn't been around lately. Besides, I don't want to do anything to annoy him, at least until the divorce is final."

"That's only a month away, Abby." Matt smiled. "And once it's final, it'd be nice to be able to take you out in public."

Abby leaned toward him and wreathed her arms around his neck. "It would be very nice. Just . . . let's wait and see, okay, Matt? I don't know how Gary will react when it's final."

His mouth tightened, but his hands were gentle as they stroked her arms. "I've been as patient as I know how, Abby, but there's no way I'm prepared to keep our lives on hold indefinitely just to keep Gary from blowing a fuse. I can handle him."

"It isn't indefinitely. I just want to avoid trouble if at all possible, Matt."

"There won't be any trouble. I'll just kick his ass."

Abby smiled. "Let's wait and see. Another month. That isn't so long, is it?"

"That depends on what you're waiting for." He kissed her, taking his time about it, then eased her back onto the pillows and leaned over her. "I'm waiting for something I've wanted for a long, long time. You."

"You've got me. All the rest is just a formality."

He brushed a strand of bright red hair back from her face. "I also want Gary out of your life, with no excuses to call you or knock on your door. I want to have the right to tell him to go to hell."

"Given the chance, you'll do that whether you have the right or not," she said dryly.

"True." Matt kissed her again.

"Just be patient a little while longer."

"Okay, okay." He sat up, then got to his feet. "I've got to get back to the office."

"Matt . . ." She hesitated. "This psychic—"

"So-called."

"Did you ever hear the rumors about her aunt? About Miss Melton?"

"What about her?"

"Well, that she knew things. Things she shouldn't have been able to know."

Matt stared down at her, brows raised. "I heard talk. So what? She was a loner, kept to herself, hardly came into town—and when she did, she barely spoke to anyone and was usually dressed oddly for a woman her age. People were bound to talk. It doesn't mean anything, Abby."

Abby smiled. "I guess not. But, Matt—if Cassie Neill can help you, let her. Don't ignore what she has to say."

"You don't usually tell me how to do my job," he noted dryly.

"I'm not now. But I know how stubborn you can be. You've made up your mind she's a phony, haven't you?"

"Maybe."

"Admit it, Matt. You wouldn't even have given her the time of day if Ben hadn't insisted. You know he's no gullible fool."

"No, but he isn't thinking with his head. Not where Cassie Neill is concerned. Beats me what he sees in her, but the lady has certainly grabbed his attention."

Abby opened her mouth, then closed it and shook her head. After that brief pause she merely said, "Just don't let a preconceived idea get in your way, Matt, that's all I'm saying."

"No, I won't." He bent and kissed her one last time,

then laughed a little as he headed for the door. "I had no idea you believed in that stuff."

When she was alone in the bedroom, Abby gazed toward the door and murmured, "Oh, I believe in it, Matt. I believe in it."

Ivy Jameson was having a bad day. In fact, she'd had a bad week.

On Monday she'd had the unpleasant duty of taking her mother's old cat to the vet to have him euthanized; Wednesday had come the notice from the North Carolina Department of Revenue claiming she owed back taxes; yesterday she'd had to tear the hide off a TV repairman who obviously didn't know his ass from a three-foot hole in the ground; and today, on this pleasant, warm Friday afternoon in late February, she was being told that her ten-year-old car was on its last wheels, so to speak.

"A new transmission," Dale Newton said, consulting his clipboard. "The brakes are shot. Universal joint. The left front tire is bald—"

"Enough." She glared at him. "How much?"

The mechanic shifted uneasily. "I haven't worked up an estimate yet, Mrs. Jameson. You just asked me to check it out and see if it needed any work. It does. There's more—"

She waved him to a stop. "Just work up the estimate and then call me. But you'd better bear in mind, Dale Newton, that my late husband loaned you the money to get this garage going fifteen years ago. I expect that to make a difference. I expect some consideration for a poor widow."

"Yes, ma'am." Newton smiled weakly. "I'll have the estimate ready in a couple of hours."

"You do that."

"I can give you a loaner, Mrs. Jameson—"

"No. I hate driving a strange car. I'll walk across the street to Shelby's and call a taxi."

"I have a phone, Mrs. Jameson."

"I realize that. What you don't have is coffee. Good day, Mr. Newton."

"Ma'am." Newton watched her walk away, her back ramrod straight, and he wondered, not for the first time, if old Kenneth Jameson had died because he'd been sick—or just plain tired.

Ivy left Newton's Garage on the corner of Main Street and First, walked a block toward the center of town, and then crossed the street to Shelby's Restaurant. A landmark in Ryan's Bluff that had once been a wonderful example of the Art Deco style, and last modernized in the sixties, it had been several times redecorated through the years, and all the individual touches of various owners had left it somewhat garish. It still had a Formica counter and swivel stools at the front, and boasted clear plastic tablecloths over the linen ones.

It was a place Ivy visited regularly and just as habitually criticized, a one-time hot spot that had seen better days but still offered good, plain food and hot coffee right up until midnight, seven days a week.

"This coffee is too strong, Stuart," Ivy told the young man behind the counter.

"Yes, Mrs. Jameson. I'll make fresh."

"You do that. And put in a pinch of salt to draw the bitterness."

"Yes, ma'am."

When Cassie answered a second knock on her front door late Friday afternoon, she was surprised to find a stranger standing there, a young man wearing a dark jump suit with the name *Dan* on one pocket and *SafeNet Security* on the other. He was holding a clipboard, and spoke politely.

"Miss Neill? I'm Dan Crowder, SafeNet Security. My partner and I are here to install your security system."

She looked past him to a white van in her driveway with the security company logo on its side and another clean-cut and uniformed young man standing beside it.

"My security system?"

"Yes, ma'am. Judge Ryan sent us."

He certainly hadn't wasted any time.

Dan smiled reassuringly. "Judge Ryan said you were to call him if you had any doubts, Miss Neill."

Cassie didn't call Ben; she called the security company. As she'd expected, Dan's story was confirmed.

Cassie toyed with the idea of sending Dan and his partner away, but in the end let them in so they could commence their work. Because Ben had been right about one thing.

In a small town, it was only a matter of time before the wrong person discovered what she could do.

"Ben?"

On the point of entering the building next door to the courthouse where his office was located, Ben paused and turned to see Jill Kirkwood approaching him. He couldn't help remembering Cassie's assertion that Jill had not accepted their breakup, but still managed to smile and greet her with the same low-key easiness he'd held on to since they'd broken it off.

Since *he* had broken it off.

"Hi, Jill. What's up?"

"Is there any news on who killed Becky Smith?"

He was only a little surprised that she asked. In the brief time it had taken him to walk the two blocks from the downtown office where he'd had an earlier appointment, he had already been stopped three times by worried citizens asking the same anxious question. Still, it wasn't like Jill to be much interested in crime, even a particularly vicious one.

"Nothing new that I know of," he told her. "Matt and his deputies are working on it."

"Does he know that Becky thought she was being followed?"

"She thought—how do you know that?"

"She told me. Came into the store one day last week. Wednesday, I think it was. We got to talking, and she mentioned she'd caught a glimpse of somebody watching her. She sort of laughed about it, said something about having a secret admirer who didn't want to show his face. She wasn't worried about it, so I didn't give it a second thought."

So he did watch her before. Another bull's-eye for Cassie.

"You'd better tell Matt about it, Jill. I don't think he knows, unless somebody else told him in the last day or so."

"All right, I'll go see him." She smiled. "I was glad to meet Cassie Neill. I liked her aunt."

"Yeah, so did I."

"She hasn't been in town long, has she?"

"Cassie? About six months, I think."

"Oh. I just didn't remember seeing her before yesterday."

"I'm not surprised. She seems as much of a loner as Miss Melton was."

"Seems? You don't know her very well?"

"I met her Tuesday." He felt a flash of annoyance at being questioned but trusted he kept the reaction out of his face.

Jill laughed a little, with the bright smile and artificial ease of someone aware of crossing the line. "Sorry, I didn't mean to pry."

Obviously his poker face wasn't as good as he'd thought.

Ben said, "Don't be ridiculous. Look, why don't you go and tell Matt what you know. He needs to hear it. The sooner we get this bastard behind bars, the better it'll be for everyone in town."

"Okay. I'll see you later, Ben."

"Sure." For just an instant as she turned away, he considered warning her to be careful, but cast off the impulse as ridiculous and unnecessary. What could he say, after all? Watch out for strangers following you?

She was a smart lady, and knowing what she did about Becky being followed, she would certainly take notice—and take steps to protect herself—if she suspected the same thing was happening to her.

So Ben watched her walk away and said nothing.

Laughing at me.
 I can hear them.
 Watching me.
 Eyes following me.
 Gotta stop them.
 Gotta make them pay.
 My head hurts.
 I'll show them.
 My feet hurt. Gotta slow down. Gotta . . .

Look at that one. So proud of herself. So sure she's the best. She deserves . . . she deserves . . . she deserves . . .
My head hurts so bad.
Eyes watching me.
I wonder if they know . . .
Blood smells like coins.

FIVE

When Cassie heard the scream, it was so loud in her head that she dropped the glass she'd been holding and clapped her hands over her ears.

"No," she whispered helplessly.

Without her volition her eyes closed, and behind the lids flashed whorls of vivid colors streaked with black. A second scream made her jerk. And hurt her throat.

"No, please . . . please don't hurt me. . . ."

Abruptly Cassie was somewhere else, someone else. She felt the painful constriction of something around her wrists, felt a sharp edge at her back and cold hardness beneath her. She couldn't see, it was all black, but then the bag over her head was jerked off.

"Please don't hurt me . . . please, please don't hurt me . . . please don't—"

The mask he wore was horrible. The character might have been from some recent slasher movie, the face a human one but terribly distorted, and it made her shock intensify, her terror soar.

"Please don't hurt me! Oh, God, please don't! I won't tell anyone, I promise! I swear! Just let me go, please!"

For an eternal instant Cassie was paralyzed, completely trapped in the woman's spiraling emotions. Shock, wild terror, despair, and the cold, cold certainty that she was going to die soon and horribly clawed at her. Through the woman's tear-blurred eyes she saw that eerie mask loom above her, saw the butcher knife in his gloved hand, and her throat hurt with gasping breaths and whimpers and raw screams.

"You'll never laugh at me again," he rasped, and his arm lifted, the knife gleaming dully.

"No! Oh, Jesus—"

As his arm started downward in a vicious arc, Cassie desperately wrenched herself free of the doomed woman. But she wasn't fast enough to save herself completely. She felt the first hot agony of the knife piercing her breast, and everything went black.

"Ben."

"Matt? What is it?"

"Meet me in town. Ivy Jameson's place."

Ben switched the phone to his other hand and checked his watch. "Now? It's Sunday afternoon, she'll be—"

"She's dead, Ben."

Ben didn't even ask how. Matt's tone told him all he needed to know. "I'm on my way," he said.

Ten minutes later he parked the Jeep behind Matt's cruiser and one other in the driveway of the Jameson house on Rose Lane just two streets behind Main Street. It was usually a quiet neighborhood, the big old houses sitting peacefully on manicured lawns, the older residents happy to be no more than a short, pleasant afternoon walk from downtown.

Ben noticed that several of those older residents were on their front porches, staring at him as he got out of his Jeep. Although they were too polite or too frightened to venture closer to Ivy's house, it was obvious that their interest was intense.

One of Matt's deputies was standing by the front door and opened it for Ben as he came up on the porch. "Judge. Sheriff's inside." He looked a bit green around the gills.

Ben went into the house. He was familiar with it, as he was most of the homes of the more politically active citizens of Ryan's Bluff; Ivy Jameson's vote had been one of the hardest to get.

From the spacious entrance hall the staircase rose to the second floor, the formal dining room opened to the right, an equally formal living room to the left, and straight ahead lay the rear of the house and the kitchen. The hardwood floor gleamed, fresh flowers in a lovely crystal vase decorated the entrance hall table, and there was an air of stuffy dignity about the place.

The two men sitting on the sofa in the formal living room spoiled the atmosphere of dignity; they were in their stocking feet, faces slack and pale with shock, and the younger one was breaking Ivy's most sacrosanct house rule by smoking a cigarette jerkily, flicking the ashes into an already full crystal candy dish on the coffee table before him.

Ben knew them both. One was Ivy's brother-in-law, and the other was her nephew. Neither looked toward him, and he made no attempt to speak to them.

Another deputy standing just outside the living room doorway silently gestured toward the rear of the house.

He, also, looked queasy, and when Ben passed him, murmured, "Sheriff said to watch your step, Judge. The floor back there is . . . slippery."

It was slippery all right.

The tile floor of the kitchen was covered in blood.

"Oh, Christ," Ben muttered as he stopped in the doorway. He had observed scenes of violence before, but not many, and nothing that had prepared him for this.

Matt stood a couple of feet inside on one of the few blood-free spots on the floor. "It looks like Ivy finally pissed off the wrong person."

It was unquestionably a scene of rage. Even the white appliances were spattered with blood, and the stab wounds in Ivy's thin body were almost too numerous to count. She'd been all dressed up, probably for church earlier in the day. Her dress might have been any light color once; now it was red.

She still had one shoe on.

"Notice the way he left her?" Matt asked.

"Yeah," Ben said, trying to breathe through his mouth because the smell was overpowering. "Sitting up with her back against the leg of the work island. Her hands in her lap. Posed. Is there a coin?"

"A nickel. In her left hand." If the smell bothered Matt, it wasn't apparent.

Ben gestured. "And footprints. The killer?"

"Among others. When she didn't show up for church or Sunday dinner afterward, and didn't answer the phone, Ivy's mother sent her son-in-law and grandson over to see if anything was wrong. They came in the back door, said they were sliding all over before they knew what was happening. If we're lucky, we might get one footprint we can't match to their shoes."

Matt pointed out a bloody butcher knife on the floor a

foot or so away from Ivy's body. "No question about the murder weapon. He just grabbed a knife off the rack."

"Forced entry?"

"No sign of it. And her relatives say she always locked the back door, all the doors, that she was fanatical about it."

"So she must have let him in?"

"Looks that way."

Ben backed out of the doorway. "This smell. I can't—"

Matt followed him, avoiding the blood gingerly, and joined him in the small hallway outside the kitchen. "Doc Munro's on his way. So're my technical people. I took one look and called you first."

"Her position, the coin. It's the same killer, Matt."

"Yeah." Matt drew a breath, his face very grim. "And he barely waited three days between killings, Ben. Worse, Becky Smith and Ivy Jameson had only two things in common. They were both white and both female. Beyond that there are no similarities between them."

"I know."

"Did you notice the knife rack? We won't know for sure until her housekeeper inventories for us, but it looks like one of the big butcher knives is missing."

Ben stared at his friend in silence, unwilling to give voice to any of the disturbing possibilities in his mind.

Matt was less reluctant. "The bastard's probably taken his next weapon from this victim. Cute. Really cute."

"Jesus," Ben muttered, frustrated by the realization that the killer might have already chosen his next victim too.

"And one more thing." Matt's voice was level. "This time your psychic didn't see it coming."

·   ·   ·

By the time Ben got to Cassie's house, it was beginning to get dark. Even so, he saw her. She was sitting on the front porch, curled up in one of the two big wicker chairs placed to one side of the front door.

As Ben reached her he said, "The security system won't do much good if you're outside it, Cassie." His voice was sharper than he intended it to be.

Almost lost in a sweatshirt several sizes too big, her jean-clad legs drawn up and her arms wrapped around them, Cassie didn't glance at him. She merely said quietly, "I had to come out here. It was . . . all I could smell was blood. It wasn't so bad out here."

Ben moved the other chair so that it was facing hers and sat, literally placing himself in her line of vision. She still looked past him. No warm hand touched him. "So you knew he killed again."

"Yes." Her face was so pale, even her lips seemed drained of color.

"Why didn't you call me?"

"By the time I could, it was too late. There was nothing anyone could do for her. I'm sorry. I'm so sorry."

"Did you see anything this time? Anything that might help us catch this bastard?"

Cassie shook her head slowly. "No. He—he was wearing some kind of mask."

"How do you know that? Did he look in a mirror?"

"No. This time I . . . I didn't connect with him. I connected with her. She was . . . was crying, but I could see him. He had some kind of mask, a horrible mask. Like something a kid would wear on Halloween."

Ben frowned. "Why would he do that? He wasn't planning to leave a witness behind."

"I don't know. Except . . . the mask made her even more frightened. Maybe that was it. Maybe he wants them to be afraid."

"Or maybe he knows you're watching."

"No."

"How can you be sure of that? If you connected with her?"

"I'm sure."

Ben was silent for a moment, then said slowly, "Why did you connect with her?"

"Maybe because I had met her briefly." Cassie's voice was growing more distant, and her eyes had an odd, unfocused look to them.

"Do you connect with the victim very often?"

"Not if I can help it. As dark as the mind of a killer is, the mind of his victim is . . . almost worse. The terror and despair, the agony . . ." Cassie shook her head again slowly. "It pulls me in. They pull me in. They're so desperate, so frantic to find a way out."

He stopped himself from reaching out to her, bad as he wanted to. "I'm sorry."

She shivered visibly, and finally looked at him, saw him. But when her gaze touched him, it was cool rather than warm, and such a faint sensation, it was almost ghostly.

"I can't do it anymore." Her voice was low, hurried. "I know it's the right thing to do, I know the sight gives me a responsibility, and I've always tried . . . but I can't do it anymore. I thought I could. I thought there had been enough time . . . enough peace. I thought I was strong enough. But I'm not. I can't go through it again."

"Cassie—"

"I can't. I can't help you. I can't help myself."

"You came to me," he reminded her quietly.

"I know that. I wanted to help. But I can't. I'm sorry."

"What you saw today. Were you looking? Were you trying to tap into him—or her?"

"No."

"Then what choice do you have?"

"I can leave."

"You left L.A. What good did it do? Cassie, there are monsters everywhere."

She closed her eyes and leaned her head back against the chair.

Ben watched her for several moments, unsettled by his intense desire to touch her, hold her. He had never been attracted to emotionally fragile women, to the opposite, if anything. If he admitted the truth, any woman who was not wholly focused on her own life and career and disinterested in anything more than a casual affair had very quickly found him to be elusive and emotionally remote. As Jill could testify.

So protective impulses and urges to comfort were alien to his nature when it came to women. He preferred to spend the night in a woman's bed so that he could leave long before dawn with a minimum of fuss, and that alone said a great deal about his avoidance of involvement on any level except the physical.

Needy women were definitely not his style. Not that Cassie clung in any way or, indeed, had even reached out to him. On the contrary, she was completely self-contained, and everything about her from the avoidance of touch and even eye contact to her body language said she was literally untouchable.

He thought she needed to be held worse than anyone he'd ever known. But he didn't touch her. Because she would not have welcomed the touch, and because he shied away from offering it.

Finally, her voice drained, Cassie said, "A few years ago, a cop friend of mine gave me a quotation from Nietzsche. He told me to put it where I could see it every day, to never forget. 'Whoever fights monsters should see to it that in the process he does not become a monster.

And when you look long into the abyss, the abyss also looks into you.' " She lifted her head and looked at him with exhausted eyes. "I don't know how many more times I can do it and survive, Ben. Every time I've looked into that abyss, a piece of me stayed there."

"You could never become a monster."

"I could lose myself in one. What would be the difference?"

He leaned toward her, elbows on his knees, getting closer without actually touching her. "Cassie, you're the only one who can decide if the risks are worth taking. The risk of this madman finding out who you are before we find him. The risk of getting too deep in his head. The risk of losing something of yourself in the blackness of his soul. Only you can really know what it might cost you. And only you can decide if the price is too high."

She gazed at him almost curiously. "You pointed out one of the risks yourself. That no matter how careful I am, how skilled, the killer is more than likely to find out who I am in this small town of yours. Even so, you believe I should try to help you catch him."

Ben was silent for a moment, then said, "If you're leaving Ryan's Bluff, the discussion is over. I understand self-preservation; anyone would. I'll respect that decision, Cassie. But if you're staying here, then you have to help us catch him. Because as long as you're here, you're a potential threat to him. You can see inside his head. Sooner or later he'll find out you can do that. And he'll come after you."

"So I've convinced you, huh? That psychic ability is real?"

"Let's just say . . . I'm convinced you're real. I don't pretend to understand it, but I do believe you possess an extraordinary skill. And right now I need that skill to help me catch a monster. Before he kills anybody else in my town."

Cassie sighed. "All right." More than anything else, she sounded defeated. "What do you want me to do?"

Ben hesitated, almost wishing he had not been so persuasive. "After a lot of arguing, I finally got Matt to agree that you should go to the crime scene, see if you pick up anything." He paused, then added roughly, "But right now I think you should sleep about twelve hours. Tomorrow is soon enough."

A little laugh escaped Cassie. "Very nice of you to be concerned, but not very practical or wise. I'd say there's no time to waste. For him to kill again so soon is a very bad sign of worse things to come."

"Be that as it may, you're exhausted. If you push yourself too hard—"

"You don't have to worry. I won't collapse on you. I'm stronger than you think." She got to her feet.

Ben rose as well. "Cassie, a few more hours won't make any difference. She lived alone, and Matt has a couple of his officers standing guard, so the scene won't be disturbed. And it's not going to be a pleasant thing to see, whether you pick up anything or not. You should rest, recover some of your strength first. I'll take you there tomorrow—" He broke off when she lifted a hand to brush back her hair and he saw the bandage. "What the hell happened?"

She looked at her hand as if it belonged to a stranger, and answered absently, "I broke a glass."

"Have you seen a doctor?"

"It wasn't a deep cut." She was obviously puzzled as her gaze returned to his face. "Her house. That's where you found her?"

"Yes. In the kitchen. Isn't that what you saw?"

Tension gathering in her voice, Cassie said, "The kitchen. No, that isn't right."

"He definitely killed her there, Cassie. There was blood everywhere, and the M.E. says that's where she died."

Cassie closed her eyes for a brief moment, then opened them and looked at him almost beseechingly. "Who died, Ben? Who was she?"

"Why—Ivy Jameson. Isn't that who—" Ben watched her sit down abruptly as though the strength had left her legs. He drew a deep breath. "You mean there's someone else?"

"Yes. There's someone else."

Ben called Matt from the Jeep once they were on their way to town, and the sheriff got there before them. He came out onto the sidewalk so quickly that Ben had barely gotten his door open. It was dark by then, but the streetlights made the sidewalk nearly as bright as day.

"Don't go in there," Matt said.

He hadn't really doubted Cassie this time, but Ben nonetheless felt a shock, and with it pangs of pain and regret. "Is she . . . ?"

Matt nodded. "The doc will have to tell us when, but I'm guessing she was killed while we were at Ivy's place. I'm sorry, Ben."

Ben gazed blindly toward the open front door of Jill Kirkwood's store for a moment. "I should have told her to be careful."

"It wouldn't have mattered, you know that. I warned her when she came to tell me about somebody following Becky. And I'm sure she thought she was being careful. But even if the town had been under curfew, she wouldn't have hesitated to come into her store on a peaceful Sunday afternoon to catch up on paperwork."

"I have to see her."

The sheriff caught his arm. "No. There's no reason for you to go in there, Ben. My team will be here any minute, and this time they're damned well going to get a completely undisturbed crime scene." He paused, then added steadily, "You don't need to see her. You don't want to see her."

"How did he kill her?"

"Knife, same as the others. But either he killed her someplace else or she hadn't pissed him off as badly as Ivy had. Virtually no blood at the scene. Only one wound, as far as I could tell. Left breast."

Ben half turned toward the Jeep, where the dome light showed Cassie's huddled posture and pale face. She hadn't said much at all since they had left her place. He returned his gaze to the sheriff. "Cassie said Jill was tied with her back to something with a sharp edge."

"Yeah, she's sitting up against a corner of her desk. He probably had her wrists tied behind her at some point but, like the others, he left her untied and with her hands in her lap."

"The coin?"

"A quarter." The sheriff paused. "Mind if I ask a few questions now?"

Ben knew whom those questions would be directed to, and it wasn't himself. But before he could reply, Cassie got out of the Jeep and came around it to join them.

Quietly she said, "Ask away, Sheriff."

"Where were you today?"

"At home. Alone, until Ben arrived a little while ago."

"You're saying you have no alibi." The sheriff's voice was mechanical.

"For Christ's sake, Matt," Ben snapped, "surely you don't believe Cassie killed three women!"

The sheriff looked at him briefly, then returned his gaze to Cassie. "And where is your car, Miss Neill?"

Matter-of-factly she said, "So you're having me watched. I thought you might be. My car is here in town, Sheriff, as you obviously know. I had it towed in yesterday morning when I discovered it wouldn't start. It's at that garage one block back from Main Street."

"And you refused a loaner."

"I didn't need one. There was nowhere I wanted or needed to go in the few days the car would be here."

As alibis went, it wasn't bad.

Ben said, "She couldn't have walked that far, Matt, not if—not if Jill was killed in the last few hours."

"Yeah, I know. Besides—" Matt glanced at Ben as he broke off, and it was Cassie who finished the sentence.

"It's not likely I'd have the physical strength to drive a butcher knife in someone's chest to the hilt," she said, still matter-of-fact.

"No," the sheriff said. "It isn't. Possible, but when I add that fact to others, it's very unlikely that you're our killer."

Ben felt sickened. "The knife. How do you know—"

"It's still in her, Ben. It looks like the missing knife from Ivy's kitchen."

"Christ."

The sheriff kept his gaze on Cassie. "So you saw Jill being killed, but Ivy Jameson's murder was a complete surprise to you."

"I never knew Miss Jameson, though I had heard of her. I met Jill once, briefly. It was enough for a connection, obviously, because I tapped into her mind, not his."

"Why not his? He killed twice today, leaving a bloody

mess behind at Ivy's. Why weren't you aware he was doing that?"

Cassie shook her head. "I don't know."

Whatever the sheriff might have said to that was postponed as a squad car and a black paneled van arrived, blue lights flashing.

"Take her home, Ben, while I get my people working on the crime scene. Tomorrow is soon enough to find out if she can tell us anything helpful."

"She" went back around the Jeep and got in without another word.

Ben wanted to censure his friend for his chilly attitude toward Cassie but knew it wouldn't help matters. So all he said was "I'll be back when I've taken Cassie home."

"Don't rush. I said you didn't need to see this one, Ben, and I meant it."

"It's my job to view crime scenes, Matt."

"Not when you were personally involved with the victim. Bad idea."

"We were not personally involved, not anymore. It was months ago."

"Still."

"I can handle it," Ben said flatly.

"Will you, for once in our lives, take my advice and my professional opinion and stay the hell away from this crime scene?"

"And when I prosecute the bastard in court? You don't think I'll need details from this crime scene?"

"I think you can get what you need from photographs and reports. Ben, I am asking you, as sheriff and as your friend, to let us handle this." Without waiting for an answer, Matt turned away and went to meet his team.

Ben watched them go into the store, then got into the Jeep and started the engine.

"He's right," Cassie said.

"I can handle it," Ben repeated.

"Probably. But why should you have to? Why put yourself through that if there's a choice?"

"Maybe there isn't a choice. It's my job, Cassie."

She didn't respond until the lights of town faded into the night behind them. "Ask yourself if Jill would have wanted you to see her like that. And if you have any doubts, the answer is no."

She was right, and Ben knew it. "All right." He was silent for a few more miles, then said, "I'm sorry about the way Matt treats you. He's just pigheaded. And all this is a lot more than he bargained for."

"I know."

"Don't let him get to you."

"He isn't. I've run into the same kind of attitude before, believe me. It's perfectly natural for him to mistrust me."

"He just can't believe we have a monster here."

"It isn't an easy thing to believe."

Ben realized his shock was wearing off just enough to let horror creep in. "My God. Three women murdered in less than a week. We have no idea who killed them or why. And we have no idea how many more he'll kill before we catch him. You were right. A serial killer."

"I'm afraid so."

"Becky . . . Ivy . . . Jill. Aside from being female and white, they had virtually nothing in common."

"Did they go to the same church?"

Ben thought about it. "No. Becky and Jill did, the same Baptist church I belong to, but Ivy was a Methodist. Why?"

"I don't know. Something about the way he had those coins laid out, as though they were on an altar or something, made me think of church." Cassie shook her head. "At this point I'm just guessing."

"Keep going, you might hit on something."

"Something helpful, you mean? Probably not without more information. The mind of a serial killer is so . . . unique, so subjective, it's almost impossible to generalize beyond a few basic suppositions. And we already know those. White male, since he's killing white females. Young, possibly abused background. But apart from those facts, this man's motivations are bound to be completely unique to him and his experiences. Guessing about them is not going to be productive, not until we know a lot more than we do now."

"There must be a pattern."

"There is—to him. But whether we'll even recognize his reasoning is doubtful. There's no logic in madness."

"So to catch a madman, we have to think like a madman?"

"I wouldn't advise it," Cassie said very quietly. "That abyss is darker and colder than you can even imagine."

SIX

They reached Cassie's house a few minutes later without further discussing the situation. With no reason to hurry back to town, and all too aware of how sleepless the night ahead was likely to be for him, Ben had no intention of just dropping her off and leaving. But he was acutely aware of Cassie's weariness—of spirit as well as body—and doubted she would welcome even casual company.

He was wrong.

"I could use some coffee. How about you?" she asked, unlocking the door.

"I'd love some, thanks."

Cassie disarmed the security system with the tentative touch of someone to whom the steps were still unfamiliar, then led the way to her bright and cheerful kitchen.

Ben was too restless to sit while she made the coffee but wasn't aware he was prowling the room until she spoke again.

"It wasn't your fault."

He checked the back door, making sure it was locked and the new dead bolt thrown. "What wasn't?"

"Jill's death."

He turned to find her leaning back against the sink, arms crossed, watching him gravely. He started to deny that it was bothering him but couldn't. "I should have warned her."

"It wouldn't have mattered. Like the sheriff said, it would never have occurred to her that she should be especially careful going to her store on a Sunday afternoon. Nobody can be on guard all the time."

"You can, apparently." Why did her reserve, her aloofness, bother him so much?

"That's different."

"Is it?"

Her shoulders lifted in a little shrug and her gaze fell away from his. "Yes. But we aren't talking about me. There was nothing you could have done to save Jill. Accept that."

"And move on?"

"We don't have a choice. Death takes people away from us all our lives. We have to move on. Or die ourselves."

"I know, I know." It was Ben's turn to shrug. "But it doesn't help, knowing that. She was thirty-two years old, Cassie. Just thirty-two years old. She lived here all her life, and she thought she was safe. She should have been safe."

"It isn't your fault that she wasn't."

"Then whose fault was it?"

"His. That monster out there. And if he isn't stopped, he'll be responsible for even more deaths."

"He'll also be responsible for destroying this town. It's already started. Matt's had to put on more people just to answer the phone since word of Ivy's murder got out.

When the morning paper announces Jill's death . . . Things are going to get very tense very fast around here. Three murders in four days. Three women brutally killed, one in her own kitchen."

Cassie turned away to pour the coffee, and said very quietly, "The townspeople are going to be looking for someone to blame for those deaths."

"I know."

"Are there any likely targets?" She set his cup on the counter near him, then retreated a few steps with her own.

"You mean the easy targets? The homeless, the disturbed or mentally disabled, those with criminal records?"

"Yes."

"Not many." Ben picked up his cup and sipped the hot coffee, leaning a hip against the counter as she did. "We don't have homeless in any real sense. The churches in the area are pretty good at helping people in need. As for the disturbed or disabled, there are a few of those middle-aged men you see in most small towns, not 'slow' enough to be unemployable, but not bright enough to be trained for anything but pushing a broom. And there's one woman who's been a well-known character in this town for at least ten years. She escapes her son's watchful eye from time to time and wanders around downtown picking up invisible things from the sidewalk." Ben paused and shook his head. "Nobody knows what she thinks she's picking up, but if you try to stop her, she cries as if her heart's breaking."

Cassie looked down at her coffee. "The wreck of a life."

"Her son says she just went away one day."

"I wonder why," Cassie murmured. "Something like that, there ought to at least be a trigger."

"If something definitive happened, I don't know what

it was. The family keeps pretty much to themselves, and they don't welcome questions. It's a common enough trait around here."

Cassie nodded distractedly. Then she seemed to rouse herself from pity and focus on the practical. "I would say she seems an unlikely target, but those men . . . The sheriff might want to keep an eye on them."

"He will. We've both seen a crowd turn ugly and start looking around for a target. That isn't something you forget, believe me."

"What about people with criminal records?"

"We have our share. The habituals commit mostly petty stuff though—housebreaking, fighting with their neighbors or their girlfriends' ex-lovers, drunk and disorderly. The sort of troublemakers who have their own bunks in Matt's jail and make regular visits on Saturday nights. As for anything else, crimes of real violence are rare around here. I've prosecuted a couple of manslaughter cases, but liquor and spite were involved both times. Convenience-store holdups, a few half-assed bank robberies over the years. But no crime to even hint there's someone living here in this town—or this county—who's capable of butchering three women." Ben sighed. "That high-tech forensics van Matt managed to wring out of his budget last year was mostly gathering dust. Until Thursday."

"So there's no one target a panicked town would immediately look to."

"Not that I know of."

"Except for me."

He waited until she looked him in the eye, then agreed. "Except you. But I'd say the possibility of anything happening to you because of that is very slight. Cassie, I don't doubt that when word finally gets out about you, there'll be suspicion. But in all honesty, even a panicked town would have to be totally out of its collective mind to suspect you of three especially vicious murders. It doesn't always take muscle to kill, but Jill studied karate as a kid, and Ivy quite obviously fought like a wildcat. You couldn't have killed them, and it's obvious."

"A reasonable argument. But the need to blame that grows out of panic is seldom based on logic, and you know it."

"I know it. Even so, I doubt anyone will seriously suspect you. Oh, they'll look at you and talk about you and wonder, and you'll probably get at least a few nasty phone calls accusing you of being a witch or worse, but I don't believe this town will condemn you as a killer."

Cassie returned her gaze to her coffee.

"He's the one you have to worry about. That madman out there. The threat to you is from him."

"I know."

"I talked to Matt about it this afternoon, and he's agreed to say nothing to anyone about you helping us. Neither will I, of course. The longer we can keep it quiet, the less chance there is of the bastard finding out about you."

She smiled faintly. "So you think we've got—what?—forty-eight hours or so before the whole town knows?"

Rueful, he said, "About that, probably. Secrets do tend to get out in small towns."

"Well, I'll cross that bridge when I get to it."

"Just be careful, will you, please?"

"I will." She raised her cup in a small salute. "Thanks for sending out the security people, by the way. The place is like a fortress now."

"I wish I could believe it would keep you safe."

Cassie met his gaze fleetingly and set her cup on the counter with a sound of finality. "I'll be fine."

Ben might have obediently taken his leave, but she reached up to brush back a strand of hair, and once again the gesture drew his attention to her bandaged hand.

"You're bleeding," he said.

Cassie looked at her hand, where a thin line of red stained the white gauze. "Damn."

He put his cup on the counter and stepped toward her, reaching out without thought. "Let me look—"

She took a step back. "No. No, thank you. I can take care of it myself."

Ben forced himself to stand still. "Cassie, you're so tired, I seriously doubt you could read anybody right now. But whether you can or not, somebody needs to look at that cut. Me or a doctor, take your pick. I can have one out here in half an hour. Of course, he'd probably insist on a tetanus shot. They usually do. Better to be safe than sorry, they say. Me, on the other hand, I'd more than likely just put on fresh antiseptic and re-bandage it. But it's your choice."

Cassie stared at him. "Did anybody ever mention that you can be officious as hell sometimes?"

"Matt likes to mention it." Ben smiled.

She smiled back, if a bit tentatively. Then she drew a breath and visibly braced herself. "All right."

Determined not to make a big deal out of it in his own mind as well as hers, Ben asked briskly, "Where's your first aid kit?"

"In that cabinet by the back door."

"I'll get it. Sit down at the table and start taking the bandage off, okay?"

By the time he joined her with the kit, she had the gauze unwound, revealing a long, thin slash across her palm that was bleeding sluggishly.

Cassie said, "Funny, I didn't notice before. The cut exactly follows my fate line. If I were superstitious, I'd probably worry about that."

"Do you tell fortunes too?" Ben asked lightly, removing what he needed from the first aid box.

"I've never been able to predict the future. I told you that when we met. But my mother could, and I was told Aunt Alex could."

"Really? I heard a couple of odd stories about her seeming to know things she shouldn't have known but just chalked it up to rumors. She was so seldom in town that few people knew her except to say hello."

Cassie shrugged. "I don't know the extent of her abilities. My mother refused to talk about her, and her own instances of precognition were few and far between."

"So her principal ability was like yours, the ability to tap into another mind?"

"Yes."

Judging that the time was right, Ben said, "Let's see that hand." And immediately added, "So, do you have a secondary ability?"

Cassie's hesitation was almost imperceptible. She placed her hand palm up in his and said steadily, "If I do, I haven't discovered it yet. But then, I haven't looked."

Ben held her cool hand in his and kept his gaze on it as he wiped fresh blood from the wound, but virtually all his attention was focused on her voice, his awareness filled with this first physical touch. "Why haven't you looked? Afraid of what you might find?"

"Let's just say that the primary ability is enough to deal with. I don't want another."

Ben nodded, then said, "I don't think this is deep enough to need stitches, you were right about that. I'll put on some antiseptic and a fresh bandage. You said you cut it on a broken glass?"

"Yes. A clean glass. So no fear of tetanus."

Ben opened a tube of antiseptic and began to apply the cream to her hand. Unwilling to allow a silence to grow between them, he said, "Earlier, you referred to your ability as 'the sight.' That's an ancient name for it, isn't it?"

"I suppose. It was always called that in my family."

He glanced up from her hand. "Always?" She was looking at him with an unusually steady gaze, her eyes impenetrable and her expression calm; he had no idea whether she was able to read him, and he didn't feel her gaze as he sometimes did. Was it because she was actually touching him?

Cassie nodded slowly. "It's like one of those stories you see in fiction. I'm not the seventh daughter of a seventh daughter, but the sight has been in my family for generations, almost always handed down from mother to daughter."

"What about the sons?"

"There haven't been any in the last few generations of my mother's line. Further back, I'm not sure. According to the family stories, it was a female gift exclusively."

Ben smiled. "Maybe to level the playing field?"

"The boys got the muscle and the girls got the sight?" Cassie smiled as well. "Maybe."

He returned his attention to her hand, putting a clean gauze pad in place over the wound and then winding gauze around her hand to secure it. "So if you have a daughter, she's likely to be psychic."

"I suppose," Cassie said.

With more reluctance than he wanted to show or admit to himself, Ben released her hand. "All done. That wasn't so bad, was it?"

"Thank you."

"You're welcome." He kept his voice light. "So, could you read me?"

Cassie didn't answer for a moment, gazing down at her hand as she flexed the fingers slowly. Then she looked up, a very faint frown between her brows. "No. No, I couldn't."

"Not at all?"

She shook her head. "Not at all. A very . . . closed book."

Ben was a little surprised at first, but then wondered if he should have been. "Like I said, you're probably too tired to read anybody tonight."

For an instant her eyes seemed to bore into his, and he felt that touch again, still cool but so firm this time that he almost glanced down to see if she had reached across the table and laid her hand on his chest.

Then Cassie was smiling just a little, and her voice was casual. "You're right. I am tired."

"I'll go, and let you get some rest."

Cassie didn't protest. She walked him to the front door. "It would probably be a good idea for me to see Miss Jameson's house tomorrow. I don't know if I'll be able to pick up anything, but I should try."

"I'll come get you—since you're without a car. Early afternoon all right?"

"Yes, fine."

"Good. Sleep late, okay? Get some rest."

"I will. Good night, Ben."

"See you tomorrow."

Cassie watched him until he reached his Jeep, then closed the door and locked it, and set the security system. She went back to the kitchen, put away the first aid kit, and rinsed out the used coffee cups, the actions automatic. She hadn't eaten anything since breakfast, but wasn't hungry now and definitely didn't want to bother fixing anything.

Her hand ached, but that was her own fault. It hadn't been hurting until she'd dug her nails into the gauze to re-open the wound just before calling Ben's attention to it.

For all the good it did.

She hadn't really suspected Ben of being the killer, but she'd seen too many outwardly decent men with black souls to discount anyone, at least until she was able to see inside their minds. Unfortunately she had not been able to read him—and she was afraid it was not because she was tired.

He had walls, solid and strong ones.

The kind of walls that few nonpsychics ever needed to build unless they had experienced some sort of emotional or psychic trauma.

Had Ben? Was there, in that seemingly open and honest man, some secret hurt or experience that had left him guarded and wary at the deepest levels of himself? Nothing in his background suggested that, but Cassie knew only too well how inadequate was the public information about a life lived.

It was the most likely explanation, that Ben's walls came from some injury or bitterly learned knowledge in his past. The only nonpsychic guarded minds she had encountered had owed their walls to trauma rather than to design.

He was not psychic.

He was also not the killer.

Cassie owed that certainty partly to her psychic ability. It had come to her as she had watched him gently examine her hand—the sudden memory of the killer who had stood over Jill Kirkwood, gloved hand raised to plunge the knife into her body.

His sleeve had fallen back, revealing his wrist, and on the inside had been a distinct scar.

Ben had no such scar.

It was a relief, but Cassie was not much cheered by it. She dreaded the coming days. Though Ben had shown some awareness of and sensitivity to the fact that this was

and would be an ordeal for her, he couldn't really understand what it would cost her.

But he'd been right in telling her that if she remained
in Ryan's Bluff, she had to help them. Not only because
it was her responsibility to help, as her mother had
drummed into her from childhood, but also because she
was in line to become a target for this killer, and stopping
him was the only way to save her own life.

She was tempted to run. More than tempted. But Ben
had also been right in pointing out that there were monsters everywhere. Besides, she had found the first real
peace of her life in this place, and gratitude also drove her
to help.

If she could. If anyone could.

Cassie made herself a cup of hot tea and soaked for
a while in a hot bath, not thinking very much about
anything. Then she went to bed early, praying she
wouldn't dream.

That particular prayer went unanswered.

Oh, Christ, he hated the dreams!
   Why wouldn't they leave him alone?
   And the voices.
   Why wouldn't they stop talking to him?
   He just wanted to sleep. He just wanted to rest.
   Why were they making him do these things?
   *His hands smelled like . . . coins. His clothes. He
thought his hair did too. Like coins.*
   Like blood.
   Shh. No more voices.
   Not tonight.
   No more dreams.
   He was so tired.

FEBRUARY 22, 1999

It was Sheriff Dunbar who came to get her the next after-noon, and he looked no happier about it than Cassie felt.

"Ben got tied up in court," he said by way of a greet-ing. "He'll meet us at Ivy's place."

"I see."

"If you're ready, of course."

Cassie thought that if he were any more polite, his face would break. "I'm ready. Just let me lock up."

Five minutes later they were in his cruiser and headed toward town. And the silence was vast.

Despite her casual words to Ben, Cassie was hyper-aware of the sheriff's suspicion and mistrust. She had formed good relationships with a number of cops over the years, but it was true that the first reaction tended to be the sheriff's, and it was always difficult for her.

In the beginning it had deeply upset her that her first role in an investigation was invariably that of suspect; hardheaded and rational cops viewed her descriptions of crimes and victims as obvious proof she had been present in the flesh, and they were difficult to persuade other-wise. It was often only when cast-iron proof in the shape of unbreakable alibis surfaced that some policemen learned, if not to trust her, then at least to believe she was no killer.

As far as Matt Dunbar was concerned, a fair alibi for at least one of the murders was obviously not good enough. Either that, or . . .

"You think I'm conning Ben, don't you? That I'm con-ning both of you."

"It crossed my mind," he replied bluntly.

"What would I have to gain?"

He sent her a quick glance, and his smile was cynical.

"How should I know? Maybe you're after fame. Or maybe you just like playing with people."

Cassie felt a spurt of amusement. "Let me guess. Somebody dragged you into a lot of fortune tellers' tents when you were a kid, right?"

"Close, but no cigar. Let's just say I've known a few people in my life who were royally taken by con artists posing as psychics."

Amusement dying, Cassie said, "I'm sorry. No wonder you're suspicious. But I'm not like that, Sheriff. I don't sit in a tent or a room hung with velvet and gaze into a crystal ball. I don't tell anybody how to make their life better, or claim to see a tall, dark stranger in their future. I don't pick lottery numbers or racehorses, or the sequence of cards at blackjack. And I never, ever take money for using this . . . gift of mine. Didn't all those testimonials give you pause?"

"There's more than one way to con somebody. And more than one reason to do it."

"Meaning I conned them? All those rational, suspicious cops? Do you really believe that?"

Dryly he said, "I think there's at least as much a chance of that as there is that you're genuine."

"So I'm definitely on probation as far as you're concerned."

"Definitely."

Cassie nodded. "Some people are never able to accept psychic ability, and some are afraid of it once they realize it's real." She turned her head and looked at him thoughtfully. "But it would make things easier on both of us, I think, if you could begin to believe that it's not a con."

"And how do you propose to accomplish that? Going to tell me what color panties Abby had on last night?"

"Green," Cassie said. When he glared at her, she grimaced. "Sorry. I know you were being sarcastic. But it was practically branded on your forehead in neon, Sheriff. If you want to test me, you'll have to do better than that."

"Test you," he said slowly.

"Why not? You won't be the first to do it, and I expect you won't be the last. You can go the old think-of-something-I-couldn't-possibly-know route, or you can get more inventive, spring a test on me when I'm not expecting it. I don't really care. Just bear in mind that there are psychic abilities I definitely don't have. I can't foretell the future, and I can't move anything with my mind."

"You can just crawl into somebody else's mind."

"Some minds. Not all." She hesitated, then said, "I can't read Ben."

"Not even when you touch him?"

"Not even then."

The sheriff was silent for a moment, then muttered, "That rings truer than anything you've said yet."

She looked at him curiously. "Really? Why?"

It was his turn to hesitate, but then he shrugged without answering.

Cassie didn't push him, because his thoughts were so clear he might as well have spoken aloud. He was thinking that Ben had never let anybody really get close, from the time they were kids. That his old man was one of those emotional tyrants you read so much about, especially in stories set in the South, a highly respected judge himself with an iron will and the absolute conviction that his word was law. Matt suspected that one of the reasons Ben had stepped down from the bench himself was that his father had died and so was no longer able to influence his only son.

Cassie rubbed her forehead and tried to shut off the easy connection with the sheriff, but before she could she was also gifted with the information that Ben had been a late child born of the old judge's second and much younger wife, Mary—whom Matt thought of as one of those pretty, childlike women who would either fascinate a man or else drive him mad.

"Headache?" the sheriff asked.

"You could say that," Cassie murmured, resisting the impulse to tell him to stop thinking so damn loud and wondering if Ben had any idea that here was one friend whose shrewd understanding nevertheless left him wondering what it was that Ben Ryan wanted out of life for himself.

A closed book indeed.

The sheriff was silent for several minutes, then muttered beneath his breath, "Green panties."

"They were, weren't they? And bra to match?"

"Yes. Dammit."

SEVEN

The blood in Ivy Jameson's kitchen had dried, and the smell of it was musty and faint. But it remained a scene of violence, and Cassie was overwhelmingly conscious of that the moment she stepped through the doorway.

"We have the murder weapon," Sheriff Dunbar said from his position inside the room to the right of the door. "If it would help to touch it?"

"No." Cassie slowly looked around. "Not if it has her blood on it." She wasn't aware of anything unusual at first. But then she felt a slight but increasing pressure, against her chest or inside it, and breathing seemed more difficult than it had a moment before.

"Cassie?" Ben was standing just behind her, in the doorway. "Are you all right?"

"I don't know. Yes. Yes, I'm fine." She continued to gaze around slowly, unwilling to tell him it was getting harder and harder for her to breathe. Her gaze focused on a pool of dried blood near the work island that was dark and slick looking, and when she blinked it suddenly turned scarlet.

The image was fleeting, a jolt of color gone before she could fully take it in. But when she looked at the blood spattered across the white refrigerator, it, too, turned briefly scarlet. And then a movement caught her eye, and she turned her head to watch scarlet blood drip from the edge of the work island and onto the tile floor.

"Jesus," she whispered.

"Cassie? What is it?"

"Shh. Don't say anything. This is . . . this has never happened to me before. When I look at it, I see the blood dripping, as if it's fresh. Splashes and smears of color all over the room, bright and wet." She closed her eyes and opened them, but the blood remained red, so red it hurt to look at it, and when she tried to turn her head away, it was as if she caught a flash of movement from the corner of her eye.

Every time she turned her head back and forth, that flash of movement was there, just out of her range of vision, teasing her by vanishing when she tried to focus on it.

Then a scream ripped through her head so loudly and violently it was like a blow, and for a single eternal instant she saw Ivy Jameson sitting on the bloody floor of her kitchen, her back up against the leg of the work island, her once-white dress horribly stained—and her open eyes staring across the room at Cassie with reproach.

Cassie wanted to run from that awful condemnation, to escape the dreadful knowledge in Ivy's gaze. But suddenly the pressure on her chest became crushing, there was no air, no air at all, and the scarlet and white kitchen was engulfed by a wave of total darkness.

The silence was absolute, and it was so peaceful, Cassie was tempted to remain there. There were horrors waiting for her outside the tranquil darkness, waking nightmares she was not ready to face. But then someone began calling her name, the sound intruding on peace, and she knew she had to respond.

"Cassie?"

She opened her eyes and was instantly alert, not at all drained or exhausted by what had happened. She found herself lying on a sofa in a very formal living room. Ben was sitting on the edge near her hips and held one of her hands in his.

Cassie tensed automatically to draw her hand away, but then she realized she was still unable to read him. His hand felt very warm.

"Told you she'd be all right," the sheriff said laconically from a nearby chair.

"Are you?" Ben asked her, gaze intent on her face.

Cassie nodded slowly. "Yes. Yes, I'm fine."

He helped her to sit up but didn't release her hand or move away until it became obvious she was indeed all right. He stayed beside her on the couch, half turned so he could watch her more closely. "You want to tell us what happened?"

"I don't know what happened. Just that it's never happened before."

"What never happened before?" the sheriff demanded. "All you said was that you saw the blood turn wet and red, and then you fainted gracefully into Ben's arms."

Cassie ignored his mockery and looked at him rather than at Ben when she said, "I saw the bloodstains turn wet and red—some even dripped from the island onto the floor. And then, for just a moment, I saw Ivy Jameson. Sitting on the floor, her back against the leg of the island, her dress red with blood. She was looking across the room at me almost . . . accusingly."

"So whose head were you in?"

"I don't know. It was as if I were standing in that room just moments after the killer left."

"How do you explain it?" Ben asked.

"I can't explain it. Unless . . ."

"Unless?" the sheriff prompted.

Cassie gazed into the distance, thinking, then said, "Unless someone else did that. Stood in the doorway only minutes after the murder. Someone I've connected to without realizing. Maybe I was . . . reliving someone's memory."

The sheriff shook his head. "You seem to have *connected* to an awful lot of people, if you ask me."

Ignoring him, Ben asked, "Was it Matt? You were able to read him earlier. Could you have picked up these images from his experience when he first arrived here in the house and saw her?"

"I don't know." She looked at the sheriff. "Except for her body being gone, is the room just the way you found it?"

"Almost." He didn't elaborate.

Cassie got up. "I need to see it again."

"Are you sure?" Ben asked. "The first time hit you pretty hard."

"I'm sure." She led the way back to the kitchen, stopping just inside the doorway as she had before. This time both men remained behind her.

Cassie concentrated on remembering what she had seen, comparing the details with the room as she saw it now. "Her body was there, at the corner of the island nearest the stove. A foot or so away . . . there was a knife. A butcher knife, covered in blood." Her gaze roamed slowly around the room. "There were footprints in the blood near the back door, but . . . the footprints on this side of the room weren't there. That's the only other difference I see."

"Then you weren't seeing Matt's first look into the room," Ben said.

She turned to the two men. "No?"

Ben was staring at the sheriff. "No. The footprints on this side of the room were made by Ivy's relatives when they found her. Before they called Matt."

"So I saw the room before they entered it."

"I'd say so, yes."

"Then someone else must have been here."

The sheriff scowled at her. "Why couldn't it have been the killer standing there? Assuming any of this bullshit is true, that is."

"I don't think it was him. I didn't get a sense of him, the way I have before. As a matter of fact . . . I didn't get a sense of anyone. No personality, I mean."

"Then what makes you so sure somebody else was here?"

Cassie thought about it but finally had to shake her head in defeat. "I don't know. Just . . . by process of elimination. I've never been able to tap into a *place,* not like that. To see, so vividly, something that had already happened, I had to be seeing through somebody's eyes, through their memories. Somebody standing right here, just inside the doorway. After Mrs. Jameson was killed, but before her relatives got here."

Slowly Ben said, "In plenty of near-death experiences, people report being out of their bodies, hovering nearby and looking at themselves. Is it at all possible that you saw this room through Ivy's eyes after her murder?"

"That," the sheriff said, "is the creepiest thing I've heard yet."

Ben was gazing at Cassie. "But is it possible?"

"I don't know." She agreed with the sheriff. It was a creepy possibility. "If so, it would be a first for me."

Sheriff Dunbar shook his head. "Either way, I don't

see that this is getting us anywhere. There's no evidence there was anybody other than the killer and Ivy in this house until her relatives arrived. In the meantime, I have three bodies and a town full of people beginning to panic. Unless you can tell me something helpful, I think I'll go back to my good old-fashioned police methods and try to find this bastard before he kills anybody else."

Cassie nodded. "Two things. Before he . . . before he killed Jill Kirkwood, he said something to her. He said, 'You'll never laugh at me again.' "

"Laughing at people wasn't Jill's style," Ben said immediately.

"In his mind she had laughed at him, belittled him. Maybe they all had, at least as far as he was concerned," Cassie said. "For what it's worth."

"And the other thing?" the sheriff asked.

"That may be more helpful. He held the knife in his right hand, and on the inside of that wrist was a scar. I think he's tried to kill himself, at least once."

"Just when did you remember seeing that?"

"Last night." Cassie shrugged. "I would have called you, but I knew I'd see you today." And she knew he was disinclined to believe her anyway. It was obvious.

Still, the sheriff was grudgingly pleased by something concrete. "Okay, I'll add those details to what little we've got so far."

"Are you going to call the FBI?" Ben asked.

"Not yet."

"Matt—"

"Don't tell me my job, Ben."

"Look, at least get in touch with that violent-crimes task force operating out of Charlotte. They have more resources, Matt. They can help."

"Their resources don't mean jackshit." The sheriff's jaw was set stubbornly. "You know and I know that this killer is not going to be found in anybody's computer database, Ben. He's home grown."

Cassie divided her attention between them. "Then you're sure he's not a stranger, a newcomer in town?"

"Positive."

"Matt, there's no way we can be positive."

"I'm positive. Ivy's relatives swear she would never have opened a door to a stranger, much less invite one into her kitchen."

"She could have let him in the front door."

"And then put the chain back on the way her nephew and brother-in-law found it later? No. She knew him, Ben. She let the bastard into the house through her back door, and she felt so unthreatened by him that he was able to cross the room and pick up one of her own butcher knives."

Ben frowned but shook his head. "What about Becky? Cassie thinks she didn't know her killer."

Cassie said, "She didn't say his name at a point when she should have. So she probably didn't know it. But that's just an assumption on my part."

The sheriff said, "That doesn't mean he's a stranger to the area. Small town or not, none of us knows every one of our fellow citizens."

Ben granted the point with a nod but said, "Still, we can't be sure, Matt. And even if you're right about it, the task force has other resources we could use. They have experts—in forensics and behavioral science to name just two."

"I can and will handle this investigation," the sheriff said flatly. "I'm not handing it off to the FBI, a task force, or to anyone else. Remember when they came cruising in here a few years ago, Ben? The FBI and DEA, tracking drug runners up from Florida and convinced the operation was based around here? I've never seen such a mess in my life. The rights of decent citizens trampled without so much as a by-your-leave, property destroyed, people up in arms. My father had a heart attack before it was all over and done with."

Sheriff Dunbar shook his head. "Unh-unh, no way am I going to let anything like that happen again, not in my town." With barely a pause he added, "Now, if you two don't mind, I say we get out of here. I need to lock up the place and get back to the office. And I'm sure both of you have better things to do with the rest of your afternoon."

Cassie didn't protest, and Ben didn't say anything else until they got into his Jeep.

Then, watching the sheriff's cruiser drive away, he shook his head. "I'm afraid it *was* a mess. And it left a bad taste in the mouth for most of the people around here. As nervous as this town is getting, Matt won't be criticized for not turning to outsiders for help."

"Can he handle this on his own?"

Ben started the engine and put the Jeep in gear. "I don't know. He's no fool, and he's got plenty of smart people working for him, but this is something outside his experience. He never worked homicide during his training as a cop, and he sure as hell never dealt with a serial killer."

"He made a good argument for Mrs. Jameson's killer not being a stranger to her. Logical and reasonable. You still don't agree?"

"I just don't agree that it's definitive. There's a chance, however unlikely, that Ivy let a stranger in, or at least opened the door to one. And you say the man who killed Jill wore a mask. She sure as hell wouldn't have opened the door to a masked man, so I have to wonder if her door was even locked. Maybe she was careless and didn't lock it behind her when she went in. Maybe Ivy was careless for once. It happens."

"To both of them on the same day?"

Ben grimaced. "Unlikely, yes. But possible."

After a moment's thought Cassie said, "I have to say he convinced me. And a man who was a stranger to Becky could still be someone Mrs. Jameson knew. If he is local, sooner or later there's bound to be some connection between the killer and at least one of his victims. I guess we'll just have to wait and see if Sheriff Dunbar's investigation turns up anything."

"Such as more bodies?" Ben's voice was grim.

"Maybe he'll find the connection, if there is one. Or evidence that points to a particular man. If he's right about this killer being from the area, then he probably has a much better understanding of the people here—and any potential suspect—than outside law enforcement officials could ever get."

"He understands the people here, but I doubt he has any special insight into the mind of this killer." Ben sent her a quick glance. "Your help could prove invaluable, Cassie. That hasn't changed."

Without responding to that, she said, "If you could just take me as far as the garage, I'd appreciate it. They called this morning to say my car was ready, so I said I'd pick it up."

Ben turned the Jeep in the direction of the garage but said, "Should you be driving? You were out cold for nearly five minutes."

Cassie was a little startled. "So long? I hadn't realized. But it's all right, I feel fine. Whatever happened back there didn't take nearly as much out of me as the usual . . . connections do."

"Could have fooled me. You went white as a sheet before you passed out."

There was a note in his voice that made her feel suddenly self-conscious, but Cassie managed to keep her own voice casual. "Shock, I imagine. Seeing her sitting there, the way she seemed to be looking at me, was so unexpected." She paused. "What if someone else was there? Why wouldn't they have come forward?"

"Probably afraid of being a suspect. And I really don't like the idea of a witness to a crime scene who's out there possibly telling friends and family what that crime scene looked like. So far we've been able to keep certain details quiet. If word gets out about the way the victims were found posed, the coins in their hands, the weapons used, it could make it more difficult to prosecute the case if and when it comes to court."

"I don't suppose you're worried about a copycat killer," Cassie said absently.

"Not really. Assuming Matt's right, I find it just barely credible that this sleepy little town could produce one vicious killer. Two operating at the same time would surprise me very much."

"Well, maybe whoever it was who might have witnessed the murder scene will be too frightened to talk about it."

"Maybe. But secrets tend not to stay secret for very long in this town."

Cassie thought about that after he dropped her off at the garage. She paid her bill and waited for her car to be driven around front, and it didn't take a psychic to sense the unease of the mechanics. All they could talk about were the murders, and speculation was running rife.

"It's gotta be a stranger. I mean, who around here would do such a thing?" one mechanic standing a few feet from Cassie demanded of his companion.

"I know plenty who could have murdered Ivy," the second man said with a snort. Then he sobered and added, "But not the other two, not Miss Kirkwood or Becky."

"You think it was the same guy?"

"Well, it musta been. I heard that the sheriff found 'em all holding flowers. Is that sick, or what?"

"Flowers? I heard it was candles."

"Candles? Now, what kind of sense does that make? Honestly, Tom, you'd believe anything anybody told you. . . ."

The discussion faded away as they walked toward the back, and since Cassie's car was delivered to her then, she left the garage and drove toward her next stop, the supermarket. She had decided to run a few errands since she was in town anyway. And, in all honesty, she also wanted to get a sense of the mood of the townspeople.

The cashier at the supermarket, unlike the mechanics, was not disposed to be fascinated by the subject. When the customer in front of Cassie asked what she thought of the murders, the teenager looked as if she would burst into tears.

"Oh, Mrs. Holland, it's so awful! Becky was in school with my sister, and Miss Kirkwood was just the nicest lady. And I heard . . . I heard they had awful things done to them, just awful! I'm so scared, all the girls are so scared!"

The customer murmured a few reassuring words, but it was clear she was none too confident in her own optimism; Cassie noticed that she glanced around her warily as she pushed her shopping cart from the store.

Cassie had bought a few perishables, but it was a chilly day, and she didn't worry when she parked her car downtown, locked it up, and went for a stroll. She window-shopped, and she listened to the people around her talk, winding up in a booth in the drugstore.

The young counterman, whose name according to the pin on his shirt pocket was Mike, was obviously excited by the fact that he had actually been questioned by deputies. He eagerly shared the experience with her as he poured the coffee she had ordered.

"On account of Becky working here and all," he explained. "And they wanted to know if we'd noticed anybody following or watching her, or if she'd told us somebody had."

"And had she?" Cassie asked, more because he so clearly wanted to talk about it than because she did.

"Not a word to any of us." Mike polished the counter in front of Cassie industriously. "Not that I talked to her much since her job was back in the office, but Mrs. Selby says Becky never told her either. And none of us ever noticed her being watched or followed, nothing like that." He lowered his voice conspiratorially. "And now there's Mrs. Jameson and Miss Kirkwood too. It's just horrible, isn't it?"

"Yes," Cassie said. "Horrible." Before he could prolong the conversation, she retreated to a booth with the day's newspaper and her coffee.

The newspaper articles were fairly restrained given the unusual violence of the crimes. The latest murders had made the front page, and the story was the headline, but the tone of the piece was low-key and just reported the facts as they were known. Two women murdered, presumably within hours of each other and less than a mile apart. Assailant unknown. The Sheriff's Department was investigating, and if anyone had anything to report, they could call the department, number provided.

Inside the newspaper, on the editorial page, a far more worried voice wondered if there should be a curfew, more deputies patrolling, and more "openness" from the sheriff. The intimation was that he was keeping to himself details of the crimes, and that those details, if known, might enable the good citizens of Ryan's Bluff to better protect themselves. Perhaps they should not have elected someone with a bare dozen years of police experience, no matter who his father had been. . . .

"Ouch," Cassie murmured, wondering if Sheriff Dunbar's methodical police work was going to prove a political liability to him in the near future.

She knew from her own research that Dunbar had gained his police experience in Atlanta, rising to detective shortly before he had returned home to Ryan's Bluff when his father had announced his retirement as sheriff.

An unkind soul might indeed have said that Matt Dunbar had won the election on his name alone, but that would have been untrue. He was qualified for his job, that was certain. And he had fairly good political instincts, though word had it he had run afoul of the town council at least once since taking office.

In any case, there was probably no one better qualified for the job of sheriff in the county, certainly not better qualified to investigate a series of murders, so the stinging editorial held a note of spite rather than reason.

Or a note of panic.

A few pages later there were articles about both Ivy Jameson and Jill Kirkwood, human-interest pieces about the lives of the two women. Ivy's history and good works were stiffly presented with an air of pious resolution, while Jill's life story was told with warmth and genuine regret.

Two women, one widely despised and the other highly regarded. And one young girl who had, by all accounts, never harmed a soul. All horribly murdered in the same small town within days of one another.

Cassie thought the newspaper had done a fine job in getting so much information in print in a Monday edition when the two latest murders had taken place the day before, but she didn't doubt that upcoming editions would sound much less detached. The days ahead promised to be rough.

She laid the paper aside and sipped her coffee thoughtfully, vaguely aware of the people moving about in the drugstore—she didn't dare call it a pharmacy, since no one else did—shopping or just visiting with each other. This was a central gathering spot for downtown, a fact Cassie had discovered early on.

But there were few people in the soda fountain side of the store, so Cassie instantly sensed when someone paused beside her booth. She looked up to see a stunning redhead, too model-gorgeous to belong in this small town.

In a rather roundabout way Cassie recognized her.

"Miss Neill? My name is Abby. Abby Montgomery. I knew your aunt. May I talk to you?"

Green panties. Cassie pushed the knowledge away, reflecting, not for the first time, that psychic abilities could provide certain facts that were nothing but embarrassing.

She gestured toward the other side of the booth. "Please, have a seat. And I'm Cassie."

"Thanks." Abby sat down with her own coffee. She was smiling, but though her gaze was direct, her green eyes were enigmatic.

Without even trying, Cassie knew that here was another mind she would find it impossible to tap into, and that certainty made her feel much more sociable than was usual for her.

It was nice not to have to worry overmuch about keeping her own guard up.

"So you knew Aunt Alex."

"Yes. We met by chance a few months before she died. At least—I thought it was by chance."

"It wasn't?"

Abby hesitated, then let out a little laugh. "Looking back, I think she wanted to meet me. She had something she wanted to tell me."

"Oh?"

"Yes. My destiny."

"I see." Cassie didn't ask what the prediction had been. Instead, she said, "I was told Aunt Alex had the gift of prophecy."

"You were told?"

Cassie had little doubt that Matt Dunbar had discussed her abilities with his lover; he was a very open man in virtually every way, and his nature would be to confide in the woman he loved. So she was certain that Abby knew she was—or claimed to be—psychic. She suspected that this meeting was in the nature of a test. Or a confirmation.

Cassie said, "I was only a little girl when my mother and Aunt Alex quarreled, and I never saw or heard from her again. Until I got word of her death and learned I'd inherited her property here. So all I really know about her are the few things I overheard as a child."

"Then you don't know if she was always right?"

Abby's voice was as calm as Cassie's had been, but there was something in the tension of her posture and the white-knuckled grip on her coffee cup that betrayed strong emotion.

Careful now, Cassie said, "No psychic is always a hundred percent right. The things we see are often subjective, sometimes symbolic images that we filter through our own knowledge and experiences. If anything, we're translators, attempting to decipher a language we only partly understand."

Abby smiled wryly. "So the answer is no."

"No, I don't know if Aunt Alex was always right—but I doubt very much if she was."

"She said . . . she told me there was a difference between a prediction and a prophecy. Is that right?"

"Precognition isn't really my bailiwick, but my mother always said they were different. That a prediction is a fluid thing, a vision of an event that might sometimes be influenced by people and their choices, so that the outcome couldn't be clearly seen. A prophecy, she said, is far more concrete. It's a true vision of the future, impossible to alter unless someone with certain knowledge interfered."

"Certain knowledge?"

Cassie nodded. "Suppose a psychic had a prophetic vision of a newspaper headline that stated a hundred people died in a hotel fire. She knows she won't be believed if she tries to warn them, so she does the only thing she can. Goes to the hotel and sets off a fire alarm before the actual fire is discovered. The people get out. But the hotel burns just the same. The headline she saw will never exist. But the event that generated it will happen."

Abby was listening so intently that she was actually leaning forward over the table. "Then a prophecy can be changed, but only partly."

"That's what I've been told. The problem for the psychic is knowing whether her interference will alter the prophecy—or bring it about just as she saw it."

"How can she know that?"

"According to some, she can't. I'd lean that way myself. Interpreting what you see is difficult enough. Trying to figure out if your own warning or interference is the catalyst that will bring about the very outcome you're trying to avoid . . . I just don't see how it's possible to do anything but guess. And if the stakes are high enough, a wrong guess could have a very costly price tag."

"Yes." Abby dropped her gaze to her coffee. "Yes, I see that."

Cassie hesitated, then said, "If you don't mind my asking, what did Aunt Alex tell you? A prediction of your destiny? Or a prophecy?"

Abby drew a breath and met Cassie's gaze, a little smile wavering on her lips. "A prophecy. She said—she told me I would die at the hands of a madman."

EIGHT

After he dropped off Cassie at the garage, Ben had a brief meeting at his office with the public defender about an upcoming case, then fielded several calls from concerned citizens regarding the murders.

Or, more specifically, what he was going to do about them.

His job demanded tact and patience, and he used both. But as he hung up the phone after the third call, he was uneasily aware that the mood of the town was already beginning to shift from panic to anger.

And there were too damned many guns in too many angry hands.

Knowing that Eric Stephens would be calling him soon to find out what he should print in the newspaper in response to citizen demands for official advice on how to be safer, he began jotting down a list on a legal pad. Matt would be asked first, of course, and he would offer these same practical suggestions before getting impatient and telling Eric to "ask Ben" so he could get back to his investigation.

Matt usually knew the right answers but seldom trusted his own instincts. Sometimes it worried Ben.

Janice buzzed from her office. "A call, Judge. It's your mother."

"Thanks, Janice." He picked up the receiver. "Hi, Mary. What's up?" He had called his mother by her name—at her request—from the time he was a boy. The habit was so ingrained now, he seldom even thought about it.

"Ben, these awful murders . . ." The little-girl, breathless voice that his father had at first found charming and then, as the years passed, utterly exasperating, was filled with worry and horror. "And Jill! The poor, poor thing!"

"I know, Mary. We'll catch him, don't worry."

"Is it true Ivy Jameson was killed in her own kitchen?"

"I'm afraid so."

"And Jill in her shop! Ben, what kind of monster could be doing this?"

Avoiding the obvious retort that if they knew that, the monster would be more easily captured, Ben said patiently, "I don't want you to upset yourself, Mary. You've got a good security system and the dogs—keep them with you when you're out in the garden."

"It's just that I'm so far from town," she said.

Ben started to repeat that she would be fine, but then remembered his missed opportunity to warn Jill. Could he live with himself if something like that happened again? "I'll tell you what. I should be finished here by five at the latest. I'll come out to the house and check all the locks, make sure the security system is working properly, all right?"

"And stay to supper? I'll fix that chicken dish you like so much."

He thought fleetingly of his half-formed intention to call Cassie and offer to bring Chinese takeout to her place that evening, and bit back a sigh. "Sure. That sounds great, Mary. I should be there between five-thirty and six."

"Bring some wine," she chirped merrily. "See you then."

"Right." Ben hung up the phone and rubbed the back of his neck wearily. He didn't feel a bit disloyal to his father in wishing his mother would find a kind widower and remarry. She needed a man around, and failing a romantic interest, she naturally turned to her son. For everything.

It wasn't a role Ben enjoyed.

Growing up the only child of a young, emotionally volatile mother and a much older, coldly distant, manipulative father, he had, more often than not, felt like a punching bag. It hadn't helped that his own personality was an uneasy mixture of his genetic heritage; every bit as emotionally sensitive and impulsive as his mother, he had also inherited his father's intellectual detachment, innate wariness, and ability to cloak his feelings behind either charm or coldness.

The mix made him a good lawyer.

He wasn't at all sure it made him a good man.

He was certain it made him a lousy lover.

Jill had deserved better. All she had wanted from him had been emotional closeness, an intimacy beyond the physical, and since they had been seeing each other for several months by that point, she had certainly been entitled to ask.

In response, he had only grown cooler and more distant, burying himself in work and offering her less and less of his time, his attention. Himself.

Even then Ben had realized what he was doing, yet he'd been powerless to do anything else. He had valued her love, but her conspicuous need of him had made him feel obligated. Not obligated to commit himself to her, but to open himself to her, and it was something he was simply unable to do.

He didn't know why that was true. But he did know that Jill had not been the only woman in his life whose attempts to get closer to him had been rebuffed, only the most recent.

After weeks of distancing himself he had coolly suggested that their relationship was simply not working. Jill hadn't been very surprised, and she hadn't subjected him to an emotional scene, but her unhappiness had been obvious.

She had deserved better.

Ben felt that he'd abandoned her twice. First because he hadn't been able to love her, and then before her death, when a warning from him might have made a difference.

"Judge?"

He looked up with a start to find his secretary standing in the open doorway. "Yes, Janice?"

"The sheriff called while you were on with your mother. He wants you to come by his office before six if you can. Says he's found out something interesting about a piece of evidence in these murders."

"Tell Sheriff Dunbar," Cassie said immediately. A prediction about dying at the hands of a madman would be terrifying enough to live with normally, she thought, but with a serial killer stalking the town, it became more than imperative that Abby take some steps to protect herself. And even though they had just met, Cassie had seen too many scenes of violence recently not to feel a chill of fear for Abby.

Abby's smile wavered even more. "What makes you think I haven't already?"

"A hunch."

"Pretty good one."

"Why haven't you told him?"

"Because he wouldn't believe it. He's an atheist, did you know that?"

Cassie shook her head.

"Yes. He goes to church because it's politically expedient, but he considers religion nothing more than myth and superstition." She paused, then added, "In other words, on a par with psychic ability."

"If there is no God, there can be no magic," Cassie murmured.

"Something like that."

Cassie sighed. "It's so difficult for most people to believe that it's just another sense, like sight or hearing. That *they* don't have it because nothing in their genetic makeup or experience triggered that part of their brain to begin working instead of lying dormant. I have black hair and gray eyes and psychic ability. All perfectly normal for me, all handed down in my family for generations. If they could just understand there's nothing magical about it."

"Matt will probably never understand," Abby said. "It's just too alien to him. He wouldn't be listening to you at all if it weren't for Ben. But even when they were kids, Ben was always the one trying new things and Matt always followed Ben's lead." She lowered her voice. "Plus, you knew we were seeing each other, and that shook him up more than he'll admit. But he's not at all inclined to put any faith in psychic ability."

"Surely he'd heed a threat to you?"

"He'd think Miss Melton was just trying to scare me—for some undoubtedly mercenary reason. He never knew your aunt, and he'd never believe how upset she was when she told me, how reluctant."

Cassie shook her head. "That's the part I don't understand."

"You mean, why she'd tell me I was doomed?"

"Exactly. As a rule, prophecies tend to herald some kind of tragedy, but no responsible psychic would offer such a warning to someone if there was nothing they could do to change a terrible fate." Cassie kept her voice matter-of-fact.

Abby frowned. "I hardly knew her, of course, but I got the distinct feeling it was something she didn't want to tell me. She seemed to force herself to get the words out. And she kept repeating that the future was never static, that human will could influence fate."

"Then she thought you could change what she saw."

"Or else just wanted to soften the blow."

Cassie shook her head. "If that were the case, why tell you at all? I can't believe she was cruel, and to offer you a bleak and unalterable vision of the future would definitely be cruel. No, my guess is that she told you because she thought if you knew, you could do something to avoid the fate she saw for you."

"Such as?"

"I wish I knew. Sometimes avoiding an event is as simple as turning left instead of right at the next traffic light you encounter." She sighed. "I'm sorry, I wish there was something more helpful I could tell you, but even if I had my aunt's gift, I'd still have to interpret what I saw. There are so many possible outcomes for any situation."

"That's what your aunt said."

"I don't know what I'd do in your shoes," Cassie said. "But telling the sheriff would be a good start. He told me he'd known a few people who were deceived by psychics, but surely he'd pay attention to a warning concerning you, especially when it was given by a woman with nothing to gain."

"He's more likely to get mad at me for taking the warning seriously. To him, it's always some kind of con." Abby paused, then added, "He's convinced you're conning them."

"I know."

"He's a good man. But he can be stubborn as hell."

Cassie smiled. "His mistrust doesn't bother me much. Or hasn't so far. So far, it hasn't been costly."

"You think it will be?"

"If I manage to pick up some useful information and he ignores it because he doesn't trust me . . . you bet it could be costly." She shook her head. "But right now I'm more concerned about you. Reading the good sheriff told me more than you'd probably like about your personal life. I know you have a husband you're separated from, and I know he's capable of violence. Add to that one maniac who's killed three women so far, and I'd say it might be a good time for you to take a vacation and go lie on a beach somewhere."

Abby's unsteady smile returned. "And what if my leaving here and going somewhere else is just another step toward my fate?"

"That's a possibility. But I'd have to say the odds are more in your favor on that beach."

"Maybe. But I can't leave."

"Then at least tell the sheriff. If you can't make him believe that my aunt could see into the future, at least convince him her warning frightened you. Maybe he can take steps to make your life safer."

"And maybe it would just be one more thing for him to worry about. I'm being careful. And that's all I can do."

Cassie admired her calm. Since she had lived often with the knowledge that some madman could possibly zero in on her, that her odds of becoming a victim were better than most, she knew only too well how debilitating that constant threat was.

Even more, she knew how it felt to live with a prophecy of doom. She almost told Abby, almost confided that her only experience with precognition had been a vision of her own fate that promised violence and destruction. But in the end she kept that knowledge to herself.

She had run three thousand miles only to find herself once again entangled in an investigation of crimes of violence; for her, running had not been an escape. There was nothing to be gained by telling Abby that.

"Do you have a dog?" she asked instead.

"No."

"Maybe you should get one. Or borrow one."

"Do you have one?"

Cassie smiled. "No. But Ben said I should get one—and he was right. Look, do you want to take a trip with me out to the animal shelter?"

"The coins," Matt said.

"What about them?" Ben sat down in one of the visitors' chairs in front of the sheriff's desk.

"We may have caught a break with them. The silver dollar found in Becky's hand turns out to be a pretty rare specimen. I don't understand the technical details, something about a flaw in the mold. They were never circulated, and only a few thousand were minted before the mistake was caught."

"A few thousand?"

"I know it sounds like a lot, but they all went to collectors, Ben, and they're very valuable."

"Does that mean they're traceable?"

"It means they might be. I've got somebody working on that now."

"How about the other coins?"

Matt shook his head. "We're still checking on those, but they look damn close to mint quality to me. If so, if he's using only uncirculated coins, then they've pretty well got to be from somebody's collection."

"We have any coin collectors in town?"

"Yeah, several that we know of. It isn't exactly an uncommon hobby. We're quietly pulling together a list."

"And then?"

"Start asking questions, as discreetly as possible. I don't want everybody in town knowing that coins are part of the murder investigation, so we've cooked up a story about a stolen coin collection. It won't fool anyone for long, but with luck it'll give us a head start."

"Maybe not much of one," Ben said. "From what I've been hearing today, rumors are already circulating that the victims were holding something when they were found."

"Shit."

"We both knew it was just a matter of time."

"Yeah, but I was hoping for days rather than hours. Dammit, how did that get out? My people have been threatened with fines and/or jail time if I find out anybody discussed this investigation outside the office."

Ben shrugged. "Osmosis. If there's a secret in this town, it will get out. Guaranteed."

Matt scowled at him. "That psychic of yours hasn't been talking, has she?"

"I doubt it. When are you going to get off her case, Matt? She's done nothing except try to help."

"Like that business a few hours ago? The killer's right-handed and probably tried to kill himself at some point by slashing his wrists?"

"You didn't believe her?"

"No."

"Tell me you at least added 'right-handed' and 'possible attempted suicide scar' to your list of identifying characteristics."

"I did. But I'm not expecting either to help. Right-handed I'd already gotten from Doc Munro anyway, a fact he gleaned logically from the wounds. As for that supposed scar—this is a town where more than half the men work in mills and plants, and injuries to the hands and lower arms are common. I think she realized that. I think she guessed right-handed because it's likely, and added the scar in for color."

"What is she going to have to do to convince you she's genuine?"

"A lot more than she has done."

Ben rose to his feet, shaking his head. "You're so damned stubborn. It'll cost you one day, Matt."

"Maybe. But not today. I'll call you if we find out anything else."

"Do that. I'll be out at Mary's this evening, but I don't plan to stay more than a couple of hours."

"She nervous?"

"Of course. I promised to check out her security system."

"Tell her I'm stepping up the regular patrols out there as of tonight."

"I will. Thanks."

"Don't mention it." Matt smiled faintly.

Ben lifted a hand in farewell and left the sheriff's office. Not one to put off unpleasant duties, he drove out of town to the house where he'd grown up. His father had insisted on calling the big, bastard-Tudor house and its hundred acres of rolling pastureland an estate, but Ben refused to.

He also refused to call it home.

He pressed the button on the intercom rather than

ringing the doorbell and wasn't surprised when his mother's cheerful voice bade him enter. The door wasn't locked. However, since he was greeted in the foyer by two enormous mastiffs, it could hardly be said the house was unprotected.

"Hey, guys." He patted the broad, heavy heads of the two dogs who were clearly delighted to see him. His mother had named them Butch and Sundance, and either would instantly die to protect her, but otherwise they were placid and friendly dogs who enjoyed familiar visitors.

They walked on either side of Ben as he went through the house to the kitchen, where he found his mother.

"The breeder has a new litter of puppies," Mary Ryan said as soon as they came in. "You should get one, Ben. You love dogs and they love you."

"I don't need a mastiff in my apartment," he told her, patient with an old argument.

"You could pick a smaller breed."

"I don't need a dog in my apartment. With my hours, it wouldn't be fair to keep any kind of pet."

She sent him a glance from her position at the center work island, where she was chopping ingredients for a salad. She was a tall, slender woman who had passed on to her son her own gleaming dark hair and hazel eyes. Her little-girl voice was incongruous; a husky, smoky voice would have been more in keeping with her looks. She was not yet sixty, and looked twenty years younger.

"You need a companion, Ben," she said. "You spend too much time alone."

"You haven't seen my workload lately," he retorted. She was, of course, discussing his wifeless state, though she invariably approached the subject indirectly. Knowing she would go on and on discussing it unless he distracted her, he set the bottle of wine he'd brought on the counter, took off his suit jacket and draped it over a barstool at the island, and said, "I'll go ahead and check all the windows and doors, all right?"

"Supper will be ready in twenty minutes."

He hoped the subject was going to be dropped, but when they were sitting at the informal breakfast table half an hour later, she brought it up again.

"A kitten, then. Maybe two of them. Cats are quite happy being left on their own for hours, and at least there'd be someone for you when you came home."

Ben sipped his wine to give himself a moment, then said calmly, "Mary, I promise you I don't lack for company. I've just been very busy lately and haven't had much time for dating."

She grimaced slightly when he bluntly replaced cats with women, but followed his lead to ask a direct question of her own. "What about Alexandra Melton's niece?"

He was startled. "How the hell did you hear about her?"

"Louise told me. You know we always do the flowers for the church on Saturday. She said she'd seen you at least twice with Alexandra Melton's niece, that there was no mistaking the girl. Is she as interesting as her aunt was, Ben?"

"I hardly knew Miss Melton."

"And her niece?"

"I barely know her."

"But what's she *like*?"

Ben gave up; Mary, for all her childish voice and moods, could be as relentless as water dripping on stone when she wanted something. "She looks a lot like Miss Melton, yes. Black hair, gray eyes. Smaller, though, and more fragile."

"Alexandra was a bit fey. Is her niece? And what is her name anyway?"

"Her name is Cassie Neill." Ben frowned. "I wasn't aware you knew Miss Melton except by name."

"We talked a few times over the years. For heaven's sake, Ben, you can't live in a town this size and not know most of the people, not if you've been here nearly forty years."

He nodded but said, "What do you mean by 'fey'?"

"Well, just that. She knew things. Once, she told me to hurry home because Gretchen—Butch and Sunny's mother, you remember her—was having her puppies and there was trouble. There was too. I lost her and had to hand-rear the boys."

One of the boys thumped his tail against the tile floor, and the other yawned hugely as Ben glanced at them. Looking back at his mother, he said, "I'd heard a few stories about her seeming to know things and didn't really believe them. But Cassie says her aunt was supposed to be able to predict the future."

"Then maybe she could. Can Cassie?"

Ben shook his head. "No."

"Because you don't believe it's possible, or because she told you she couldn't?" Mary asked, intent.

"Because she told me she couldn't." Ben didn't see any reason to tell his mother that Cassie's psychic skills lay in quite another direction.

Mary was disappointed. "Oh. I was hoping maybe she could."

"So she could tell your fortune?" Ben asked dryly.

Mary lifted her chin. "As a matter of fact, Alexandra did that. After the thing with the puppies, I asked her if she could tell me anything about my future. She sort of laughed, and then she said that because of my son, I'd meet a tall, dark, and handsome man I'd fall madly in love with and soon marry."

It sounded so much like the sort of stock prediction

common in sideshow fortune tellers' tents that Ben could say only, "Oh, for God's sake, Mary."

"It might come true, you don't know."

Ben sighed. "Sure it might."

She stared at him. "You know, son, you are far too cynical even for a lawyer."

Since she called him "son" only when she was seriously annoyed with him, and since Mary annoyed with him could lead to uncomfortable interludes in his life, Ben said contritely, "I know. Sorry, Mary. I'm just not sure I believe in precognition, that's all." And it was the truth, even if not all of it.

Somewhat mollified, she said, "You should open up your mind, Ben. Your imagination."

"I'll work on that."

She eyed him. "You're just humoring me."

"For your sake, I hope Miss Melton's prediction comes true. If I notice a tall, dark stranger lurking around, I'll definitely invite him here for supper."

"Now I know you're just humoring me." But she seemed more amused than annoyed.

Accustomed to her swift changes of mood, Ben merely said, "Not at all. Fix this chicken dish for him, and I can guarantee he'll be impressed. You're a great cook and you know it."

"Umm." She sipped her wine, her eyes bright as she watched him across the table. "Can Cassie cook?"

"I wouldn't know."

"You like her, don't you?"

"Yes, I like her." He kept his voice patient and matter-of-fact. "No more and no less." *Liar.* "Stop matchmaking, Mary. The last time—" He bit off the rest, but it was too late.

Mary's face changed, and her eyes filled with quick tears. "I was so hoping you and Jill would stay together.

She was such a sweet girl, Ben. Even after you broke up she came to visit me and talk about you. . . ."

He hadn't known that. It seemed that Cassie had been right yet again when she had told him that Jill was an ex-lover not yet ready to let go. "Mary—"

"Who could have done that to such a sweet girl, Ben? And Ivy and that poor girl Becky? What's happening to this town? Who will that monster kill next?"

"Everything will be all right, Mary."

"But—"

"Listen to me. Everything will be all right." Recognizing the signs of rising hysteria in his mother, he set himself to the task of reassuring her. He kept his voice level and calm, his words encouraging, and refused to allow her to work herself into a state of panic that would demand sedatives and his presence in the house overnight; it was a condition he knew her quite capable of achieving.

And not for the first time he felt a flash of reluctant sympathy for his dead father.

NINE

"You're in my way, you know." Cassie gently nudged the German shepherd–collie mix to one side so she could open the bottom drawer of the storage chest.

Max whined softly and sat down, watching her with bright, attentive eyes. After a couple of nights and days together, they were growing accustomed to each other, but the young dog was clearly worried by the fact that Cassie was spending so much time digging through drawers and closets. Not that he could be blamed for that, since his original owners had abandoned him when they moved away.

Cassie spared a moment to stroke his head and murmur reassuringly. She had tried explaining that she would not leave him as his former people had, but discovered not only that canine minds were unreadable—at least by her—but also that it was difficult to explain verbally to a dog that she was only sorting through her aunt's things, boxing up what was to be thrown away, given away, or stored.

She wondered if Abby was having an easier time with the full-blooded Irish setter she had fallen in love with.

"Well, maybe I've done enough today anyway," she decided. "There are those boxes full of papers downstairs— I can go through them tonight and it probably won't upset you too much. In the meantime, why don't we go for a walk?"

The magic words lifted Max's head eagerly, and he preceded her out of this spare bedroom and downstairs. Cassie didn't put the dog on a leash; she had already discovered that he'd had basic obedience training and, besides, he tended to stick quite close to her when they were out.

She got her quilted jacket off the stand by the front door. It was only three in the afternoon, but the forecast was for snow and both the icy air and low, thick gray clouds said that the weather bureau might have gotten it right this time.

It was the kind of weather Cassie loved. She shoved her hands into the pockets of her coat and struck out across the fields near the house, walking slowly as she divided her attention between Max's happy exploration of every rock and hole in the ground and the spare, naked beauty of her surroundings.

It was easy to forget about . . . other things.

The killer had remained quiet these last days. As far as they knew, he had not killed again—and Cassie had not gotten so much as a whisper from his mind.

That was a silence she could only be happy about.

If the investigation was making progress, she didn't know any of the details. The sheriff had not been in touch. Ben had called the previous afternoon, to check on her he said, and he was relieved to hear she had adopted a dog. He hadn't been able to tell her anything about the investigation; another tricky case was keeping him in court more than he had expected, and he'd gotten little opportunity to talk to Matt. He had sounded tired and a little restless.

The newspaper hadn't had much to say either beyond a few stark facts. Becky Smith had been buried, but funerals for the other two victims were postponed indefinitely while the search for evidence continued.

Probably smart of the sheriff, but the lack of closure was not helping the mood of the townspeople. With two bodies lying in refrigerated storage at one of the local undertaker's and a visibly increased police presence throughout the county, no one was going to forget the potential threat. No curfew had been declared, but the newspaper reported unusually quiet streets after dark and women traveling in pairs, groups, or with male escorts virtually at all times.

If Cassie had been an optimist, she might have brought herself to hope that the killer had left and moved on to other hunting grounds. She was not an optimist. And she was more than half convinced the sheriff was right, that this killer was local, someone born and bred in the area. And still there.

Somewhere.

Realizing what she was doing, acknowledging silently that it was not, after all, so easy to forget, Cassie pushed thoughts of the killer firmly from her mind.

"Enough," she said out loud.

Max dashed up to her with a stick, and she spent the next fifteen minutes or so throwing it for him. She tired of the game before he did; he was still carrying the stick in his mouth when Cassie started back toward the house.

He dropped it the instant he saw the Jeep parked in the driveway, and his full-throated barks rang out across the field, oddly hollow in the cold, still air. Cassie saw Ben come down the steps from the porch and look in their direction, and caught Max by the collar to keep him by her side.

"Max, heel," she told him firmly. He stopped barking but was growling low in his throat by the time they got within a few feet of the visitor.

"Hi," she greeted Ben.

"Hi." He was eyeing the dog. "Well, he's big enough. Does he bite?"

"I don't know yet, though the shelter said he was gentle as a lamb the whole time they had him." Cassie glanced down at the still-growling dog. "Abandoned by people who apparently just didn't want to move him along with the furniture."

"It happens, sad to say. At least our shelter doesn't put them to sleep."

"That's what they told me." And that the younger Judge Ryan had been partly responsible for the shelter's policy of never euthanizing healthy animals—an interesting insight into his character. "Abby adopted one too, did you know?"

"Matt mentioned it." Ben smiled. "A very large Irish setter who loves to sleep with Abby. Matt wasn't entirely happy about that."

"I'll bet." Cassie wondered if Abby had confided in the sheriff about the prophecy but decided not to ask.

Max's growl got louder.

"You'd better introduce us," Ben said.

Cassie had little experience with dogs, but knew instinctively how it needed to be done. She told Max to sit, keeping one hand on the dog, and gestured for Ben to step closer. When he did, and after only the slightest hesitation, she reached out and took his hand. It was very warm, even on this cold winter day.

"Max, this is Ben," she said steadily. "He's a friend." She guided Ben's hand close enough for the dog to sniff. Max either liked the way this new person smelled or else accepted Cassie's reassuring touch; his tail thumped against the frozen ground and the growling stopped.

Ben petted the dog with a casual yet experienced ease and spoke to him kindly. By the time he straightened, Max was completely relaxed.

"So far so good," Cassie said. She released the collar, and they watched as he went to investigate the tires of the Jeep.

"We'll see how he greets me next time." Ben paused. "Does he sleep with you?"

Cassie decided not to take the question too personally. "He has a bed of his own beside mine. So far, he's stayed in it."

Ben nodded. "I'm glad you got him."

"So am I." It was the truth. She had discovered it was pleasant to have an attentive and undemanding companion who listened when she talked. And it had surprised her how much she had talked to the animal.

"I'm sorry to drop in on you without calling." Ben's voice held that same restless note she had heard when he had called the previous night. "But I was out this way, and—"

Cassie allowed the silence to last only a moment. "It's cold out here. Why don't we go inside? It'll just take a few minutes to warm up the coffee."

"That sounds good. Thanks."

Max left off investigating the Jeep to accompany them, and as usual followed Cassie into the kitchen.

"He sticks close," Ben observed from the doorway.

"So far." She glanced at Ben, reading more tension

in his posture, and said, "I was planning to light a fire in the living room fireplace. How are you at getting them started?"

"Fair." He smiled.

"Then you get the job. It always takes me way too much newspaper and kindling."

"I'll see what I can do."

By the time Cassie came into the living room carrying a tray, Ben had the fire going briskly. He had shed his suit jacket and rolled up his shirt-sleeves, and was standing by the fireplace, loosening his tie. Cassie put the tray on the coffee table and sat down at one end of the sofa.

"I think there's a knack to lighting fires," she said, pouring the coffee. "I don't have it. You obviously do. Thanks."

"My pleasure." Ben watched Max carry a rawhide bone in from the kitchen, eye the fire distrustfully for a moment, then collapse on a rug not too far from Cassie.

"We're getting into a routine," she said. "I give him a rawhide bone about this time, and it takes him the rest of the night to demolish it." She held out Ben's cup, and when he came to take it, added, "Have a seat."

He chose the other end of the sofa, and sat half turned so he could look at her. "I hope I'm not disrupting your routine."

"No. I've been sorting through some of Aunt Alex's things, but taking my time." She gestured toward a large box occupying a nearby chair. "That's mostly papers, correspondence and the like. I'll probably go through it tonight. But there's no hurry."

"So you haven't been bothered by anything else?"

Cassie shook her head and sipped her coffee. "No, nothing. I would have called the sheriff and offered to try again, but I imagine he's determined to try all the normal lines of investigation first. He won't look to me until he gets really desperate."

Ben didn't smile. "Do you think he will?"

"If you mean do I think the killing is over—no, I don't."

"Why not? Maybe three satisfied him."

"I don't think so. There's a . . . need in this one, a hunger. Killing appeases something inside him. The terror of his victims appeases something inside him. But he isn't sated yet. He'll kill again."

"It's like waiting for the other shoe to drop," Ben said. "Matt's investigation hasn't uncovered anything new, or at least not anything helpful. No witnesses have come forward. There are no viable suspects. And the whole town is holding its breath."

Cassie refused to say it for him. She merely waited.

Ben shook his head. "Maybe Matt's willing to wait and depend on traditional police methods, but I'm not. Not when there's another option. Cassie, would you try again? See if you can pick up any new information, something that might help us catch this bastard before he kills again?"

"What would the sheriff say about that?"

"He said plenty," Ben replied with a grimace. "Especially when I said I didn't want to bring you to his office and draw attention with everybody in town so edgy and watchful. He refused to come out here, and didn't want to let me bring something you could touch. But he finally gave in, probably to get me out of his office."

"So you weren't just in the neighborhood, huh?"

He hesitated. "I would have called first, but I wanted to see you before I asked you to try again, make sure you weren't as drained as you were before. To be honest, I drove around for half an hour before I could convince myself I had to ask you."

Cassie could believe that. It explained his disquiet since arriving; he was beginning to understand how much it took out of her, and he was torn between need and the reluctance to cause hurt.

"It's all right, you know," she said. "I did agree to try to help."

He gave her a quick look. "You wanted to stop, Cassie, we both know that."

"And we also both know I don't have a choice. Not if I stay here." She paused. "And I'm staying here. So let's see whatever it is you've brought for me to touch."

Ben set his cup on the coffee table and went to get his jacket from a chair near the fireplace. When he came back to the sofa, he was holding a small plastic bag labeled EVIDENCE. Inside the bag was a scrap of drab-colored cloth.

"Matt said this might tell you something."

Cassie put her cup on the coffee table and then took the bag from him and opened it. She braced herself mentally, closed her eyes, then held the scrap of cloth between her fingers.

Ben watched her. Since the night she had been unable to read him even after touching him, he thought she was a bit less wary in his presence; she was definitely making eye contact more often than she had at first.

But she was still very much shut inside herself, guarded and watchful. Her smiles were almost always brief, her eyes unreadable. And though the strain he had seen at their first meeting was still visible in the faint shadows under her eyes, she seemed somehow less torn by it, as though acceptance of the situation had bred a kind of peace.

Or a kind of fatalism.

That bothered Ben, this feeling that Cassie was resigned to a fate she was convinced lay in store for her. She had not had to tell him that the fate she saw for herself was not a happy one; it had been obvious. And that had been the reason he had driven around arguing with himself before finally coming to her. Not because an attempt would most likely drain her, but because he couldn't shake the feeling that with each attempt she was moving nearer a destiny that would take her far beyond his reach, maybe beyond anyone's reach.

And she knew it.

He made himself put that aside for the moment, and was about to ask her if she sensed anything, when her sudden smile threw him off balance.

"Cassie? Does it tell you anything?"

She opened her eyes, the smile lingering. "As a matter of fact, it does." She returned the scrap to the plastic bag and dropped it carelessly onto the sofa between them. "It tells me the good sheriff has a sense of humor as well as a suspicious nature. I wasn't entirely sure about that."

"What are you talking about?"

"It's a test, Ben. A test for me." She was still smiling. "I invited him to do it, actually, so I can't complain."

Ben picked up the evidence bag. "Are you telling me this didn't come from any of the crime scenes?"

"Afraid not."

"Then where the hell did it come from?"

"As I said, the sheriff has a sense of humor. That scrap of material is from his own Boy Scout uniform."

"Son of a *bitch*."

"Don't be too hard on him. I knew he wouldn't refuse a challenge and I gave him one. To test me unexpectedly. That's why he refused to come along, of course. He's such an open book, I would easily have read his intentions. He's sure I can do that, even if he'd argue there's nothing paranormal about it. This way, he's not here, and even if I could read you, you had no idea the so-called evidence wasn't genuine."

Grimly Ben said, "I certainly didn't."

Cassie shrugged. "Well, I passed his little test. It won't convince him, but it should at least give him pause. Maybe in the end that'll be worth something."

Ben heard himself say, "What is the end, Cassie? Can you tell me that?"

She looked away, amusement fading. "I told you I can't see the future."

"But you saw yours. Your fate."

"That's different."

"Is it? Can you tell me your fate isn't tangled up with this investigation?"

Her profile was still, expressionless, as she gazed toward the fireplace, and her voice was calm when she said, "I can't tell you anything about my fate."

"Why not?"

"Because it's mine. Because telling you could somehow be the spur to make it all happen just as I saw it."

"And what if not telling me is the spur? Can you be sure it isn't?"

"No."

"Then—"

"I had to make a choice, Ben. Act in any way to try to change what I saw, or not act. I acted. I ran three thousand miles. And in running, in acting to try to change what had to be, I put myself right back into the kind of situation I was running from." She turned her head and looked at him at last, smiling faintly. "I don't think I'll act anymore."

"You acted by agreeing to help us."

"No, that was just one foot following the other. I'm here. Trying to help is the logical, natural thing to do. I'm not trying to change fate. I'm just doing what I have to do."

"You saw your own death, didn't you?"

"No."

He frowned at her. "You're lying to me."

"No, I'm not. I did not see my own death."

"Then what did you—"

"Ben, I don't want to talk about this. It won't do either of us any good. Just . . . stop feeling guilty for pressing me to help, all right?"

"Is it that obvious?"

"To me it is. Can we change the subject now?"

He nodded slowly. "All right. Tell me something. When you took my hand outside a little while ago, were you able to read me?"

"No."

"Then it wasn't because you were tired before."

"No, it wasn't. I can't read you. You have walls."

His gaze was intent. "What does that mean?"

Cassie hesitated. "I'm not so sure you want to talk about this."

"Why wouldn't I?"

"Because . . . it's been my experience that people have walls for a reason. To protect themselves. To keep other people out. To . . . reveal as little of themselves as possible."

"Are you saying these walls exist because I deliberately built them?"

"Deliberately—probably. Consciously, probably not. Ben, I'm not making some kind of an accusation. We all have defense mechanisms." She watched him with a slight frown, aware that she had touched a nerve and uncertain whether to continue. But something in his eyes made her go on. "Most of us learn early to hide things about ourselves, to disguise what others see, and only those closest to us ever realize it. It's human nature. But for some people, hiding or disguising what's there is impossible, for one reason or another. Maybe because the inner pain is too great, or maybe just because the personality is particularly sensitive and empathetic. It feels so much and so deeply that it has no defenses. So the mind, if it's strong enough, builds walls to protect itself."

Cassie shook her head. "Just like the defense mechanisms other people use, the walls usually pass unrecognized, even unnoticed except by those closest to you."

"Unless you happen to meet a psychic," Ben said.

"Psychics look beneath the surface. It's what we do."

"And beneath my surface is a wall."

"That bothers you."

"Shouldn't it?"

Slowly Cassie said, "It's there for a reason, Ben. It was put there for a reason. If and when it's no longer needed, it won't be there anymore."

Ben drew a breath. "I see."

Cassie realized she had not in any way reassured him, but she didn't know what else to say.

"I suppose I should be grateful. If not for my walls, you'd still be avoiding my eyes and doing your best not to touch me."

She nodded. "Probably. Your walls mean I don't have to work so hard to keep my own in place. From my point of view, it's a welcome respite. Nice to be able to talk to someone and not have to worry about listening with the wrong sense. So far, it's just you, Abby—and Max."

"You can't read Abby?"

"No."

"She wouldn't have struck me as the kind of person who'd need walls," he mused.

Cassie smiled. "Which only proves that hers work."

"I guess so." He hesitated, then said reluctantly, "I should probably go and let you get back to your sorting."

Old and solitary instincts prompted Cassie to agree

that he should leave, but newer urges got in the way. His eyes were attentive, and that restlessness was back in his voice, and she didn't have to read his mind to know that he did not want to leave her just yet.

She wondered when it had gotten hard to breathe, and was vaguely surprised her voice sounded normal when she said, "If you don't have other plans, I fixed a huge pot of soup yesterday, far too much for Max and me. You could stay awhile, help us finish it."

In the momentary silence between them, they could hear the whine of the wind as it built outside, and a sudden quiet rattle against the windowpanes announced the arrival of sleet.

"It sounds like a perfect night for soup," Ben said. "What can I do to help?"

He moved very carefully, wary of the dog's keen ears even with the noise of the building storm. Caution told him to stay back, but he wanted to get closer, close enough to see inside.

So cozy in there. A nice fire in the fireplace. Lights and the appetizing aroma of good food making the kitchen warm and snug. Quiet voices that were comfortable with each other and yet aware, the edges of their words blurred with longing.

They were oblivious of his watching eyes.

He stood outside, his collar turned up and hat pulled low to protect his face from the stinging sleet. It was cold. His feet were cold. But he remained where he was for a long time, watching.

She was protected.

Not that it mattered.

. . . .

"Why didn't you tell me before now?" Matt demanded.

Abby shrugged. "Because I didn't think you'd take it seriously."

"Until a killer started butchering women?"

She winced but nodded.

Matt shoved his plate back and made a rough sound. "You should have told me, dammit."

"So you could do what? A week ago you would have scoffed, told me I was foolish for letting some cockeyed prediction bother me. Since then, what would you have done? Told me to get security installed, get a dog, be careful—all of which I've done."

Matt glanced at the big red dog sprawled near Abby's side of the kitchen table and could hardly help but say, "I wouldn't have told you to get a dog. At least, not one so attached to you."

She smiled. "I like my males possessive. But don't worry. I've had a talk with Bryce. He won't try to get between us in bed again."

Matt wasn't at all sure that "having a talk" with a dog could possibly do much good, and once more turned a jaundiced eye toward the Irish setter. "Yeah, right. Bryce. What kind of name is that for a dog?"

"Blame his former owners, not me."

The beautiful dog lifted his head and looked at each of them briefly, tail thumping against the floor, then stretched out again with a gusty sigh.

Matt returned his gaze to Abby. "He'd damned well better protect you, is all I've got to say."

"I'm sure he'll do his best," she replied, rising to carry her plate to the sink.

Matt followed suit with his own. "You could move in with me. My place has better security—and I'd be there with you every night."

"Not until the divorce is final, Matt."

"What would a few weeks matter?"

"I told you. I want to wait and see how Gary reacts when the divorce is final."

"And what if he reacts violently? Honey, the town's like a powder keg, everybody's tense and jumpy. Gary may not need much to push him over the edge."

She managed a smile. "That's exactly why I don't intend to push him until I absolutely have to."

"And if I have to, I'll lock his ass up in my jail until he learns how to be reasonable."

"And the hell with due process?"

"You could file charges against him."

"No. No, I won't do that. Not unless he forces me to."

Matt put his hands on her shoulders and turned her to face him. "Abby, I know you say Gary hit you just that once, the night you told him to get out, but I've always been sure you weren't telling me everything."

Her gaze was fixed on his loosened tie. "I told you the truth about that night."

"About that night, yes. But not the truth about it being the first time he hit you."

Despite her best efforts, Abby felt her eyes sting as they filled with tears. Shame crawled inside her. She hadn't wanted Matt to know what a weak creature she was.

"Honey . . ." He gently tipped her chin up so she'd look at him. "You don't have to tell me about it until you're ready. But I want you to know something. Nobody has to tell me what kind of guts it took for you to throw him out. And nobody has to tell me how scared you were when you did it."

Abby blinked back the tears. "I can't talk about him to you, Matt. I just can't."

"Okay. Okay, sweetheart." He pulled her into his arms and kissed her. The dog didn't growl in protest this

time, so things were definitely improving on that end. But
Abby was just a bit too tense in his arms, and the embers
of rage glowed deep inside Matt. Given the chance, he
knew he'd beat Gary Montgomery to a bloody pulp.

"I could stay here tonight," he offered huskily.

"No, you couldn't. Not all night." But her arms
slid up around his neck, and her body was relaxing, soft-
ening against his. "For a while though. You can stay for
a while."

And it seemed her talk with Bryce had done some good
after all. The dog didn't even follow them to the bedroom.

It was still well before midnight when Matt reluctantly
pulled himself from Abby's bed and dressed. She got up
as well, because she wasn't yet ready for sleep and she
needed to reset the security system behind him. She didn't
bother to dress, just pulled on a robe and belted it tightly,
then walked him to the front door.

"Look how much it's snowed. Be careful driving
home," she told him.

"I will. And you be careful, especially later, when you
let the dog out," Matt told her.

"I will, don't worry."

He kissed her a last time, then left, waiting on the
front porch until he heard her throw the dead bolt.

Abby went back into the kitchen. "You're a good
boy," she told Bryce, who was still lying patiently near
the table. "Just let me finish cleaning up in here, and I'll
take you out one last time tonight."

Like any housebroken dog, Bryce recognized the word
"out" and sat up eagerly. But he was a very patient dog
and whined only once while she finished cleaning up
from supper.

"All right, let's go." She decided to take him through

the back door so that he could run free in her fenced yard; that way, she didn't have to get dressed and could wait on the porch for him until he was ready to come in.

With the dog at her side, she went to the back door and put the security system in a standby mode, then unlocked the door and pulled it open.

She was barely able to grab Bryce by the collar, when he lunged with a deep-throated snarl at the man standing on the top step.

"Gary," she said.

TEN

"All I know is what the sheriff and Judge Ryan said in the paper," Hannah Payne told her boyfriend worriedly as they sat in the kitchen drinking coffee and finishing the last of the muffins she'd fixed earlier. Joe was about to leave for his third-shift job at the plant, and she was up because he was about to leave her alone in the house they shared.

"Baby, he just wants to scare you girls into being careful, that's all," Joe said patiently. "And he's right. But s'long as you *are* careful and don't go anyplace by yourself, you'll be fine. I checked all the doors and windows, locked everything up tight. You've got a dependable car, a cell phone, a pistol in the nightstand drawer, and Beason."

Half asleep under the kitchen table, the big mongrel thumped his tail against the floor in a brief response.

"I know, but—"

"Take him with you when you leave the house, and be sure you drive with all the doors locked. Don't open the doors here to anyone but me or your sister. Let the machine screen all the calls, and don't pick up if you don't know who it is." He smiled at her. "Just be careful, Hannah. If you're really scared, I'll take you and Beason over to your sister's every night when I leave for work, and you can stay with them till morning."

"No, I don't want to do that. You know we always end up in a fuss over something stupid if we spend too much time together. I'll be okay here with Beason."

"You sure?" He watched her intently. "I don't know if I can, but if you want I'll try to get some time off maybe next week. We could drive up into the mountains. Unless they catch this bastard before then."

"Well, let's wait and see."

"I need to go ahead and put in for the time."

Hannah considered, then nodded. "I think I'd like to get out of town for a while. Even if they do catch him."

"Okay, I'll see if personnel can schedule me off for a few days. Just stop worrying, baby, okay?"

"I'll try. But I need to get groceries tomorrow morning," she said.

"I'll be home by eight-thirty. I'll take you."

"You need to sleep."

"I can sleep later. Now, come on—and lock the door behind me."

Hannah went with him to the front door of their small house and kissed him good-bye, perhaps clinging a bit more than was her habit. "Drive carefully. It's still snowing."

"I will, don't worry." Joe patted her on the bottom and whispered a lewd suggestion in her ear, which made her smile and remind him they didn't have time and he was going to be late for work. He grinned and winked at her.

And then he was gone.

Hannah locked the door behind him and checked the locks twice. She took Beason with her when she finally went to bed, even though he was supposed to stay in his bed in the living room.

She turned on the TV and watched a very old movie just so she wouldn't have to listen to the thick silence of the snowy night.

"Gary," Abby said.

He kept his gaze on the dog and didn't venture to cross the threshold. "Where the hell did you get that?" he demanded.

Abby was about to answer him, when it occurred to her that she didn't have to. "Gary, what are you doing here? It's nearly midnight." She made no attempt to quiet the tense, growling dog at her side.

Gary tore his gaze from the dog and smiled at her. It was the charming smile she had fallen for as an eighteen-year-old girl too young and inexperienced to worry about his brooding silences and bursts of jealous rage. He had been a strikingly handsome man then; at forty, he was thickening—around the middle and in his features. Too many years of indulging his temper and his appetites had left their mark.

"I just came to see you, Abby. What's wrong with that?"

She had been terrified, and fought not to let him see her overwhelming relief. He didn't know about Matt, at least not yet. If he had, he wouldn't have been able to keep quiet about it; in Gary, jealousy was immediate and unmistakable.

Abby drew a breath and kept her voice even and without emotion. "Gary, it's late, the weather's lousy, and I'm tired. And if that isn't enough, you must remember what Judge Ryan told you. You don't live here anymore, and if you keep showing up here unannounced, I'll get a restraining order. You don't want me to do that, do you? Talk about our business in court for everybody to know?"

It was the only real leverage she had against him, and she used it cautiously so as not to use it up. Gary was a vice president at one of the local businesses, a real estate development company that was highly respected and very prominent in town, and his reputation meant a great deal to him. A divorce was one thing; a divorce from a wife claiming physical and emotional abuse during a thirteen-year marriage was something else entirely.

She had gone to Ben Ryan the day after she'd ordered Gary—at the point of his own gun—to leave. He had listened to her story, the whole sad and messy story Matt still didn't know, and had given her both genuine compassion and excellent legal advice. Even more, he had paid Gary a discreet visit and had made it very plain to her husband that he could either quietly agree to an uncontested divorce, or find himself charged with assault and battery and divorced on the grounds of extreme cruelty.

In the months since then, Gary had been relatively co-operative, though at first prone to show up at the house from time to time. When she had gotten involved with Matt only a few months after her separation, Abby had grown fearful that her volatile husband would appear at just the wrong moment; combine Gary's violent jealousy with Matt's fierce protectiveness and the meeting could only end in tragedy.

Once again she had gone to Ben, though this time withholding the relevant fact of her involvement with another man. And once again he had visited Gary, this time to explain that unsolicited visits would not be tolerated.

Gary had been very quiet since then.

Too quiet.

Now he scowled at her. "I suppose you'll go running to Ryan again, just because I wanted to see you. It's a sad thing when a man can't talk to his own wife, Abby."

Bryce's growls grew louder as he either sensed her growing tension or heard the menace in Gary's voice.

Abby allowed the dog's growls to fill the silence for a moment, then said, "Gary, our divorce will be final in just about three weeks. I am not your wife, not anymore. There's nothing you have to say to me that I'm the least bit interested in hearing. Except good-bye. Please close the gate as you leave."

His scowl intensified, but his voice was low, almost gentle. "You really shouldn't talk to me like that, Abby. Until those final papers are signed, you're still my wife. And a wife should never say such things to her husband. Not if she knows what's good for her."

Abby felt an all-too-familiar chill of fear and fought to keep him from seeing how easily he could still manipulate her emotions. "In thirty seconds I'm going to let go of this dog. From the sound of him, I don't think he'll need any encouragement at all to take a few pieces out of you. And while he's doing it, I'll be calling the sheriff."

Maybe he remembered that shotgun she had pointed at him on his last night in this house, or maybe Gary simply recognized that Abby was not going to back down this time. In any case, he was the one who retreated, slowly, down the steps.

"And Gary?"

He looked at her, silent, face hard.

"Just so you know—if anything happens to this dog, like poison, for instance, or a stray shot from some anonymous hunter's gun, or even a car that doesn't stop, I'm going to give your name to the sheriff."

His expression darkened just a bit, proving to Abby

that she did indeed know her husband. Then he swore beneath his breath and stalked away. She heard the gate open, and then close with a loud click.

Abby stood stiffly, listening until she heard a car start up nearby, then the crunch of tires on the snowy street and the engine fading into the distance.

Then she slumped against the doorjamb.

She really needed to get a padlock for the gate, a strong one. And the security company had recommended shrubbery lights and a post lamp at the front walkway, so that no one could approach the house at night unseen. Burglars, they'd said, tended to avoid houses with good perimeter lighting.

She wondered if violent ex-husbands would.

Bryce was whimpering softly, obviously disturbed. Abby managed to get hold of herself enough to take him out onto the porch. But the dog refused to move more than a few feet away from her, lifting his leg against the nearest bush and returning quickly to her. Maybe it was the cold or the snow still drifting lazily downward that made him disinclined to linger. Or maybe he simply knew that he needed to remain close.

Abby brought him back inside and locked the door, then reset the security system.

"Tomorrow," she told the dog as she dried his feet and brushed a bit of snow from his glossy red coat, "we're calling the security company and getting those lights put in. And we'll get a padlock for the back gate."

Her voice was calm, but her heart still thudded, and that horrible cold knot of anxiety that Gary always created lay huge and heavy in the pit of her stomach.

She was afraid. She hated to be afraid.

"I don't want to scare you, Abby. But you have to be careful. I saw a possible future for you, and it isn't good.

*There's a chance . . . I saw him kill you, Abby. I couldn't
see his face, and I don't know who he is, but he was enraged, cursing, and his hands were on your throat."*

"What? What are you saying?"

*"I'm sorry, I'm so sorry. You have to be careful. He's a
madman, sick in his mind, and he'll kill you unless—"*

"Unless?"

*"The future is not static, Abby. Even prophecies are
not always what the seer interprets them to be."*

That had been Alexandra Melton's warning, and all
she would say. Since Abby had only a few days earlier
thrown her abusive husband out of the house, she had
been half convinced it had been her own fear and anxiety
the older woman sensed, that the "prophecy" had arisen
from that.

Still, she had continued to be wary, to take care. Given
Gary's propensity toward violence, it had been obvious
to her that if Alexandra had indeed seen a future event,
the madman in her vision would certainly be him.

Until, as Matt had baldly stated, a killer had begun
butchering women. Now she had to be wary, not only of
her ex-husband, but of virtually every other man as well.

They were certainly not reassuring thoughts that followed Abby to bed that night. And when Bryce looked at
her with pleading eyes, she allowed the big dog to stretch
out happily beside her.

She kept her hand on him all night.

FEBRUARY 25, 1999

Cassie woke in the morning with a sense of expectancy.
She lay in bed for some minutes, thinking, aware from
the brightness of the room that it had snowed consider-

ably more during the night, but in no hurry to get up and look. Her sleep had been unusually restful, dreamless as far as she remembered, and she felt better than she had in a long, long time.

The evening with Ben had been surprising. As he had noted, she was able to relax her guard in his company, yet even as her "extra" senses lay peacefully dormant, the other five had awakened with a vengeance. She had been hyper-aware of him, of his voice, his movements and gestures, his smiles.

Especially his smiles.

And oddly aware of *his* awareness. She found that strange because it was something completely new for her. Always before, either she could read a man—such as the sheriff—or she could not. If she could not, it meant he was a closed book to her, revealing nothing of himself that was not visible.

Perhaps because of the violent male minds she had routinely dipped into her entire adult life, Cassie had seldom felt more than a fleeting interest in any man personally. And even when the natural urges and drives of a healthy young female body had presented themselves, she'd had little difficulty in pushing them from her consciousness.

When one's only experience of sex lay in horrible mental images of unspeakable violence and death accompanied by terror and agony, it was virtually reflexive to completely avoid even the possibility of becoming involved with any man.

So Cassie knew herself to be dangerously isolated and inexperienced when it came to saner human emotions, and ridiculously ignorant about the physical side of a normal male-female relationship.

Ben was attracted to her, she was sure of it. She knew

she was attracted to him. Instincts she hardly understood told her that the attraction was strong and intensifying, and that it was only a matter of time before . . .

Before what? Before they ended up in bed together? Before they fell in love? Before he swept her off her feet and into some absurd emotional fairy tale she hadn't believed in since she was eight and possibly not even then?

Cassie threw back the covers as she sat up, her earlier sense of happy expectancy deflated. She was, she told herself, being an absolute idiot. For the first time in her adult life, she had been thrown into the company of a handsome, sexy man whose mind was closed to her and who had shown her what was undoubtedly only ordinarily polite attention, and her imagination was running away with her.

Ben needed her to help catch a madman threatening his town, and that was the only reason he needed her. His devotion to this town and its people was strong, his abhorrence of insane killers even stronger, and in her abilities lay possible tools for him to use to protect the former and destroy the latter.

That was all.

Having reached that conclusion, Cassie tried to stop thinking about it. About him. She got up and dressed, then put the coffee on, got her boots from the laundry room, and took Max out for his morning run.

It had snowed about four inches, not so much that it made walking difficult but just enough to cover the winter-flattened grass of the fields with a blanket of pristine white. The bare limbs of the hardwood trees were frosted with a thin layer, while the pines so common in the state bore the weight of snow on drooping boughs that appeared to slump in weariness.

Cassie watched Max dash around happily, then lifted her gaze to the mountains. Ryan's Bluff was nestled in a valley high up against a shoulder of the Appalachians; normally the view of the mountains was pleasant and often a bit hazy, but today the dull green and brown was dusted with snow and the cold, clear air made the hulking shapes seem to loom nearer than they actually were.

As she stared up at them, Cassie's smile of pleasure faded. For the first time, they felt threatening, brooding down on the valley and the town with an almost malevolent stare.

Watching her.

Just as she had in Ivy Jameson's kitchen, she felt a pressure in or on her chest, at first barely noticeable but intensifying slowly. The chill of the ground seemed to sweep upward from her boots in a wave that left behind it cold flesh and quivering muscles.

The crisp white landscape surrounding her took on a dingy gray hue, as though a fog had moved in, and a dull, roaring sound grew louder in her ears. She had the sense of something beating up against her like fluttering wings, trying to get in, and the touch of it was as icy as the grave.

The sensations were so unsettling and unfamiliar that Cassie didn't know what to do. She was afraid to lower her guard, to open herself up and let whatever it was touch her mind. But as wary and fearful as she was, experience had taught her that struggling against any attempt to contact her would only prolong the situation—and possibly make it impossible for her to control what happened.

If she *could* control it.

Cassie drew a breath and let it out slowly, watching it turn to mist before her face. Then she closed her eyes and opened herself to whatever it was that demanded her attention.

·   ·   ·   ·

Ben tossed the plastic evidence bag onto Sheriff Dunbar's desk and said, "Cassie may not mind, but I really don't appreciate your sense of humor, Matt."

"Excuse me?" Matt was wonderfully polite.

"Don't play innocent, it's not your best face. That scrap of cloth is from your old Boy Scout uniform."

"So she got that, huh?" Matt said as Ben sat down in his visitor's chair.

"She got it. Said the cloth was only evidence of your sense of humor—which she had doubted until then."

Matt smiled, but then quickly frowned.

"She said it wouldn't convince you." Ben was watching him. "But that it might at least give you pause. For Christ's sake, Matt, what's it going to take?"

Matt ignored the question. "Following up on the coins hasn't given us squat. For one thing, all the collectors we've talked to so far have been middle-aged or older. All apparently happily married with kids. And not so much as a traffic ticket among them."

"And so nowhere near the profile."

"If I accept the profile, yes."

"Do you? And will you finally admit we have a serial killer?"

Matt hesitated. "I may be stubborn, but I'm no fool, Ben. The only real connection between the three victims is their sex and race—and the fact that we can't find, in any of their pasts, an enemy angry enough or with any other kind of motive to kill any of them. Which means it's looking more and more likely all three were killed by a stranger, or at least by someone they hardly knew."

"Which points to a serial killer."

"I don't see any other option, goddammit." Matt sighed explosively. "They used to call them stranger killings, did you know that? Before somebody coined the term 'serial killer.' The most difficult kind of murder to solve because the killer has no tangible connection with his victim."

Ben nodded. "I've been doing some reading on the subject, especially since Ivy and Jill were killed. Sounds like you have as well."

"For all the good it's done me. All I end up with is that pathetically thin profile your damned psychic offered after Becky was killed. White male between twenty-four and thirty-two, probably single and unlikely to be involved with a woman, probably from an abusive background with at least one domineering parent, probably with sexual problems. Hell, I *probably* speak to the guy when I pass him on the streets!"

Ben could understand the sheriff's frustration, because he shared it.

"Worst of all," Matt said gloomily, "yesterday I heard at least three people mention the phrase 'serial killer,' and once that spreads, things are going to get crazy around here very fast. Say we've got a murderer running around and people get upset. Say it's a serial killer and they go nuts. It's like yelling *Shark!* at the beach."

"Most of the women seem to be taking care, at least we've got that," Ben offered. "I don't think I've seen one walking alone all week."

Matt grunted. "It's not much to brag about, Ben. The bald truth is that we're no closer to finding this guy than we were last week when Becky was killed. And you know as well as I do that the longer we go on without a break in the case, the less likely it is that we'll ever get this bastard. We catch killers because they leave evidence we can interpret or they do something stupid. This one has done neither. Maybe he'll kill again and get cocky enough to leave us some helpful evidence. Or maybe three was his limit and now he's just sitting back, watching us stumble around in the dark."

"Cassie thinks he isn't finished yet."

"Oh, shit." The sheriff didn't sound so much disgusted as despairing.

Keeping his tone as neutral as possible, Ben said, "If we're going to take advantage of her abilities, we'd better do it soon. The longer this goes on, the more likely it is that this bastard could catch Cassie in his mind and recognize her as a threat."

Matt stared at him. "You've been reading up on psychics as well as serial killers, haven't you?"

Ben didn't deny it. "The consensus seems to be that some people are abnormally sensitive to the electromagnetic energies of the brain. Through one conduit or another they're able to tap into the energies of other people's minds and read them, interpret them as thoughts and images, and even emotions."

"What do you mean by 'conduit'?" This sounded more like science and a lot less like magic, so Matt was at least inclined to listen.

"What Cassie called 'connections.' Physical touch, either of a person or some object he or she has touched, is most common. It's rare for a psychic to be able to tap into another mind without being in some kind of contact. But for a very few psychics—and I think Cassie's among them—once that contact has occurred and lasted long enough, it seems to leave a sort of map or trail behind, like a faint stream of energy connecting the two minds. After that, it's possible for the psychic to follow the trail virtually at will."

Ben paused. "Unfortunately it's also possible for the target mind to identify that connection—maybe even follow it back to the psychic."

"Even if he isn't psychic?" Matt asked intently.

"There's some speculation that the mind of a serial killer is so abnormal that their thoughts literally 'misfire' so that the electromagnetic energy spills into the brain and causes changes at the molecular level. Just the way a head injury can trigger latent psychic abilities by jolting the brain, so can these misfires. Over a period of time the serial killer can actually become psychic. If that's so, and if this killer is as young as Cassie believes, it may be only a matter of time before he can follow the trail back to her."

"Assuming he doesn't read her name in the paper first," Matt commented dryly.

"That's the other risk, and probably a more likely one. Sooner or later word will get around that Cassie is psychic and that we've been talking to her."

"Won't that look just dandy at the next election."

"If we put this killer behind bars," Ben reminded him, "I doubt very much the voters will care how we did it."

"Maybe. But in the meantime, we'll take a lot of flak. And your psychic will take center stage."

"Stop calling her my psychic. You know her name."

Matt eyed him. "Touchy, aren't you?"

"This is not about me. Are you going to ask Cassie for help or aren't you?"

Rather mildly Matt said, "Yes, I am."

Ben blinked. "And just when did you make up your mind about that?"

Matt fingered the evidence bag still lying on the blotter in front of him. "When you told me she knew this came from my old Boy Scout uniform. Like you said— like *she* said—I'm not convinced. But I can't think of a single trick or deception to explain how she could identify this correctly. Except that she *knew*. Taken with the rest, it's enough to make me want to find out what else she knows."

"It's about time."

"Well, don't just sit there staring at me. Call her."

.   .   .

At first Cassie was aware of nothing except the cold. Far beyond the chill of snow and wind, this cold was absolute. It felt, she imagined, the way the biting touch of deep space would feel against cringing human flesh. She had the hazy idea that even the blood in her veins was slowing, turning to slush as the cold reached it.

The fluttering sensation returned, intensified for a moment, then faded, and she felt something else.

Some*one* else.

Cassie opened her eyes slowly. Around her the air remained gray and foggy. She was distantly aware of the dog barking frantically but didn't see him. She turned her head slowly, toward the woods, where more pines than hardwood trees made the area dark and gloomy with the canopy of their heavy branches.

The people were standing just inside the woods.

There must have been a dozen of them, mostly women but a few men as well, and at least one young boy. They watched her with eyes as profoundly reproachful as those Ivy Jameson had aimed across her kitchen at Cassie days before.

When they started moving slowly toward her, Cassie saw the wounds. One woman's throat gaped open. Another's head was misshapen, a horrible depression of the skull crying mutely of a heavy object and terrible force. One man carried his own bloody arm, while another held his hands protectively over the inches-wide gash that opened him from chest to crotch.

They walked toward her steadily, emerging from the shadows of the woods and into the field with its gray snow and foggy air, and that appalling coldness came off them in waves that were almost visible.

They left no footprints in the snow.

Cassie heard a faint whimpering sound and realized it was coming from her own throat. It was a pathetic substitute for the scream crawling around deeper inside her. She was frozen, immobile. She couldn't run away or back away or even throw up an arm to try to protect herself.

All she could do was stand there and wait for them to reach her.

To touch her.

ELEVEN

When Cassie opened her eyes, she wasn't immediately sure either where she was or how she had gotten there. The tiled ceiling above her looked vaguely familiar, and she eventually identified it as that of the living room of Aunt Alex's house.

Her house.

Odd. The last thing she remembered was . . . getting up that morning. Putting the coffee on—she could smell it—and taking Max out for his run. And then . . .

Nothing.

"So you're back."

She turned her head toward the voice and realized several things simultaneously. She was wrapped from head to foot in a thick blanket, she was lying on the sofa with her head and shoulders propped up with pillows, and she was so incredibly cold that shivers racked her body in waves.

The sheriff stood at the fireplace, in which a fire blazed. He had one shoulder propped against the mantel, his hands in the pockets of his black jacket, and one eye on the big dog that sat only a couple of feet away, staring at him with a distinctly hostile attitude.

"Ben didn't have time to introduce us," Matt told her somewhat dryly as her gaze shifted to the dog. "Good thing this mutt already knew him, though. Otherwise neither of us would have been able to get near you."

"Near me? Where was I?" Her voice sounded a bit shaky, she thought, but considering the chills, that was hardly surprising.

He took her bafflement in stride. "Out in the field north of here, about a hundred yards from the house. Lying unconscious in the snow, with the dog standing guard over you and barking his head off."

"Unconscious?" She thought about that, then shook her head. "Where's Ben?"

"In the kitchen. Either hot chocolate or hot soup, whichever he could fix the quickest." Conversationally Matt went on. "When you didn't answer your phone, Ben was convinced something had happened. So we came out here. Heard the dog as soon as we got out of the car, and spotted you a couple of minutes later. When we got to you and managed to get past the dog, it was obvious you weren't in good shape. You were about two shades paler than the snow, your pulse was faint and about twenty beats a minute, and you were barely breathing. If I hadn't been able to convince Ben you just needed to get warm, you'd be on your way to the hospital right now."

"How did you know that's all I needed?"

Matt frowned slightly. "That's hard to explain. I just looked at you, and I could swear I heard a voice in my head saying the word 'cold' over and over. Your voice."

That didn't surprise Cassie very much. Even though she still didn't remember what had happened, if she had reached out unconsciously for help, it would have been the sheriff, with his unshuttered mind, who would have been able to hear her.

"Thank you, Sheriff," she said.

"Don't mention it. And the name's Matt."

She decided not to question his apparent change of sentiments. Instead, she said to the softly growling dog, "Max, he's a friend. Be a good boy and lie down."

The dog turned his alert attention to her but obediently lay down where he was, his tail thumping the floor.

"Thank you," Matt said. "He was making me nervous."

Before Cassie could respond, Ben came into the room carrying a mug. He wasn't dressed for court; the casual jeans and sweatshirt he wore took years off his age and made him seem unnervingly approachable.

He had obviously heard their voices and wasn't surprised to find her awake, but his face was grim. The gaze he fixed on her was so intense, she had to look away.

He sat down on the sofa alongside her legs and held the mug to her lips. "Drink this, Cassie. It'll help warm you."

It was hot chocolate, and it was either very good or she was very cold and thirsty. She took a couple of swallows, then managed to get her hands out from under the blanket and took the mug from him. It was no accident that she didn't touch him at all in the process.

"Thanks, I can manage."

Ben didn't protest or even comment. He just sat there, one hand on the back of the sofa and the other on his knee, and stared at her without speaking. She knew he was staring, because she could feel it.

Matt said, "So far, she doesn't remember what happened out there."

"What do you remember?" Ben asked her.

Cassie frowned at the mug. The hot liquid was warming both her chilled hands and her shivering body, but she knew it would be a long time before she felt warm again. "I remember going out to take Max for his morning run. I remember walking away from the house, looking up at the mountains. . . ."

"Cassie?"

She caught her breath, her eyes closing as sensations and images stepped out of hiding in her mind. "Oh, God. I remember," she whispered.

"Tell us." Ben's voice was quiet.

It took a moment for Cassie to get her voice under control, and when she finally began speaking, she reported her experience without emotion. It wasn't until she reached the end of the story that her voice broke slightly.

"They were coming toward me and . . . and I couldn't run away. I couldn't even scream. I just kept getting colder and more terrified the closer they got. Then . . . just before they reached me . . . everything went black. I don't remember anything else."

She didn't have to look at Matt to know that he was torn between bafflement and disbelief. She sneaked a glance at Ben and found him still watching her, his expression no less grim than it had been, his eyes unreadable. She had no idea what he was thinking or feeling.

Matt said, "So these people were ghosts?"

"I guess."

"You *guess*?"

Cassie turned her gaze to the sheriff, finding it easier to meet his incredulous eyes than Ben's unfathomable ones. "Yes, I guess. I don't know for sure, because this has never happened to me before." She drew a breath. "Look, my abilities have never allowed me to—to cross beyond death. I'm not a medium. I pick up thoughts from living beings, images from events that are happening or have recently happened. I don't know anything about ghosts."

"What about what you saw at Ivy's house? You said it was possible you could have been seeing what her—what her spirit saw moments after her death."

She hesitated. "I said it was possible, but I didn't believe it. Even though it felt so strange, I was sure what I saw that day came from the memories of a living person who stood there and looked at the murder scene. But . . ."

"But?"

"But . . . some of the things I felt today were similar to what I felt that day, and I don't think they were memories." She shook her head. "I just don't know."

"If what you saw were ghosts," Ben said, "who were they?"

"I didn't recognize any of them. But they'd all been murdered, I think."

Matt swore under his breath. "I thought you said this killer of ours was new at the job. If he's killed a dozen people—"

Cassie hesitated again, then shook her head. "I don't think they were his victims. I mean . . . when I stood in Mrs. Jameson's kitchen, it was as if I tapped into somebody studying the scene. Almost as if I saw it the way he had, from his perspective. The dripping blood so vividly scarlet, the body with its eyes turned toward me in reproach. It was very dramatic, those images, almost as if the whole thing had been . . . staged to elicit a strong emotional response.

"I had that same feeling today, or almost. As if I were seeing something conjured out of some black hell of fantasy. Not the ghosts of victims past, but more like . . . a cast of characters he was imagining."

"The ghosts of victims future?" Ben said.

"Maybe." She didn't look at him. "But it was more like some adolescent psychopath's . . . wet dream." Even as the words left her lips, Cassie felt a flash of pained humor. Virginal she might be, but innocent she definitely was not. A line from an old movie sprang into her head, something about being an unholy mess of a girl.

That was her.

The silence dragged on for just a moment too long, and it was Cassie who broke it by saying calmly, "Now that I think about it, their coming toward me like that, bleeding and carrying parts of themselves, reminds me of a horror movie I saw years ago, about the dead being reanimated. Our killer might well enjoy dreams like that."

"So now you're in his dreams?" Matt demanded.

"Could be. I was up early, maybe he slept late. And dreamed."

"And you tapped in." Ben's voice was still quiet.

Matt made a little sound that was a combination of amusement and despair. "Cassie, you're making it real hard for me to believe any of this."

"I know. I'm sorry." She turned her head and smiled faintly at him. "Nothing's ever as simple as you want it to be."

"Ain't it the truth. Look—we came out here because I was going to ask you to try to tap into this guy again, but obviously—"

"I can try."

Ben said, "You're still shivering."

Cassie didn't look at him. "I'm fine. A little cold, but not even tired."

Matt glanced from her face to Ben's and hesitated. "We can wait and do it tomorrow. Lying out there in the snow didn't do you any good at all, no matter what caused it."

"I'd rather try now." Cassie kept her voice level. "I

need to be in control of this, or at least as much as I can be. I need to be the one instigating the contact."

Matt waited a moment, but when Ben said nothing, agreed with a nod. "I have one of the coins with me. But . . ."

"But?"

"Well, Ben said he thought that eventually you'd be able to tap into this guy at will without touching something he touched. I'm just wondering if you can do that now."

Cassie glanced at Ben, then handed the mug to him, again taking care not to touch him. "Let's try."

"Have you ever done it before?" Ben asked, sounding a bit rough around the edges.

"No. Never tried to before. But since his unconscious mind seems to be reaching me all too easily, I'm curious to find out if I can."

Matt finally left the fireplace, hitching a wing chair closer to the sofa, where he'd have a clear view of Cassie. He pulled out his notebook and a pen with a muttered "Just in case," and then waited expectantly.

Ben set the mug on the coffee table but didn't move from his place beside her on the couch.

Cassie put her hands back under the blanket and closed her eyes, trying to relax, to concentrate. It was difficult with Ben so close. He virtually trapped her on the sofa, but years of practice enabled her to push away even that distracting realization.

Imagery had always helped Cassie to focus on what she was trying to do, though holding some object had tended to speed the process so that her images were swiftly replaced by those seen through the eyes of killers.

This time she conjured the image of a path through a peaceful forest and began following it. Nothing yanked at her. No dark voice whispered to her. As she walked, she looked around, interested but at ease. Whenever she came to a path leading in a different direction, she allowed her instincts to decide whether she should take it, sometimes doing so and other times walking past. The cheerful bird sounds began to fade, and the woods grew darker.

"Cassie?" Ben's voice, curiously distant and hollow in the forest.

"I'm not there yet," she told him, vaguely aware that he was coming with her on the journey.

"Where are you?"

"Following the path." She felt herself frown. "It's an odd path."

"In what way?"

"Dunno, exactly. Just feels strange."

"Tell me."

She sighed a bit impatiently. "The ground is all spongy. And it smells odd, like . . . like inside a musty closet. And the light seems to be coming from two different directions. I'm casting two shadows. Isn't that strange?"

"Do you hear anything?"

"I did hear the birds. But now there's just the music."

"What music?"

"I think it's from a music box. I can't remember the tune though. I should, but I can't."

"All right. If you remember, tell me."

"I will." She walked on, noting without any sense of uneasiness the way the trees around her began to assume twisted shapes like nothing in nature. "Hmm."

"Cassie?"

"What?"

"Where are you?"

She was about to report that she was still in the forest, but before she could she came to a distinct fork in the path. Her instincts had nothing to say about the matter, so Cassie flipped a mental coin and picked the right-hand path.

"Cassie, talk to me."

"The path forked. Two roads diverged in a wood . . . I went right. It was the less-traveled path."

"Cassie, I think it's time to turn around and come back."

She realized he was worried and tried to make her voice reassuring. "I'm all right. And, besides, I'm nearly there."

"What do you see?"

"A door."

"In the middle of the woods?"

Until he asked the question, Cassie hadn't considered it odd. But now she stared at the very large door that appeared to be made of solid oak. "Hmm. I could go around it, but I think I'm supposed to go through it."

"Be careful."

It took some time to find the knob, especially since it wasn't a knob at all but a lever hidden cunningly in the wood. She pressed it with a sense of triumph and then pushed open the door.

The forest was gone. Ahead of her stretched a bare hallway with doors opening off to the left and right. It smelled even more like the inside of a long-forgotten closet. With a sigh she started walking.

"Cassie?"

"There's a hallway with lots of doors. I'm walking straight down the hall. Damn. This is much faster when I have a guide."

"A guide?"

"Something of his. Never mind. I've gone this far, and—" She had opened the door at the end of the long hallway, and the instant she did, the journey was complete. "Oh."

"Cassie? What is it?"

No hallway. No woods. No comforting images. Just

the oppressive weight of him around her, the unnerving awareness of another consciousness surrounding her own, and seeing what he saw because she had no other choice.

"It's him." All traces of reassurance and lightness were stripped from her.

"Where is he?"

"A room. Just a room. Drawn curtains. Lamps. There's a bed. He's sitting on the bed."

"What's he doing, Cassie?"

She had come upon him so suddenly that she was wary of giving away her presence, and so tried to keep very still and quiet. "He's . . . making something."

"What is he making?"

She was silent for a few beats, and then her breath caught in her throat. "It's a piece of wire with a wooden handle on each end. He's making a garrote."

"Are you sure?"

"Very sure. I've . . . seen one before."

"All right. Can you look around, Cassie? Can you tell us more?"

"I can only see what he sees, and he's looking at his hands, watching them . . . caress the weapon. He likes it."

"Look at his hands. Study them. What can you tell us about them?"

"Young. Strong. No scars except . . . the inside of each wrist. He bites his nails, but they're clean. Nothing else."

"Do you know what he's thinking?"

"I'm afraid to listen."

"You have to," a new voice ordered.

"Matt, stay out of this! Cassie, don't listen to him unless you're sure you can do it safely."

"I think I can hide from him. But . . ."

"But what?"

She felt forlorn. "Nothing. I'll listen."

"Be *careful*."

Cassie made herself very small and very still, and cautiously listened. At first the racket of his thoughts was like static on a radio, crackling painfully in her mind, but slowly the snapping and popping faded as she was able to sift through all the background noise.

"He's . . . thinking about what he's going to do . . . to her."

"To who? Who is he thinking about, Cassie?"

"He's— There's no identity. Just *her*. That's the way he thinks of her. *She* is going to be sorry. *She* is going to be so surprised. *She* . . . is going to die for a long time."

"Shit."

"*Matt*. Cassie, is he thinking anything else that might help us? About a place or a particular day?"

"Just . . . soon. He's eager to . . . to do it. And this time he wants his hands on her when she dies. That's why the garrote. He wants to feel her . . . Oh, *Christ*—"

Cassie crept from his mind as fast as she dared, and once she was out, the hallway and the forest path sped by in a blur. And then she was back inside herself. Her body felt cold and queasy and much more tired than it had before, but at least she was back.

"Cassie?"

She opened her eyes slowly and looked at Ben. He was unusually pale, she realized. Had her horror sounded as overwhelming as it had felt?

"I'm sorry." Her voice sounded damnably weak, but there was nothing she could do about it. "I had to . . . I couldn't stay there."

It was Matt who asked, "What was he thinking? What was it you couldn't bear to hear?"

She drew a breath and tried to hold her voice steady.

"This one he means to . . . to rape. He wants to be inside her when she dies."

Ben made a rough sound, but Cassie kept her gaze on the sheriff.

Matt's face was grim. "But you have no idea who it is he'll go after?"

"No. I think he's already picked her though. The sense of anticipation was strong. It was like the feeling I got the first time, when he was watching Becky. I'm sorry, Matt. Maybe if I'd been able to stay with him, he would have thought about what she looked like, or where she was when he watched her. I could try again—"

"No." Ben's voice was level. "Not now. You might not have been tired before, but you're exhausted now. And you're still shivering."

Cassie still refused to look at him. "I didn't give you anything helpful. I have to try again, and soon, or else he'll kill that poor girl—and God knows how many others."

"Killing yourself won't help us."

"I know my own limits. And I'm stronger than I look."

"Are you?"

"Yes."

The sheriff's gaze had been shifting from one to the other as they spoke, but when Ben didn't respond to her last flat statement, Matt said, "If we're lucky, a few hours won't make a difference. Why don't you get some rest, and we'll try again later this afternoon? The stronger you are, the better our chances of learning something useful. Right?"

Cassie wasn't an idiot. "Yes. All right."

Ben said, "Promise you won't try on your own. Without a lifeline."

Cassie wanted to point out that most of her contact with the killer had taken place without benefit of a lifeline, but something in Ben's voice warned her he wouldn't be happy with that reminder. "All right."

"Promise."

"I just did."

Ben drew an audible breath, then said, "Matt, would you give us a minute, please?"

"Sure. I'll wait in the car."

Cassie watched the sheriff leave the room. She listened to the front door close quietly behind him. And when the silence had dragged on too long, she finally looked at Ben.

"What's going on?" he asked quietly.

"What do you mean?" Her voice sounded evasive even to her.

Ben frowned. "You want a list? All right. Last night you were perfectly comfortable with me, today you are obviously not. You don't want to meet my eyes. You don't want to touch me. You're a million miles away. Cassie, I don't have to be psychic to know something's changed. What is it?"

For just an instant Cassie was tempted to tell him the truth. *I was mooning over you like a silly schoolgirl and now I've stopped, that's all.* But even though it was her nature to be honest, she found herself unable to tell him that.

Instead, she heard herself say coolly, "Nothing's changed, Ben."

"And last night?"

She wasn't entirely sure what he was asking but answered anyway. "I think they call that the quiet before the storm." She shrugged, conscious once again that she was wrapped in a blanket, virtually immobile. And he was too close. It made her feel restless. And it made her talk too much. "For a little while, I . . . forgot about that madman out there. I forgot about responsibilities and keeping my guard up and—and the necessity of being alone."

"Who says being alone is a necessity?"

"It is. For me it is. Always has been." She wanted to keep it light, make it casual, but knew she sounded just plain miserable when she added, "Oh, just go away, Ben. Please."

He leaned toward her suddenly, one hand lifting to touch her face. "Don't ask me to do that, Cassie."

She went utterly still, staring up at him. His face was somehow different, as though some part of him she'd never seen lay exposed on the surface. She didn't know what it was she saw, but it stirred something in her that had never been awakened before.

"What is it about you?" he murmured, obviously more to himself than to her. "So guarded and wary, so aloof and afraid to be touched. Yet I can't help wanting to touch you. Needing to. Maybe you can't read my mind, but I can't get you out of it, Cassie."

His fingers traced the line of her brow and jaw, his thumb brushing across her cheekbone, and when her body shivered in reaction, Cassie understood that one of them was playing with fire.

"You . . . really should go," she managed to say unsteadily.

"I know." Ben's hand now cupped her cheek, his thumb rubbing slowly back and forth across her lips and his eyes intently following the movements. "Believe me, I know. I know the timing's lousy, that it'll take all your emotional energy to do what we're asking you to do. I know you're tired right now. I even know I'll probably make you a lousy lover, given my track record. I know all the logical, practical reasons I should go away and leave you alone."

"But?" She was surprised the word emerged coherently. His husky voice was as much a caress as the touch of his fingers and her body, which had felt so cold only moments before, now seemed feverish.

"But I'm having a hard time convincing myself to be sensible about it." His mouth brushed hers very lightly and then retreated. "I want you, Cassie. I didn't plan on this, and God knows how it'll end, but I want you. And . . . I have this feeling that if I let go of you now, I'll lose you for good."

"I'm . . . not going anywhere."

"You've been trying to hold me off, shut me out. Do you think I can't feel it?"

Cassie resisted the urge to press her face against his caressing hand. "For your sake as much as mine. Trust me, Ben, I'm the one who'd make a lousy lover. I wouldn't be good for you. I wouldn't be good for any man."

"Maybe I'm willing to risk it."

"Maybe I'm not."

His eyes were heavy-lidded and darkened, and so intense they seemed to pull at her. "Somehow, I don't think either of us has a choice."

There was something almost reluctant in his voice, and it made her say, "You don't know me."

"I know all I need to know."

"No, you don't. You don't know, Ben. I have too much baggage. Too many monsters dragging at my heels." She swallowed hard. "I can't—"

His mouth covered hers, warm and hard and so unexpectedly familiar that she was helpless to prevent her own instant response.

Hardly aware of moving, Cassie got her arms out from under the blanket and reached up to him. One of her hands pressed against his chest as though holding him off, but the other slid from his shoulder to the nape of his neck. Her touch was tentative but not shy, and when he lifted his head she made a sound of disappointment.

"Can't you?" he murmured.

"You aren't playing fair," she told him, bemused by the husky sound of her own voice.

"I'm not playing. Cassie, listen to me. For just a minute, forget about the rotten timing. Forget about that maniac out there. Forget about everything except the two people in this room."

That was not very hard to do, she thought. In fact, it was frighteningly easy. "All right."

"Tell me you don't want me."

She drew a breath and let it out slowly. "You know damned well I can't do that."

He smiled. "Good. Then we go on from there."

Go on where? But she didn't ask what she suspected was an unanswerable question. Instead, she said, "Do you have any idea how crazy this is?"

"You'd be surprised." He kissed her, briefly but not lightly, then eased away from her. "I'd better go and let you get some rest, especially if Matt and I are coming back in a few hours."

She'd forgotten about that. She'd also forgotten that the sheriff waited outside, presumably in his cruiser with the engine running. Remembering made her protest die in her throat. "Right. Right."

Ben seemed a little amused, but his eyes were still darkened and his face still bore that oddly naked look she couldn't quite define. "I'll call before we come out here, but I'm guessing it'll be around four or five."

"Okay. I'll be here."

He took a step away but then hesitated. "Remember your promise. Don't try to reach this guy without a lifeline."

"No, I won't."

He didn't say good-bye. She watched him until he was out of sight and listened to the front door open and close. Then she just lay there on the couch, no longer cold or even tired, but uneasily aware that she had just turned an unexpected corner.

And had no idea what was waiting for her.

Matt folded up his newspaper when Ben got into the cruiser and lost no time turning the vehicle around and pointing it back toward town. Neither spoke until Cassie's snowy driveway lay behind them, and then the conversation was brief.

"If you want my advice—" Matt began.

"I don't."

The sheriff glanced at his friend, then murmured, "Okay. Then I'll just drive."

TWELVE

The Plantation Inn was not bad as motels went, though Bishop could have done without the plastic palms that seemed to sprout from every corner. Still, his room was clean and comfortable, limited room service was available—when the restaurant next door closed, you were on your own—and the desk clerk had been reassuringly knowledgeable when he had asked her about fax lines and data ports.

Accustomed to living out of a suitcase, he didn't bother to unpack his clothing, but he did get his laptop out and set it up on the fair-sized desk by the window, where the promised data port was available. By the time room service delivered his lunch, he had logged on and downloaded his mail and faxes from the office, as well as tapped into a North Carolina database that gave him access to past and current issues of virtually all publications from the area.

He ate a club sandwich while reading relevant articles and editorials from the previous week's editions of the local paper, then checked several larger newspapers throughout the state. He found that recent news from Ryan's Bluff was not mentioned anywhere else.

So. The sheriff had his town buttoned up tightly. At least for now.

Instead of speculating on that interesting fact, Bishop reread the information he had gathered earlier concerning Alexandra Melton. There was little enough of it, just deed and title information on her property, and the major points of her will. It did not appear that she had involved herself in any meaningful sense in town affairs, since her name made the local newspaper only when she died.

But Bishop's information went back further than Alexandra Melton's life in Ryan's Bluff. In fact, it went back more than thirty years. In his file were a number of detailed reports, including several from various West Coast hospitals and at least half a dozen from law enforcement organizations. He just glanced over those, since the information was familiar to him, but spent some minutes looking at a detailed family tree going back nearly two hundred years.

Except for husbands, the tree was almost entirely female. There had been few sons born to this line of women for generations, and seldom more than one daughter.

Cassie Neill's name occupied one of only two boxes representing the current and only surviving generation.

After studying the tree for a time, Bishop closed the file and shut down his computer. He called room service to come get his tray, changed into the very casual clothing that was suitable for exploration, and left the motel.

He drove to the downtown area, since the Plantation Inn was some miles away. Snowplows had been at work to scrape aside the scant few inches of snow, even though the temperature had risen enough to begin melting it anyway; he avoided the slush in the gutters when he parked his car near the drugstore and got out.

For a few moments Bishop stood near his car and just looked around. There was a fair amount of activity on this Friday afternoon. Shoppers moved in and out of the stores, the car lot on one end of town seemed to be having some sort of loud and colorful promotion involving the giveaway of a television set, and the two restaurants he could see appeared to be doing brisk business.

But he noticed immediately that no woman walked alone, and that the few children about were kept close to their parents. And that it was quieter than it should have been, with conversations kept low and no audible laughter. Not too many smiling faces, which he knew was unusual in this part of the country. And more than one passerby gave him a distinctly suspicious glance.

He wouldn't have much time, he knew, before somebody official asked him what he was doing in town.

Bishop began strolling down the street, visiting several stores, making small purchases at each, and speaking politely if not affably to the clerks who waited on him. Aware that he had a face designed by fate to make others nervous at the best of times, he made no attempt to ask questions but, rather, listened in on various conversations going on around him. Or at least to those that didn't stop abruptly whenever someone caught sight of him, as they invariably did.

He heard the phrase "serial killer" spoken at least half a dozen times. He also heard several men declare that they were armed and ready should the bastard come after *their* women.

It was a promise that did not appear to reassure those of their women present to hear it.

Bishop ended up in the drugstore, with coffee and a talkative young counterman who offered speculation about the three recent murders with ghoulish fascination. Neither encouraging nor discouraging, Bishop listened, saying only that it seemed like too nice a town to have such goings-on.

Apparently feeling that this placid reaction implied criticism, Mike the counterman was quick to add the information that they also had a witch.

Bishop sipped his coffee. "Really?"

"Yeah. Everybody's talking about her." Mike industriously polished the counter in front of his customer, just in case his boss was watching. "Some say it's her fault, these killings, but I got it from one of the sheriff's deputies straight that she couldn't have done it. With her own hands, I mean. Too little. Besides, I think she had an alibi when Miss Kirkwood was killed."

"If that's so, why would anyone blame her?" Bishop asked mildly.

"Well, because she's a witch." Mike lowered his voice. "Way I heard it, she knew there was going to be a killing and warned the sheriff about it. Judge Ryan too."

"Then why didn't they stop it?"

"Didn't believe her, is what I hear. Well, I mean— would you? But then Becky was killed, so I guess she knew what she was talking about, at least that time. What I want to know is, how's she doing it?"

"You mean—how does ESP work?"

Mike shook his head impatiently. "Naw. I mean, does she have a crystal ball? Some of them tarot cards? Or does she need the blood of a chicken or something like that? Keith Hollifield, over by the plant, he's missing a few chickens just since last week, and he's been putting it around that maybe the witch needs them to see the future."

"Has anyone asked her?" Bishop's ironic tone was lost on the young counterman.

"Not that I know of," Mike replied earnestly. "But I think the sheriff should, don't you?"

"Absolutely." Bishop paid his check for the coffee and left Mike a reasonable tip, then strolled from the drugstore.

A sheriff's deputy lounging against a light post outside straightened, eyed him speculatively, then politely asked if he was a stranger in town.

Out of time.

Smiling faintly, Bishop produced his identification.

The deputy's eyes widened. "Um. You'll be wanting to talk to the sheriff, I expect."

"Eventually," Bishop said. "But not just yet."

Though the temperature hovered just far enough above freezing to begin melting the snow, the picture outside Cassie's kitchen windows was still a winter wonderland when she sat down to a late breakfast. Ben and the sheriff had been gone nearly two hours, but it had taken her some time to rouse herself enough to get up from the sofa. And when she did finally get up, she discovered that she was more tired than she had realized, and still a bit cold.

A hot bath helped warm her, and by the time she apologetically fixed Max's breakfast and something for herself, she was feeling better. Physically at least.

She wasn't sure about emotionally.

Years of experience had taught her not to dwell on the horrific images and thoughts that came to her tele-pathically, so it was easy enough for her to think about the killer with a hard-won degree of detachment. But knowing he had chosen his next target and that he planned new torments for her was not so easy to dismiss from her mind.

Not easy, but entirely necessary in order for her to find some sort of peace. But this time it required more than concentration; it required distracting herself with thoughts that were, in their own way, nearly as emotionally upsetting.

Thoughts about Ben, and about what seemed to be growing between them.

Cassie was still astonished to recall her response to him, and even more surprised by his desire. She didn't know how to explain it, any of it. With what she'd learned of men and the things too many were capable of, she had thought it virtually impossible to contemplate a relationship with this . . . this absurdly dreamy longing. With curiosity and eagerness.

A sexual relationship, she assumed. Ben had made it clear he wanted her, though she was uncertain as to why that would be so. She was no fool—and she had read too many male minds not to know that they simply did not look at her and feel desire. She was too thin, not at all pretty, weighed down with the baggage of nightmarish abilities, and laughably lacking in experience when it came to romantic relationships.

In short, she was no bargain.

And Ben . . . No question that he could get virtually any woman he wanted, and probably always had, despite the walls that kept him distant emotionally. He was handsome, intelligent, sexy, both compassionate and kind. He was an important man in town, a man people looked up to. And he was an elected official, which meant his life was open to public scrutiny.

Something she doubted he had considered.

No, it just didn't make sense. There were myriad reasons that she would be attracted to him, but not a single one to explain his interest in her.

Except maybe as a novelty.

Cassie considered that with all the detachment she could muster. A novelty? Something entirely different from what he was accustomed to and, therefore, of interest? A woman who found his walls a relief when they might well have presented a problem for him in other relationships? She supposed it was possible, but if his attraction sprang from something so insignificant, he surely would have decided to wait until the threat to his town was past.

He must have known she wasn't going to be running off with somebody else in the interim.

Cassie stood at her kitchen window with her coffee and stared out at the pretty, peaceful scene, all too aware that once again her sense of expectancy had vanished.

To Max, who was sticking close, she said, "I can talk myself out of a good mood faster than anyone else I know."

Max thumped his tail against the floor and gazed up at her intently.

"He just feels sorry for me, that's what it is. Or maybe he's just one of those men who gets a charge out of thin, pale women always falling unconscious practically at their feet. Makes them feel extra macho or something. Although I wouldn't have said he needed that."

Max whined, and Cassie reached down to scratch him between the ears.

"I've got to stop being unconscious around him. That's the second time he's carried me, and I missed it again. A woman dreams all her life of being swept up into a man's arms, and when it happens—twice— she's unconscious."

Max licked her hand.

"Thank you," she said dryly. "I appreciate the sympathy. But the truth is . . . I don't know what the truth is. All I know is that I'm about a breath away from making a fool of myself over him. And that scares me to death."

Max nudged her hand firmly, obviously asking for more of the pleasant scratching between his ears. Cassie obliged.

"But you want to know what the really sad thing is? The sad thing is that I don't think being scared is going to stop me. I don't think anything is going to stop me. I think I'm going to make a fool of myself over him."

Whatever Max might have responded, the ringing phone startled them both and cut off Cassie's confidences. She picked up the extension in the kitchen, said hello, and heard the unmistakable gruff voice of her aunt's elderly lawyer.

"Miss Neill?"

"Hello, Mr. McDaniel. More papers to sign?"

"Er—no, Miss Neill. No, probate was wound up quite satisfactorily." Phillip McDaniel cleared his throat. "Miss Neill, would it be convenient for me to come and see you after lunch? It won't take long, but if you could spare me a few minutes, I would greatly appreciate it."

Cassie frowned slightly, although she couldn't have said why. "I could come into town to your office, Mr. McDaniel, if it's important. For you to come all the way out here—"

"I assure you, Miss Neill, I would prefer to come to you. If it's convenient, that is."

"Of course. But what is this about?"

He made several vague noises, then said, "Merely a small matter which—well, I would prefer to discuss it in person, Miss Neill. Shall we say around two-thirty?"

"All right, fine. I'll see you then."

Cassie hung up the phone and looked at Max. "Well, what do you think about that?"

Max moved closer and nudged her hand, asking for more scratching.

Deanna Ramsay hated living in a small town. She hated living so near the mountains. She hated living in the

South. In fact, she pretty much hated her life. Especially now that some maniac was out there stalking women and scaring everybody so much that they'd gone paranoid. Her parents wouldn't let her leave the house without an escort; the principal wouldn't let any of the girls leave school grounds without an escort; deputies were everywhere in town and pounced the instant a body ventured a step or two *away* from the escort. . . .

"I hate my life," she announced in disgust.

Her best friend, Sue Adams, giggled. "Just because Deputy Sanford scolded you and ordered us to wait in the drugstore for Larry!"

Deanna heaved an impatient sigh. "No, not because of him. He's a dork. I hate my life because my life is entirely hateful. Look, if we have to wait in here for my brother to get back, let's at least have a Coke."

They ordered two Cokes from Mike and retired with them to the booth at the back, which was their spot.

"I don't know why you're so upset," Sue said. "At least you have a brother to take you places—and at least he *will*. Both my sisters are still children, I won't have my license for more than another year, and Mama gets hysterical if I even *mention* the *possibility* of going on a date."

"So does my mom. You'd think we were prisoners!"

"Well," Sue said reasonably, "we *are* prisoners. More or less. Neither one of us is sixteen yet, we don't have cars, or jobs *or* boyfriends—"

Deanna glared at her and said in a lofty tone, "Speak for yourself."

"On which point?" Sue demanded.

"Never you mind. Let's just say that if you were half the friend you claim to be, you'd talk my brother into taking us to the mall when he gets here, and then keep him occupied while I . . . run a little errand."

"But we're supposed to go straight back home!"

"And back into prison for the entire weekend, because Larry has to work and you know nobody else will take us anywhere."

"Well, but—"

"Well, but nothing. I'm sick and tired of the whole thing. This has been the most boring week on record. I want to *do* something. What's the use of a day off from school if we have to sit at home all morning and then spend half the afternoon waiting for Larry in the drugstore?"

Sue stared at her. "What are you up to, Dee?"

Deanna shook her head but smiled portentously. "Like I said, I just want to stretch my legs at the mall. But Larry'll never take us if I ask, so you do it."

Sue began to feel apprehensive. "Dee, there's a real killer out there. And nobody knows who he'll go after next."

"Oh, for God's sake, Sue, I'm not going to wander down any dark alleys, or even leave the mall. I'll be right there, practically in your sight, safely inside and surrounded by other people. I just don't want my big brother looking over my shoulder, that's all."

"Who're you meeting?" Sue demanded.

Deanna conjured an innocent face. She'd practiced the expression for a good hour that morning while putting on her makeup. "I'm not meeting anybody."

"I don't believe you."

"Well, pardon me if I don't care." Seeing that she was about to seriously offend her henchwoman, Deanna relented. "Spend the night with me tonight and I'll tell you everything, okay? Just ask Larry to take us to the mall before we go home. Please?"

"Why won't you tell me now?"

"Because. Come on, Sue, you owe me a favor. Didn't I do your history homework last week?"

Sue had an uneasy feeling the two "favors" hardly balanced out but found herself giving in the way she always did with Deanna. "You'll tell me the truth tonight? Swear?"

"I swear."

After a moment Sue gave in. "All right. I just know I'm going to be sorry—but all right."

Deanna smiled blindingly. "You won't be sorry!"

"Judge Ryan?"

Ben was accustomed to being stopped from time to time whenever he was out in public, but today it had taken him double the usual time just to walk from his parking place to the courthouse.

He had made it as far as the third step this time.

Wishing he had taken the back way in, he turned to find one of the more vocal citizens of the town approaching determinedly.

"What can I do for you, Mr. King?" He and Aaron had known each other for twenty years, but Aaron liked titles, insisting they denoted respect. He would have continued calling himself Major after his army service but had discovered to his chagrin that others only found it amusing.

"Judge, is what I've been hearing true?"

"That depends on what you've been hearing." Ben made sure his tone was easy rather than sardonic.

Aaron scowled. "What I've been hearing is that Sheriff Dunbar—and you—have been allowing some woman claiming to be a fortune teller to advise you."

Ben was resigned; it was the fourth time he had heard

some variation of the truth. "And where did you hear that, Mr. King?"

"From at least three different people since yesterday. Is it true, Judge?"

"Not precisely."

"Then what, precisely, is the truth?"

Ben paused a beat, briefly considered how much damage one angry voter with influence could do when election time rolled around again, then consigned the risk to the limbo of things unimportant and unregretted.

"The truth, Mr. King, is that Sheriff Dunbar and I are investigating three particularly vicious murders. We are using all means at our disposal to gather information that might prove helpful in that investigation, as is our job. We are not gazing into crystal balls or reading tarot cards, nor are we talking to anyone who does."

Aaron ignored the denial. "I heard it was Alexandra Melton's niece."

Ben felt a chill. If this man had heard so specific a piece of gossip, then others had as well. Which meant it was only a matter of time before Cassie's identity was common knowledge throughout the town.

"Is it true?" Aaron demanded.

Ben wasn't a politician for nothing. "Is it true she's a fortune teller? Of course not."

Aaron's scowl deepened. "She doesn't claim to be able to see the future?"

"No, she does not."

"But you and the sheriff have been talking to her about these killings?"

"*If* we have, the interviews are part of an ongoing investigation and hardly subject to public discussion, Mr. King. As you, of course, know."

Aaron also respected—to excess, in Ben's opinion—the red tape of a bureaucracy, and so found himself caught between rampant curiosity and the unhappy knowledge that he was in no way part of the official loop of persons involved in the investigation. He drew himself up to his full height—which was a good five inches shorter than Ben's—and said self-righteously, "I have no intention of interfering in the official investigation, Judge."

"I'm glad to hear it."

Aaron wasn't finished. "But if it should come to light that you and the sheriff have allowed yourselves to be deceived by a charlatan into pursuing false leads, placing even more of our women in danger from the resulting delay in apprehending this killer—then, Judge, then I won't hesitate to add my voice to those calling for your resignations."

Ben wasn't tempted to laugh, even though the speech had obviously been rehearsed and was delivered with condescending relish. Aaron King was a pompous windbag, but he had the knack of rallying others around him, and considering the tension of the townspeople, it was likely he could gather quite a mob to demand action if the investigation didn't soon result in an arrest. Especially if there was another murder.

Calmly Ben responded, "And rightly so, Mr. King. If we don't do our jobs, we should step down. But, I assure you, we are doing our jobs. Thank you for your opinion and your interest. I'll pass on both to Sheriff Dunbar."

Faced with courtesy, Aaron could only incline his head in stately acceptance, execute a turn with military precision, and march away—a grand departure somewhat spoiled by the fact that he slipped on a patch of ice in a shady spot on the walkway and nearly fell on his ass.

Ben still wasn't tempted to laugh. In fact, he felt more than a little grim, and not because he feared losing his job.

Cassie was becoming all too visible, and despite

the wild mix of rumor and speculation concerning the extent of her abilities, it would not require confirmation for at least one citizen of the town to view her as a dangerous threat.

And he had more than a job to lose.

Abby probably wouldn't have felt brave enough to leave the house on Friday afternoon, not after Gary's sudden and menacing appearance the night before, if it hadn't been for Bryce. But luckily for her, the dog was not only companionable, he was also well trained.

It was also lucky for her that the snow had closed numerous businesses for the day, including the financial services office where she worked, because otherwise she might have upset her boss by bringing her dog along.

"I'll be much less jumpy by Monday," she told Bryce that afternoon as she backed her car out of the driveway. "We'll have a nice, peaceful weekend, and on Monday the security company will install all the new lights. But right now we have to go out to the mall and get that padlock. And some chew toys so you won't eat any more of my slippers."

The Irish setter sat up like people in the passenger seat beside her and lolled his tongue out in a happy grin. He loved riding in the car.

He wouldn't much like waiting in the car, Abby knew, but the mall didn't allow pets. It would be for only half an hour though, just long enough for her to do her shopping.

The mall was safe enough, certainly.

It was two-thirty on the dot when Phillip McDaniel rang Cassie's doorbell. Since she had expected him to be prompt—he didn't seem to know how to be anything else—Cassie was opening the door while his finger was still on the button.

"Hello, Mr. McDaniel. Come in, please."

"Thank you." He stepped inside, eyed the growling dog at her side, and said, "You can let go of him, Miss Neill. Dogs never bite me. I have no idea why, but there it is." He was a tall and painfully thin man of perhaps seventy, with a snowy goatee and a full head of white hair, and there was an air of dignified elegance about him.

Maybe it was that gentle composure that prevented dogs from attacking. Or maybe it was just because there was so little meat on his bones.

Reluctant to put either theory to the test, Cassie performed the usual introductions, and Max followed them quite happily into the living room.

"Let me take your coat," she said to the lawyer. He was the sort of man who wore a trench coat on chilly days; today it was accompanied by a muffler and kid gloves.

But McDaniel shook his head and gave her a pained look out of grave eyes. "I can stay only a moment, Miss Neill. And, truthfully, you may order me to go when I have explained my errand."

"Good heavens," Cassie said mildly. "Why would I do that, Mr. McDaniel?"

"Because I am guilty of a terrible breach of trust, to say nothing of duty and responsibility."

He said it as though he fully expected to be keelhauled or drawn and quartered for the crime, but since Cassie liked him and since she couldn't imagine him deliberately harming anyone, she didn't hesitate to say, "I'm sure whatever you did was quite unintentional, Mr. McDaniel."

"That hardly absolves me."

"Well, why don't you tell me what it is, and then we can put it behind us."

He drew a sealed envelope from the inside pocket of his coat and handed it to her. "This was given to me by your aunt some months before her death, Miss Neill."

Cassie looked at her name scrawled across the envelope in what she recognized as her aunt's hand, and then looked inquiringly at the lawyer. "And it was somehow forgotten during probate? That's quite all right, Mr. McDaniel. I'm sure it's just a personal letter I probably wouldn't have read until now anyway, so no harm done."

"Indeed, she assured me it was a personal message for you, but . . ." McDaniel shook his head. "I'm afraid there has been harm, Miss Neill, although I don't know—" He drew a breath. "Your aunt gave me the envelope with very specific instructions, and I gave her my word I would obey those instructions."

"Which were?"

"To place the envelope in your hands on the twelfth of February of this year."

Cassie blinked. "I see. That would have been . . . about two weeks ago."

"Hence my failure. Miss Neill, I am so sorry. As you know, your aunt was one of my last clients, taken on at her insistence even though I was on the point of retiring when she came to me and asked that I handle her will and estate planning. In the last year I've been gradually closing out my offices, and I'm afraid your aunt's envelope and the instructions simply got lost in the shuffle." He sighed. "My memory isn't what it once was, and I'm afraid I completely forgot about it."

She knew he was deeply upset by his failure and quickly said, "It could have happened to anyone, Mr. McDaniel. Please don't worry about it. I'm sure my aunt wouldn't be at all upset—it's only a two-week delay, after all. What could that matter?"

"I'm afraid it may matter very much, Miss Neill,

although I can't, of course, know how. Miss Melton assured me that there was nothing of legal significance in the envelope, only a personal message for you, but she was most insistent that it be delivered on the twelfth of February. Not before and not after. The date seemed highly significant to her. And, perhaps, to you."

Cassie eyed him consideringly. "She told you that? That the date would mean something to me?"

"Not precisely." He was uncomfortable. "But I was aware that Miss Melton occasionally—knew things. Her intensity convinced me that her message to you might be in the nature of advice or, even, a warning of some kind."

"I wouldn't have said you were the type of man who'd believe in things like that," Cassie said.

"Normally I'm not. But she—really, Miss Neill, she seemed quite desperate. I'm afraid the message was terribly important to her."

"Well, why don't I—" As Cassie went to open the envelope, McDaniel's outstretched hand stopped her.

"Your aunt wished you to read it when you were alone, Miss Neill. She was quite specific about that instruction."

Cassie didn't know whether to be amused or worried, but the latter emotion was beginning to take precedence. "I see. Well, then that's what I'll do. Did she leave any further instructions?"

"Not with me," McDaniel replied. "I am so sorry, Miss Neill." He began to back away. "I'll let myself out."

Cassie found herself staring at empty space and blinked when the closing of the front door was followed quickly by the sound of a car engine starting. For an older gentleman, he could move when he wanted to.

She sat down on the sofa and stared at the envelope.

"What do you think, Max? Is it a case of better late than never? Or should I throw this into the fire unread?"

Max whuffed softly and thumped his tail against the floor.

"The twelfth of February. Two weeks ago. What was I doing about two weeks—"

What she had been doing was coping with the sudden terrible knowledge that a killer was stalking his first victim in this sleepy little town.

With fingers that had turned numb, Cassie tore open the envelope and unfolded a single sheet of notepaper. The message sprawled across it was brief and to the point.

Cassie,
   Whatever happens, stay away from Ben Ryan. He'll destroy you.
                                        Alex

THIRTEEN

It should have been simple. Cassie had not seen or spoken to her aunt for more than twenty-five years; in fact, she barely remembered her. There had been no birthday or Christmas cards, and not even the notification of her sister's violent death had compelled Alex Melton to contact her niece.

Only after her own death, in the shape of her will and now this message, did Cassie hear from her aunt.

It should have been a simple decision to ignore this "warning."

But it wasn't.

As voices from the dead went, Alex Melton's was as eerie and as terrifying as anything Cassie could have imagined, and as badly as she wanted to, she could not ignore it.

He'll destroy you.

Alex Melton had been desperate that her niece receive this warning, her attorney said—and he was not a man to use such words lightly. She had been desperate enough to leave the warning with very specific instructions that it be delivered on a precise day. The very day that Ben Ryan's name had occurred to Cassie as a possible ally in her attempt to convince Sheriff Dunbar that a killer was about to strike.

If Cassie had received the warning then . . . what? She thought she probably would have reconsidered her idea of going to see him. She had been so wary of getting involved once again in a murder investigation, so reluctant to put herself through it all once again. It would not have taken much to make her withdraw into her quiet, peaceful isolation. Guilty conscience partly absolved because she had, after all, tried to warn the sheriff.

But now?

Two weeks had changed so many things. The killer had struck three times, and she knew he was about to strike again. The sheriff was willing to listen now, maybe even to believe in what she could tell him, and that might make a difference. And she was committed now, determined to try her best to help catch the killer. And there was Ben.

Ben, who wanted her. Ben, who made her feel things she had never felt before and wanted so badly to feel again. Ben, who could touch her without threatening her walls.

He'll destroy you.

Ben destroy her? How?

Someone unfamiliar with psychics and their abilities would have immediately thought of the killer terrorizing this town, and assumed that either Ben was the killer or that her involvement with him would somehow deliver her into the hands of the killer.

But Cassie knew Ben was not the killer. Even more, she knew that her aunt's choice of words was important; if Alex had seen her niece's death, she would have used that word. But she had not.

He'll destroy you.

Not kill her, or cause her to be killed. Destroy her. And in that word lay a wealth of frightening possibilities. Because there were fates worse than death. Much worse.

"I didn't see him," she murmured to Max. "When I saw my fate, I didn't see Ben. He won't be part of that, won't cause it to happen, surely."

What she had seen had been a jumble of images and emotions, leaving her with only the certainty that the abilities she had lived with since childhood would be her doom. That she would, in stealing the shadows of yet another dangerously insane mind, become lost herself in the terrible, hungry darkness of that lunatic consciousness. Lost forever.

Death would be simple—and preferable—by comparison.

He'll destroy you.

. . . destroy you.

. . . destroy . . .

For a long time Cassie sat staring at the note, her eyes skimming the words again and again, her brain trying to take in all the implications. She felt colder than she had that morning. She felt more alone than she had since she had first run to this place looking for peace.

Her aunt had certainly not feared that she would get her heart broken. Rejection by a lover, while destructive, seldom destroyed. And yet, somehow, in some way, Alex had been convinced that unless she stayed away from him, Ben would destroy her.

"Dammit, Alex, why didn't you explain?" she murmured. But even as the words left her lips, Cassie knew the answer. Predicting the future was a tricky business, and more often than not the worst thing a psychic could do was offer explicit details even if she was sure of them.

Precognitive visions tended to be shrouded in symbolism, with interpretation uncertain and conclusions risky. Alex could have *known* with absolute certainty that Ben Ryan had the ability or potential to destroy her niece without being at all sure how that could or would come about.

So the simplest and most direct warning was the safest. Stay away from him. He'll destroy you.

"Too late," Cassie said to her aunt and to herself. "Whatever is meant to happen . . . will happen."

Running three thousand miles hadn't changed that. This warning would not change that.

She turned her head and gazed at the box full of papers that had been sitting in a nearby chair for days now, waiting for her attention. She had avoided the task just as she had avoided reading her aunt's journals. She had kept herself distant from her aunt's personality whenever possible, preferring not to know about the woman who had quarreled so bitterly with her sister that they had never spoken again.

Alex Melton's silence upon being notified of her sister's murder had hurt Cassie deeply.

And yet despite her own unwillingness to remain ignorant of who Alexandra Melton had been, her aunt's personality had refused to remain a mystery, because she had left clues behind and because other people had spoken of her. Evidence such as all the unopened craft kits Alex had bought from Jill, the purchases obviously used as excuses for visits, indicated a surprising shyness. Her warning to Abby, reluctant and troubled, was clear evidence to Cassie both of her aunt's sense of responsibility and her reluctance to meddle in other lives.

There had been other indications of personality during the months Cassie had spent in her aunt's home. From the way she had decorated and the books she had read to her extensive collection of movies on videotape—

a passion Cassie shared—Alex Melton's taste and preferences had gradually seeped into Cassie's awareness.

Yet she still had no idea why her mother and aunt had quarreled. She had no idea if Alex had left her this house and property only because she was the sole survivor of the family or if some other reason had prompted the bequest.

And she had no idea how to interpret a specific and yet enigmatic warning delivered from beyond the grave.

Gazing at the box filled with papers that might hold some vital clue in understanding her aunt's warning, Cassie wondered if her own reluctance to know Alex Melton might prove more costly than she could ever have imagined.

She got up from the sofa, went to the fireplace, and looked down at the note and envelope in her hand. Her hesitation was a brief one. She tossed them into the fire and watched them burn.

Then she got the box filled with her aunt's papers and began trying to understand a life.

"All right," Larry Ramsay said as he escorted the girls into the mall. "We're here." He adopted the long-suffering tone common to put-upon males who would much rather be somewhere else, preferably tinkering with an engine.

"I really appreciate this, Larry," Sue said, not quite batting her eyes.

"No problem," he said politely.

"It's just that I really do need to check about that software program today so I'll have the weekend to work on the project. So I'm really grateful."

Deanna stifled a giggle. Though Larry appeared oblivious—perhaps not unexpectedly since he was ten years older—it was no secret to Deanna that her best friend had a crush on her brother. She was mildly interested on most days but today had her mind most definitely on her own troubles.

"It's okay," Larry said, only his sister hearing the touch of impatience in his voice. "Radio Shack is—"

"Sue, didn't you say you saw the program at that computer store at the other end of the mall?" Deanna asked quickly.

"Oh, yeah—I did see it there," Sue agreed obediently.

"Then, let's go." Larry gestured for the girls to precede him but stuck close as they joined the other brave souls who had ventured out to the mall.

Deanna glanced surreptitiously at her watch. Three-thirty. She still had a few minutes. She hoped the computer store was as crowded as it usually was. It would be much easier for her to slip away for a few minutes if that was the case. Even though Larry tended to get absorbed in computer stuff, and even though Sue had promised to ask his advice about that program she was considering, Deanna knew her absence would be much less likely to be noticed if the store was busy.

And there was that little alcove between the store and one of the exits, which was perfect.

Just perfect.

Hannah Payne knew it probably wasn't smart to go to the mall by herself after promising Joe she wouldn't stir outside the house alone, and it took her some time to talk herself into it. But in the end, boredom and necessity won out over caution. Since he hadn't gotten to bed until after their morning trip to the grocery store, Joe would sleep until nearly suppertime; Hannah was expecting a long and dreary afternoon to stretch out before her.

Besides, the worries and what-ifs that were frightening in the wee hours of the night, when a body was alone in the house and jumping at shadows, looked absurd in the bright light of day with the world awake and going about its business as usual.

And, anyway, when they were out earlier, she'd forgotten she needed to pick up some material she'd ordered from the fabric store at the mall.

Hannah was a seamstress, talented enough to make a nice living at it, and she had lately tried her hand at designing a few outfits for one of the stores in town. The interest in her work was promising, and she wanted to get a few more things made as quickly as possible. So she needed that material.

She probably should have taken Beason with her, but the dog was an uneasy traveler and prone to bark constantly if left in the car by himself, so she went alone. She left Joe a note explaining where she was going just in case he woke up while she was gone, and she locked the car doors and kept an alert eye out for strangers.

But she encountered no strangers and nothing suspicious, arriving at the mall without incident.

It was just past three-thirty when she parked her car as close as possible to the main entrance and went in.

Canned music blared from the speakers, seemingly louder than usual because the crowds were thinner and quieter than usual. And everybody was visibly nervous.

The sight amused him. The shoppers spoke to one another warily if at all, their gazes suspicious. Children were kept close to their mothers' sides, and it was plainly apparent that both more husbands and fewer teenagers were present at the mall than was usual on a Friday afternoon.

But she was here.
And that was all that really mattered.

Ben drove his Jeep out to Cassie's place, while Matt arrived separately in his cruiser. The sheriff had not blinked
when Ben made the suggestion, and he had not protested;
Ben had an uneasy feeling that his own voice had been a
bit forceful, perhaps even defiant. And that Matt understood all too well where Ben's motives lay.

It was a hell of a thing when a man with walls so thick
that a psychic couldn't see past them still managed to
wear his hopes on his sleeve.

Hopes he didn't want to think too much about. He
was beginning to think he was obsessed with Cassie, and
that bothered him a great deal. He had always been able
to take relationships lightly, be casual about a physical
need that had never really touched his emotions, but it
was different with Cassie. The physical need was there,
certainly, but it was more than matched by a riot of emotions he hardly knew how to deal with.

It was simpler to just try to ignore them, at least for
the present.

Cassie greeted them at the front door, the alert dog as
usual at her side. She was smiling faintly and her voice
was calm, but Ben knew immediately that she was even
further away from him than she had been before they'd
talked that morning. She was shut inside herself, remote,
and when her gaze rested on him briefly, he didn't feel a
warm hand—or even a cool one.

Second thoughts? Or something else?

With Matt close behind him as they went into the living room, Ben could hardly ask. Instead, looking at the
neat stacks of papers on the coffee table and remember-

ing what she had said about her plans to go through her aunt's papers, he said, "You've been busy."

Cassie gave the dog a soft command to lie down, and he did on what was obviously his rug near the fireplace. If she was aware of tension in Ben's voice, it wasn't apparent in her own serene reply. "I thought it was time to get this done. I even started reading one of Aunt Alex's journals."

"Did she say why she scared the hell out of Abby?" Matt demanded.

Cassie looked at him. "So she told you."

"Yes, she told me."

"And?"

"And what? Do I believe your aunt saw the future? No, I don't. Do I believe Abby could be in danger? Yes, I do. Aside from this maniac we have running around, Gary Montgomery is a sadistic son of a bitch who's convinced Abby belongs to him and who is entirely likely to commit a violent act against her if he gets the chance."

Ben glanced at him but didn't comment.

Cassie said, "I'm glad she told you. As for Aunt Alex—so far I haven't even reached her move out here. The first journal starts more than thirty years ago."

"Skip ahead," Matt advised.

"Sorry, I'm one of those people who finds it physically impossible to skip ahead when reading a story. And this is quite a story." She shook her head. "In any case, I doubt she'll explain in her journal why she told Abby what she did. She just wanted to warn her, Matt, that's all. Because she thought Abby could do something to change her own future if she knew what to expect."

There was a grim set to Matt's jaw. "Maybe."

Cassie looked at him a moment. "The coffee's hot, if either of you—?"

Matt shook his head and Ben said no thanks.

"All right. Then why don't I try again to reach the killer."

It wasn't a question, but Ben felt a strong urge to protest. He didn't like Cassie's remoteness, and he didn't like the fact that too many people in the town suspected that Alexandra Melton's niece was involved in the investigation.

"I don't think this is a good idea," he said.

Cassie gestured for them to sit, taking for herself a chair at right angles to the sofa. "Why not?" she asked mildly.

Ben glanced at Matt, then sat at the end of the sofa nearest Cassie while the sheriff took the other chair. "Because people are beginning to talk, Cassie. And they know your name."

She didn't change expression. "Well, we expected that. All the more reason for me to try again. If he doesn't already know about me, he will soon."

It was Matt who said, "And when he does know about you? Will he be able to—to block you when you try to contact him?"

Cassie shrugged. "I don't know. There have been a few in the past who were able to sense it when I tried to touch their minds, and one or two were able to block me at least partially. If he finds out about me, he could try that—although keeping those blocks in place continually will be all but impossible. Sooner or later I'll be able to get in."

"And then?" Ben was gazing at her steadily. "He'll be able to follow the trail back to you, won't he? He'll be able to reach into your mind."

"Maybe. But even if he can do that, he doesn't kill with his mind."

"Are you sure of that?" Ben demanded.

Cassie returned his stare for a moment, then looked at Matt. "Correct me if I'm wrong, but so far you have no evidence pointing to the identity of the killer."

"You're not wrong," Matt said.

"And I assume you're not willing to bet the lives of your fellow citizens on the hope that the killer has decided to abandon this nasty little habit of his?"

"My mama might have raised a stubborn man, but she didn't raise a fool."

"Then I say the risk is an acceptable one."

"Cassie—" Ben started to protest.

"And it's my risk." She looked steadily at him. "In ten years of working with the police, the only killer ever to backtrack and identify me telepathically was the man who killed my mother. He's dead."

"But he came after you."

"Physically. Just as this one might whenever he finds out who I am. That threat exists no matter what I do, especially if people in town are beginning to talk about me. So I'd just as soon try to figure out who he is before he has time to come looking for me."

Put that way, Ben could hardly object. But he was still uneasy, more so with every passing minute.

Taking his silence for assent, Cassie sat back in her chair, getting comfortable. She closed her eyes. "It shouldn't take nearly as long to reach him this time. I know the way now. . . ." Her voice faded on the last words.

Ben allowed several beats of silence to pass, watching that still, pale face. All it took to alert him was a flicker behind her eyelids. "Cassie? Tell me what you see."

A slight frown drew her brows together and her lips parted on an indrawn breath. "He's . . . walking. There are people all around him."

"Where is he, Cassie?"

"Stores. A fountain."

"Jesus," Matt said. "The mall."

"Cassie? What is he doing? Is he just shopping, is that why he's there? Or—"

"He has a hand in his pocket. He's . . . fingering the garrote. He's looking for her."

Matt was about to reach for his walkie-talkie but froze suddenly, his gaze riveted to Cassie's face. "Jesus," he repeated, softly this time.

Her eyes were open. She stared straight ahead, unblinking, blind to everything except the telepathic view from a killer's eyes. And her pupils were dilated, so enormous that only a thin ring of pale gray showed around them, like ice rimming two holes into nothing.

Ben felt a jolt of pure fear. At that moment he believed as he never had before that Cassie was no longer in the room. She was somewhere else, and where she was was dark and cold and crazy.

And only the thinnest and most fragile of ties kept her anchored to the body awaiting her return.

Abby glanced at her watch and, seeing that it was nearly four, quickened her pace. Shopping was taking longer than she had expected. Poor Bryce was waiting in the car, no doubt impatiently, and though the rawhide chew toys she had bought him would atone for temporary abandonment, she didn't want to stay away any longer.

Besides, it would be dark soon, and even with the powerful lights in the parking lot, she did not want to walk out there after darkness fell.

Just one more quick stop, and then she could go. . . .

·   ·   ·

Max got up from the rug near the fire where he'd quietly lain all this time and came to sit near Cassie's chair. His eyes were fixed on her, and he whined softly. Every inch of his body spoke of tension and worry.

"Cassie?" Ben's voice was hoarse, and he cleared his throat. "Cassie? Talk to me. Where are you?"

Her head moved very slightly, as if in response to his voice, but she never blinked or showed any expression, and her voice remained flat and totally without emotion. "I'm in him. He's . . . excited. His heart is pounding. There's so much danger, taking her here. But he likes that. He likes the challenge. The anticipation."

Matt hesitated, one hand on his walkie-talkie. "Ben. I need a description," he said softly. "If I send my people in there in force, we'll cause a panic. He'll be able to disappear in the mess."

Ben nodded. "Cassie? Is he looking toward any of the stores? Is there a reflection?"

Her brows drew together again, but those wide, empty eyes never changed. "Just . . . glimpses. Distorted. I think he has on . . . a blue jacket. Like a . . . team jacket. There's a white letter, I think. Maybe an R."

Ben glanced at Matt, reading the sheriff's dismay even as he felt his own. The largest and oldest of the three county high schools boasted blue team jackets with white lettering, and they were so commonly seen in the area, it was something of a joke. Hundreds of male students, past and present, wore the damned things.

Ben had one himself, packed away in a trunk out at the old house.

"Cassie, can you see anything else? What color is his hair?"

"He's wearing a hat. I think. A . . . baseball cap."

Yet another common sight in the area. Ben wanted to swear violently but forced himself to stay steady. He didn't like the growing pallor of Cassie's face or her utter stillness, sensing more than seeing that she was losing strength with every minute that passed.

"We need to know what he looks like, Cassie. Can you help us know that?"

She was silent for a moment. "I don't think— He isn't looking at the stores any longer. Just straight ahead, because . . . Oh. He's getting more excited. It's filling his mind, all his plans for her. He . . . has a safe place he can take her, so nobody will . . . will hear her, and it's all ready for them. He wants to make her strip for him first, so he can watch. And then—"

"Cassie. Who is he thinking about? Who is she?"

"The bitch."

"What's her name, Cassie?"

"Bitches don't have names." That assertion was particularly chilling delivered in her soft, toneless voice. But not nearly as chilling as her next words. "Bitches are only good for fucking. And for killing."

"Cassie—"

"Especially for killing. I like to see them bleed."

"It's nearly four," Sue hissed to her best friend. "If you're going to do something, do it now."

"You just hold Larry's attention for a few minutes," Deanna murmured in response, and wandered one row over to gaze at a fine display of modems.

Obedient, Sue carried the computer program she was considering over to where Larry stood near the door. Within five minutes he was returning to the software display with her, shaking his head at her ignorance.

Giggling, Deanna slipped out of the store.

·   ·   ·

"Cassie, listen to me. Are you listening? Pull back. Pull back, Cassie." It was not something she had warned him about, but Ben knew instinctively that if her voice had merged with the killer's until they spoke as one, then she was definitely in too deep.

"*You could never become a monster.*"

"*I could lose myself in one. What would be the difference?*"

Jesus Christ.

"I like to see them—"

"*Cassie.* Pull back. *Do it.* Now!"

There was an instant of silence, and then she said, "All right. He's . . . still walking. But faster now. I think . . . he knows where she is."

Ben was only vaguely aware of Matt on his walkie-talkie, sending his officers to every exit of the mall. All his concentration was focused on Cassie. He had the terrifying notion that if he so much as looked away from her, he would lose her forever.

"Cassie? Where is he now? Can you tell us?"

"He . . . just passed the food court."

"Going which way?"

"I don't know."

"Cassie?"

"I don't know. I've never been there before." Exhaustion was beginning to drag at every word.

Ben kept his voice calm. "Try to see the name of one of the stores, Cassie. Can you see?"

"There's a . . . shoe store beside . . . a music store. And across is a . . . bookstore."

"Matt, he's heading toward the north end," Ben said to the sheriff without taking his eyes from her. "Cassie?"

"I'm still here," she said distantly. "His feet are hurting. His boots are too tight. Isn't that funny?"

"Cassie, is he watching anyone?"

"No. She's . . . he knows where she'll be."

"Is he thinking about it? Where she'll be?"

"No, he's just—" Cassie's voice broke off abruptly. She didn't even seem to be breathing. Then her eyes closed, her head jerked as though she'd been slapped, and a cry of pain escaped her.

FOURTEEN

Hannah Payne glanced at her watch and swore beneath her breath when she saw it was almost four o'clock. She'd tried to hurry, but Connie *would* insist on talking to her in detail about every piece of material as she cut it.

And now just look at the time! If she didn't get a move on, there was no way she'd have time to get Joe's supper fixed and on the table by the time he woke up.

Her arms full of material and mind filled with the pros and cons of various excuses, Hannah took her usual shortcut past several boarded-up stores currently being remodeled and headed for one of the lesser-used exits that only a former employee of one of the stores in the mall would know about.

Her summer job had been at the food court.

All too conscious of time passing, Hannah was hurrying when she rounded a corner, which was why she didn't see him until she literally ran into him.

"Hello," he drawled.

·   ·   ·

"Cassie? Cassie!"

Ben was on the point of grabbing her and shaking her when she finally lifted her head and opened her eyes. The pupils were normal once more, but he thought he had never seen such weariness.

"What happened?" he asked, quieter now, hardly aware that he was on one knee by her chair.

"He pushed me out," Cassie whispered.

"What?"

"He knows who I am."

Ben reached for her hand and found it icy. He rubbed it between his. "Are you sure?"

She leaned her head back against the chair, gazing at him without expression. "I don't know how, but . . . he realized I was with him. He was so quick, and I . . . I couldn't hide myself. I heard him. . . . He thought my name just as he pushed me out of his mind."

"Christ," Ben muttered.

Matt was on his feet. "Cassie, is there anything else you can tell me about him? My people will be covering all the mall exits within ten minutes, but telling them to stop any male wearing a Central High jacket is just too vague even if we narrow it to males accompanied by females. Is there anything else you can tell me? Anything at all?"

Cassie looked at him with those exhausted eyes and said, "I think they're already too late."

Deanna Ramsay turned with a welcoming smile that rapidly died. "Oh. It's you. Do you want something?"

"Funny you should ask," he replied.

•   •   •

"You didn't have to stay," Cassie said. She sipped the hot coffee Ben had given her and eyed him over the rim of the cup. "I'll be all right."

"You're welcome," he said.

She didn't smile. With an afghan wrapped around her and the hot coffee inside her, she was warmer than she had been, but she was so drained, she just wanted to curl up and sleep.

And, please God, not dream.

"Matt could probably use your help," she told Ben.

"Matt has two dozen deputies and all the mall security out there helping him. I'd just get in his way." He paused. "I'm not going anywhere, Cassie."

She drew a breath and concentrated on forming the words. "I need to sleep about twelve hours."

"All right." He put his cup down, reached for hers and put it also on the coffee table, then came to her and lifted her out of her chair, afghan and all.

"What're you—"

"You could never manage the stairs," he told her, managing them easily even bearing her weight.

Cassie's thinking was fuzzy, but she decided that she didn't like being carried by a man when she was too damned tired to enjoy the experience. But all she said was "Why can't you just leave me alone?"

"Which bedroom?" he asked, apparently unmoved by her shaky question.

Cassie sighed and rested her head on his shoulder. "The big front one. I have to take Max out."

"I'll take him out. Don't worry."

"He needs to be fed."

"I said don't worry, Cassie. About anything. Just sleep."

Already half there, she murmured, "Yes, but you can't spend the night here. What would people say?"

"Go to sleep, love."

She tried to say that he shouldn't call her "love" and he certainly shouldn't spend the night in her house, but the only thing that emerged was a sensual little murmur that would have embarrassed her if she had been able to think about it. But thinking was beyond her. Her eyes had closed, and when she felt the softness of her bed beneath her, Cassie just sighed and let go, falling into sleep as though into a deep well.

Ben removed her shoes and used the afghan as an extra blanket when he covered her. He turned on the lamp on her nightstand since it was getting dark but left the light low. She was deeply asleep already, her fragile body completely limp, and for a moment he stood beside her bed and just gazed down at her.

How many more of these dreadful psychic journeys could she take before they destroyed her? Not many. He had known the attempts drained her energy and strength, but until that day he had not known they also consumed her very life force.

And he had not known that the possibility of losing her forever would be a knife in his heart.

He heard a quiet sound and turned his head to find Max standing in the doorway, staring at him with anxious eyes. Ben sent a last look at Cassie and then went to the dog and nudged him into the hallway so he could draw the door almost closed.

"Come on, boy," he said. "Let's go downstairs and leave her in peace."

At least, whatever peace she could find in her dreams.

"Any luck?" Ben asked the sheriff when Matt was called to his cruiser's phone.

"Yeah, and all bad. We've got a missing girl, Ben."

"Who is it?"

"A teenager named Deanna Ramsay. She came to the mall with a friend, and they were escorted by her older brother. The friend is hysterical, but from what I've been able to get out of her, it seems Deanna talked her friend into distracting her brother so she could slip away. She intended to meet someone, the friend claims, but she doesn't know who. The brother swears she couldn't have gone missing more than ten minutes before we got here. We're searching the place, and we've searched every male in the right age group with or without a Central jacket." Matt paused, then added flatly, "Nothing."

Sitting on Cassie's sofa with her dog's head in his lap, Ben stared at the leaping flames in the fireplace and tried to think of something positive to say. Nothing came to mind.

"Shit," he said finally.

"My sentiments exactly." Matt sounded too tired to swear. "My deputies are going to keep searching the area, and we've got a growing group of volunteers standing by if we have to start beating the bushes around here. I've called John Logan, and he's on his way out here with his dogs. The girl left a pair of gloves in her brother's car, so we'll have her scent. But I'm betting the bastard got her in a vehicle of some kind, so the trail will end a few yards from one of the exits."

He drew a breath. "Nobody saw anything unusual, nobody heard anything unusual. I'm about to head out to the Ramsay place with Larry, break the news to their parents."

"If they haven't heard already."

Matt grunted an agreement. "How's Cassie?"

"Asleep. Or maybe I should say unconscious. She said she needed about twelve hours, but I'll be surprised if she wakes up before late tomorrow morning."

"You staying out there tonight?"

"Yes."

Matt didn't comment, saying merely, "Okay, I'll call you there if I have any news tonight or in the morning."

"If you need my help—"

"No, we've got enough eyes for a search. There's nothing you can do here." Grimly he added, "So far this bastard's been leaving his bodies where we can find them quickly, but if Cassie was right about his plans for this one . . ."

"We may be in for a long wait," Ben finished.

"Yeah. And in the meantime, I don't much like the mood of our volunteers, Ben. We've had to disarm more than half of them already. If we have to use them to search, and if that girl's body is found, I'm going to have a mob on my hands."

"I know."

"And now Eric is threatening to put out a special edition of the paper tomorrow, and I just can't make him see it'll only fan the flames."

"I'll call him."

"Yeah, okay." Matt let out a weary breath. "And I'll call you if there's any news."

"Watch your step, Matt."

"I will." Matt hung up the phone and backed away to close the cruiser's door, then looked at Abby, where she leaned against the rear fender with her dog at her side. Before Matt could speak, she did.

"I should go home." Her gaze moved restlessly over the people milling all around the parking lot, where lights were beginning to flicker on as darkness rapidly approached. There were plenty of uniformed sheriff's deputies coming and going from the mall and questioning people in the parking lot, but there were even more concerned citizens just standing around, taking it all in. "You have work to do, and I'm just in the way."

Matt stepped closer, not touching her even though he wanted to. He had gone cold to his bones when he had seen her among the mall shoppers and realized how close she had been to an insane killer. "You could never be in the way." He knew why she was worried, of course, and her next words confirmed it.

"Matt, if somebody sees me just hanging around you and starts to wonder . . ."

Roughly he said, "I don't want to let you out of my sight."

Her tense expression softened. "I'll be fine. I'll take Bryce home and we'll lock ourselves in the house. And wait for you."

He didn't like it but knew he didn't have much choice. "All right." Because he couldn't help himself, he lifted a hand to touch her cheek briefly. "But, for God's sake, be careful."

"I will. You too."

Matt watched her all the way to her car, and it wasn't until she drove past him and lifted a hand in farewell that he turned back to his duties, reluctantly pushing her out of his thoughts.

Unseen by either of them, Gary Montgomery sat in his car gripping the steering wheel with white-knuckled fingers and watched his wife drive away. Then he turned his gaze to the sheriff busily directing his men.

"Son of a bitch," he muttered. "Son of a *bitch*."

· · ·

"I'm glad I scared you," Joe Mooney declared stolidly, escorting Hannah to her car. "Jesus, Hannah, you weren't even looking where you were going!"

"I was in a hurry." She knew only too well that this time she wouldn't be able to defend her actions. That poor girl, snatched from the mall in broad daylight—and the monster that took her might well have passed Hannah only minutes before! She shivered.

"I don't know what I'm going to do with you," Joe said.

Hannah suddenly felt like crying. "Can you stay home tonight, Joe? Please?"

He gazed down at her as they reached her car. Even though he knew the third shift at the plant would be short a number of workers on this night as more than one man stayed home, he said, "I've got a sick day coming. Get in the car, honey, and I'll follow you back to the house."

Hannah threw her arms around his neck, scattering fabric all over the pavement.

As Matt had predicted, John Logan's bloodhounds could follow a trail only a few yards from one of the mall exits, where Deanna Ramsay's abductor had obviously forced her into a waiting car. The mall property had been thoroughly searched, and with the girl's trail vanishing into thin air, there was nothing for the sheriff to do but disband the waiting group of volunteer searchers and send his officers out to patrol the town in the hope of seeing something—anything—suspicious.

The volunteers were reluctant to go even with Matt's assurances that he'd call them if it was decided a search was in order for the following day. There was a great deal of grumbling and growling from the group, and Matt was careful to make sure that they did indeed disperse and go their separate ways before he and most of his officers also left the mall.

The officers scattered, some to return to the office but most to begin patrolling. Matt's mercifully brief trip out to the Ramsay place had dashed his faint hopes that the girl had somehow gotten herself safely home; he had left a couple of his people gathering the names and numbers of Deanna's friends from her stricken parents so that every possible avenue of information could be followed.

He didn't expect it to help.

Deanna Ramsay had been abducted by a monster smart enough not to leave a trail, and the next they knew of him would undoubtedly be when her body was found.

Her raped and tortured body, if Cassie was right.

Her demonstration that day had very definitely given him pause. Even a skeptic would have been forced to say that she had been in the grip of something extraordinary, and he doubted he would ever forget that horrifying emptiness he had seen in her unseeing eyes.

He wondered if Ben had any idea what he was getting himself into.

The station was quiet with so many of his deputies out questioning Deanna's friends and looking for some hint of where her abductor had taken her, and Matt welcomed the relative silence. He needed to think.

He went into his office and closed the door. He called Abby first to make sure she had arrived home safely and that she was securely locked inside, and told her that if he could get to her place tonight, it would be before midnight; if he wasn't there by then, he wouldn't be coming tonight.

As always, Abby understood.

Matt spent the next hour and more at his desk going over every note and report concerning the three murders. He looked at photographs, studied the coins and the knives found at the scene, read every last detail of the autopsies.

When he finished, he was no closer to knowing who had killed the three women and, apparently, abducted Deanna Ramsay.

A knock at his door interrupted his brooding, for which he was grateful, and he looked up to find one of his deputies, Sharon Watkins, looking at him questioningly.

"What is it, Sharon? Any news?"

"Not about the Ramsay girl, no," she replied.

"I'm afraid to ask what else has happened."

"Nothing—that I know of. There's someone here to see you, Sheriff. He doesn't have an appointment, but I think you'll want to see him."

"This can't be good," Matt muttered.

"It isn't." Her expression told him she was glad it was his problem rather than hers.

Matt gave her a wry smile. "All right, send him in."

He absently tidied the files on his desk and rose to his feet as Sharon showed the visitor into his office. And he didn't need to hear the man's introduction or see his badge to know exactly what he was looking at.

"Sheriff Dunbar? My name is Noah Bishop. I'm with the FBI."

He was a tall man, lean but with the wide shoulders and athletic carriage that spoke of a great deal of physical strength. He had black hair boasting a rather dramatic widow's peak, piercing gray eyes, and a strikingly handsome face marred by a jagged scar that ran from the corner of his left eye almost to the corner of his mouth.

It was not a face that inspired comfort.

"Agent Bishop." Matt gestured to a visitor's chair, then reclaimed his own. "What can I do for the FBI?"

"Relax, Sheriff." Bishop smiled. "I didn't come down here to stick my nose into your investigation." His voice was cool but matter-of-fact.

"No?"

"No. This is your jurisdiction. The FBI would be happy to offer its expertise, especially if you do indeed have a serial killer operating in the area, but we have learned in such situations as this that it's more politic to wait until we're invited."

"Glad to hear it."

If Matt's brevity disturbed the agent, it wasn't apparent. "Then we understand each other."

Matt inclined his head. "Care to tell me how you heard about our little investigation?"

"The local newspaper."

"Which you have delivered to you in Virginia?"

Bishop smiled again. It was rather frightening. "I have access to certain computer data banks, including one in this state. Your local paper, like so many others, archives its issues for research—and posterity. Once the phrase 'serial killer' was used, it showed up on my system when I did a routine search for information."

"The Internet," Matt said with ironic admiration. "It's just wonderful."

"It does tend to make secrecy difficult." Without waiting for a response to that provocative statement, Bishop went on calmly. "As I said, Sheriff, the FBI would be happy to offer any aid or advice you might require. However, I'm not here primarily because of your investigation, but on a related matter."

"Which is?"

"I'd like to talk to you about Cassandra Neill."

FEBRUARY 27, 1999

When Cassie woke, it was with the leaden sensation of
having slept a long, long time. She lay there for a while, not
particularly concerned about anything, staring drowsily
up at the ceiling. But then the niggling suspicion that she
had slept in her clothes intruded, and she finally forced
herself to sit up and push back the covers.

Yes, she *had* slept in her clothes.

Why on earth had she done that?

The clock on her nightstand told her it was a bit
after nine in the morning. She was reasonably sure it
was Saturday.

And somebody was frying bacon in her kitchen.

Bewilderment rather than anxiety was uppermost in
Cassie's mind. It took her several minutes of careful
thought to recall what had happened the previous afternoon, and when she did she realized that Ben must indeed have stayed all night.

After carrying her to bed. And leaving her there.

She pushed that realization away and the covers with
it, sliding stiffly out of bed and standing on the rug beside
it for a moment as she automatically assessed her condition. Her thinking was still a bit fuzzy. Her muscles, having obviously remained in one exhausted position all
night, complained with every movement, and her growling stomach told her it had been too long since her last
meal, but other than that she felt surprisingly well.

A long, hot shower took care of the stiff muscles and
cleared her head, and by the time she was dressed and on
her way downstairs, her head was clearer and she felt
ready to face just about anything. Even a prosecuting attorney frying bacon in her kitchen.

He had the table already set for two, and her portable

radio was quietly playing oldies in the background. It was a cheerful, welcoming scene.

"Good morning," he said when she came in. "The coffee's hot."

"Good morning." She headed for the coffee, desperately in need of caffeine and hoping it didn't show.

Max, sprawled out near the back door with a rawhide treat between his front paws, thumped his tail in welcome but didn't stop chewing. The honeymoon, Cassie decided, was definitely over.

"I hope you don't mind, but I've made myself at home," Ben said casually and without looking at her.

"How could I mind?" she murmured.

"I imagine you might." His voice remained conversational. "Yesterday you told me to leave."

She vaguely recalled that. "I told you to leave me alone. You did."

He sent her a glance that was no less sharp for being brief. "How do you feel?"

"Better. Sleep usually helps." Though not usually sixteen hours' worth. Sipping her coffee, Cassie looked at Ben, noting both his ease in the kitchen and the fact that he had changed clothes since yesterday. Where had he slept?

"Do you like pancakes?" he asked. "Say yes."

"Yes." She went to get syrup and butter from the refrigerator, then poured orange juice for them both as he finished cooking.

She wanted to ask him about the poor girl who'd been taken yesterday, but her mind shied away from it. There was nothing she could do, she reminded herself fiercely. Not for that girl. Not now.

She remained silent while Ben transferred the food to the table and they both sat down to eat. The silence between them stretched out for most of the meal. It didn't seem to bother Ben at all. Cassie was in no hurry to break it; she was not uncomfortable with him, though she was highly conscious of his every movement. She just didn't know what to say to him.

They were nearly finished when she finally spoke. "This is good. Thanks."

"I specialize in breakfasts and steaks. Other than that . . ." He shrugged, smiling.

She thought that expertise had probably taken him as far as he wanted it to but didn't say it aloud. Instead, driven, she said, "That girl—"

"They haven't found her yet."

"I could—"

"No," Ben said. "You couldn't."

"I'm all right now."

"Maybe." He shook his head, watching her intently. "And maybe not. Do you remember it all, Cassie?"

"More or less."

"Do you remember speaking in the first person, in the killer's words?"

She felt a chill. "No."

"You did. I managed to pull you back, but—" He drew a breath. "Now I understand what you meant when you said you needed a lifeline."

Cassie didn't ask what, specifically, she had said. Instead, she shook her head and murmured, "Every case is a bit different, but . . . I don't understand anything about this one. Peculiar things have been happening almost from the beginning."

He hesitated. "Something else. Your eyes were open during most of the contact. That isn't usual, is it?"

"No."

"Your pupils were so dilated, there was almost no color showing at all."

Cassie felt more disturbed by what she heard in his voice than by the anomalous occurrence he described. "I can't explain it. The difference I felt was . . . a matter of degree."

"What do you mean?"

"I mean the contact itself didn't feel different, just the depth of it. Almost instantly I was deep in his mind, his consciousness, so quick, it was like flipping a switch."

"Because you knew the way after finding him the last time?"

"I guess." But that didn't feel right somehow, and she went on slowly. "If I didn't know better, I'd swear he . . . pulled me in. That he wanted me to know where he was and what he was doing. That he deliberately let me know that much before he pushed me out."

"Why isn't that possible?"

"Well, because . . . there was no awareness of me. None at all, not until that very last second when he suddenly *looked* at me and then pushed me out."

"You said he knew you."

"Yes. He . . . he said my name in his mind."

"Cassie."

She heard that whisper once again in her mind, and a shiver rippled through her. She had never before been caught like that in another mind; a dark inner eye had turned toward her with such swift accuracy that she had felt pinned in place.

Trapped.

That was what she could never tell Ben. That she knew with utter certainty she would never have been able to escape from the insane strength of that other mind if he had not contemptuously thrown her free.

FIFTEEN

"Cassie?"

She summoned a smile. "As I said, he knows who I am now. But we expected that sooner or later."

"Do you think he'll block you from now on?"

"He couldn't do it continually. Eventually even the strongest mind gets tired or distracted and the guard slips. I'll be able to get back in."

"And if you can? Will he know you're there?"

Cassie hesitated. "I don't know. I've always been able to hide my presence before. I . . . must have been distracted somehow this time, and that's how he caught me."

"What if he catches you again? Can he hurt you?"

"With his mind?" She tried to make sure her voice didn't sound evasive. "All he did this time was push me out. It's the natural thing to do."

"We're dealing with an unnatural mind, Cassie."

"Yes. I know."

Ben stared at her, then pushed his plate away with a smothered oath. In a very steady voice he said, "Even if he can't hurt you, how many more times do you think you can do this without killing yourself?"

"As many as I have to." Cassie got up and carried her plate to the sink.

He followed with his own plate. "I don't think so, Cassie. Do you realize you scared the life out of me yesterday? I thought I was going to lose you forever."

She fixed a fresh cup of coffee to give herself a moment to think. It didn't help. "I'm sorry." Her own voice sounded more puzzled than apologetic to her; she wondered how it sounded to him.

Obviously not apologetic.

"Dammit, Cassie! Stop acting like I shouldn't care if you put yourself in danger."

She poured milk into her coffee, stirring it with careful concentration. "It's my risk to take. I told you that."

"And I'm not concerned in the matter?"

She took a moment to respond. "What do you want me to say, Ben?"

He put his hands on her shoulders and turned her to face him. "Look at me."

She did, but reluctantly.

He gave her a little shake. "Stop shutting me out."

"I'm not."

"You've been miles away from me since Matt and I came back yesterday afternoon. I want to know why. Is it because I told you how I felt? Are you having second thoughts about getting involved with me?"

He'll destroy you.

Cassie wondered if she could even try to save herself. "Ben, you must see it—it's no good."

"Why?" he demanded bluntly.

"My God, aren't all the reasons obvious?"

"Not to me. So tell me."

She drew a breath. "For one thing, I'd make a

lousy lover. Ben, I've been inside too many male minds filled with nothing but violence and hate. I can't just push all that aside, pretend I never saw it, that it never terrified me."

"You've never been in my mind," he said quietly.

"I know that." She steadied her voice with an effort. "And I know those other minds, those . . . urges and actions are abnormal. Most men never feel such violence. But accepting that in my own mind doesn't help. I still . . . I can't help being afraid. Don't you see? There's no trust left in me."

"I don't believe that."

"You have to. It's true."

"Cassie, I would never deliberately hurt you."

"I'm sure you mean that." She avoided his gaze.

"But you don't believe it's the truth."

"I told you. I can't trust anymore. I don't want to get involved, not with anyone. Ben, please, just—let it go, okay?"

He ignored the plea. "Is it because you can't read me? Because you can't be sure there's no violence in me?"

"I don't know. Maybe." She had to wonder if it would make things easier if she could read Ben. Or harder.

His fingers tightened on her shoulders. "Cassie—"

The telephone rang, making her jump, but she was glad to have a reason to move away from him, if only as far as the kitchen wall phone. She picked up the receiver and said hello, hoping she didn't sound as shaky as she thought she did.

"Cassie, it's Matt. Is Ben still there?"

"Yes. Hang on a second." She held out the receiver, and when he took it immediately moved away and busied herself loading the dishwasher.

"Matt? Have you found her?" Ben kept his gaze on Cassie and shook his head when she looked up questioningly. Then he frowned as the sheriff continued to speak. "I don't know if that's such a good idea, Matt. We'll just feed the gossip if Cassie comes to your office openly. I know. Yes, I realize that, but—" He listened for a moment longer, then said, "All right. We're on our way."

He hung up the phone and directed all his attention at Cassie. "You heard. He wants to talk to us in his office. I don't know why he didn't want to tell me over the phone, but he was right when he pointed out that your involvement in the investigation is an open secret by now."

Cassie closed the dishwasher. "I'll get my jacket." She kept her tone as indifferent as she could manage. "Would you let Max out for a minute, please? I'd like to leave him in the house."

Ben did as she asked without comment, and by the time she was ready to leave, so was he. He joined her at the front door, picking up a small leather bag she hadn't noticed sitting by the stairs. Cassie didn't ask, but he explained anyway.

"Since my days in the circuit court, I've always carried a packed overnight bag with me in the Jeep. I never knew when I might have to spend a night away from home."

Cassie set the security system without comment, and they went out to his Jeep. The silence between them was not a comfortable one, and it was broken only once between her house and their arrival at the Sheriff's Department.

"What can I do to teach you to trust me?" Ben asked.

Cassie didn't tell him that if she had not already trusted him, she would never have been able to accept him as a lifeline.

He'll destroy you.

It was probably already too late, but she had to try. No matter how much it hurt.

"Nothing," she answered.

． ． ．

Abby had listened to the radio all morning, but the local station reported hour by hour that the missing Ryan's Bluff teenager had not yet been found. The Sheriff's Department was asking that anyone with any knowledge or information please come forward, and in the meantime urged everyone to remain calm. Deputies were out in force.

Abby was restless. She hadn't talked to Matt since the previous evening and had slept badly, yet she had been up with the chickens despite feeling tired and out of sorts. She had busied herself all morning by performing her usual weekend chores, but all the housecleaning and washing was done long before noon, and nothing else served to occupy her attention.

The weather was dreary, cold, and overcast, threatening some kind of precipitation all morning, and the last of the snow clung to spots here and there as if inviting more to join it. The radio said the roads were clear but followed that report by stating that the Sheriff's Department was asking everyone to stay off the roads unless they had to be out.

Abby could imagine the calls Matt must be getting, from panicky citizens to furious merchants; no matter what he did, somebody would be unhappy with him, and if he couldn't quickly make the streets safe for everyone . . .

She was worried about him. He hadn't bargained for this kind of situation, and nothing in his experience had prepared him for it. He was an intelligent man and a shrewd cop, and he would not make many mistakes—but those he made would be out of the conviction that he knew what was best for the town.

The problem was, in this situation there was no

"best," no right answer for the town—except to catch a particularly brutal, undoubtedly insane killer.

Abby went cold just thinking of Matt in that confrontation. Because he would be there, of course. If they were able to locate the killer, Matt would be first through the door—not because it was his job, but because it was his nature.

The phone rang, and Abby went eagerly to answer it, hoping Matt had found a moment to call. She really needed to hear his voice.

"Hello?"

No one responded, but the line was not silent. Instead, there were sounds of breathing, faint but unmistakable.

"Hello?" Abby repeated, unease growing. "Is anybody there?"

"*Abby.*"

Just that, just her name whispered. Then a click, and the dial tone.

Ben felt as well as saw Cassie stiffen the moment she preceded him into Matt's office. But that was her only visible reaction as she looked at the man lounging against the filing cabinet beside the sheriff's desk.

"Hello, Bishop," she said, calm.

"Cassie." The well-dressed man with the sharp gray eyes smiled, an expression that did not lend the slightest bit of charm to his scarred face.

As Cassie settled into the visitor's chair farthest away from Bishop, Matt introduced Ben to the agent, his own feelings clear in the flatness of his voice.

Ben wasn't dismayed to find an FBI agent in his town, but he was wary—though not for the same reason Matt was. "Agent Bishop," he said as they shook hands.

"Judge Ryan."

When Matt nodded toward the other visitor's chair, Ben took it. There was a leather sofa along the wall beside Bishop, and Ben wondered if the agent remained on his feet because he felt it gave him a tactical advantage.

Matt said, "Agent Bishop found out about our situation here thanks to newspaper archives and a North Carolina database."

"And came to offer his expertise?"

"In a manner of speaking."

Bishop said, "This isn't an official visit, Judge. As a matter of fact, I'm currently on a sabbatical."

"I wasn't aware the Bureau offered its agents sabbaticals."

"It's an uncommon practice. It might be more accurate to say that I had accrued a substantial amount of vacation and leave time over the years."

Ben glanced at a silent and distant Matt, then looked at Cassie, who was gazing at Matt's desk. The tension in her slight body was visible, even though her face remained expressionless.

Ben had the feeling he was the only one in the room who didn't know what was going on.

"Okay," he said, returning his gaze to the agent. "So how does that explain your presence here? Just happened to be in the area, or is chasing after serial killers a hobby of yours?"

"You might say that chasing after alleged psychics is a hobby of mine."

"Alleged?"

"That's right. There are so many charlatans, you know. So many so-called telepaths whose claims can't be scientifically documented."

"He means me." Cassie looked up for the first time,

her gaze fixing on Bishop. "I don't perform well in a laboratory setting." Her voice was cool.

"That's one way of putting it," Bishop murmured.

"The tests were poorly designed and you know it. But it was my fault for even agreeing to be tested." Her shoulders lifted and fell. "I've stopped trying to prove myself to you, Bishop."

"Have you?"

Two pairs of gray eyes locked together, and Ben could almost feel the struggle of wills. Then Cassie looked at Matt and said, "I don't know what he's told you, but I can guess he had nothing good to say about me. Want to hear my side of the story?"

Matt nodded.

"Okay. A couple of years ago Agent Bishop was called into a missing persons case in San Francisco. The missing woman's husband was quite wealthy and politically powerful, which was why the FBI was called in even though there was no evidence of a kidnapping. Days went by, then weeks, but neither the police nor Bishop and his people could find a trace of the lady.

"Her sister, in the meantime, contacted me. She had heard of me through mutual acquaintances, and believed I might be able to help find her sister. So I flew to San Francisco and went to the house where the missing woman had lived."

"And?" Matt prompted.

"And I knew she was dead." In a wry tone she added, "The police were, naturally, suspicious when I made that claim. But when they started looking for a body, they found one. Just where the husband had dumped it."

"He hasn't gone to trial yet," Bishop said.

"You know and I know he killed her."

"Maybe."

Cassie glanced at the agent, then returned her gaze to Matt. "At any rate, Agent Bishop asked me to allow myself to be tested. I refused, and went back to L.A."

"Why did you refuse?" Matt asked.

"Advice from my mother. It was her belief that until medical science learned a lot more about the brain, psychic ability would never be understood. What science cannot understand it tends to try its best to disprove. The whole process leads to a great deal of tension and pressure, both of which interfere with psychic ability."

Bishop made a skeptical sound.

Cassie didn't rise to the bait. "Anyway, as I said, I went home. A couple of months later I was asked to advise in a murder case. And Agent Bishop turned up—like a bad penny."

"I resent that," he murmured.

Cassie ignored him. "It was a difficult case complicated even more by the fact that I had the flu and should have refused to get involved. That's no excuse, but it is part of the reason I failed."

"How did you fail?" Matt asked.

"Misinterpreted something I saw. What I told them led the police to concentrate on the wrong suspect, and the real killer had time to kill again. Which he did." She looked steadily at the sheriff. "It wasn't the first time something like that happened, and it won't be the last. No psychic is a hundred percent right a hundred percent of the time."

Again Cassie gave a little shrug. "There were a few more cases after that, some I was able to help solve and some I wasn't. Bishop kept turning up, kept asking me to allow myself to be tested. So I finally did. And I flunked all the tests. As I said, I don't perform well in a laboratory setting. I always did choke at exams."

"You graduated college," Bishop pointed out. "Eventually you had to pass those exams."

"Putting myself through that earned me a degree. Putting myself through your tests again would earn me absolutely nothing."

"Except scientific validity and recognition."

"And then what? Go on the talk shows? Find myself getting tons of mail from poor lost souls who think I might be able to help them? Sit in more laboratories while more scientists devise more tests to measure and weigh and define my abilities? Why? Despite what you think, Bishop, I don't want to be recognized. I don't want to be validated. And I sure as hell don't want to be famous."

"Then," he said softly, gesturing around them, "why do this? Why involve yourself in police investigations?"

"Because I can help. Not all the time, but sometimes. Because I was raised to believe it's my responsibility. And because I can't *not* involve myself." She drew a breath and added quietly, "And I really couldn't care less whether or not my reasons satisfy you."

"They satisfy me," Matt said, surprising everyone.

"And me," Ben agreed, tired of feeling invisible in the room.

Cassie glanced at him for the first time, something he couldn't read flickering in her eyes. Then she looked at Matt. "In that case, I say we have more important things to talk about. Is there still no word on that poor girl?"

"No, nothing. Do you think you'd have any luck trying to connect with the killer again?"

Before Ben could object, Cassie said, "I've already tried a couple of times today, and—"

"What?" He stared at her. "When? And without a lifeline? Dammit, Cassie!"

She avoided his gaze once more. "Not long after I woke up this morning, and in the car coming here. There was no danger. It would have been a shallow contact—if I'd been able to get through. I wasn't able. He's keeping me out."

"Convenient," Bishop murmured. For someone who'd more or less been told to mind his own business, he didn't appear to be discouraged or disgruntled, merely calm and watchful.

Matt glanced at him, then said to Cassie, "How about trying to reach the girl? I still have the gloves she left in her brother's car yesterday."

Cassie nodded without hesitation. "I'll try."

The sheriff jerked his head toward the agent. "Want him gone?"

"No, he can stay." She smiled faintly. "One of the things that intrigues him about me—I do perform well outside laboratories."

Bishop made no comment.

Matt reached into his center desk drawer and drew out a plastic bag with a pair of delicate ladies' gloves inside. He pushed the bag across to Cassie. "I'm assuming you could reach her if she's still alive. What if she's already dead?"

"I may get nothing. Or I may know where she is." She had not yet reached for the bag.

"How?" Ben asked her. "If there's no mind there to tap into, how do you know?"

Cassie turned her head and looked at him with an odd little smile. "I have no idea. Sometimes I just know."

He watched as she reached for the bag, opened it, and drew out the pair of gloves. Head bent, she held them in her lap, fingers toying with them. Ben saw her eyes close.

He waited a minute or so, then said, "Cassie? What do you see?"

She didn't respond.

"Cassie?"

"Poor thing." Her voice was soft.

The sheriff muttered, "Shit."

Ben kept his voice steady. "Can you see her, Cassie? Where is she?"

"She's . . . in a building. A barn. It hasn't been used for a long time, I think. There used to be pasture all around it, but now everything's overgrown. . . ."

Cassie lifted her head and opened her eyes. She was pale but calm. She slid the gloves back into the plastic bag and pushed it across the desk to the sheriff. "I can show you the way," she told him.

Ben wanted to protest, but he knew it would be almost impossible for Cassie to pinpoint the location on any map; there were far too many abandoned barns in far too many overgrown pastures in the area.

Ben and Cassie went in his Jeep, with the sheriff and Bishop following in Matt's cruiser. Ben and Matt agreed that the fewer people who knew they were searching for a body, the better. At least until it was found.

As they headed north out of town at Cassie's direction, Ben said, "I'm surprised Matt's letting Bishop tag along. In fact, I'm surprised he's giving him the time of day."

"If I know Bishop, he probably implied that the Bureau would be very interested in these murders—if they knew about them. The other newspapers in the state too. Although, of course, if he's busy following the investigation, he won't have time to report in or call anybody."

"You seem to know him very well."

Cassie glanced at him. "I can't read him, if that's what you're asking."

"Even when you touch him?"

"I've never touched him."

Ben digested that. "So he has walls too, huh?"

"Big, thick ones." Cassie paused. "Turn up here to the left. Beside that fence."

He did so. "What's he after, Cassie?"

"I don't know. If I had to guess, I'd say proof. On the other hand, I've always had the idea he's looking for something he really doesn't expect to find in a lab or on a score sheet."

"For instance?"

"I don't know. As I said, it's just an idea. Wait—slow down a bit. See that dirt road up ahead? Turn onto it."

From the gathering tension in her voice, Ben knew they were getting close, so he fell silent and concentrated on following her directions. Several miles and a few more turns later, he stopped the Jeep on a fairly narrow dirt road. Cassie pointed, and he could see through the trees a ramshackle building that had probably once been a barn.

Uncertainly she said, "I don't think the killer came from this direction, but—"

"In case he did, we'll stop here to avoid screwing up any tracks."

Matt's cruiser pulled in behind them, and the sheriff and FBI agent got out and approached the Jeep, both on Ben's side.

"Is this it?" Matt asked.

Ben pointed and related what Cassie thought about the killer's approach.

"Okay. You two wait here."

"Matt?" Cassie leaned forward a bit so she could see him. "This time he arranged the body for . . . for maximum shock effect. Brace yourself."

He nodded. He and Bishop disappeared into the trees.

Ben looked at Cassie. "Were you right? About what he intended to do to her?"

Cassie drew a breath and let it out slowly. "Not entirely. He had a few more plans I didn't know about."

"What do you mean?"

She turned her head and looked at him with haunted eyes. "He cut her up, Ben. She's in pieces."

SIXTEEN

The news that the horribly mutilated body of fifteen-year-old Deanna Ramsay had been found spread through Ryan's Bluff like wildfire. By the time Cassie and Ben got back to the Sheriff's Department less than an hour after the body was found, a small crowd was already gathering; by the time the black van belonging to a local undertaker passed through town a few minutes later escorted by a couple of deputies, the crowd had doubled.

With the sheriff still at the crime scene, Ben went out to talk to them. Cassie remained inside and didn't hear what he said, but she watched from the window in Matt's office, and she wasn't surprised when the visibly agitated group calmed somewhat and eventually began to disperse.

"The man has a golden tongue."

Cassie turned from the window to find a female deputy standing in the doorway. Her name tag read SHARON WATKINS.

"But how long will they listen to him?" Cassie asked.

Sharon smiled. "They're listening today. That's really

all we can hope for." She hesitated. "We have some pretty good coffee out here, if you'd like a cup."

Cassie appreciated the offer, especially since she knew most of the deputies viewed her with uneasiness if not outright suspicion. "Thank you."

"I'll get the judge some too. I figure he'll stay here at least until the sheriff gets back."

"I think that's the plan." Ben had already made numerous phone calls in a concerted effort to keep the lid on the growing panic and anger of the town.

"He'll have to talk to the mayor again." Sharon sighed as she turned away. "He's already called twice in the last five minutes. The man needs a hobby."

Or a town where no killers lurked, Cassie thought. She hadn't met Mayor Ruppe, but from what she had heard she got the feeling the first-term mayor had a great deal of charm and very little common sense. Which was undoubtedly why he leaned heavily on the advice and help of other leaders of the town, particularly Ben and Matt.

Cassie returned her gaze to the window to watch Ben speak to the few lingering members of the crowd, then went back to her seat on the leather sofa. She would have preferred to be home, but Ben had asked her to stay with him, and she had agreed more because she hoped she might be of some help than because it was a comfortable or safe place to be.

She knew he was worried about her, that he didn't want her alone in her isolated house—even with a protective dog and a good security system. Her most recent contact with the killer had unsettled him as much as it had her, she thought. He was also very obviously feeling decidedly edgy about Bishop.

She couldn't help him there. The agent made her feel edgy herself, and always had.

Cassie leaned her head back against the sofa and closed her eyes—then just as quickly opened them again. The trouble with closing her eyes was that she kept seeing the remains of that poor girl scattered all over that barn. Even with her experience of horrible sights and her hard-won ability to detach herself somewhat, this one was so brutal and dehumanizing that it was branded on her mind's eye in a way she would never entirely escape. But when her eyes were open she could look consciously at something else.

Anything else. The map behind Matt's desk made a good focus. Salem County. One of the larger counties in the state, and shaped vaguely like a triangle . . .

Cassie shook her head irritably. There was some damned song in her head, a tune she couldn't identify that kept playing over and over again, fading into silence, only to return. It was one of those maddening tricks of the mind that tended to come when there was too much to think about.

Sharon returned with coffee and the offer of sending out for a late lunch if and when it was wanted. Cassie thanked her, and the deputy returned to her desk a couple of minutes before Ben came back into Matt's office.

Cassie indicated the cup Sharon had left for him, then said, "It looked pretty ugly out there for a while."

Ben sat down behind Matt's desk. "It'll be a lot worse if we ever get a suspect in custody. That's as close as I ever want to come to facing a lynch mob."

"They listened to you. They left."

"This time," Ben said, unknowingly echoing Deputy Watkins. "But if we don't catch this bastard, and soon . . ."

"He's still blocking me."

"Dammit, Cassie, stop trying to contact him without a lifeline."

"I told you it isn't dangerous." She shook her head,

avoiding his gaze. "And I have to keep trying. What else am I here for, Ben? So far, all I've been able to do is tell Matt where to look for the bodies. I've been a lot of help."

"You've done everything you could."

"Have I?" Cassie stared down at her coffee. "I'm not so sure."

"You seem very tense. What's bothering you?" he asked.

"I don't know. Just a feeling."

He waited, watching her.

Slowly Cassie said, "He had to be in a frenzy this time, you know. To do what he did to that poor girl."

Ben hadn't viewed the murder scene, but he had seen Matt's sickened face and Bishop's stony one as well as Cassie's haunted eyes; he could only imagine the carnage that must have lain waiting for them in that barn.

"Don't think about it," he said.

"I don't have a choice. It isn't something I can put out of my mind. Eventually maybe, but not yet." She shrugged jerkily. "If I can just make sense of it . . ."

"How can any of this make sense?"

"Even madmen have their own mad logic." She looked at him, frowning. "Maybe that's what's bothering me."

"What?"

"Well . . . it's like he's blowing hot and cold. One victim is found far from where she was killed, the crime scene neat, her body virtually unmarked except for the wound that killed her, no murder weapon anywhere to be seen. The next is found in the room where she was killed, blood everywhere, the weapon a knife he found and left right there. Then he picks up another knife and takes it to use on his third victim, who is found where she was killed, but again the scene is neat and calm. And now this. He made the weapon that killed her and took it with him after he was done with her—but killing her wasn't enough. Raping her wasn't enough. He had to cut her into pieces. . . ."

Ben drew a breath. "It takes more than a kitchen knife to hack a body into pieces."

"He used an ax," Cassie said. "And left it at the scene. He took the garrote with him, but left the ax in that barn."

Ben didn't ask her how she knew that. Instead, keeping his voice as composed as hers was, he said, "Seemingly calm and controlled when he kills one victim, then frenzied when he kills the next. As if he needs those violent outbursts?"

"I don't know. But it bothers me. I'd say he was trying to disguise some of his kills, but leaving the coins at the scene is as good as a signature, and he has to know that."

Matt had told them tonelessly that the killer had left his usual coin after killing Deanna Ramsay. It was a penny, placed on her forehead between gouged-out eyes.

Cassie rubbed her own forehead fretfully as she considered the mad logic of a madman, and Ben felt a little chill as he imagined a coin lying coldly against her skin.

He didn't want to let her out of his sight. It wasn't just because the killer knew who she was now; it was also because Cassie seemed hell-bent on contacting the bastard again and was far too willing to do so without a lifeline.

At least, without him as her lifeline. He was afraid that was it. Cassie had withdrawn so completely from him, she would not accept any kind of contact with him even to save her life. If it could save her life.

"There's something I'm missing," she said almost to herself. "Something . . . I just don't know what it is."

"As much as I hate the very possibility, have you considered that there might be two killers?"

Cassie nodded immediately. "Sure. But I'm positive the same man killed these women, all of them."

Ben knew that Matt had reached the same conclusion thanks to what little forensic evidence they'd managed to gather added to the presence of the coins and the identical way in which the first three bodies had been found posed. And they'd found a bloody footprint at this latest scene that Matt was certain would match one of those found in Ivy Jameson's bloody kitchen. To Matt the facts added up to one killer.

"I just wish I knew what was bothering me," Cassie murmured.

"You're still tired," Ben said.

"I slept more than twelve hours."

"Maybe it wasn't enough."

Cassie's smile was slight and fleeting. "It's never enough. I'm fine, Ben. I told you I wouldn't collapse, and I won't. I'm stronger than I seem."

"I just—"

"I know. You're worried about me. Don't be."

Lightly he said, "For somebody with walls, I don't hide some things too well."

Cassie said nothing, just stared at her coffee.

Was he being too watchful, too protective? Ben didn't know. It was the first time in his life he had found himself coping with an almost overpowering urge to shield a woman; he suspected he was neither hiding it nor handling it too well.

Especially given Cassie's prickly and independent nature.

He had told himself that morning to back off and give her the time and room she obviously needed, but gazing at her now, he was very conscious of minutes ticking away. Something told him that even if backing off and giving her time was the smart thing to do, it was not the right thing to do, because time was something they simply did not have.

"We've never had a chance, have we?" he heard himself say.

She looked at him, those eyes touching him as though with a warm hand, and the wariness he saw there hurt him. She didn't ask, but her brows rose in an almost indifferent question.

"We've never had a chance to . . . be ordinary. Just two people drawn to each other. We can't even seem to talk about ordinary things. All we talk about are killers."

Cassie smiled just a little, sadly, and he wanted badly to go put his arms around her. "I tried to warn you," she said.

"Cassie—"

She shook her head. "It doesn't matter."

"It matters to *me*."

"Catching a killer matters to you, Ben." Her voice was suddenly remote. "Making your town safe again matters to you. And maybe . . . maybe I matter to you."

"There's no maybe about it," he said roughly.

She accepted that without any visible reaction. "All right. But it's a question of priorities, isn't it? Nothing can be . . . can be settled until this killer is caught. All your energy, and all of mine, has to focus on that."

"And afterward? When the killer is caught? What then, Cassie?"

"I don't know." There was something painfully honest in the apprehension in her gaze. "I don't know how you'll feel. How I'll feel. I don't even know if either of us will have the energy left to give a damn."

"This is not going to just go away, if that's what you think. *Is* that what you think? That I want you because we're both involved in this investigation, that it's propinquity?"

"Stranger things have happened," she murmured.

Ben shook his head. "You're wrong. For one thing, I'm not in the habit of coming on to the nearest available woman. Cassie, why are you looking for excuses?"

"Excuses?"

"That's what it sounds like to me. One reason after another to hold me at arm's length until—what? Until I lose patience and give up?"

Cassie was spared having to answer when the phone rang.

"Dammit," Ben muttered, as Cassie answered the phone.

"I think the mayor wants to talk to you," Cassie said, and both of them heard the relief in her voice.

Hannah Payne hummed softly to herself as she pinned the pattern to material spread out on the living room floor. She should have been in her sewing room, of course, the extra bedroom that Joe had fixed up for her. But he was napping in their bedroom right next door, since he had to go in to work that night, and she didn't want to disturb him.

From time to time she felt a little chill of worry over that missing girl, but Joe had been right when he'd told her she would just upset herself if she listened to the radio all day waiting to hear about the poor thing.

There was nothing she could do to help, after all.

Snug in her own safe little world, Hannah worked contentedly, disturbed only when the phone rang just after two o'clock. She lunged to grab the receiver before it could ring again and wake Joe.

"Hello?"

Silence.

"Hello? Is anyone there?"

Soft music began to play.

Hannah began to be afraid, even though she couldn't

have said why. It was a music box, she realized; nothing else had quite the same tinkling sound. Just a music box, and someone was obviously playing a joke on her.

"Hello? Who's there?" She didn't recognize the tune—
"*Bitch.*"

With a gasp Hannah hung up the phone. She sat there on the floor, feeling very, very cold. Just a joke, of course. Somebody was being bad, being mean, that was all it was. That was all.

Joe wasn't going to like it when she asked him to stay home from work another night.

It was three o'clock that afternoon when Abby pulled her car to the curb in front of the Sheriff's Department, left Bryce inside, and came up the walkway to the steps.

Cassie was sitting on the fourth one.

"Hi," Abby said.

Cassie echoed the greeting, then added, "Matt isn't back yet."

"He's still out there with—with the Ramsay girl?"

"Where she was killed, yeah. They sent her body back to town about an hour ago, but the crime scene unit is still out there collecting evidence. Or what they hope will be evidence."

"That FBI agent still around?"

Cassie wasn't surprised that the other woman knew. "Out there with Matt and the rest."

"Word has it he's from one of those serial killer task forces the FBI sends around the country."

"He isn't. Though I believe he spent some time in Behavioral Sciences at Quantico."

Abby eyed her. "Then why is he here? Nobody believes Matt called the Bureau, least of all me."

"He didn't." Cassie smiled and briefly explained her history with the agent, finishing with, "He'll stick around, watching and listening and offering unsolicited advice. Probably drive Matt nuts—even though he really is pretty good at figuring out murders. But I guess you could say he's here for me if for anything."

"I see. And what does Ben say about that?"

"Not much so far." Cassie jerked a thumb over her shoulder. "The mayor and three members of the town council are in there talking to him right now. I was just in the way, *and* the focus of intense curiosity, so I came out here for some fresh air."

Abby sat on the step beside her. "Has Ben kept you hanging around here all day?"

"Well, I've suggested taking a cab home, and one of the deputies offered to drive me, but Ben needed to stay here until Matt gets back and he asked me to stick around." She shrugged. "Maybe I can help."

"And maybe he just wants you with him."

Cassie turned her gaze out toward Main Street, absently focusing on a woman a couple of blocks down who seemed to be picking up litter from the sidewalk. "I don't know why he would. We either spend our time discussing the finer points of lunatic killers and their methods or else end up in a—a senseless debate neither of us can seem to win. One of us pushes, and one of us backs away. It's like some frustrating dance."

"One of those, huh? I've been there."

"He's a very stubborn man. Not as stubborn as your Matt, maybe, but—"

"Nobody is as stubborn as Matt." There was a touch of amusement in Abby's voice. "As for Ben, the word I'd use to describe him would probably be 'determined.' "

Cassie sent her a glance. "Yeah?"

"Definitely. As far as I can tell, nothing much has ever stood in his way when he wanted something."

"I suppose that goes for women too?"

Abby pursed her lips thoughtfully. "I imagine so, though to be fair, he hasn't exactly cut a heartless swath through the county. He's usually had a girlfriend but seems to prefer them one at a time—and they seem to stay friendly with him once it's over."

"Figures." Cassie sounded disgruntled.

Abby hid a grin. "Well, he's a nice guy."

"I know. I know he is." Cassie sighed and watched her breath turn to drifting mist. It had warmed up during the afternoon and the skies had cleared somewhat, so sitting on the front steps of the Sheriff's Department was actually rather pleasant, but it was still a winter day and there was still a chill in the air.

"And not at all bad looking," Abby went on, warming to her theme. "Of course, some women don't care for dark men, and I suppose it could be argued that since he's still single at—let's see, he's Matt's age, so he must be about thirty-six or -seven—then he probably has a few intimacy issues lying about. But maybe I've seen too many talk shows."

Cassie smiled, continuing to watch the woman moving slowly toward them along the sidewalk, bending from time to time to pick up something from the pavement. "Intimacy issues, huh? Yeah, well, he isn't the only one."

"You can tell me it's none of my business if you like, but which one of you is backing away?"

"Me, at the moment."

"Ah. You don't like dark men?"

Cassie kept it light. "It's lawyers. I mean, I know he's been a judge, and now he's a prosecutor, but all those lawyer jokes just get to you after a while."

"And he's a politician too," Abby noted sympathetically.

"Worse and worse."

"I suppose you could try reforming him."

"Oh, no. Any woman who tries to reform a man deserves everything she gets."

Abby laughed.

Cassie smiled, then said, "Abby, who is that woman? The one coming toward us?"

Abby looked. "Oh. That's Lucy Shaw, poor thing."

"What is she picking up? I thought it was litter, but—"

"Nobody knows what she *thinks* she's picking up. Whenever she manages to escape her son's watchful eye, she ends up roaming the streets picking up invisible things until he comes looking for her."

Remembering, Cassie said, "Oh, yes, Ben told me about her. And nobody knows what did this to her?"

"Not that I've ever heard. I just assumed it was Alzheimer's, even though she couldn't have been much past forty when I first noticed her roaming the streets."

"She looks about seventy now," Cassie murmured.

"I know, but she's younger. When she was a young woman, she was famous for her needlework. Apparently she still does some in lucid moments, because her son usually sells a few pieces at the church bazaar every year." Abby paused, then added, "I should go call him now. She never seems to wander into traffic or get hurt in any way, but she isn't dressed warmly enough to be out here."

Lucy Shaw was wearing faded jeans neatly rolled up above her ankles and a cotton cardigan over a T-shirt. Untied and ancient Reeboks flapped on her sockless feet. Her mostly gray hair was untidy but not witchy, and she was almost painfully thin.

She turned up the walkway that led to the Sheriff's Department. She had been moving steadily and straight down the street, but now she moved much quicker, bending only once to pick up whatever her mind told her was so important. She held one hand cupped close to her body, as though holding small items, and her other hand curved around it protectively. She stopped near the foot of the steps, straightened, and stared at them with vacant eyes.

Gently Abby said, "Miss Lucy, you shouldn't be out on such a cold day."

Those faded blue eyes sharpened, stared at her for a moment, then shifted to Cassie. "They're all over." Her voice was paper-thin and whispery. "Scattered all over. I have to pick them up."

"Of course you do," Cassie said quietly.

"You understand?"

"Yes. Yes, of course."

"It wasn't my fault. I swear, it wasn't my fault."

"No one blames you," Abby soothed.

"You don't know." The faded eyes returned to Cassie's face. "But *you* do. You know the truth, don't you? You can see the face he hides from everybody else. His true face."

Cassie and Abby exchanged glances, and then Cassie said, "The face who hides, Miss Lucy? Who are you talking about?"

"Him." She leaned toward them and whispered fearfully, "He's the devil."

"Miss Lucy—" Abby began.

Lucy Shaw reached out suddenly, one hand gripping Cassie's knee with unexpected strength. "Stop him," she hissed. "You have to."

Cassie caught her breath and stared into the old woman's eyes.

Then, as abruptly as it had begun, Lucy Shaw's moment of lucidity was over. Her eyes seemed to film over, and her hand fell away from Cassie. She stepped back, her hands cupped protectively once again near her middle, and said fretfully, "I have to pick them up. All of them. I have to. . . ."

Quick footsteps thudded up the walkway, and a thin man of about forty-five who bore an unmistakable resemblance to Lucy Shaw caught her arm. "Mama. Come along home, Mama."

"I have to pick them up," Lucy told him anxiously.

"Yes. We'll pick them up at home, Mama."

Abby said, "I was about to call you, Russell."

"She didn't mean to bother you." His voice was a bit rough, his tone defensive.

"We know that, Russell, we were just worried about her."

"Thanks," he said, but he was scowling. His eyes shifted away from Cassie and his grip tightened on his mother's arm. "Come along now," he said gently enough.

"They're scattered all over," she murmured sadly.

"Yes, Mama. I know."

The two reached the end of the walkway and turned back the way Lucy had come. When they reached the corner, they turned and vanished.

"Where do they live?" Cassie asked.

"Two streets back from Main. Close enough." Abby looked at Cassie curiously. "You went white when she touched you. Did you—could you see anything?"

Cassie didn't reply for a moment, and when she did her voice was abstracted. "Have you ever tried to see something in the face of a shattered mirror?"

"Is that what a broken mind looks like to you? A shattered mirror?"

"Hers does."

"Did you see anything in it?"

"No, nothing clearly enough to identify. Except—" Cassie looked at Abby, frowning. "Except kittens."

"Kittens?"

"Yeah. Kittens."

Abby had intended to tell Matt about the phone call she had received, but she was reluctant to hang around the Sheriff's Department, waiting for him. When he still hadn't returned by four o'clock, when the clouds began rolling in and the chill in the air deepened, she decided enough was enough.

"I'll tell him you were here," Cassie said, then eyed her in sudden realization. "Why were you here? I mean, considering how careful you two usually are to avoid attention."

"No reason."

"Uh-huh. What is it, Abby?"

"I got a call. Just some nut breathing heavily into the phone, that's all." And whispering her name. "It was probably just Gary playing games. Look, I don't want to worry Matt. I just wanted to see him."

"I'll tell him about the call," Cassie said. "Abby, this is no time to hold back when something spooky happens. Even if it is *just* your ex tormenting you, Matt needs to know. In the meantime, you keep Bryce with you."

It was good advice, and Abby took it.

She drove back home, not quite as restless or uneasy as she had been earlier, but not entirely calm either. She wanted to see Matt. And she was reasonably sure she would see him that night; she knew him, and knew he would come as soon as possible after Cassie told him about the call.

Besides which, they hadn't seen each other since those

tense few minutes at the mall the previous day, and Matt seldom let two nights pass without them being together.

He would be upset after the day he'd had, and he would be tired. And hungry. Abby raided her freezer for the ingredients for a stew, and within an hour had it bubbling on the stove.

When the phone rang, she didn't hesitate to pick it up. She never got the chance to say hello.

"You bitch!" Gary snarled. "Did you think I wouldn't find out about him?"

SEVENTEEN

Cassie came downstairs and announced as she entered the living room, "I've made up the bed in that other front bedroom."

Standing by the fireplace, Ben scowled. "You shouldn't have bothered. I told you the sofa in here would be fine."

"If you insist on staying here, that's a perfectly good guest room, and you'll use it. You can't have gotten any rest at all on that sofa last night. It isn't comfortable for sleeping, and it's inches too short for you."

Ben considered telling her that since he had been unable to sleep anyway and had gone to check on her an average of once an hour all night, the comfort of the sofa had not been an issue. But she had been distant and distracted since they returned to her house, and he was wary of saying the wrong thing.

Finally he quietly said, "Thank you."

They had brought Chinese takeout food with them from town when Matt's return to the station around six had allowed Ben to leave, and he still hadn't gotten over the fact that Cassie had not argued when he stated his intention of spending the night.

Cassie had merely nodded acceptance. She even went with him to his apartment, looking around curiously while he repacked his overnight bag.

He had no idea what she'd thought or felt about his place; she had made no comment.

Now, with the remains of their meal cleared away and sleet rattling against the dark windowpanes as a long evening stretched ahead of them, he was as uncertain of her mood as he had been all day. The only thing he was reasonably sure of was that she was far away from him.

She curled up in the armchair she seemed to favor, glanced toward Max lying in his accustomed spot and working on the nightly rawhide bone, and said idly to Ben, "I don't know how you usually spend your Saturday nights, but there are lots of books here, and movies on tape. There's even a stack of jigsaw puzzles in that front closet. All pretty tame, I guess."

Ben put another log on the fire, then sat down on the sofa a couple of feet away from her and gazed at her steadily. "I'd rather just talk. Unless you're too tired."

"Talk about what?"

"You."

She smiled. "You know all about me. You had your secretary research me, remember?"

"Tell me what she didn't find out," he invited, refusing to be discouraged.

"There's nothing to tell." Cassie looked back at the fireplace.

Ben tried to keep it casual. "I don't even know what your major was in college, or how you supported yourself in the years since."

"Double major, psychology and English lit. I had some income from Mother's estate, I told you that. It was enough to live on." She was matter-of-fact, almost indifferent. "To supplement that, I read scripts. Easy work that let me stay home and avoid people."

"Except when you helped the police."

"Except then." A slight frown disturbed her face. "I was never career minded. I just wanted to be left alone."

"And now?"

"And now I have this." She gestured at the room around them. "Thanks to Aunt Alex. And she left me lots of books and tapes and craft kits to occupy my time. If I'm very lucky, when this killer is caught there won't be another murder in these parts for years and years."

"So you'll be left in peace."

"Is that too much to ask?"

"What about a family, Cassie? What about that psychic daughter you could have one day?"

"No. No family. No daughter. Pass this curse on?" Her smile was twisted, more with regret than with conviction, Ben thought. "I don't think so."

"Maybe she wouldn't consider it a curse."

Cassie shrugged. "Maybe. And maybe the world would be different. Maybe people wouldn't be driven to hurt each other. Maybe a cure would be found for insanity, and there'd be no more monsters cutting up teenagers. And maybe the sun would rise in the west."

"You said you couldn't see the future."

"I can't."

"Then how can you be so cynical about it?"

"Experience with the past."

Ben went back to the fireplace, to replace a log that had fallen out onto the hearth. But he remained there, gazing down into the flames.

Cassie didn't have to be psychic to read his thoughts. "I know," she said softly. "I'm such a downer. It's hard to be an optimist when you live your life with monsters."

"Trying to scare me off?" Ben asked without taking his eyes from the fire.

"Just . . . telling it like it is." Cassie leaned her head back against the chair and watched him. There was a dull ache deep inside her, as if her very bones hurt, and staring at him did nothing to ease the pain.

He'll destroy you.

Would he? And would she care very much if he did?

Cassie knew she was a fatalist. She had good reason to be. For all her efforts over the years, all the horrendous, exhausting hours spent stealing into the minds of madmen and watching through their eyes acts of unbelievable evil, nothing much had changed.

Evil killed. Innocents died.

And she told the police where to find the bodies.

So, yes, she understood fate. She believed in fate. She had discovered the futility of trying to fight fate.

"Cassie?"

She wondered what her own expression was like to make his so disturbed. And she wondered why she was even struggling against something that had to be.

"Telling it like it is," she repeated slowly.

Ben came to sit down on the coffee table directly in front of her, leaning forward so that almost no space separated them. And even that vanished when he reached out to put a hand on her knee. "Cassie, I don't have to be psychic to see that you're in pain. What is it? Is it me? Am I causing this?"

For a fleeting instant Cassie remembered another hand clutching her desperately, but the image faded as she looked into Ben's hazel eyes and felt the warmth of his hand even through the heavy denim of her jeans. His hands were always so warm.

So warm.

"Of course it's you," she murmured, smiling.

"I don't want to hurt you," he said, not reassured by the smile.

"Then kiss me."

Ben got to his feet, caught her hands, and pulled her up. "It's not that I want to refuse," he said in the tone of a man who wanted to be completely understood, "but what just happened here? Because I could have sworn you thought this was a bad idea."

"A woman's allowed to change her mind. It says so in the rule book."

"Ah." Ben's arms went around her, and he was smiling but his eyes were grave. "So now you think this is a good idea."

Cassie wasn't about to lie to him. "I think . . . I never really had a choice." She looked at her hands resting on his chest, felt the warmth and strength of him, and let her body lean into his because it needed to.

"Cassie—"

"I trust you," she said, because it was true. "And I . . . need you." She needed his warmth, his caring. Most of all, she needed to know, just once in her life, what it felt like to be a woman a man desired. She reached up, her fingers touching his mouth, her gaze searching his face intently. "I need you, Ben."

Ben had the uneasy idea that he was seeing Cassie's fatalism at work once more, but it would have taken a stronger man than he was to draw away from her because of that. He had wanted her since the day she had first walked into his office, wary and withdrawn and tormented, her haunted eyes tugging at something deep inside him, and even if she had doubts he had none—not about this.

His head bent and his mouth covered hers hungrily. There was nothing gentle in the kiss, nothing hesitant, and Cassie responded instantly, rising on her toes to fit herself more intimately against him, her mouth opening eagerly beneath his. She felt so fragile in his arms, yet there was a steely strength as well, and unquestionably the desire of a woman. It was an enormously seductive combination.

Entirely willing to be seduced, Ben nevertheless managed to ask hoarsely, "Are you sure?"

There was a restless urgency in her voice when she answered, "I've never been so sure about anything in my life."

It was more than enough. Ben kissed her again, then lifted her into his arms and carried her upstairs.

"To be honest, I was almost relieved," Abby told Matt, sincere but also trying to keep him calm. "The fact that Gary called instead of storming over here I take as a good sign."

"How the hell do you figure that?" Matt had finally stopped pacing the kitchen and swearing under his breath, but it was clear he wanted nothing better than to break something Gary-shaped with his bare hands.

"I think if he'd found out I was seeing anybody but you, he would have come after me. But you give him pause. You're bigger than he is, younger, in much better shape—and you wear a gun. I don't think he wants to take you on, Matt."

Matt pulled her into his arms and held her tightly. "That doesn't mean he won't try something a lot nastier than phone calls when he's sure I won't be around. Goddammit, Abby, this time I won't take no for an answer. Either I stay here or you move in with me."

She couldn't help but laugh, albeit shakily. "You

won't get no for an answer. Now that Gary knows, I don't care who else finds out."

"Good." He kissed her, taking his time about it.

When she could speak a few words coherently, Abby said, "You must be tired. Aren't you tired?"

"Not that tired." He nuzzled his face against her neck, inhaling her scent because he loved it, then forced himself to raise his head. "But I am starving. Until I smelled that stew, I hadn't realized how long it's been since breakfast."

"Breakfast? Honestly, Matt—" She eased from his embrace and got busy putting supper on the table.

Neither of them brought up the reason his appetite had been gone for the entire day; it wasn't until the meal was finished and the dishes cleared away that Abby brought up the subject.

"You don't have to go back to the office tonight, do you?"

"No, there's nothing I can do there." His tone was bleak.

"Cassie said the killer wouldn't leave enough evidence to make himself identifiable—was she right about that?"

"So far." Despite his earlier words, he looked very tired. "If we can ever get a viable suspect, we might have enough to nail his ass. He didn't wear a condom when he raped the Ramsay girl."

Abby tried hard to match his seeming detachment. "So he might be a—what do you call it?—a secretor?"

"Maybe. But even if he isn't, with all the advances in DNA testing, we should be able to get just about everything except his name and address from the semen." He added, "Not that DNA evidence always convinces a jury, as we well know, but I'm counting on Ben to make damned sure this one doesn't slip through our fingers if we make it that far."

"If?"

Matt sighed heavily. "We might never catch him, Abby. I haven't wanted to admit it even to myself, but the simple truth is that serial killers tend to get caught only if they screw up—and they seldom screw up."

"But this is such a small town, a town where everyone knows his neighbor. How can a—a monster hide here?"

"In plain sight. Going about his business just like the rest of us, and probably with a smile on his face." Matt shook his head. "He won't have two heads, or a forked tail—or anything else to warn the world he's an evil bastard."

Abby was silent for a minute, then said, "Was that FBI agent any help?"

"Some. He knows a bit about serial killers, and more than a bit about murder investigations. I figured he'd just get in my way, but so far he hasn't tried to take over the case. Not really surprising, I guess, since his main interest is Cassie."

"That's what she said. But what is he doing, Matt? I mean, does he want to find some kind of evidence that she's genuine? Or that she isn't?"

"According to Bishop, he's just observing. I can't make out whether he believes in her or not. He says his interest in Cassie goes back a few years, that investigations she gets involved in tend to be—I think the phrase he used was 'unusually interesting.' So he keeps an eye on her in his free time. I did point out that Cassie would most probably have a solid case for harassment if she decided to protest his observing, but he didn't seem too worried."

"How about Cassie?"

"Tense when he's around, but not especially upset, far as I can see."

Abby hesitated. "Do you think that maybe it isn't Cassie's psychic abilities Bishop is interested in?"

Matt sipped his coffee. "I wouldn't be surprised if Ben's afraid it's something like that."

"But what do *you* think?"

"Bishop doesn't give away much, so I couldn't say what his feelings are. As for Cassie, Ben's the one she watches when he isn't watching her."

"I like her," Abby said.

Matt looked at her with brooding eyes. "Yeah, so do I."

"But?"

He shook his head. "No buts. It's just that I'm wondering what all this is doing to her. To them."

"It can't be easy for either of them."

"No. And even without this situation, I'd say both of them have a few problems to work through."

Abby lifted an eyebrow. "Cassie's problems I can guess. But Ben? He's always seemed very centered, very balanced and emotionally stable."

"He has, hasn't he?" Matt shook his head. "We all have problems. Ben has his. But in one way Cassie may turn out to be the best thing that's ever happened to him. Thanks to her, I think he's finally beginning to figure out the difference between being needed by a woman and having a needy woman hung around his neck."

"You mean Mary?"

"I do. Granted the old judge was a cold fish, but if Mary had been more mature, she wouldn't have clung to Ben all these years trying to get the emotional security she needed. With her hung around his neck, especially since the old judge died, it's no wonder the last thing he wanted from any other woman was even the hint she might need more from him than he was willing to give."

"Makes sense, I guess. And you think Cassie is asking for something he is willing to give?"

Slowly Matt said, "I think Cassie is asking absolutely

nothing of Ben, despite the fact that it's painfully obvious how alone she is in her life. And maybe that's it. Maybe for once Ben's the one who needs more than he's being offered."

"From what she told me, I gather Cassie is trying not to get involved with him."

"Oh, hell, they're already involved. He's over there tonight, just like he was last night—and will be tomorrow night. Watching over her."

"Ben's never struck me as especially protective of the ladies he was interested in."

"You noticed that, huh?"

Abby smiled. "Does he know yet?"

"I don't think so. And I'd bet a year's pay that Cassie isn't sure whether he feels responsible for her or is just trying to get in her panties."

Abby had to laugh.

Matt smiled in response but then sobered. "I think that lady has seen too many monsters up close and personal. And even though yours truly is an open book to her, she says she can't read Ben, and I'm guessing that'll just make it harder for her to let him get close."

"And the longer this killer stays on the loose . . ."

"The worse it'll be for both of them. Right now, as tenuous and fragile as it is, Cassie's connection to the killer is our best lead." Matt paused. "And the killer knows it."

He wound the music box carefully and let it play, smiling as the two dancers twirled and bobbed around each other in their eternal circle.

He was tired and needed to sleep, because there would be so much to do tomorrow. But not just yet.

First he had to open his treasure box and look at each and every item, just as he always did before bed.

Becky Smith's necklace.

Ivy Jameson's peacock pin.

Jill Kirkwood's lace-trimmed handkerchief.

That was somewhat crumpled, since he had come into it a few nights before, but the sticky evidence of his devotion only made his smile widen.

He held his most recent trophy in his hands and studied it in the lamplight. Deanna Ramsay's panties. He liked the silky feel of them in his fingers. He liked the pretty blue and green flowers printed on the material. He liked the way they smelled.

He held the panties to his nose for a few minutes, eyes closed, breathing in, then put them tenderly into his treasure box with the other items.

He closed the box, then carried it to the dresser and placed it alongside the square of black velvet that occupied the center space beneath the mirror.

There were only two coins left, the dime and the fifty-cent piece.

He frowned down at them for a moment, trying to remember why they were so important.

Oh, yes. Tokens of his affection. He had to leave tokens of his affection with the ladies. That was . . . important.

He mustn't forget how important.

Two more, then.

He had already selected them. And he knew what he would do to them. It was going to be so much fun. The only question was, which one would be first?

Eeny, meeny, miny, mo . . . catch a lady by the toe . . . if she hollers . . . don't let her go. . . .

He lifted his eyes and gazed into the mirror, sad but unsurprised when nobody looked back.

*   *   *

Cassie woke with a start but had no idea what had jarred her from a blissful sleep. Then, even as Ben rose on an elbow beside her, she remembered.

"Hey." He touched her face with gentle fingers. "Are you all right?"

His hands were always so warm. She loved that. She wanted to purr like a cat whenever he touched her.

She thought she should probably be embarrassed by that.

"I'm fine," she said at last.

"You cried out in your sleep."

Cassie studied his face in the lamplight, memorizing it with an intensity she was hardly aware of. "Just a bad dream, I guess."

"You don't remember?"

"Not really. There was something about a mirror. And I couldn't get away from the music." She frowned suddenly. "Still can't."

"What music?"

"There's been a tune in my head on and off all day. It's vaguely familiar, but I can't remember what it is."

"Maybe I'd recognize it."

Cassie smiled at him. "Trust me, you don't want me to try humming. I'm tone deaf."

"Really?" He relaxed beside her, his head propped up on one hand while the other rested lightly on her stomach. "That's hard to believe. You have such a musical voice."

"Must be genetics, then. I couldn't carry a tune in a bucket with a lid on it." Cassie couldn't remember him pulling the covers up over them, but she was glad he had. She wasn't exactly embarrassed, but she did feel a bit self-conscious lying there next to him, naked.

A bit? God.

It was the most astonishing thing, passion. No wonder

so much was written about it. For the first time in her life, Cassie now understood how people could claim that passion had made them mindless.

"Cassie?"

She blinked up at him. "Hmm?"

"You went away. Where did you go?"

Cassie wondered if her eyes had crossed. Even the memory of passion was astonishing. She cleared her throat. "Nowhere in particular. What time is it?"

He glanced past her toward the nightstand. "Just after eleven."

"I should take Max out."

"I'll do that. Later." Ben leaned down and kissed her slowly and thoroughly.

By the time he lifted his head, Cassie's arms were up around his neck, and she was reasonably sure she was purring. Where had the damned covers come from? She wanted them gone.

Ben seemed to have the same idea. He pushed the blankets and sheet down until they rode somewhere around his hips, leaving Cassie bare much lower down. His eyes were on her small, pale breasts, and then his hand was touching them.

Cassie heard a muted sound escape her, and was helpless to stop it. The most casual of touches was something she was acutely aware of; the stark intimacy of his hands on her naked body was something she could feel all the way to her soul.

She wasn't aware that her eyes had closed, that her nails bit into the hard muscles of his shoulders. The bed was gone, the room, the house. The world. All she knew was his warm hand stroking her flesh, creating pleasure she had never even imagined herself capable of feeling. Her breasts were hot and aching, her belly empty, and when his hand slid down between her legs, she thought she would die.

He caressed her with certain knowledge, building her desire higher and higher until she could barely endure the sharply winding tension. She wanted to plead with him to stop torturing her, but all that emerged was a wordless whimper.

Then she felt him between her thighs, felt the slow, inexorable push of his hard flesh inside her body, and the soft sound she made was triumph and need.

"Open your eyes, love," he murmured. "Look at me."

His face was taut, eyes darkened and absorbed as they locked with hers, and Cassie was astonished all over again. She couldn't read his mind, yet somehow saw deeper, and that incredibly intimate communication made her pleasure spiral even higher as their bodies moved together.

"Ben," she whispered, obeying the compulsion to say his name, hearing the panic in her voice.

"I'm here." His lips touched hers, toyed with hers, his forearms beneath her shoulders, fingers tangled in her hair. Those gleaming, darkened eyes were heavy-lidded, fixed on hers. His hips moved in a quickening rhythm.

The tension inside Cassie became unendurable, yet she had no choice but to endure it. Her senses were spinning out of control, her body caught up in a desperate headlong rush toward completion, and she clung to Ben as the only anchor left to her in an ocean of impossible sensation.

When release finally came, it swept over her with the force of a tidal wave, the pleasure stealing her breath and almost stopping her heart, and it left Cassie dazed and shaken. She barely had the strength to hold Ben as he shuddered and groaned with his own climax, and all she could think of was how close she had come to never knowing this.

It was a long time before either of them could move, and then it was Ben who eased his weight onto his elbows and looked down at her with eyes that were still dark and intent.

Beyond any ability to be coy, Cassie said, "Wow."

A glitter of amusement lit his eyes. "I would say thank you, but it was definitely a mutual effort." His voice was husky.

"Is it . . . always like that?" The first time had been astonishing enough; Cassie wasn't sure she could survive if it just kept on getting more powerful.

"It never has been before," Ben said, and kissed her lazily.

Cassie tightened her legs when he would have lifted himself away. "Don't go."

"I'm too heavy, love."

"No, you aren't." She wondered if he was even conscious of the endearment.

"Are you sure?"

"Positive." She wanted to feel as much of him against her as possible for as long as possible.

Ben was more than willing to stay where he was for a little while at least. He kissed her again because he had to, and kept his fingers threaded through her silky hair as if, he vaguely realized, he expected her to try to escape him.

He thought she probably would.

Even then, with her body cradling his in the sated aftermath of the most incredible lovemaking he had ever experienced, there was something in her eyes that told him she was drifting away from him again, retreating in some way he could see and feel but not quite define.

He wanted to grab and hold on tight, but every instinct warned him that to do so would only push her away from him even faster and farther. The realization made something hurt inside his chest.

"You're frowning," she murmured, fingers gently smoothing his forehead.

"Am I?" He turned his head to kiss the inside of her wrist, where it was warm and soft.

"Is something wrong, Ben?"

He kept it light. "I think we should get a pet door installed for Max. Because I really don't want to leave you."

She smiled, but before she could reply they both heard a soft sound from the doorway. They turned their heads to see the dog standing there, tail waving slowly and with an almost apologetic look on his face.

"Speak of the devil," Ben said, and very reluctantly eased away from Cassie.

By the time he let the dog out for a last run, reset the security system, and made sure the fire they had earlier abandoned in the fireplace was banked for the night, Ben wouldn't have been surprised to find Cassie asleep again. But she was only drowsy, and came into his arms eagerly as soon as he slid into bed beside her.

"What kept you?" she murmured. "While you were gone, the music came back."

"Max wanted another rawhide bone." Ben kissed her, hardly surprised to find that he wanted her again and every bit as urgently as the first time.

Cassie wreathed her arms around his neck. "Stop talking about the dog."

Both of them forgot the dog.

And the music.

His shoulder made a comfortable pillow, and his body against hers was a pleasure Cassie thought she could drown herself in. She was vaguely aware of sleet rattling

against the windowpanes, of the occasional whine of the
wind, but most of her consciousness was focused on the
deep and even sounds of Ben's breathing.

He'll destroy you, came the whisper from the grave.

"I don't care," Cassie whispered in reply.

EIGHTEEN

"I wish you'd come to the station with me," Matt said restlessly, watching Abby pour herself a second cup of coffee.

"Any other Sunday, I would. But Anne can't be there today, and I have to play the organ. Matt, surely you aren't worried about me being at the church? There'll be people all around, you know that."

"Ivy Jameson was killed before she could get to church last Sunday."

"Well, you've already said you're taking me, so I should get there safely." She smiled at him. "And since you're taking me, you can come pick me up afterward."

"You don't have to worry about that."

Abby reached across the table to touch his hand. "I'll be fine, Matt. And you need to be at the station, we both know that. If what you suspect is right, you need to check all the notes on the first three murders."

"I don't know if it'll get us anywhere," he confessed.

"Maybe a step or two closer to understanding the son of a bitch. But I have to check it out."

Reluctantly Abby said, "And you'll have the autopsy report on the Ramsay girl to go over as well."

He grimaced. "I'm not looking forward to that. And I don't expect it to help us much. Even though she was left in pieces, you could still see the ligature mark on her neck. I figure the report will tell me Cassie was right about that as well. He strangled the girl with a garrote."

"What about Cassie?" Abby said. "Are you still planning to ask her and Ben to come to the station?"

"If I'm right about the missing articles. Don't know that it'll help, but I think we need to talk over a few things. And maybe Cassie will be able to contact the killer."

"What about Bishop?"

Matt shrugged. "It was what he noticed at the murder scene yesterday that got me started thinking. His expertise may come in handy, and at this point I'm not too proud to ask for help—as long as he doesn't drag the Bureau in with him. So, sure, why not?"

In fact, Matt called Bishop's motel room from his cruiser as he drove Abby to church, and the agent arrived at the station just minutes after Matt settled at his desk.

"Postmortem?" Bishop asked, noting the papers the sheriff was studying.

"Yeah. She was strangled with a thin wire or something similar. Cassie was right about that. And something else. He killed the girl while he was raping her."

Bishop sat down on the leather sofa. "A first for him, right?"

"Right. No established sexual contact with the first three victims—although Cassie says this sort of murder is always sexual, and the reading I've done seems to agree with her. You've seen the reports. What do you think?"

"She's right. It's about power, and that usually translates into sexual domination." The agent thought a moment. "A bit surprising that he apparently didn't attempt sexual domination with the first three, but he may well have achieved satisfaction observing their terror before and during the murders."

It was Matt's turn to consider. "Cassie also claims that when Jill Kirkwood was killed—third victim—the killer wore some kind of Halloween mask. We have no idea if he also wore one when he killed the first two victims—or the fourth, for that matter."

"He may have tried the mask to elicit more terror from his victim. If that's so, if he wore it only that time, and not before or after, then he may be only beginning to shape and perfect his M.O."

"What a cheerful possibility," Matt said.

"A reasonable one, I'm afraid. He kills because he likes to kill, and each experience gives him more ideas for his next murder." Bishop's voice was remote. "We may never know what triggered his compulsion, what pushed him over the line from fantasizing to acting out his fantasies, but whatever's driving him is obviously growing stronger and more complex. The first victim was not physically tortured, though we can assume he did his best to terrify her emotionally before he cut her throat. The second victim either fought him—with a certain amount of success—or else he fully intended to allow himself a bloody rampage just to find out how it felt."

"Christ," Matt muttered.

"Interesting that he followed that indulgence with a much calmer and quieter murder, and that he may have worn a mask expressly designed to terrify his victim. He was undoubtedly exhausted after killing the Jameson woman, yet he was obviously unsatisfied."

Matt snorted. "Ivy probably never satisfied a man in her life—even with her death."

Bishop smiled faintly. "Yes, she's the victim who stands out among the rest, doesn't she?"

Matt leaned back in his chair. "Are you saying that might mean something?"

"I wouldn't be surprised. The other victims ranged in age from fifteen to thirty-two—Jameson was considerably older. The other victims were quite attractive by any yardstick—Jameson was not. She was the only one killed in her home, and she may have let the killer into the house. And while the Ramsay girl was dismembered in an apparently violent rage, it's important to note that he killed her first. Jameson died in the struggle that left the crime scene a bloody mess."

"So he may have had some reason to hate Ivy in particular, which is why he chose her—is that what you mean?"

"It's a possibility. The other three victims seem to have been chosen by some combination of appearance and vulnerability, but Jameson doesn't fit into that. Wouldn't hurt to try to figure out why."

Matt nodded. "Okay. I'll send a few of my people out to question the neighbors and her acquaintances one more time. Ivy pissed off people on a regular basis though, so narrowing the field might take a while."

"In the meantime, have you found out whether there were missing items from the first three victims?"

"Yeah, it looks like there are—and I could kick myself for not asking sooner."

"It won't make any difference until you have a viable suspect. It probably won't tell us anything helpful about the killer, or offer any indication of where we might look for him. But it will provide a few nails in his coffin once we have him in custody."

"If we ever do." Matt paused, then went on briskly.

"We can't be absolutely positive, but last night and this morning I've had my people double-checking with the families and, in the case of Jill Kirkwood, searching her home. Becky Smith, according to her mother, almost always wore a thin gold chain. It wasn't found on the body and isn't in her jewelry box at home. Ivy's mother claims she always wore a peacock pin to church, and there's been no sign of one. Panties are missing from the Ramsay girl's effects, so we can assume that he took something from Jill Kirkwood as well, even though we have no clue as to what that is."

"Trophies," Bishop said. "He'll have the items in his possession, probably in a drawer or box."

"Like you said, it'll help. If we catch him." Matt sighed.

"You'll catch him. The one mistake he's consistently made is to operate in a small area within a close knit community. Sooner or later he'll have an identifiable connection to one of his victims."

"Yeah," Matt said. "But how many victims will he get before we get him?"

There wasn't a lot of traffic on the roads because of a night of sleet and a cold, overcast morning, but that was all to the good. And he doubted they would be expecting anything so soon, so that was good as well.

But the best thing of all, he thought, was that they would never, in a million years, expect him to lure his target from such an unquestionably safe haven.

The church bells began to ring, and he smiled.

They spent most of Sunday morning in bed, getting up around ten only after Max insisted, in canine terms, that enough was enough. But it wasn't until they had finished their late breakfast and cleaned up the kitchen that Cassie reluctantly brought up a touchy subject.

"I really should try again."

Ben's mouth tightened, but his voice was calm when he said, "You tried yesterday when Matt got back to his office, and you were still being blocked. Why would today be different?"

"Ben, he can't keep blocking me indefinitely. Sooner or later I'll be able to get through. Frankly I'd rather it was sooner. Don't you want this to be over?"

"Of course I do. It's just that it takes so much out of you, Cassie."

"Only when I actually make contact." She gazed at him steadily. "Testing the waters isn't hard at all. And we have to know. If he's stalking somebody else. If he's planning to kill again soon."

"Cassie—"

"Once, just once, I'd like to be able to tell Matt something other than where to find the latest body."

Ben came to her and wrapped his arms around her, holding her close. "I know."

She rested her cheek against him, her own arms lifting in a gesture that was still tentative and sliding around his waist. She wondered if he had any idea at all that he was the first person since her mother's death to offer a comforting hug. "There can't be any peace as long as he's out there."

"I know."

"And almost anything would be better than this damned music," she said somewhat ruefully.

"That's still bugging you?"

"Umm." She drew away from him, not made uncomfortable by the physical contact, but so unaccustomed that she was hyper-aware of it. "The moment I'm not thinking about anything, it creeps back in."

"Identify the song and it'll go away."

"Probably." Cassie shook her head. "Never mind, I just need to concentrate on something."

Ben didn't protest again. They left Max in the kitchen working on a rawhide treat while they went into the living room so Cassie could get comfortable. When she did have something to concentrate on, focusing on the effort to touch the killer's mind, she once more encountered a block she was unable to get past.

"Damn."

"You said he couldn't block you indefinitely," Ben reminded her.

"I know. But the block feels awfully solid." She reached up to rub her forehead. "This damned *music*."

"Do you often get an unidentifiable tune in your head?"

"No, almost never." She stared at him, suddenly very uneasy. "Almost never. When you're tone deaf, music isn't something that sticks in your mind. And this sounds like it's coming from a music box. I haven't listened to a music box in a long, long time."

Before Ben could respond the phone rang. Cassie had to get up from the sofa to reach the receiver, since it was on a side table.

"Hello?"

Ben saw her face tighten as she listened for a moment. Then she cradled the receiver. He was on his feet and moving toward her without thought.

"Cassie?"

"Wrong number," she said softly.

He put his hands on her shoulders and turned her to face him. "I don't think so. What did they say?"

"Nothing important." She let out a small laugh that

sounded more resigned than amused. "Remember you said I'd probably get a few calls from upset and suspicious citizens? That was one. But don't worry. I've been called worse things than a witch, believe me."

"Dammit." Ben pulled her into his arms and held her. "There had to be a few, I guess. But most of the people around here are pretty tolerant, Cassie. They're just afraid and panicked right now."

"I know. I'm all right, really."

He drew back just far enough to be able to kiss her, the first reassuring touch rapidly becoming something else. His hands slid down her back to her hips, holding her tighter against him, and Cassie made a muted sound of pure pleasure.

She felt a little embarrassed when he raised his head to smile down at her, but the look in his eyes was familiar evidence of his own arousal.

"Have I mentioned that I have a very difficult time keeping my hands off you?" he asked, his hands moving caressingly.

Cassie cleared her throat, but her voice still emerged huskily. "You haven't, no. But I've sort of noticed since last night."

"I've said it before. For a man with thick walls, there's a lot I can't seem to hide."

She considered that. "To be honest, I'm glad. I'm not experienced in these matters, so I'm very grateful you haven't kept me guessing."

He chuckled. "No, I haven't done that."

"Because of my lack of experience?" she asked curiously.

"Because I can't keep my hands off you." He kissed her again, hunger unmistakable. Against her mouth he added hoarsely, "I am so glad you changed your mind about us. I don't know how much longer I could have stood it."

Cassie slid her arms up around his neck, rising on tip-toe because the fit was better. Much better. "It's probably a good thing I can't read you."

"Why?" He was exploring her throat.

"Never mind."

Ben raised his head and looked at her. "Why?" he repeated.

She was embarrassed now. "Let's just say I'm having a hard time understanding why you want me."

"If you're talking about all that baggage again, I don't know why you thought it would keep me away. Everybody past the age of twenty-one has baggage of some kind. Or should." He shrugged. "God knows you haven't seemed too worried about mine."

Cassie was glad he was focused on the emotional aspects; she really didn't want to have to explain that it was his physical passion for her she found somewhat baffling. "How bad can yours be?" she asked, easing further away from the question of desire.

"Oh, mine's textbook." He returned to exploring her throat. "Domineering father, childlike mother who didn't have the faintest idea how to be a parent. Boring stuff." His voice was deliberately light, almost flippant.

"Looks to me like you grew up just fine despite that," she told him, allowing her fingers to venture into his hair and enjoying the sensations.

"Mmm. And yet . . . there are these walls."

"They seem to worry you a lot more than they do me," she commented absently, wondering if Max would be very upset if they went back to bed.

"I hope that's a good sign rather than a bad one."

Cassie was saved from having to reply when he kissed her, and her response was even more passionate, because this talk of baggage and walls had reminded her that fate would seldom be denied.

When the phone rang again, she could have sworn aloud, and Ben did. And he was the one who answered it—with considerable annoyance that was heightened by his suspicion that it was another crank call.

"Am I interrupting something?" Matt asked, and then went on immediately. "Never mind. Sorry to intrude on your love life, but we have this killer running around. You may remember."

"I do," Ben told him. "What's up?"

"A couple of maybe interesting developments. I think we should have a council of war. Can you and Cassie come to the office?"

Ben resisted the impulse to say no. With Cassie in his arms, her slender body pressed fully against his, it was more than a little difficult to think about anything else.

"Ben?"

Recalling that the killer knew who Cassie was and posed a huge threat to her safety made him answer, "We're on our way."

"Be careful on the roads. Slippery as hell out there."

"Right."

As he hung up the phone, Cassie said dryly, "I gather we're leaving?"

"Yes, dammit." Ben held her against him for a moment longer, then eased away. And it didn't take a psychic to see his reluctance. "Matt wants to talk to us. And he'd better have something important to say."

Cassie sighed. "I'll get my jacket."

"Abby?" Hannah Payne stood in the doorway of one of the classrooms and looked in to see Abby collecting the lesson books left behind by her Sunday school class.

"Hi, Hannah. What's up?"

"Kate and Donna are handling the nursery during preaching, so I'm free. Do you need me to do anything?"

"There's nothing I can think of—unless you want to finish up in here while I go upstairs and make sure the music is in place."

"Sure, happy to."

"Okay, thanks. See you upstairs."

Alone in the basement room, Hannah gathered the lesson books and put them away in a cabinet, then straightened the chairs and picked up a pair of gloves somebody had dropped. Men's gloves, black leather, and very nice. She turned one in her hands, studying it, wondering if Joe would like a pair for his birthday the following month. He didn't usually wear gloves, but . . .

The wetness she felt on two of the fingers stained her own hand pink. Staring, Hannah felt a chill of unease. Just paint, probably, or . . . something like that.

A sound from the doorway spun her around with her heart in her throat.

"What have you got there?" he asked.

"No luck, huh?" Matt asked.

"No, sorry." This time Cassie and Ben were on the leather sofa while Bishop occupied one of the visitors' chairs in the sheriff's office. Cassie had just attempted once more to contact the killer's mind, without success.

Matt shrugged. "Worth a try."

"I'll try again later," Cassie said.

He nodded. "Well, like I told you two, we have a bit more on the killer—we think. He's collecting trophies. And *maybe* he killed Ivy Jameson out of spite. We've got a growing list of people Ivy pissed off in the weeks before she was killed, so it looks like the trick there is going to be narrowing the list to something manageable."

The music in Cassie's head was beginning to madden her, but she said, "Matt, remember what I told you yesterday, what Lucy Shaw said to me?"

"I remember. That somebody was the devil."

"What do you think about that?"

He lifted an eyebrow at her. "Not much, I have to say. She's on the shady side of crazy, Cassie, and has been for more than ten years."

"What about her son?"

"What about him?"

"Is there—does he have any connection to any of the victims?" She rubbed her forehead irritably.

"Russell? Not that I know of."

Almost to herself she muttered, "He had a jacket on yesterday, so I didn't see his wrists . . . but the hands could have been right. I think."

Ben was watching her closely. "But you said you didn't see anything in Lucy's mind you could identify except kittens."

"No, I didn't. It's just a feeling." She returned his gaze, frowning. "I've missed something, I know I have. And there was something about meeting Lucy and her son that's really bothering me. Something I saw—or didn't see. Or just didn't understand."

Ben looked at the sheriff. "Who's their doctor, Matt, do you know?"

"Munro, I think. Why?"

"Will he be in church?"

Matt shook his head. "After doing that autopsy first thing this morning, I figure he'll be at his desk drinking straight scotch. What do you want me to ask him?"

"If Russell Shaw ever tried to commit suicide."

Matt pursed his lips, then reached for the phone.

Bishop, who had heard Lucy Shaw's story the previous day, said to Cassie, "Serial killers are rarely insane in any clinical sense, so it's highly unlikely he could have inherited a mental illness from his mother."

"That isn't what I'm thinking."

"What, then?"

"Ever since Ben told me about her, I've wondered what it was that triggered Lucy's illness. And after meeting her, I don't think she has Alzheimer's, or senility, or anything like that. I think something *happened* to her, some kind of shock that shattered her mind."

Ben said, "Such as discovering that she might have spawned a psychopath in the shape of her son?"

"Could be." Cassie rubbed her forehead again.

"The music again?"

"Yes, dammit."

"Music?" Bishop was still watching her. "You're hearing music in your mind?"

"Yes, but I haven't gone crazy, so don't get your hopes up."

Matt hung up the phone and said, "Doc's going to check his records. He made noises about confidentiality, but if he finds what we're looking for, he'll call back."

Bishop said to Cassie, "How long have you been hearing the music?"

"Off and on since yesterday morning."

"Since you woke up after the last contact with the killer's mind? After he caught you there?"

Cassie nodded slowly. "Yes. Since then."

Her head hurt. There was something over her head, her face, some dark material. For an instant the fear of smothering was uppermost in her mind, but then she realized that her wrists were bound behind her back. She was sitting on something cold and hard, and behind her was . . . She made her fingers explore hesitantly, and identified what felt like exposed pipe, cold and impossible to budge. Her wrists were bound together on the other side of the pipe, with a belt she thought. That wouldn't budge either, though she tried. And—

She heard the music first. Muffled by the bag over her head, the tinkling sound nevertheless identified it as coming from a music box. And it was playing . . . *Swan Lake.* Behind it, beyond it, was another sound, a muffled roaring sound that she knew she ought to be able to identify but couldn't.

That realization had barely registered in her mind, when she heard another sound, the faint scuffling of shoes against a rough floor, and she understood with a jolt of terror that she was not alone. He was there.

Instinctively, in total panic, she wrenched against the belt binding her wrists, succeeding in doing nothing except hurting herself. And drawing his attention.

"Oh, so you're awake, are you?"

"Please," she heard herself say shakily. "Please don't hurt me. Don't—"

The bag was jerked off her head, and she blinked in the sudden wash of light. At first all she saw were bare bulbs hanging down and, across the room, some hulking machinery with a small glass window that showed a fire inside.

A fire?

"I'm so glad you're awake." His voice was incongruously cheerful.

She looked up at him, focused on his face, and felt nothing but uncomprehending surprise. "You?"

"I just love the first moment of astonishment," he said, then bent down and slapped her across the face brutally with the flat of his big hand. "And the first moment of fear."

"Could the music be coming from him?" Bishop asked.

"He isn't psychic, not yet," Cassie objected, "so how could he be sending me anything?"

"Maybe he isn't sending it. Maybe he's put it in his mind—the way any person might recite a rhyme or count or calculate—in order to block out something. You. Maybe you've been touching his mind all along, and he's fighting to keep you out."

"Is that possible?" Ben asked her.

"I don't know. I suppose so. It might be a clever way to keep me out without expending much effort, distracting me with the music."

Matt said, "Does that mean you might be able to get through now?"

"I can try."

She did try, but knowledge that the killer could be using that endless tune to distract her was no help at all. "He has solid walls," she said, opening her eyes with a sigh. "And I don't understand that. There's no way he could have built them so quickly, not to protect himself from a recently perceived threat. And he didn't have them earlier, or I wouldn't have connected to him the way I did."

The phone rang then, and Matt answered it quickly. He said hello, then "yeah" a couple of times, his eyes narrowing. It was a short conversation, and when he hung up after a brief thanks, he was grim.

"What?" Ben demanded.

"Russell Shaw never tried to commit suicide as far as Doc Munro knows."

"But?" Ben asked, hearing the word in his friend's voice.

"But his son did. Mike Shaw apparently slit his wrists about twelve years ago, when he was only fourteen."

"His son?" Cassie echoed. "Lucy's grandson?"

"Yeah. The mother died in childbirth with Mike; Russell and Lucy raised him. He lived with them until about a year ago, then moved into one of those shacks out by the old mill about a mile from town."

"Is there any chance I could have met him?" Cassie asked Ben.

Grimly he said, "A good chance, though you probably wouldn't have paid much attention. Mike Shaw is the first-shift counterman at the drugstore."

"I've met him," Bishop said. "He struck me as having a ghoulish interest in the murders."

"He'd be off on Sundays," Cassie mused, recalling that the drugstore was closed then.

"And one other day." Ben looked at Matt. "Can we find out if he was off on Friday at the time the Ramsay girl was taken?"

"Yeah, easy enough once church lets out and his boss is back home, but . . ." Matt hunted through the file folders on his desk and opened one of them. "I seem to recall . . . oh, shit. Bingo."

"What?" Ben asked quickly.

"Mike Shaw is one of the people her mother mentioned had a disagreement with Ivy Jameson a few days before she was killed. Seems she ate at the drugstore and wasn't at all pleased with Mike's cooking. Ripped him to shreds—as only Ivy could—in front of his boss and half a dozen customers."

Bishop said, "I would say that probably upset him quite a bit."

"He's the right age," Ben noted. "And plenty strong enough physically."

Matt frowned. "Say we find out he was off on Friday. Does that give us enough to search his place? Will Judge Hayes sign a warrant, Ben?"

"In this case? Yes," Ben said. "He'll sign a warrant."

"Mike, why are you doing this?" She kept her voice as steady as possible, even though she had never been so terrified in her life.

He made a "tsk" sound and shook his head. "Because I can, of course. Because I want to." His attention was caught by the slowing of the music box, and he walked quickly across the concrete floor to a heavy old table where the box was sitting. He picked it up and wound it, then set it back on the table. "There," he murmured to himself.

There was an old iron cot a few feet away from her against one cinder-block wall, and she glanced toward it, fear spiraling. Surely he didn't mean to . . . "Mike—"

"I want you to shut up now." His tone was pleasant. "Just shut up and watch." He opened a battered leather duffel bag that was also on the table and began removing things from it.

A butcher knife.

A hatchet.

A power drill.

"Oh, God," she whispered.

"I wonder if there's a receptacle down here," he muttered, staring around with a scowl. "Dammit. Should have checked that."

"Mike—"

"Oh, look—there's a receptacle." He turned his head and smiled at her. "Right behind you."

•   •   •

His intercom buzzed, and Matt reached for the button impatiently. "Yeah?"

"Sheriff, a lady named Hannah Payne is on the line for you," Sharon Watkins said. "She says it's important and—I think you'd better talk to her."

Sharon had more experience in the department than he did, so Matt tended to respect her judgment. "All right."

"Line four."

"Thanks, Sharon." He punched the correct line and then turned on the speaker. "Sheriff Dunbar. You wanted to speak to me, Miss Payne?"

"Oh—yes, Sheriff, I did." Hers was a young voice, and uncertain, and also very frightened.

Matt consciously gentled his own voice. "What about, Miss Payne?"

"Well, it's . . . Joe came into the classroom when I found them, and he says I probably shouldn't bother you, and on a Sunday and all, but I'm just so worried, Sheriff! They were just there, in the classroom like he forgot them, and I think there's blood on them and—and now she's gone!"

Patient, Matt said, "Start at the beginning, Miss Payne. Where are you, and what did you find?"

"Oh, I'm at the church, Sheriff—Oak Creek Baptist. And I found a pair of black gloves in one of the Sunday school classrooms. A man's gloves, and I think they have blood on them, because they're all wet and it's coming off pink on my hands."

Tension crept into Matt's voice. "I see. Is there a label in the gloves, Miss Payne? Do you have any idea who they might belong to?"

"Well, that's why I'm worried. Because the initials inside say MS, all nicely embroidered the way Miss Lucy can do, and he's in her Sunday school class, so it must be

Mike. But he isn't upstairs in preaching, because I checked. And she's gone too, when she was supposed to play the organ, and I *know* she wouldn't have left without getting somebody else to play, not when she told me she was going to check on the music—"

"Hannah." Matt's voice was insistent. "Who's gone? Who are you talking about?"

"Abby. Mrs. Montgomery."

NINETEEN

"See, you really shouldn't have been mean to me, Abby," Mike said gently.

"Mean to you? Mike, when was I ever mean to you?" The only clear thought Abby had was to keep him talking, to stall, delay the inevitable. She had no idea what time it was, how long before Matt came to pick her up and found her missing from church. How would he find her in this place—wherever it was? A basement, she thought, but where was it? There was nothing familiar that she could see, no sight or sound to tell her what building loomed above this dim and musty-smelling room.

"That loan." He picked up the butcher knife and held it point up to study the shiny blade. "The loan I needed to get that cool 'ninety-five Mustang back before Christmas. You really should have given me the money, Abby."

She didn't bother to explain income versus debt to him. Instead, she said strongly, "I'm sorry, Mike."

"Yeah, sure you are. Now."

She swallowed hard, almost hypnotized by the way he kept turning the blade of the butcher knife. *Keep talking.*

Just keep talking. "What about Jill Kirkwood? How was she mean to you, Mike?"

"She laughed at me. Her and Becky, they both laughed at me. I saw them." He put the knife down for a moment to once more wind the music box, then picked up the knife and frowned at it.

"How do you know they were talking about you, Mike?"

His head snapped around with the speed of a striking cobra, and his young, pleasant face was twisted into an ugly mask of bitter hate. "Can't you hear good? I *saw* them. Heads together, giggling. Of course they were talking about me. Laughing at me. But they're not laughing now, are they, Abby? And I bet you wish you'd loaned me that money now, don't you?"

"Yes," she whispered. "Yes, Mike, I do."

Matt's fear was a palpable force in the room, and it was almost impossible for Cassie to close out his emotions, but she tried.

"Music," she murmured, her eyes closed. "I keep getting flashes of a music box. I think he's playing it, but— Damn. *Damn.* I can't get through."

"Oh, Christ," Matt said hollowly.

"Can you reach Abby?" Ben asked quietly.

"Not with her walls."

"Even now?"

"Especially now. They've been built up over years, over a lifetime, designed to protect the mind and spirit, so the habit is to withdraw even more thoroughly inside them when there's trouble. Damn. If I can just find a way past the music . . ."

It was Bishop who said, "Don't try to get past it. Let it carry you in. Concentrate on the music box."

She opened her eyes and stared at him a moment, then shut them and concentrated fiercely. "The music . . . the music . . . the box . . . I can see it. There are two dancers twirling around each other, bobbing. . . ."

Abby looked at the music box because it terrified her so much to look at the knife he held. It was one of those cheap little music boxes that tended to be gifts early in a little girl's life, cardboard covered with ribbed pink paper that was stained and faded. The lid was mirrored on the inside, and the mirror was cracked in at least three places. In the box between two removable velvet-covered trays two tiny dancer figurines bobbed and twirled around each other in jerky accompaniment to the tinkling music.

Swan Lake, she thought. Swan song. Was Mike clever enough for that? She didn't think so. The box was probably just something from his childhood, the significance of which she would never know. . . .

Matt, where are you?

"I think we've talked enough," Mike said, turning to smile at her. He was holding the butcher knife.

Abby swallowed. "The music box, Mike. It's slowing down again."

He looked over his shoulder, then turned back to pick up the box. "Mustn't let that happen," he murmured. "Mustn't let the music stop."

Cassie frowned. "Can't let the music stop. He can't let the music stop. He wants her to hear the music, to listen to it, because . . . because then she . . . he . . . won't let me in. That's it. He's playing the music to shut me out. But I can feel him now. I can feel his heart beating. . . ."

Ben said, "Cassie? Can you see what he sees? Can you see where he is?"

She tilted her head a bit, as though listening, then said, "He's still in the church. The old boiler room in the sub-basement. It's soundproof, and he knows nobody will ever think to search for them there, especially since he's shut me out. . . ."

"The church is five minutes away." Matt was out of his chair and bolting for the door even as Cassie's voice trailed off, with Bishop right behind him. It was the agent who snapped softly, "Start bringing her out, *now*."

Ben nodded but kept his eyes on Cassie's pale face. "Cassie? I want you to come back to me, love."

"I don't want to. . . . Abby is so alone. . . ."

"Cassie, you can't help her now. Come back."

"But . . . he's getting ready. He didn't have time to get the cot ready when he brought it here early this morning. So now he is. Tying the ropes to the frame for her wrists and ankles. He wants to play with her for a long, long time."

Ben knew time was running out, for Abby and for Cassie, but he had to ask, "Has he hurt her yet? Has he hurt Abby?"

"He knocked her out so no one would know he grabbed her. But she's awake now. She's trying to talk to him, to reason with him. He doesn't mind, because he thinks he has all the time in the world. But he's . . . getting more excited. He likes watching her try to save herself. He wonders if—if she'll scream the way the last bitch did. He liked that. . . ." Her voice trailed away, and she caught her breath.

"What is it, Cassie? What do you see?"

"Not see. Feel. His boots are too tight. They're still too tight." Cassie looked puzzled. "Why doesn't he take them off?" She fell silent, brows drawn together.

"Cassie? That's enough, Cassie. You have to get out of his mind now. You have to come back to me."

For a moment it seemed Cassie would continue to resist his command, but then she let herself relax taut muscles. A moment later she opened her eyes slowly, and even more slowly turned her head to look at him. "Matt better hurry," she whispered.

Ben pulled her into his arms, feeling her shiver against him. "He'll get there in time," he said, wishing he could be as sure of that as he sounded.

The cruiser took the corner on two wheels. Bishop hung on until all four wheels were on the street again, and then returned to checking out his weapon.

"How many doors?" he asked.

"Just one."

The sheriff's voice was level with the sort of calm more dangerous than nitroglycerin in a paper cup, and Bishop shot him a quick, accessing look. "Windows?"

"No. It's a sub-basement. The only way in is through one heavy wooden door at the base of a flight of wooden steps we access from the primary basement."

"Can the door be locked?"

"Not from the inside. With the old furnace in that room, it's a safety issue. Unless the bastard has added his own hardware, of course."

"I hate to assume he hasn't," Bishop said.

"Then we won't. We assume he's got the door locked or barred from the inside. Which means we have one shot—and only one—to surprise him. If we don't get through the first time, he knows we're out there and he has time to hold a knife to Abby's throat."

If he hasn't already. But Bishop didn't say that, of course.

.   .   .

He used the butcher knife to cut lengths of rope from a heavy coil, then left the knife on the table beside the music box. It had taken him several minutes, but he had the cot ready now, with the lengths of rope tied to the iron frame to bind her wrists and ankles. He had wound the music box several more times while working, not once losing patience with the interruptions.

That single-mindedness terrified Abby more than anything else.

Matt, where are you?

She had tried her best to loosen the belt wrapped around her wrists, but once again had done nothing except hurt herself. The pipe behind her was solidly in the wall and in the cement floor, and God knew how deep in the earth beneath it. There was no way she could free herself.

Mike went to wind the music box again. He picked up the butcher knife for a moment and stared at it, then put it down beside the box and came toward her.

"Don't—"

Ignoring her strangled plea, he hunkered beside her and reached around to her wrists. For an instant the belt tightened almost unbearably, then loosened abruptly. Abby knew at once that she was still helpless; as the blood rushed into her numbed fingers, they tingled and throbbed and were virtually useless. And when Mike grabbed her arms and hauled her up with dreadful strength, her knees buckled and she sagged against him.

"Mike, please don't hurt me." Her voice shook with terror, and the sound of her own paralyzing fear brought back vivid memories of her cowering beneath Gary's punishing fists, pleading with him to stop, not to hurt her anymore.

Nobody had come to save her then.

Nobody would come to save her now.

As Mike began to drag her toward the cot, Abby found the strength to dig in her heels, to struggle against him. "No! God damn you, it's not going to be that easy!"

She caught him off guard and got one wild swing at his jaw that actually connected and rocked his head back. For a second his grip loosened, and Abby wrenched herself away.

She got two stumbling steps away before she felt his hands close around her throat from behind, felt herself jerked back against the solid wall of muscle that was his chest.

"Bitch," he snarled, fingers tightening. "Fucking bitch! I'll teach you. I'll teach you—"

Her fingers plucked desperately at his in a vain attempt to loosen them. Blackness swam across her vision, and she sagged once more against him as the newly found strength drained out of her legs in a rush.

"I saw him kill you, Abby. I couldn't see his face, and I don't know who he is, but he was enraged, cursing, and his hands were on your throat."

Oh, God. Alexandra had been right after all. Fate couldn't be changed. . . .

It was very quiet when they reached the heavy oak door, and the light from the basement above barely illuminated the wooden steps behind them. Matt was acutely conscious of every soft creak beneath the feet of the deputy a few steps behind him and Bishop. His fears fixed on what lay beyond, Matt curled his fingers over the knob and turned it slowly. But when he leaned against the unlocked door, it refused to budge. Still moving slowly despite every instinct screaming inside him, he eased back.

Bishop bent down and used a tiny penlight to study the door. "Looks like a new bolt might have been installed on the inside," he whispered.

Matt looked at the shotgun the agent carried, and tried to swallow the dryness of terror. "Then we'll have to blast our way in."

"If we're quick enough, the surprise should give us a few seconds before he can act."

A *few seconds*.

Dear God.

Matt looked at the pistol in his hand. He thumbed off the safety and held it ready. "You blast the door, I go in first."

They shifted position, and Bishop aimed his shotgun. "Ready?"

"Go."

The sudden roar of the shotgun was deafening. Bishop followed it with a powerful kick to the door, and it crashed open.

Matt was moving even as he registered the scene inside, even as he saw that most of his worst fears had come true.

Near the center of the room, Abby slumped back against Mike Shaw, her throat surrounded by his powerful hands. Her own hands fell limply at her sides and her knees buckled as the life was squeezed out of her.

An animal-like bellow escaping from somewhere deep inside him, Matt charged across the few feet separating him and Abby. His wild gaze was on her, but he saw Mike start to turn, his young face twisted into a horrible mask of rage.

Matt didn't hesitate. He swung his gun and slammed the butt against the bridge of Mike's nose. His fingers instantly released Abby to claw at his own face. Then, before he could do more than draw a lungful of breath to howl in pain, Matt kicked the back of his knee, and he went sprawling.

Matt left him for Bishop and the deputies. He dropped to the floor beside Abby's limp body and gathered her into his arms, feeling himself begin to shake.

"Abby? Honey, please—"

At first Abby thought it was all over. But then she heard an ungodly noise, was dimly aware of Mike jerking behind her, of his fingers tightening almost convulsively. There was no more air, and the blackness filled everything, and she was falling.

"Abby . . . *Abby*! Honey, open your eyes. Look at me, Abby! Look at me—"

Matt's voice.

She tried to swallow and found that her throat hurt terribly. Tried to open her eyes and had to fight against the weight holding them shut. He was cradling her in his arms, his expression so fierce that it would have frightened her if any other man had worn it. But it was easy for Abby to smile at Matt.

"Hello," she whispered through her very sore throat.

He groaned and gathered her even closer, and over his shoulder Abby saw Mike sprawled out on the floor, cursing steadily while his hands were being cuffed behind his back by one of Matt's deputies. His nose was bleeding.

Bishop stood near the table, looking down at the music box that no longer played, at the butcher knife Mike had been too many steps away from. The agent was holding a shotgun, which explained the explosion of sound Abby vaguely recalled hearing. They must have used that to blast through the door—and distract Mike long enough to let them get inside the room.

Talk about an eleventh-hour rescue.

Abby managed to get her arms up around Matt's neck and whispered, "What do you know. This time somebody came."

MARCH 1, 1999

"The really unexpected thing," Ben said after hanging up the phone the next afternoon, "is that Hannah Payne probably saved her own life as well as Abby's. Matt says they found Polaroids at Mike Shaw's house—all the victims before and after he grabbed them. And he had one each of Abby and Hannah. So she was intended to be next. She told Matt she got a creepy phone call the other day, the same as Abby did. Abby thought hers came from Gary, but he swore not."

"Before or after Matt hit him?"

Ben chuckled. "After, I think. Gary Montgomery is a very subdued man, I'd say. Matt made it perfectly plain to him that if Abby gets so much as a hangnail in the next thirty or forty years, Gary is dead meat. And given the fact that Matt was just this side of sane after nearly losing her to a serial killer, I have no doubts that Gary believed every word."

"Neither do I."

Ben sat down beside her on the sofa and shook his head. "I still can't get over it. Mike Shaw, a serial killer. Christ, he worked on my campaign."

"Is he saying anything?"

"Not much, no. And since the county public defender has already announced she'll resign before taking him on as a client, and his father refuses to hire any other attorney—not that one has come forward to offer—questioning him is a bit of a problem."

"How will it be solved?"

"We're going outside the county to somebody who won't have to live here after the trial. Judge Hayes already has calls in to a couple of good lawyers, and one of them's bound to take the case—for the notoriety, if nothing else. Then again, when the news breaks in the major newspapers, there'll probably be at least a few hotshots outside the state who'll sell their souls for the case."

"But you'll prosecute?"

"Damned right. His lawyer will argue for a change of venue, but no matter where the case is tried, I will prosecute."

"Good. Did I hear you say something about Bishop?"

"Matt says he's sticking around for a while. Lending his expertise in gathering and cataloging all the evidence they're turning up at Mike's house." Ben paused, then went on carefully. "Which, of course, wouldn't have anything to do with you. Him staying, I mean."

Cassie looked at him, smiling faintly. "Not a thing."

He eyed her. "Uh-huh."

"Don't you have to be in court today? I mean, I know the county prosecutor has a certain amount of leeway, but most of them work Mondays, I thought."

"I'm taking some well-deserved time off before getting to work on the biggest case this county has ever seen. The legal system won't grind to a halt without me for a few days."

Cassie was thoughtful. "I see. Which, of course, wouldn't have anything to do with me."

"It's Max. I can't bear to abandon him."

She glanced toward the dog, who was snoring softly on his rug near the fireplace. "Yes, he's obviously the clinging sort."

Ben grinned at her. "Okay, okay. We both know you're not. And I know you're not in danger any longer, not even from crank calls, given that the mayor is ready to hand you the key to the town after Matt made it clear you saved Abby's life and helped him catch the killer."

"I hope you'll tell His Honor I don't want the key to the town." Cassie was uncomfortable both with that idea and with the growing certainty that Ben had something on his mind. "I'm glad I was able to help there at the end, but nothing's really changed, Ben."

"Hasn't it?" He was grave now, watchful.

"No. I'm not part of the town. I moved out here for peace and quiet, just like my aunt did." Cassie shrugged. "She managed to live here for twenty years without getting involved, and I imagine I will too."

"You're already involved, Cassie. You did something Alexandra never did—put yourself at risk for the people here."

"I didn't have much choice. You know that."

"You had a choice. You could have run away, avoided the whole problem and left it up to us to catch Mike. But you stayed, and you helped."

She drew a breath. "You also know it was an—an extraordinary event, probably once in a lifetime for this town. It won't happen again."

"So you mean to bury yourself out here? Go into town only when you have to? Take Alexandra's place as the town eccentric?"

"There are worse fates," she murmured.

"What about us, Cassie?"

She turned her head to look at the fire they had going because it was a cold day with occasional snow flurries, and thought again of her aunt's prediction about Abby's ultimate fate. Alex had been wrong, or knowing about it had somehow enabled Abby to change what might otherwise have happened.

She might have been wrong about Ben too. And Cassie might have been wrong when she had seen her own fate. There was, at least, a chance of that.

Wasn't there?

"Cassie?"

She was afraid to look at him. "I don't know. I guess I just assumed it would—would go on for a while. Until you got tired of me."

"Tired of you?" He put his hands on her shoulders and turned her to face him. "Cassie, are you under the impression this is just an affair?"

She stared at him. "What else could it be?"

"Something a lot more permanent." He touched her face with gentle fingers, brushed back a strand of silky black hair. "I hope."

Of all the possibilities she might have considered, that one had never even occurred to her—and Cassie was more than a little surprised it had occurred to him. Slowly she said, "I think it's a little early to be talking about anything permanent, don't you? I mean, neither one of us was looking for any kind of commitment."

"Maybe not, but—"

"Ben, you know there's no maybe about it. I've been . . . shying away from people most of my life, and it's obvious you aren't ready for any kind of long-term commitment."

"How is it obvious?" Then he realized. "Oh. My walls."

It didn't take a psychic to see that the reminder disturbed him, and Cassie conjured a rueful smile. "We're still getting to know each other, still learning to trust. Let's give us time, Ben, okay? Time without . . . outside pressures like serial killers pushing us toward something we're not ready for yet. There's no hurry, is there?"

"I suppose not." He pulled her into his arms, smiling but with something of a frown lingering in his eyes. "As long as you don't intend to kick me out of your bed anytime soon."

"That," Cassie said, sliding her arms up around his neck, "was never part of my plan."

It was after dark when Ben woke in the lamplit bedroom to find himself alone. He got dressed and went downstairs, discovering Cassie in the living room. The smell of something good cooking wafted from the kitchen, and she was busy packing away the stacks of papers and journals that had lain on the coffee table for the past few days.

He paused for a moment in the doorway to watch her, conscious of a constriction in his chest and a cold knot of unease in the pit of his stomach. Had he made a mistake? His common sense had told him to wait, to be careful not to make demands, but other instincts had insisted that Cassie know how he felt.

Ben thought she cared for him. He thought that given her past and almost pathological reluctance to allow anyone even the most casual of physical contact, she would have been unable to accept him as her lover if she had not cared. If she had not trusted him at least partly. But he also knew that Cassie's past experiences with the dark violence of too many male minds made it almost impossible for her to completely trust a man, especially when she could not read him.

His damned walls.

She would not commit herself to him until she was sure of him, and his walls made that impossible. Even if he managed to pull the walls down, Ben wasn't sure it would bring Cassie to his side and his life for good. She had been alone for a long time, had convinced herself that being alone was the best way for her. Would she—could she—change her life so drastically by accepting him and all the people and responsibilities he would bring with him?

He didn't know.

Ben arranged his features to express pleasant companionship and went into the living room. "You abandoned me," he accused Cassie lightly.

She smiled. "I got hungry, sorry. Spaghetti. I hope you like it."

"Love it." He wanted to touch her but forced himself not to make his need for her so damned obvious. "What are you doing in here?"

"Packing away this stuff."

"I thought you were going to read the journals."

Cassie sent him a glance he couldn't interpret to save his life, and murmured, "Sometimes it's best not to know how things turn out."

"Are we talking about Alexandra?"

She looked at the journal in her hand, then added it to the other stuff in the box. "Of course."

He didn't think so but accepted what she said, wary of pushing her when she seemed so elusive. "Well, you can always read them later."

"Yes. Later." Cassie closed the box, then looked at him, smiling. "The sauce should be ready if you are."

"I'm ready."

He moved very carefully, wary of the dog's keen ears even with the noise of sleet and wind. Caution told him to stay back, but he wanted to get closer, close enough to see inside.

So cozy in there. A nice fire in the fireplace. Lights and the appetizing aroma of good food making the kitchen warm and snug. Quiet voices that were comfortable with each other and yet aware, the edges of their words blurred with longing, with hope and uncertainty and fear.

They were completely wrapped up in each other.

They were oblivious of his watching eyes.

He stood outside, his collar turned up and hat pulled low to protect his face from the stinging sleet. It was cold. The ground was frozen, and his feet were cold inside the thin shoes. But he remained where he was for a long time, watching.

She hadn't understood. All his work, and she hadn't understood.

Hadn't understood he had done it all for her.

But she would.

Soon.

MARCH 2, 1999

"So much for time off," Ben said, knotting his tie as Cassie lay in bed, watching him. "Trust Judge Hayes to make me come back to work."

"Well, he's right," she said. "Now that Mike Shaw has a lawyer, and most of the evidence has been collected from his house, it's time for you to go to work."

"Do you have to be so reasonable?" Ben came to sit on the edge of the bed, smiling down at her. "I'm being driven out of a very warm bed on a very cold morning, and I intend to bitch about it."

She reached up to touch his face in one of those hesitant little gestures that always stopped his heart. "The warm bed will be here waiting for you when you get back. That is—"

"Oh, I'm definitely coming back," he assured her.

"For lunch if I can manage it. By five if I can't. Either way, I'll bring takeout. Any preferences?"

"No. I'm easy to please."

"Yes," he said, bending to kiss her, "you are. Try to go back to sleep, love. I'll take Max out and feed him before I leave. See you later."

Cassie listened to the faint sounds of his leaving, then curled up with her arms wrapped around his pillow and breathed in the faint scent of him that clung to the linen. Already he was marking his presence in her life. Her bed smelled of him, and the scent of his aftershave lingered in the room. His toiletries were on the bathroom counter beside hers. One of his shirts lay across the chair in the corner.

Something permanent?

She shied away from thinking about that because it was so astonishing and potentially wonderful—and she didn't trust the possibility of it. Her life had taught her that wonderful things simply did not happen to her, and she had learned to eye happy surprises with suspicion.

There was always a catch.

But until she discovered what that was, Cassie just wanted to enjoy the moment, to luxuriate in contentment. She was in a warm bed where a warm man had lain beside her all night, and every muscle in her body was blissfully weary.

He was a very . . . passionate man.

Smiling to herself as she remembered that passion, Cassie drifted off to sleep.

When the ringing woke her, she thought it was her alarm, and peered at the nightstand resentfully. But then the phone rang again, and she pulled herself across the bed to answer it.

"Hello?"

"Cassie, will you please tell Ben to get his ass over

here?" Matt requested in a harassed voice. "That damned defense lawyer made some phone calls on his way here, and now I'm hip-deep in the media. The *national* media. I don't want to talk to them, that's Ben's job, dammit."

She reached to turn the clock toward her, and a cold hand closed around her heart. "Matt . . . he left here more than two hours ago."

TWENTY

There was a long silence, and then Matt said carefully, "The roads are a mess. Maybe he stopped to pull somebody out of a ditch. He has chains in that Jeep of his, and a winch. That's probably it. I'll send a patrol car out that way."

"He would have called. He would have called one of us."

"Maybe he hasn't had time. Don't make yourself crazy before we know if there's a reason."

Cassie's throat was so dry, she could hardly swallow. "I'm coming to town," she said.

"Cassie, listen to me. I wasn't kidding about the media. There are three news vans parked in front of the station, and the place is crawling with press. You do not want to be here."

"Matt—"

"You stay put. I'll check it out and call you the minute I know something."

"Hurry," she whispered. "Please hurry."

For an endless hour Cassie paced the floor and bit her

nails, her imagination going wild. Even though she knew it would be impossible, she tried to reach out to Ben, telling herself it simply wasn't conceivable that something could have happened to him without her knowing about it. She would have felt it, surely.

All she felt was terror, and it was all hers.

When Matt's cruiser pulled up in her driveway, Cassie knew the news would be bad. Numb with dread, she went out onto the porch to meet Matt and Bishop, and their faces told her that her instincts were right.

"He's not dead," she said.

"No, he's not dead. At least—we don't think so." Matt took her arm and led her back into the house, and the physical contact made her acutely aware of his worry.

Cassie sat down on the sofa, staring from one man to the other. "What do you mean, you don't think so?"

Matt sat down beside her. "We found the Jeep but not Ben. It looks like he stopped to clear a fallen tree from the road. Idiot. The Jeep could have made it over easily. He was thinking about whoever came along behind him."

"I don't understand," Cassie said. "If he wasn't with the Jeep, then where is he? What happened?"

From his position on his feet near the fireplace, Bishop said, "There were tire tracks showing another vehicle came up behind his. And that tree didn't come down naturally."

"You mean—some kind of trap?"

Matt nodded. "We think so, Cassie. It looks like someone else stopped, ostensibly to help Ben. Then grabbed him, probably after knocking him out. There's— We found a little blood at the scene." Quickly he went on. "I have some of my people crawling all over the scene, and I sent for the tracking dogs, but I'm not expecting them to pick up much of a trail. Back at the station they're pulling files and cross-checking to see if we can come up with anybody who might have had an especially strong grudge against Ben."

Cassie tried to concentrate. "Who? Who would have done something like this?"

"Like any other prosecutor and former judge, Ben's made his share of enemies, and while any of them might have run him off the road, setting a trap like this is way beyond what I'd expect. This was . . . I don't know . . . personal somehow." Matt exchanged a glance with Bishop, then said, "We found something on the front seat of the Jeep."

"What?"

Matt reached into the pocket of his jacket and pulled out a plastic evidence bag. Inside was a single red rose, painstakingly fashioned from tissue paper.

"Oh, my God," Cassie whispered.

The headache had lessened to no more than a dull throb, and the blood had dried on the side of his face, but Ben still felt lousy. Every time he turned his head too fast, dizziness swept over him and nausea churned in his stomach, and shouting a few times in the vain hope somebody other than his captor would hear had earned him nothing except more pain and queasiness. Cold and stiff, he kept flexing his fingers in the hope of warding off total numbness and in the effort to loosen the ropes binding his wrists to the arms of the chair where he sat.

He had studied every inch of the room, and there wasn't much to see. It was mostly barren, the two windows heavily curtained, the ancient carpet on the floor stained and threadbare. One other chair sat by the closed door. There was a fireplace where a low fire burned and took the edge off the chill; the only other light came from an incongruously elegant torchère between the windows.

So all he could say for sure about where he was being held was that there was some electricity, even if it wasn't being wasted on heat. That and his present position told him his captor wasn't much concerned about the well-being of his hostage. The iron chair Ben was tied to was dead center in the room and bolted to the floor, and several attempts had convinced him it would take more than muscle to budge it. He was glad his wrists were tied to each arm of the chair rather than behind his back, but if the position was more comfortable, it didn't provide extra leverage to dislodge the chair.

He thought he had loosened the ropes a bit though. Unless that was only wishful thinking.

The initial shock of finding himself helpless had finally passed, and he was left with anger and bewilderment; fear, he thought, would undoubtedly come later. What occupied his mind in those first long minutes of silence was the question of who hated him enough to do this.

He had a hazy memory of stopping the Jeep to clear away a tree fallen across the road, but nothing beyond that. He could only assume that someone had come up behind him and hit him with something heavy.

But who?

He had put away a few people in his time, but Ben couldn't think of anyone with a resentment powerful enough to arrange his kidnapping. The timing also struck him as extremely odd; with virtually everyone in the county overwhelmingly relieved by the capture of a serial killer, who would be concentrating on old grudges?

He kept working to loosen the ropes, taking advantage of being alone in the room because he had a fair idea that wouldn't last long. And it didn't.

When the man walked into the room a few minutes later, pushing some kind of rolling cart covered with a white cloth, Ben's first realization was that he was a total stranger. He was a medium-sized man on the wiry side, not particularly tall or particularly powerful in appearance, with straight hair-colored hair and the pasty skin of someone who didn't spend much time outdoors. The only unusual physical characteristic Ben noticed was that he had incongruously large hands and feet, both of which lent him a slightly ludicrous air. His features were regular, even pleasant, and he wore a small half-smile.

It was the smile that made Ben suddenly, acutely, aware of the chill in the room.

"Hello, Judge. That's what they call you, isn't it? Judge?" His voice was deep, the tone amiable.

"Some do." All his instincts told Ben to hold on to both his wits and his temper, to keep his body relaxed and his own voice calm. But the hair on the back of his neck was standing straight out.

"Oh, I think most do. And I think you like it."

"What do I call you?" Ben asked.

The man smiled, revealing even white teeth. "What is that thing you see on T-shirts everywhere these days? Bob's wife, Bob's boss, Bob's brother. Just call me Bob."

"Okay, Bob. Should I know what it is I've done to piss you off?"

"Should—but don't." He got the chair that was by the door and placed it in front of Ben a few feet away, beside the covered cart, and sat down. The picture of relaxed interest, he clasped his big hands together in his lap and continued to smile pleasantly at his captive.

"Do we play a guessing game?"

"Bob" shook his head. "Oh, I'm quite willing to tell you, Judge. That's the whole point of this, after all. No one should ever die without knowing why."

"So tell me."

"The oldest male game in the world, Judge. Rivalry."

"I see. So what are we competing for?"

"Why, for her, of course. For Cassie."

Ben controlled the urge to lunge at the other man, and kept his voice cool. "And here I thought all I had to worry about was an FBI agent."

Bob's smile widened. "Bishop? Neither of us has to worry about him, not where Cassie's concerned. He's not in love with her. He likes to believe he understands her, but he doesn't really. I'm the only one who really understands Cassie."

That his captor knew Bishop was bad enough; the caressing way his voice dropped whenever he said Cassie's name was beginning to make Ben's skin crawl. "What gives you this special insight?" he asked.

"It's very simple, Judge. I understand Cassie because, unlike you or Bishop or any other man in her life, I'm a part of her. I've been inside her head for years."

Matt said, "Bishop had much the same reaction and refused to explain. So why don't you? What does this paper flower mean to both of you?"

Cassie swallowed hard and forced herself to remain calm. "It started . . . more than four years ago. The L.A. police called me in on a series of murders. It was unusual because the killer hit all age groups, from little girls to elderly women, and all races. The victims had nothing in common except that they were female. He killed them in different ways, tortured some but not others, hid some bodies while leaving others out in the open so they could be easily found. It seemed to be almost a game to him to keep everybody guessing. The FBI profiler they called in was tearing his hair out."

"So the police called you in," Matt said. "And?"

"He always left a paper rose on his victim's body, and I used that to connect with him. I tapped into him pretty easily just as he was stalking his next victim. The police were able to save the girl, but the killer slipped away in the confusion. And vanished."

"You mean he stopped killing?"

Cassie nodded. "For a while, at least that's what the police believe. It was more than six months later when three more bodies turned up, each left with one of his trademark paper roses. Again I was able to tap into his mind, and again he managed to slip away. For the next couple of years he'd suddenly go active, kill two or three times, then vanish before anybody could get close. Including me. There was no pattern we could fix on, no way we could anticipate when and where he'd begin killing again. Then . . ."

"Then?"

It was Bishop who took up the story, his voice cool. "Then he killed a series of children in rapid succession, and the entire city was going crazy. Finally, and for the first time, the killer left behind more than a rose. He left a fingerprint. The police were able to identify him as one Conrad Vasek, an escaped mental patient with the distinction of having terrified every doctor forced to try treating him in the twenty years since he was committed at the age of twelve."

Matt said, "And they had no luck finding him even though they knew who he was."

"None. The man was acknowledged as a twisted genius, psychopathic since birth but brilliant. And he loved games." Bishop's gaze shifted to Cassie. "Especially new ones."

"You weren't there," Cassie murmured, staring down at the rose.

"I heard about it afterward," Bishop said. He looked at Matt. "Just about the time Vasek killed an elderly woman and then a teenager, word leaked out to the press that the L.A. police were trying to track him using a psychic. Vasek must have seen it as a challenge. He grabbed a little girl but didn't kill her right away. Instead, when Cassie connected to him, he led the police a long and merry chase and then was somehow able to distract Cassie just long enough."

"I misinterpreted what I saw," Cassie said. "Sent the police the wrong way. When they found the little girl, her body was still warm."

"And you got the blame?" Matt demanded incredulously.

"I blamed myself. And it was . . . just too much. I couldn't handle it anymore. That's when I left L.A. and came here."

Softly Bishop said, "I wonder how long it took Vasek to find you."

Cassie stared at him, with dawning understanding. "Of course," she whispered. "That's why the light was falling from two different directions when I tried to reach Mike Shaw. That's how Mike was able to push me out with such strength, to block me for so long even though he isn't telepathic. Because it wasn't him. Somehow Vasek was linked to Mike's mind, controlling him. Vasek was controlling him all along."

"Inside her head." Ben spoke slowly.

"She didn't know I was there, of course. She thought we were in contact only whenever she was helping the police try to catch me. But I've been able to slip into her mind virtually at will for a long time now. Into her thoughts. Her dreams."

"Her nightmares." Until that moment Ben had never been able to truly see the substance, the reality, of Cassie's monsters. But then he saw. Finally he understood. And it wasn't the chill of the room that sank deeper into his bones and left shards of ice so cold they burned.

Dear God, Cassie . . .

The monster calling himself Bob continued to smile. "Her nightmares? Oh, I don't think so. All I did was . . . encourage her . . . to use her natural gifts. Remind her who she really was. That's why I followed her here. She thought she could run away from who she was, but I couldn't let her. We were meant to be together, Cassie and I, and I had to show her that. I had to show her that our minds were already joined."

"By killing more women?"

"By making certain she used her natural gifts."

Ben swallowed the bile rising up in his throat and forced himself to say calmly, "So you came here and looked for a tool you could use to attract her attention. To impress her with your own abilities. You needed someone with a weak mind you could control, someone with the instincts—if not the expertise—of a natural killer. Mike Shaw."

"You must admit, Michael was perfect. And I was quite lucky to find him in this pissant little town of yours. A sociopath more than ready for his first real kill. All he needed was a little guidance, and that was simple enough."

"How did it feel," Ben asked, "to kill by remote control?"

Bob seemed gratified by the question, clearly happy to explain. "Interesting, actually. And more satisfying than I had expected. He's totally primitive, of course, driven by rage and imagined slights, and with absolutely no finesse. I'm sure your experts will find he's clinically insane. Not too bright either, I'm afraid. But he made excellent clay I could mold to fit my needs."

"And your need was to impress Cassie."

"I wanted her to understand," Bob said reasonably. "That we were two halves of a whole, that we belonged together. I knew that from the first time she touched my mind. But she didn't seem to understand the glory of the kill, and how . . . liberating it is. So I had to show her."

"Then why use a tool?" Ben asked. If he could keep him talking, let him reveal more and more of himself, then maybe, just maybe a weakness would become apparent. Something Ben could work on, as he worked on witnesses in a courtroom to get what he needed from them.

"Why, to show Cassie how powerful I am, of course." Bob was thoughtful. "And I am, you know. Quite powerful. I had to maintain the connection with Michael most of the time in order to keep him under control, while also hiding my presence from Cassie."

"How were you able to do that?"

"The connection to Michael was simple to establish, and not terribly difficult to maintain. He just needed to be in constant physical contact with an item that belonged to me. As for hiding my presence from Cassie, I'd been practicing that for nearly three years."

"Why hide from her at all? I mean, if you were intent on impressing her, why not reveal yourself from the first?"

"To surprise her, of course." Bob's smile faded at last, and his ordinary-colored eyes took on an odd shine. "That was before I realized you were going to confuse her."

"Is that what I did?"

"We both know it is. She was completely untouched, innocent, and you ruined that. You preyed on her weak female body to scramble her instincts and senses, used your experience to teach her a passion of the flesh." For just an instant he seemed faintly distracted, as though hearing a distant sound, but then he shook his head. "You corrupted her."

"Then I'm surprised you still want her."

"I'll have to purify her, naturally. She can never return to her untouched state, but she can be made more worthy of my love."

Ben wasn't about to ask how. Instead, he said coolly, "Well, I didn't butcher other women for her, but I'm willing to bet Cassie prefers my ideas of romance to yours."

"You confused her. She was completely focused on me and what I could do when she was in California, and she would have regained that focus. If not for you." His smile was thin and particularly unpleasant. "You told her you loved her, didn't you, Judge?"

"Don't you know?" Ben taunted softly. "Weren't you in her mind when I was in her bed?"

The odd shine in those ordinary eyes intensified, but a fragment of Bob's smile remained. "You know, I sat in court one day and watched you, Judge. You're very good. Quite skilled at . . . going for the jugular. But there's something you've forgotten, I'm afraid."

"Oh? And what's that, Bob?"

Bob reached over to flip back a corner of the white cloth on the cart beside him, revealing a varied selection of implements that had only one thing in common. They were all very, very sharp. He picked up what looked like a scalpel and tested the edge with his thumb, then smiled at Ben.

"When I go for the jugular, I use a real knife."

Matt hung up the phone and turned to Cassie. "You were right about the damned boots. They practically had to cut them off Shaw, but Vasek had scrawled his name inside sure enough. How the hell—?"

"They were always too tight," Cassie murmured from her position near the fireplace, where she stood, petting Max. She couldn't sit still any longer, and for the past few minutes had been restlessly prowling the room.

Matt was baffled. "Why did Vasek have him wear his boots?"

"Connections. Vasek is an amazingly strong telepath, but what he was trying to do was incredible. To control another mind like that, even a sick and broken one . . . He needed something of his always touching Shaw, so the connection would be almost automatic. According to what the L.A. police found out about him, he's quite a bit smaller than Shaw, so none of his clothing would fit, but a physical oddity is that he has large hands and feet. Shaw could wear his boots, even though they were a bit too tight. It worked quite well."

Matt shook his head. "One of my deputies is bringing them out here. What makes you think you'll be able to connect with Vasek using the boots when the flower didn't even get you close?"

"Because he's been using them as a conduit." Cassie drew a deep breath, trying to keep herself calm and centered, trying to save her energy. "I don't know if it'll work, Matt. But I have to try."

Matt didn't ask if she'd tried to contact Ben telepathically. He knew she had, and had failed, and her desolation had been so painful to see that he had turned away.

He looked at the FBI agent and said, "What I can't understand is this. If he did all this to impress Cassie, then how does grabbing Ben and suddenly going silent figure into his plans? Is it because we caught Mike? Because his tool isn't available any longer?"

Bishop's gaze was on Cassie. "He grabbed Ryan out of

pure jealousy, I'd say. It's been fairly obvious in the last few days that Cassie's in love with him, and that he had elected himself her protector."

She flinched but said nothing.

Matt asked bluntly, "Then why not just kill Ben outright? Why take him alive?"

Even with a face as unexpressive as granite, it was still obvious that Bishop didn't want to answer that question. But finally, softly, he did. "Because he wants to play with him for a while. To appease his jealousy and to punish Cassie."

Cassie made a smothered little sound, then said, "I'm going to shut Max up in the kitchen before the deputy gets here," and hurriedly led the dog from the room.

"Next time," Matt said grimly to Bishop, "just *tell* me it's a dumb question, all right?"

"All right. Any luck with those tire tracks?"

"I've got people combing both sides of that road trying to pick them up again. With so much sleet and mud, we've at least got a shot." He fell silent for several minutes, then said, "Do you think Ben's still alive?"

"Yes."

Matt looked at him curiously. "Why?"

"Because a cat likes to torment its prey before it kills it."

"I'm sorry I asked."

Bishop shook his head. "It won't be physical torture, not at first. From what I know of Vasek, he'll want to talk, brag about what he was able to do, probably try to show himself off as a better match for Cassie. Plus, it should throw him off stride to have a male victim. Ryan can work that to his advantage if he's smart enough to use it."

Matt hoped his friend was smart enough.

When Cassie came back into the living room a few

minutes later, she was calm again. And if the two men noticed that her eyes were red-rimmed, neither commented.

"Where's that deputy?" she demanded of Matt.

"Another five minutes, Cassie. Be patient."

"I can't be patient."

"Try. And when the boots are here, assuming they
work for you, what do you mean to do? If Vasek is as
strong as you claim, how the hell can you get into his
mind without his knowing?"

"I will, that's all." Her voice was flat. "I just will."

Matt might have continued to object, but the phone
rang just then and he went quickly to answer it. "I told
everybody to shut off the walkie-talkies. The damn things
can be heard for miles," he muttered in an explanation
nobody asked for.

He said hello, then "yeah" a couple of times. Cassie
watched him and without even trying caught a few flashes
of a narrow dirt road and an old house in the distance. A
knock on the door distracted her, and by the time Bishop
answered it and brought one of Matt's deputies into the
living room, the sheriff was hanging up the phone.

"They've found the place," she said to Matt.

"Maybe." He was more grim than hopeful. "The tire
tracks match, and they lead to what's supposed to be a de-
serted house. It would help if we could have verification."

Cassie took the pair of gleaming snakeskin boots from
the young deputy, who looked bewildered but gave them
up without a protest.

Matt said to him, "Stand there in the doorway and
keep your mouth shut, Danny."

"Yes, sir."

Cassie sat down on the sofa, holding the boots in her
hands and staring at them.

Remembering what Ben usually did, Matt asked, "Will
you need a lifeline?"

"Not for this. I just want to see if I can . . ." She closed her eyes and after a moment murmured, "I can get in. There's one part of his mind he's not guarding, the part that used to be connected to Mike Shaw. It isn't a large doorway, but it's there. And it's big enough."

"Can you tell me where he is, what he's doing?" Matt asked.

She frowned slightly, then started and opened her eyes. "He almost caught me. He's quick. Very quick." She chewed on her bottom lip as she set the boots on the coffee table. Her voice was steady when she said, "I wasn't deep enough to see through his eyes. But for an instant he thought about where he was, and I saw the same house I saw in your mind, Matt."

"I was afraid of that. The house is very isolated, Cassie, practically out in the middle of a field," the sheriff said. "No cover at all." His brooding gaze shifted to Bishop. "If Vasek sees us coming, he could hold us off indefinitely. With Ben as his hostage. And if he's armed—"

"He usually is," Bishop said.

"Shit. I just don't see how we can catch him by surprise. If we go in in force, he'll easily see us coming, and have plenty of time to—"

Cassie lifted a hand to cut him off, unwilling to hear possibilities. She got to her feet and went to stand by the fireplace, already feeling cold. "He won't see you coming. I'll distract him."

"How?" Bishop demanded.

She looked at the agent. "I'll give him something else to think about. Me."

"So," Ben said, "your only way of dealing with a rival is to cut his throat, huh?"

"Not my only way. Just the best way. You have to be out of Cassie's life."

"And then she'll tumble into your arms? I don't think so."

"She will come to me quite willingly, Judge," the madman said. "Once I take care of you. Once she learns the lesson."

"The lesson being?"

"That she belongs to me. That I will not tolerate anyone else in her life. Not a lover, certainly. And if, once you're gone, she still fails to understand and I have to kill two or three of the people she considers friends, well, I'm sure that will get the point across." His smile widened. "Don't you agree?"

TWENTY-ONE

"You can't," Bishop said.

"I know you'd like to believe that, but—"

Bishop stepped toward her and grabbed her wrist to stop her when she would have turned away. "That isn't what I mean," he said roughly.

Matt saw Cassie go still, saw her stare up at the agent with surprise and something else, something he couldn't define, the emotion flitting across her delicate face like a shadow. Then Bishop was speaking again, an edge to his voice, and the moment passed.

"If you touch his mind openly, go through that narrow doorway he used with Shaw, the connection is his as well as yours. He can hold on to it. Pull you even deeper. Close off the way behind you. And what happens if the cops shoot him—kill him? We both know that's what's likely to happen, because Vasek won't let himself be taken alive. He'll make damned sure they have to kill him. And he won't let go of you. You'll be in too deep, Cassie."

Matt said, "Too deep? You mean she won't be able to get out? Even if he dies?"

Bishop released Cassie's wrist. "He could hang on even while he dies. And pull her with him."

"You don't know that." Cassie massaged her wrist absently, not looking at either of the men. "At best, it's all theoretical. Besides, I'm strong enough to pull away."

"You don't know that," Bishop retorted. "This man, this *monster*, is obsessed with you, Cassie. He followed you across three thousand miles, and when he found you, he methodically destroyed what was left of Mike Shaw's mind so he'd have a tool he could use to get your attention without exposing himself. He designed all of this, set up the situation to involve you, impress you with his cunning. Do you really think if you drop your guards and expose yourself, walk willingly into his mind, that he'll *ever* let go of you?"

"I'm strong enough," she repeated steadily.

"I don't think so."

She glanced up at him, then turned her head and gazed at the sheriff. "One thing we can all be sure of. Unless we stop Vasek, he'll kill Ben. And then he'll go on killing. More women, Matt. Maybe here, in your town. More people you know and care about. This is the best chance we'll have to get to him. You know it is."

Matt was a cop and he saw the logic. But the idea of allowing Cassie to sacrifice herself stuck in his craw. "Can't you just tease him somehow? Get his attention just long enough to let me and my people get close? It would take only a couple of minutes, five at most. Can you do that without giving him a chance to pull you in?"

"Of course I can."

"She can't," Bishop said. "It's all or nothing, Dunbar. To pull this guy's focus, she'll have to expose herself, walk in and show herself to him. And you can bet he'll grab and hold on tight. If she's inside the bastard's head and you have to kill him, she dies." Bishop smiled thinly. "But you'll save your friend. Maybe it's a price you're willing to pay."

The sheriff took a step toward the agent, but Cassie's voice fell between them, curiously soft. "Bishop, if you say one more word, I promise you'll regret it." Her gaze fixed on Matt's face, and she smiled. "You don't have to worry, Matt. I'll be just fine. No danger at all, remember that. Will you remember?"

Matt looked at her, frowning for only an instant as though troubled by something too wispy to get hold of. Then he smiled back at her. "I'll remember. No danger. You'll be fine."

"Yes, I'll be fine. The important thing is to surprise Vasek so you can save Ben." Her voice remained gentle. "So you get your people into position, and when you are, call and let me know. Then give me exactly five minutes before you make your move. All right?"

"All right, Cassie. I'll leave Danny here with my cell phone, and he'll be able to report when we're ready."

Bishop didn't say a word.

Matt said, "It'll probably take us fifteen minutes to get there and into position, Cassie. But I'll let you know. And I promise—I'll get Ben out of there alive."

"Of course you will." She said it as if there were simply no other possibility.

The sheriff nodded decisively and left the room after giving his phone to the young and puzzled deputy who remained uncertainly in the doorway.

Bishop reached for a chair and shoved it behind her. "Here—sit down before you fall down."

She did, wondering if she looked as bad as she felt. Surely not.

"Taking quite a risk, using up precious energy in order to ease the mind of the good sheriff." Bishop's voice was not quite mocking. "Does Ryan know you can do that, by the way?"

Cassie drew a deep breath. "*I* didn't know I could do that."

"Dunbar won't be happy when he realizes you tricked him."

"No, I imagine not. But he won't realize just yet. Not just yet. And by the time he does, it won't matter." She was so tired already, strained with terror and her worry for Ben. And there was so much left to do.

Bishop leaned his shoulders back against the mantel, his arms crossed over his chest, face expressionless as always. But the scar looked whitened and angry.

Cassie wondered if he knew that mark was a barometer of his emotions.

"This is an asinine scheme," he said as if it hardly mattered.

"Maybe."

"Even assuming it works and Ryan comes out of it alive, he won't thank Dunbar or me. He'll say we used you."

"He'll know better."

"Will he? You expect him to be rational, then? When he sees what you've done, what it's cost you?"

"I'll be fine."

"Do not try to trick me," Bishop said. "Climb inside my mind and I'll shove you out."

"I know."

"Do you?"

"Yes." She smiled faintly. "But don't worry. Your secret is safe with me."

For the first time, his voice softened. "Never mind me. Cassie, this is crazy. Even in top condition, with all your strength, your chances would be slim against Vasek. Like this, drained and exhausted and so scared for Ryan you're hardly thinking straight, you have zero chance of coming out of this alive."

"I have the best reason in the world to survive. Will-power counts for a lot, you know that as well as I do." She paused, then added, "But in case something happens, tell Ben . . ."

"Tell him what, dammit?" Bishop demanded roughly when her voice trailed into silence.

Cassie shook her head. "Never mind. I should have told him myself when I had the chance."

"I hate melodrama," he snapped.

Despite everything, Cassie laughed. "Yes, I rather thought you would. Don't worry, I won't subject you to any more of it."

They were silent for a few minutes, and then Bishop said abruptly, "Cassie, I want you to promise me something."

"If I can."

"Once you're in, don't let go of the lifeline. No matter what Vasek says or does, no matter what he shows you, do not let go of me."

"All right. I'll do my best."

"So will I," Bishop said grimly.

Silence fell, broken only by the crackle of the fire and the creak of Danny's shoes as he shifted uneasily from one foot to the other. Cassie sat in the chair and stared into the fire, and Bishop watched her. Danny watched them both. And he was the one who nearly jumped out of his skin when the phone in his hand rang.

He answered, listened intently, then said, "Yes, sir," and without turning off the phone said to Bishop, "I'm to leave the line open. Sheriff says they're as close as he dares get, and they'll move in in exactly five minutes."

Cassie got up and went to sit on the sofa so she could get the boots, hardly noticing when Bishop came to sit beside her.

"Don't let go of the lifeline," Bishop repeated.

She picked up the boots, held them against her with both hands, and closed her eyes. Bishop watched her, speaking the instant he saw the telltale flicker of her eyelids.

"Talk to me, Cassie. Are you in?"

"I'm in." Her voice was hollow, distant, and Bishop frowned.

"Does he know you're there?"

"Yes. Yes, he knows."

"What was the deal with the music box?" Ben asked, watching his captor pick up yet another sharp implement from the cart and study it. "Cassie thought Mike was using it to block her. But it was you, wasn't it?"

"Of course it was me. Michael has no more telepathic ability than you do. I was using it to distract Cassie—*and* to keep Michael focused on rituals. It was necessary."

"In order to maintain your control over him?"

"Why are you stalling?" Bob asked curiously. "Is another hour of life so important?"

"Did you ask that of your other victims?" Ben countered.

"A few. Most were incoherent, however, so I've never received a satisfactory answer."

Despite the chill of the room, Ben could feel sweat trickling down the side of his neck. It hadn't been difficult to keep the monster talking, but he had the uneasy idea that it was still very much a question of who was toying with whom.

He wished he could reach out to Cassie. Touch her. But even if he had known how to do that, there was no way Ben wanted her there in the room.

What he was afraid of was the very real possibility that Cassie would find her way there anyway. If she knew he was missing, she would reach out, and thanks to his walls, it wouldn't be his mind she touched. If this insane monster was even half right about the connection between him and Cassie, she would inevitably touch that dark evil.

Ben knew how much of herself she had risked for the relative strangers of Ryan's Bluff; what would she risk to save the life of a lover?

It terrified him.

All he could think to do was keep the monster talking, keep looking for a chink in that armor of self-satisfaction. And hope he could find some way to free himself before Cassie came looking for him.

"I can give you a coherent answer," he told his captor. "Another hour of life is important. Another minute. Even another second. Because as long as there's still some time, there might be enough time."

"Enough time for what?"

"Enough time for me to kill you."

Bob stared at him in astonishment for a moment, then began to laugh. But the laugh cut off abruptly, and he rose to his feet, the knife in his hand seemingly forgotten, that earlier look of distraction gripping his features. His eyes had a distant, unfocused look. And his voice dropped to that caressing note that made Ben's skin crawl and his blood run cold when Bob murmured, "Well. Hello, my love."

·   ·   ·

"He knows you're there?" Bishop demanded.

"He's . . . surprised," Cassie murmured. "He didn't think I'd noticed the boots." She was silent a moment, her features twisting in revulsion. "Oh, God. The things he thinks. His mind is so dark, so . . . evil. He has no soul."

Bishop glanced at his watch. "Can you see through his eyes, Cassie?"

"No." She sounded unsettled. "He's . . . he's holding me too deep."

"Holding you?"

Her voice was hardly a breath of sound. "He wants me to see . . . his secret places."

"Cassie, listen to me. Try to back away. Try to see through his eyes."

"I want to. I want to see Ben."

"Try. Very carefully."

There was a full minute of silence, and then she flinched. Her eyes opened, the pupils enormous and blind.

Ben knew the connection had been made, that Cassie or some part of her was there. He didn't know if she could see him, but it was obvious to him that his captor was in a kind of trance, eyes blank, all his concentration turned inward.

He wouldn't get another chance.

"Cassie?"

"He won't let me see. He . . . likes this. Likes having my voice in his mind. He wants me there . . . always. The door. He's going to shut the door—"

Bishop reached over and grasped her wrist strongly.

"Cassie? Hold on to me, Cassie. He can't close the door if you don't let him."

Her breathing slowed and grew shallow, and the pallor of her skin deepened until even her lips were drained of color. "I'm ... trying," she whispered. "He's so strong ... so strong. He's getting angry, furious that I would ... defy him. . . ."

"Hold on to me, Cassie. Don't let go."

You came to me. I knew you would.

I had to come.

Yes. We belong together.

No.

Vasek felt an instant of shock at her calm denial, then a hot and satisfying rush of rage. *Yes. We belong together.*

I belong with Ben. Utter certainty.

You're confused, my love. But it's all right. I'll show you the truth. He used his abilities to surround her presence with himself, to hold on to her and begin pulling her deeper, and to try to cut off the way behind her. Cut off her escape.

I'm not your love.

Of course you are.

No. Somehow she managed to defy him, to prevent him from capturing her. *And you're no part of me. No matter what you think. No matter how many times you believe you've slipped into my mind without me knowing.*

Vasek was more disconcerted than he wanted to admit. *You never knew. Never!*

Oh, no?

Her laughter in his mind, like quicksilver.

You never knew, he declared, but the assertion was

hollow and he heard the emptiness of it. His sense of superiority was rocked, unsteady for the first time.

Of course I knew.

I don't believe you! He tried to penetrate her certainty, probe her claims, but her presence was smooth and cool and peculiarly detached. He felt her presence but not her spirit. And only those thoughts she allowed him to see.

Rage rose higher in him, hotter, wilder. No. He wouldn't. He had never—

You lose.

Ben didn't know how he managed to loosen the ropes enough to free his wrists. Perhaps it was because this particular monster had little experience in binding his victims since he tended to kill them quickly. Perhaps he had been distracted by the anomaly of a male captive, and it made him careless. Or perhaps it was simply that Ben's desperation gave him a strength he had not known he possessed.

He bloodied his wrists doing it, but his hands were still functional when he wrenched free of the ropes and bent to untie the ones binding his ankles. He kept his eyes on the unmoving, unblinking monster, praying he'd have time to act, to cross the few feet of space between them and get his fingers around that pasty throat and choke the evil life out of the bastard.

Cassie.

He had asked her what would happen if she went too deep, and she had replied with a faint smile that she would not come back. How deep was she now? And what would happen if the monster in whose mind she was trapped died before she was able to escape?

Ben hesitated for only a second, and in that second

something heavy crashed through the windows, and two of Matt's deputies lay on the floor, guns drawn and pointed at the monster. And the monster was turning toward them, face twisting, a terrible triumph in the glance he threw Ben as his arm rose, the knife he held gleaming in a threat any cop would recognize and instinctively act to counter.

"No!" Ben shouted, lunging up from the chair.

He was too late.

"Cassie?"

The room was so deathly silent that Bishop heard the shots through the open line of the cell phone. They were close together, but he was able to count three of them, and each one made Cassie's slender body jerk. Then her eyes closed, a long breath escaped her, and she went totally limp.

Bishop eased her back against the pillows and felt for a carotid pulse. It was so faint, he could barely discern it, and her skin was like ice.

"Cassie?" He slapped her cheek sharply, getting absolutely no response. Over his shoulder to the deputy, he snapped, "Call EMS."

"My God," Danny whispered. "Look at her hair."

"Get EMS here *now*!"

MARCH 10, 1999

"I've run every test I have." The neurosurgeon Ben had flown in frowned at his clipboard. "The MRI showed no tumor, no bleeding or swelling of the brain. There's no apparent injury or trauma, no disease we can detect. She's breathing on her own. The EEG shows brain activity, though of a kind I find unusual."

Bishop, who'd been standing on the far side of the hospital bed gazing out the window, turned to look at the doctor. "Meaning?" His voice was cool.

Dr. Rhodes shook his head. "I mean there's activity in an area of the brain where there is normally little or no activity, especially during coma."

"Is that good?"

"I don't know," the doctor replied bluntly. "Just like I don't know how that white streak could have appeared in her hair instantaneously. If anyone else had told me it just appeared like that—"

"I was there," Bishop said. "It appeared in a matter of seconds as she fell unconscious. Started at the roots and went right to the ends."

Almost to himself the doctor muttered, "The medical literature says that's an old wives' tale."

"Rewrite the literature," Bishop suggested.

"I may have to. On several counts. I just don't understand what's causing this coma. There's no medical reason to account for it."

Sitting beside the bed, Ben said, "So what you're telling us is that you have no idea what's wrong with her?"

"I know she's in a coma, Judge. I don't know what caused it. I don't know how long it will last. She may recover naturally." Rhodes clearly felt helpless. "I'm sorry. There just isn't anything we can do." He looked from one man to the other, then sighed and left the room.

"She won't recover naturally," Bishop said.

"You were her lifeline." Ben's voice was harsh. "Why did you let go?"

"If I had let go, she'd be dead." In stark contrast, Bishop's voice was calm, even mild.

Ben reached over to touch Cassie's cheek gently, his eyes fixed on her face as they had been too many long hours during the last week. Her terribly still face. "Then what the hell happened?"

"I've told you. She was trapped inside the mind of a maniac when he died. She wasn't strong enough to pull herself completely free of that psychic backwash of energy."

"Completely free? Where is she?"

"Somewhere between."

A laugh escaped Ben, and it held no humor whatsoever. "Christ. That's helpful."

"You asked."

"Look, if you're going to stand there spouting bits of information like Yoda, at least tell me something I can use to get her back."

"All right. If you want her back, go after her."

"How? I'm not psychic."

Bishop moved away from the window and toward the door with a shrug. "Then she's gone. Have a memorial service for her and get on with your life."

"Bastard."

At the door the agent turned and gave Ben one last, steady look. "You're the only one she's allowed to get close to her in more than ten years. The only one with a connection to her that is literally of the flesh. And you're the only one who can bring her back." He walked out the door.

Ben stared after him for a moment, then returned his gaze to Cassie's still, pale face. He was finally getting used to the stark white streak in the black hair above her left temple, but her utter stillness was killing him.

He had tried talking to her. Pleading with her. He had watched Rhodes and the staff try various loud and seemingly painful methods to wake her, all without success. Her heart beat. She breathed. And there was activity in her brain.

But she was not here.

"*. . . a connection to her that is literally of the flesh.*"

What was that supposed to mean? That because they were lovers they shared a bond? Ben wanted to think so. But during the endless week past, when he had sat there staring at her, talking to her, trying to reach her, there had been no response at all.

The white streak had made him think of her aunt, and so in desperation he had combed through Alexandra Melton's journals, searching for something he could do to help Cassie. He had found unexpected and astonishing information, including the fact that Alexandra had left a warning for her niece to stay away from him or be destroyed.

A warning Cassie had clearly ignored.

He discovered that her mother and aunt had quarreled over how to raise her, the mother insisting her child be imbued with a strong sense of responsibility to use her talents to help others while the aunt warned of a dangerous gift that could too easily destroy—as her own psychic ability had very nearly destroyed her.

Ben thought he might have found an answer there, thought Alexandra's survival after some kind of psychic shock must bode well for Cassie. But what he discovered was that Alexandra had survived simply because her shock had not been as extreme as Cassie's; she had been pulled from an insane mind, but not a dying one.

Her journals offered Ben no help. And precious little hope.

"Ben?"

He turned his head to see Matt standing in the doorway. "No change," he reported quietly.

Matt still felt guilty at the unwitting part he had played in what had happened to Cassie, and it showed. "Abby wants to come see her. I said tomorrow would probably be better."

"Yeah."

"She said to tell you not to worry about Max, he's doing fine with us."

Ben nodded. "Thanks."

"I told Mary I'd drive her home today, but Rhodes volunteered to do that."

Despite everything, Ben felt a rueful amusement. "Is it my imagination, or did those two take one look at each other and tumble?"

"Not your imagination." Matt smiled. "Rhodes seems to be completely smitten, and Mary's been telling everybody that Alexandra Melton told her a long time ago that because of her son she'd fall in love with a tall, dark man and marry him."

"Because of me. Well, I did fly him in from Raleigh." Ben looked back at Cassie. "I'm glad that worked out for somebody."

"She'll be all right, Ben."

"I know. I know she will." He had to keep saying it. Had to keep believing it.

Matt began to turn away, then hesitated. "I know you probably don't give a damn right now, but Shaw's finally talking. And we finally know why the coins."

"Why?" Ben asked, not giving a damn.

"Vasek. Part of his sadistic fantasy was the need to leave a token of his *affection* with a victim. He knew his usual paper roses would give him away to Cassie, so he came up with the coins. They actually came from his own father's collection, locked in a bank vault for twenty years. Traceable. It's the first tangible connection between Shaw and Vasek."

"Good," Ben said.

"And we found out something else. About those kittens Cassie saw in Lucy Shaw's mind. It seems she had a cat she adored, and she was thrilled when it had kittens.

She came home from the store one day to find Mike sitting in the middle of the living room floor. Cutting the kittens into pieces with his Boy Scout knife. He was eight years old."

"Jesus Christ," Ben said.

"Yeah. Russell came home to find Lucy trying to . . . pick up all the pieces. And she's been trying ever since."

Ben gazed at Cassie's face and ached inside. Monsters. Dear God, how many stories just as horrible as that one were stored in her mind? And how incredible was it that she had still been able to walk into his office and volunteer her help in trying to stop yet another monster from terrorizing his town?

"Ben? Can I get you anything?"

"No. No, thanks, Matt."

"Okay. See you tomorrow."

"Yeah." Ben sat there for several minutes in the silence of the room, then got up and went to close the door. He returned to Cassie's bedside and his chair.

For a long time he thought about monsters invited resolutely into a tired and gentle mind, again and again despite fear. And then he thought about the walls a man built around himself as some kind of protection from a past that had been difficult but without real monsters. Walls that kept out the pain of memories but just as thoroughly kept out the healing spirit of the woman he loved.

Then he took Cassie's cool hand in his, bent his head over it, and began tearing down his walls.

EPILOGUE

"I should have realized," Cassie said, shaking her head. "It was making me uneasy that the killer seemed to be blowing hot and cold, varying his methods and the way he left his victims. I should have remembered that was Vasek's M.O."

Standing at the foot of her bed, Matt said, "Three thousand miles and months away, how could you? Besides, if he was telling Ben the truth, the bastard made damned sure you wouldn't think it was him."

"In other words," Ben said, "you are not and have never been to blame for Conrad Vasek's crimes." *Let it go,* he added silently, and when she turned her head to smile at him, he felt the warmth like a physical touch, and the bright shimmer of her amusement in his mind.

Bossy.

Never.

Admit it. You like bossing me around.

I love having you around. Big difference.

Cassie reached out a hand, and his fingers twined with hers. Aware of the sheriff's gaze, Ben didn't kiss her, but he thought about it, and Cassie's smile widened.

Oblivious of the mind-play, Matt said, "With Vasek dead, Mike Shaw has pretty much gone to pieces, and even his hotshot lawyer has admitted the only question is whether he gets the gas chamber or locked in a rubber room for the rest of his life. If my vote counts, I say I'd rather my tax dollars weren't spent on keeping him alive."

"You'll be in the majority," Ben said. "But I'm betting he won't be judged fit to stand trial."

Matt shook his head. "Then we'd better ship his ass someplace far away from Salem County. There's a lot of confusion about Vasek's role in all this, but everybody knows Mike was caught with his hands around Abby's throat." His face darkened with the memory.

Ben said, "Since we don't have a jail or hospital capable of dealing with him, I imagine he will be shipped away."

"What about Lucy?" Cassie asked Matt.

"She's finally getting the help she's needed for years. Faced with what his son has done, Russell had to finally admit it wasn't smart to keep some things in the family. He's lived all his life with the knowledge that the Shaws have had a strain of mental instability that apparently goes back several generations. He thought he could handle it, keep his mother safe and Mike from getting worse. And he might have managed it. If Vasek hadn't come looking for a tool."

Which is not your fault, Ben reminded Cassie fiercely.

I know. I know.

"Anyway, it's over now," Matt said. "Things are finally getting back to normal. And you'll be out of the hospital tomorrow. Which reminds me—Ben said you came out of this with all your psychic abilities fried."

"That," Ben said, "is not exactly how I put it."

"Well, close enough. So it's true, Cassie? You can't read me anymore?"

"I can't read anybody, apparently. Except Ben."

The sheriff grinned at his friend. "So how does it feel to be an open book?"

Ben smiled at Cassie. "Actually, it feels pretty great." And deeply, unexpectedly satisfying.

Matt shook his head. "Better you than me. Is it permanent?"

Cassie said, "After reading through Aunt Alex's journals today, I have to say it probably is. At least, to all intents and purposes. She got back some of her ability eventually, but it took nearly twenty years and she was never as strong as she had been before."

"Before what?"

"Before she was almost trapped in the mind of a madman. She didn't offer many details, but I gather that just before she quarreled with my mother, she was asked to help find a lost child. The kidnapper was totally insane, and she was adrift for a time in his mind."

"Creepy," Matt noted.

"Yes." Cassie didn't reveal to him that she had already faced and was dealing with the knowledge that Conrad Vasek had found his way into her mind uncounted times without her awareness. "Aunt Alex came out of it changed. Emotionally. Mentally. And physically." Her free hand strayed up to briefly touch the white streak at her left temple.

"How about you? Any regrets?"

"None at all."

Matt studied her. "I have to say, you look much more peaceful. I guess silence is golden, huh? I mean, except for Ben."

Cassie smiled at him. "You have no idea."

"So if I should need a little special insight in any future investigation—"

"Try tea leaves. Or a crystal ball."

"Anything but you?"

"That's the idea."

"Umm. But you are sticking around, right?"

"Yes," Ben said. "She is."

Bossy.

Never.

"Glad to hear it," Matt said seriously. He eyed them a moment, then added, "I think it's time I was leaving."

"We wouldn't want to rush you," Ben said mildly.

Matt grinned. "Okay, I'm going. But before you lock the door behind me, I should warn you that Bishop said he'd probably stop by sometime today to say good-bye."

Ben waited until his friend said his own good-byes and left to tell Cassie, "Good-bye, hell. Bishop will be very lucky if I don't deck him."

"He told you that you could get me back," Cassie reminded him, smiling.

"Yeah, but the bastard left me to figure out how by myself. If he'd told me, and right from the beginning, you wouldn't have spent a week in a coma and I wouldn't have nearly gone out of my mind worrying about you."

Cassie looked thoughtful. "Maybe we both needed that time. Me to . . . drift in limbo, where there was nothing to do but think about things, and you to find the willingness to open yourself up and reach out to me."

He lifted her hand to rub it against his cheek. "God knows why it took me so long, why I wasn't willing to admit even to myself that I loved you. The best thing that ever happened to me, and I was afraid to accept it. So afraid I almost lost you."

"You didn't lose me." Her voice was serene, like her

smile. "Things happen for a reason, Ben. Aunt Alex knew that if I became involved in the search for a killer here, Abby would be saved—but she also knew what would happen to me, that I'd be trapped by the death of the killer and, she thought, destroyed. So she tried to avoid both fates. She warned Abby, hoping she'd be able to change her own destiny. And she left a warning for me to avoid you, hoping it would keep me safe. Her warning to me should have been delivered on time, but a fluke series of events delayed it. Which gave me the opportunity to meet you and fall in love with you—the only person who really could save me. It all had to happen just as it did."

"If you say so," Ben murmured. But the terror of nearly losing her was still strong in him, and he leaned over to kiss her because he had to.

"I can come back later," Bishop said from the doorway.

Ben made a rude noise, but Cassie sent the agent a welcoming smile. "No, come in."

"If you're here to say good-bye," Ben said.

Bishop didn't appear distressed by this eagerness to see the last of him. "I am," he said calmly.

Cassie gave Ben a look, and he relented. "Thanks for your help," he said to the agent.

"And damn me for not offering it sooner. I'll take it as read, Judge."

"It's always nice to be understood."

Giving up, Cassie said to Bishop, "So you're leaving us. Another so-called psychic to debunk?"

"No, nothing so interesting, I'm afraid. I'm called back to the office on far more mundane matters."

"Well, I would say it's been a pleasure, but we both know I'd be lying. It has been interesting though. As usual."

"For me as well." Bishop eyed Ben for a moment, then told Cassie, "Be sure and invite me to the christening. In the meantime, have a nice life."

"You too." Cassie waited until he'd nearly reached the door, then said, "Bishop?"

He turned, lifting one brow questioningly.

"Good luck. I hope you find her."

That hard, scarred face was perfectly still, perfectly enigmatic. Then he nodded, more in acknowledgment than acceptance, and left.

"Find who?" Ben asked.

Cassie smiled. "Who he's looking for."

"And that is?"

"Not my story."

Ben thought about that for a moment, then blinked. "Christening?"

"I don't know why he thinks there'll be a christening," Cassie said almost absently. "He knows I'm not religious."

"Christening?"

Cassie slid her arms around his neck as Ben leaned over her, and her laugh was soft and warm. "Well, I distinctly remember as I was coming out of the coma hearing you say you were definitely ready for a long-term commitment. As a matter of fact, you were quite fierce about it."

"Yes, but— You're sure? So soon?"

"Positive. Do you mind?"

My darling . . .

I love you, Ben.

Cassie . . . my Cassie . . . I love you so much.

It was a long time later when Ben lifted his head. "A connection that is literally of the flesh. That's what he said when you were still in the coma. I thought he meant because we were lovers, but that wasn't what he meant at all. And just now he asked to be invited to the christening. He knew. Dammit, Bishop *knew*. How?"

Cassie said serenely, "I suppose he must have seen it in the tea leaves, darling. Does it matter?"

With her warm gray eyes smiling up at him, her slender body in his arms, and the astonishing intimacy of her presence glowing inside him somewhere deeper than thought, Ben decided that nothing else mattered.

Nothing at all.

In *Stealing Shadows,* Kay Hooper
introduces FBI agent Noah Bishop,
whose rare gift for seeing what others do not
helps him solve the most puzzling cases.
Now, Bishop's electrifying adventures
continue in two stand-alone tales
of psychic suspense. . . .

HIDING IN THE SHADOWS
available October 2000

OUT OF THE SHADOWS
available November 2000

Turn the page for sneak previews.

HIDING IN THE SHADOWS

She opened her eyes abruptly, as though from a nightmare, conscious of the pounding of her heart and the sound of her quick, shallow breathing in the silent room. She couldn't remember the dream, but her shaking body and runaway pulse told her it had been a bad one. She closed her eyes and for several minutes concentrated only on calming down.

Gradually her heart slowed and her breathing steadied. Okay. Okay. That was better. That was much better.

She didn't like being scared.

She opened her eyes and looked at the ceiling. Gradually a niggling awareness of something being different made her turn her head slowly on the pillow so she could look around the room.

It wasn't her room.

Her other senses began to wake then. She heard the muffled, distant sounds of activity just beyond the closed door. She smelled sickness and medicine, the distinct odors of people and machines and starch. She noted the Spartan quality of the room she was in, the hospital bed she was lying on—and the IV dripping into her arm. All of that told her she was in a hospital.

Why?

It took a surprising effort to raise her head and look down at herself; her neck felt stiff, unused, and a rush of nausea made her swallow hard. But she forced herself to look, to make sure all of her was there.

Both arms. Both legs. Nothing in a cast. Her feet moved when she willed them to. Not paralyzed then. Good.

With an effort, she raised the arm not hooked to the IV until she could see her hand. It was unnervingly small, not childlike but . . . fragile. The short nails were ragged and looked bitten, and the skin was milky-pale. She turned it slowly and stared at the palm, the pads of her fingers. No calluses, but there was a slight roughness to her skin that told her she was accustomed to work.

Afraid of what she'd find, she touched her face with light, probing fingers. The bones seemed prominent, and the skin felt soft and smooth. There was no evidence of an injury until her exploration reached her forehead and right temple. There, a square of adhesive bandage and a faint soreness underneath told her she'd suffered some kind of cut.

But not a bad one, she thought, and certainly not a big one. The bandage was small, two or three square inches.

Beyond the bandage, she found her hair limp and oily, which told her it hadn't been washed recently. She pulled at a strand and was surprised that it was long enough for her to be able to see. It was mostly straight, with only a hint of curl. And it was red. A dark and dull red.

Now why did that surprise her?

For the first time, she let herself become aware of what had been crawling in her subconscious, a cold and growing fear she dared not name. She realized she was lying perfectly still now, her arms at her sides, hands clenched into fists, staring at the ceiling as if she would find the answers there.

She wasn't injured except slightly, so why was she here? Because she was ill? What was wrong with her?

Why did her body feel so appallingly weak?

And far, far worse, why couldn't she remember—

"Oh, my God."

The nurse in the doorway came a few steps into the room, moving slowly, her eyes wide with surprise. Then professionalism obviously took over, and she swallowed and said brightly if a bit unsteadily, "You—you're awake. We were . . . beginning to wonder about you, Fa—Miss Parker."

Parker.

"I'll get the doctor."

She lay there waiting, not daring to think about the fact that she had not known her own name, still didn't beyond that simple and unfamiliar surname. It seemed an eternity she waited, while those cold and wordless terrors clawed through her mind and churned in her stomach, before a doctor appeared. He was tall, a bit on the thin side, with a sensitive mouth and very brilliant, very dark eyes.

"So you're finally awake." His voice was deep and warm, his smile friendly. He grasped her wrist lightly as he stood by the bed, discreetly taking her pulse. "Can you tell me your name?"

She wet her lips and said huskily, "Parker." Even her voice sounded rusty and unused, and her throat felt scratchy.

He didn't look surprised; possibly the nurse had confessed that she had provided that information. "What about your first name?"

She tried not to cry out in fear. "No. No, I—I don't remember that."

"Do you remember what happened to you?"

"No."

"How about telling me what year this is?"

She concentrated, fought down that cold, crawling panic. There was nothing in her mind but blankness, an emptiness that frightened her almost beyond words. No sense of identity or knowledge. Nothing.

Nothing.

"I don't remember."

"Well, try not to worry about it," he said soothingly. "A traumatic event frequently results in amnesia, but it's seldom permanent. Things will probably start to come back to you now that you're awake."

"Who are you?" she asked, because it was the least troubling question she could think of.

"My name is Dr. Burnett, Nick Burnett. I've been your doctor since you were admitted. *Your* name is Faith Parker."

Faith Parker. It didn't stir the slightest sense of familiarity in her. "Is—is it?"

He smiled gently. "Yes. You're twenty-eight years old, single, and in pretty good shape physically, though you could stand to gain a few pounds." He paused, then went on in a calm tone completely without judgment. "You were involved in a single-car accident, which the police blame on the fact that you'd had a few drinks on top of prescription muscle relaxers. The combination made you plow your car into an embankment."

She might have been listening to a description of someone else for all the memory it stirred.

The doctor continued. "It also turned out to be highly toxic to your system. You appear to be unusually sensitive to alcohol, and that, combined with the drug, put you into a coma. However, aside from the gash on your head, which we've kept covered to minimize scarring, and a few bruised ribs, which have already healed, you're fine."

There were so many questions swirling through her mind that she could only grab one at random. "Was—was anyone else hurt in the accident?"

"No. You were alone in the car, and all the car hit was the embankment."

Something he'd said a minute ago tugged at her. "You said . . . my ribs had healed by now. How long have I been here?"

"Six weeks."

She felt shock. "So long? But . . ." She wasn't even sure what she wanted to ask, but her anxiety was growing with every new fact.

"Let's try sitting up a bit, shall we?" Not waiting for her response, he used a control to raise the head of the bed a few inches. When she closed her eyes, he stopped the movement. "The dizziness should pass in a minute."

She opened her eyes slowly, finding that he was right. But there was little satisfaction in that, not with the questions and worries overwhelming her. And panic. A deep, terrifying panic. "Doctor, I can't remember anything. Not where I live or work. I don't know if I have insurance, and if I don't, I don't know how I'll pay for six weeks in a hospital. I don't even know what address to give the cab driver when I go—go home."

"Listen to me, Faith." His gentle voice was soothing. "There's no reason for you to worry, especially not about money. Arrangements have already been made to pay your hospital bill in full, and I understand that a trust fund has been set up for you. According to what I've been told, there should be plenty of money, certainly enough to live on for months while you get your life back in order."

That astonishing information bewildered her. "A trust fund? Set up for me? But who would do that?"

"A friend of yours. A good friend. She came to visit you twice a week until—" Something indefinable crossed his face and then vanished, and he went on quickly. "She wanted to make certain you got the best of care and had no worries when you left here."

"But why? The accident obviously wasn't her fault since I was alone . . ." Unless this friend had encouraged Faith to drink or hadn't taken her car keys away when she should have.

"I couldn't tell you why, Faith. Except that she was obviously concerned about you."

Faith felt a rush of pain that she couldn't remember so good a friend. "What's her name?"

"Dinah Leighton."

It meant no more to Faith than her own name.

Dr. Burnett was watching her carefully. "We have the address of your apartment, which I understand is waiting for your return. Miss Leighton seemed less certain you would want to go back to your job, which I believe is one of the reasons she wanted to make it possible for you to have the time to look around, perhaps even return to school or do something you've always wanted to do."

She felt tears prickle and burn. "Something I've always wanted to do. Except I can't seem to remember anything I've always wanted to do. Or anything I've done. Or even what I look like . . ."

He grasped her hand and held it strongly. "It will come back to you, Faith. You may never remember the hours immediately preceding and following the accident, but most of the rest will return in time. Coma does funny things to the body and the mind."

She sniffled and tried to concentrate, to hold on to facts and avoid thinking of missing memories. "What kinds of things?"

Still holding her hand, he drew a visitor's chair to the bed and sat down. "To the body, what you'd expect after a traumatic accident and weeks of inactivity. Muscle weakness. Unstable blood pressure. Dizziness and digestive upset from lying prone and having no solid food for weeks. But all those difficulties are temporary, and should disappear once you've been up and about for a few days, eating regular meals and exercising."

"What about . . . the mind? What other kinds of . . . problems can be caused by coma?" The possibilities lurking in her imagination were terrifying. What if she never regained her memory? What if she found herself unable to do the normal things people did every day, simple things like buttoning a shirt or reading a book? What if whatever skill and knowledge she'd needed in her work was gone forever and she was left with no way to earn her living in the future?

"Sometimes things we don't completely understand," the doctor confessed. "Personality changes are common. Habits and mannerisms are sometimes different. The emotions are volatile or, conversely, bland. You may find yourself getting confused at times, even after your memory returns, and panic attacks are more likely than not."

She swallowed. "Great."

Dr. Burnett smiled. "On the other hand, you may suffer no aftereffects whatsoever. You're perfectly lucid, and we've done our best to reduce muscle atrophy and other potential problems. Physical therapy should be minimal, I'd say. Once your memory returns, you may well find yourself as good as ever."

He sounded so confident that Faith let herself believe him, because the alternative was unbearable.

Trying not to think about that, she asked, "What about family? Do I have any family?"

"Miss Leighton told us you have no family in Atlanta. There was a sister, I understand, but I believe both she and your parents were killed some years ago."

"And I'm single. Do I— Is there—"

"I'm sure you must have dated," he said kindly, "but evidently there was no one special, at least not in the last few months. You've had no male visitors, no cards or letters, and only Miss Leighton sent flowers as far as I'm aware."

So she was alone, but for this remarkably good friend.

She felt very alone, and considerably frightened.

He saw it. "Everything seems overwhelming right now, I know. It's too much to process, too much to deal with. But you have time, Faith. There's no need to push yourself, and no reason to worry. Take it step by step."

Faith drew a breath. "All right. What's the first step?"

"We get you up on your feet and moving physically." He smiled and rose to his own. "But not too much today. Today, we'll have you gradually sit up, maybe try standing, and monitor your reaction to that. We'll see how your stomach reacts to a bit of solid food. How's that to start?"

She managed a smile. "Okay."

"Good." He squeezed her hand and released it, then hesitated on the point of turning away.

Seeing his face, she said warily, "What?"

"Well, since you might want to read the newspapers or watch television to catch up on things, I think I should warn you about something."

"About what?"

"Your friend Miss Leighton. She went missing about two weeks ago."

"Missing? You mean she . . . she stopped coming to visit me?"

There was sympathy in his dark eyes. "I mean she disappeared. She was reported missing, and though her car was found abandoned some time later, she hasn't been seen since."

Faith was surprised at the rush of emotions she felt. Confusion. Shock. Disappointment. Regret. And, finally, a terrible pain at the knowledge that she was now truly alone.

Dr. Burnett patted her hand, but seemed to realize that no soothing words would make her feel better. He didn't offer any, but went quietly away.

She lay there, staring up at the white, blank ceiling that was as empty as her mind.

OUT OF THE SHADOWS

"So when're the feds due in?" Alex asked Miranda as they stood near the top of the hill and watched as the lake down in the hollow was slowly crisscrossed by half a dozen small boats. The last light of the day was just making it over the mountains to paint the lake shimmering silver; another few minutes and they'd either have to put up floodlights or continue the search tomorrow.

"Anytime now."

Alex looked at her curiously. "So how come you're out here instead of back at the office waiting for them? I mean, dragging the lake is a good idea—anonymous tip or not—since we haven't found a trace of the Grainger girl anywhere in the area, but I can call in if we find anything."

Miranda's shoulders moved in an almost irritable shrug. "They'll have to drive in from Nashville, so it could be late tonight. Anyway, I left Brady on duty at the office with instructions to bring them out here if they arrive before I get back."

Still watching her, Alex asked, "Do you have any idea

how many are coming? Isn't this crack new unit supposed to be made up of a dozen or more agents?"

"I don't know for sure. There isn't much information available, even for law enforcement officials. We'll get what we get, I guess." She sounded restless, uneasy.

Alex was about to ask another question when he saw Miranda stiffen. All her attention, all her *being*, was suddenly focused elsewhere. She no longer saw the lake or the people below them, wasn't even aware of him standing beside her.

Then he saw her eyes shift sideways, as if she was intensely aware of some sound, some thing, behind her but didn't want to turn her head to look at it.

"Randy?"

She didn't respond, didn't seem to hear him.

Alex half turned to look behind them. At first, all he saw was the hilltop and light flooding over it because the sun had not yet set. Then there was an abrupt, fluid shifting of the light, and the silhouette of a tall man appeared.

Alex blinked, startled because he hadn't heard a sound. Two more silhouettes appeared on either side of the first, another man and a woman. They paused there on the crest of the hill, looking at the activity below them, and then lost the blinding halo of light as they moved down the slope toward Alex and Miranda.

The man on the left was a couple of inches shorter than the other but still plenty tall at about six feet. He was maybe thirty, on the thin side, and had nondescript brown hair. The woman was roughly the same age, not very tall, slender and blond. Both were casually dressed in dark pants and bulky sweaters.

But it was the man in the center who caught and held Alex's attention. Dressed as casually as the other two in jeans and a black leather jacket, he was a striking figure.

He was very dark, his black hair gleaming in the last of the day's light, and a perfect and distinct widow's peak crowned his high forehead. He was wide-shouldered and navigated the rock-strewn slope with far more ease than his slipping and sliding companions. As he neared them, Alex saw the vivid scar marking one side of his coldly handsome face.

He looked back at Miranda and saw that her gaze was fixed once more on the lake below. But her breath was coming quickly through parted, trembling lips, and her face was a little pale and very strained. He was astonished at how vulnerable she looked. For a moment. Just a moment.

Then she closed her eyes briefly, and when she opened them all the strain was gone. Or hidden. She looked perfectly calm, indifferent even.

Quietly, Alex said, "Randy, I think the feds are here."

"Are they?" She sounded only mildly interested. She slid her hands into the front pockets of her jeans. "They're early."

"Guess they had a fast plane."

"Guess so."

Intrigued, but willing to await events, Alex returned his attention to the approaching agents. When they were close enough, the tall man in the center spoke, his voice deep and cool but with an undercurrent of tension.

"Sheriff Knight?" His pale, oddly reflective eyes were already fixed on Miranda.

She turned to face the newcomers. "Hello, Bishop."

Alex noted that Bishop's companions didn't seem surprised that this small-town sheriff knew him, so it was left to him to ask, "You two know each other?"

"We've met," Miranda said. Without elaborating, she introduced Alex, and just as calmly Bishop introduced

Special Agents Anthony Harte and Dr. Sharon Edwards. Nobody offered to shake hands, possibly because both Miranda and Bishop kept their hands in their pockets the entire time.

"I'm the forensic pathologist you requested," Edwards offered cheerfully.

"My specialty is interpretation of data," Harte explained when Miranda's gaze turned toward him.

"Good," she said. "We have some puzzling data for you to interpret. In the meantime, just to catch you up on events, we're following a tip that our latest missing teenager might be found here in the lake."

"A tip from whom, Sheriff Knight?" Bishop asked.

"An anonymous tip."

"Phoned in to your office?"

"That's right."

"Male or female?"

Her hesitation was almost unnoticeable. "Female."

"Interesting," he said.

There had been no tone of accusation in his voice, no special defensiveness in hers, but Alex thought both existed and that puzzled him even more. Then, realizing something else, he said, "Hey, you're both chess pieces. Knight and Bishop."

Miranda looked at him, one brow rising. "How about that," she said dryly.

Alex cleared his throat. "Well, anyway. We're losing the light down on the lake, Sheriff. Want to call off the search for the day?"

"Might as well." She glanced at the agents. "If you'll excuse me for a few minutes?" She didn't wait for a response, but made her way down the slope toward the shore of the lake where the boats were already gathering.

Bishop, Alex noted, never took his eyes off Miranda.

Alex was curious enough to be nosy, but something in Bishop's face made him stick to professional inquiries. "So what's your specialty, Agent Bishop?"

"Profiler. Who took the anonymous call, Deputy Mayse?"

Alex wasn't sure he liked the question, but answered it anyway. "Sheriff Knight." Then he found himself defending where Miranda had refused to. "That's not at all unusual, in case you think it is. The sheriff makes a point of being accessible, so lots of people call her directly if they have information or questions."

Those cool, pale eyes turned to him at last, and Bishop said almost indifferently, "Typical of small towns, in my experience. Tell me, has this area been searched?"

"No. Until we got the tip about the lake, there was no reason to think the Grainger girl would be this far out of town."

"And do you think she's here?"

"The sheriff thinks there's a chance. That's good enough for me."

Bishop continued to gaze at him for a long moment, making Alex uncomfortable in a way he couldn't define. Then the agent nodded, exchanged glances with his two companions, and moved several yards away from the group to a rocky outcropping. From there he could see most of the hollow and the lake below as well as the surrounding hills.

"What's he doing?" Alex asked, keeping his voice low.

Sharon Edwards answered. "Getting the lay of the land, I guess you'd call it. Looking for . . . signs."

"Signs? It's nearly dark already, especially down there. What can he possibly see?"

"You might be surprised," Tony Harte murmured.

Alex wanted to question that, but instead said, "I gather he's in charge?"

"He's the senior agent," Edwards confirmed. "But your sheriff is the one in charge. We're just here to help, to offer our expertise and advice."

"Uh-huh."

She smiled. "Really. We have a mandate never to interfere with local law enforcement. It's the only way we can be truly useful *and* be certain we're called in when the situation warrants. If word gets around that we never ride roughshod over local authorities, we're a lot more likely to be contacted when police are confronted with our sort of cases."

Alex looked at her curiously. "*Your* sort of cases?"

"I'm sure you saw the bulletin the Bureau sent out."

"I saw it. Like most Bureau bulletins, it didn't tell me a hell of a lot."

Edwards smiled again. "They can be cryptic when they want to be. Basically, we get called in on cases with . . . unusual elements. Either the evidence just doesn't add up or is nonexistent, or there are details that seem to smack of the occult, the paranormal or inexplicable. Sometimes those elements show up early, soon after the crimes, sometimes only after local law enforcement has exhausted all of the usual avenues of investigation."

"So you guys pursue *un*usual avenues?"

"We . . . look for the less likely explanations. And some of the methods we use are more intuitive than scientific. We try to keep things informal."

"Is that why no trench coats?"

She chuckled, honestly amused. "We are considered something of a maverick group within the Bureau, so when it was suggested that we dress more casually, the powers that be gave their permission."

Alex would have asked more questions, but a hail from the lake sent him down to help some of the search teams get their gear ashore.

Gazing after him, Tony Harte said, "Think you told him enough?"

"To satisfy him?" Edwards shook her head. "Only for the moment. According to his profile, he's curious and possesses a high tolerance for unconventional methods. That's probably why he hasn't questioned his sheriff too closely about all her hunches and intuitions since she took office. But he's protective of her, and he's wary of us. He'll be cooperative as long as he's sure we're contributing to the investigation without making Sheriff Knight look bad."

Harte grunted, then glanced aside at Bishop, still standing several yards away as he looked down on the lake. "What about this sheriff? Did you know who she was?"

"I had my suspicions when I went to do a deep background check on her—and found she didn't have one."

"So it is her?"

"I think so."

"No wonder he was in such a hurry to get here. But I've seen warmer greetings between mortal enemies."

"What makes you so sure that isn't what they are—at least from her point of view?"

"Never thought I'd feel sorry for Bishop."

"I imagine he can handle his own problems." Edwards smiled faintly. "In the meantime, there's this little problem we're supposed to be helping with. Are you getting anything?"

"Nope. I was blocked just about the time we topped the hill. You?"

"The same. Remarkable, isn't it?"

Harte turned his gaze toward the lake and watched as Miranda Knight made her way up the slope. Her lovely face was singularly without expression. "Poor Bishop," he murmured.

If he knew his subordinates were discussing him, Bishop

gave no sign, but he joined them only moments before Sheriff Knight and her deputy reached them.

Deputy Mayse said, "Nothing more we can do here tonight, so—"

"We can search for an abandoned well," Bishop said. "There's one nearby."

Mayse stared at him. "How can you possibly know that?"

"He knows," Sheriff Knight said. She looked at her deputy, matter of fact. "Most of the men are probably exhausted, Alex, but ask for volunteers to search around the lake. The moon will be rising, so we'll have some light."

The deputy looked as though he wanted to question or argue, but in the end just shook his head and went back down to talk to the searchers.

Agent Harte exchanged glances with Edwards, then said, "The more people we have searching, the quicker we're likely to find something. Our gear's in the car. We'll go change into boots and get our flashlights, some rope—whatever else looks like it might be helpful."

"Better have a compass or two," Sheriff Knight said. "This is tricky terrain. It's easy to get turned around, especially in the dark."

"Understood." Harte glanced at Bishop, who was already wearing boots, then traded another look with Edwards and shrugged. They both turned and trudged back up the slope to their rental car on the other side.

With one last glance back at the two people standing several feet and a light-year or so apart, Harte muttered, "I guess it could be worse. She might have shot him on sight."

ABOUT THE AUTHOR

KAY HOOPER, who has more than four million copies of her books in print world wide, has won numerous awards and high praise for her novels. Kay lives in North Carolina, where she is currently working on her next novel.